jo............................ life: he was a diplomat. soldier, barrister, journalist, historian, p............, publisher, poet and novelist. He was born in Perth in 1875, the eldest son of a Free Church of Scotland minister, and educated at Hutcheson's Grammar School in Glasgow. He graduated from Glasgow University then took a scholarship to Oxford. During his time there – 'spent peacefully in an enclave like a monastery' – he wrote two historical novels.

In 1901 he became a barrister of the Middle Temple and a private secretary to the High Commissioner for South Africa. In 1907 he married Susan Charlotte Grosvenor; they had three sons and a daughter. After spells as a war correspondent, Lloyd George's Director of Information and a Conservative MP, Buchan moved to Canada in 1935 where he became the first Baron Tweedsmuir of Elsfield.

Despite poor health throughout his life, Buchan's literary output was remarkable – thirty novels, over sixty non-fiction books, including biographies of Sir Walter Scott and Oliver Cromwell, and seven collections of short stories. His distinctive thrillers – 'shockers' as he called them – were characterised by suspenseful atmosphere, conspiracy theories and romantic heroes, notably Richard Hannay (based on the real-life military spy William Ironside) and Sir Edward Leithen. Buchan was a favourite writer of Alfred Hitchcock, whose screen adaptation of *The Thirty-Nine Steps* was phenomenally successful.

John Buchan served as Governor-General of Canada from 1935 until his death in 1940, the year his autobiography *Memory Hold-the-door* was published.

ALLAN MASSIE is a novelist, journalist, columnist and sports writer. A Fellow of the Royal Society of Literature, he has lived in the Scottish Borders for the last thirty-five years.

This edition is dedicated to the memory of Denis Read, 1924–2017. A resident of Woodilee, Denis was a great admirer of John Buchan throughout his long involvement with the John Buchan Museum

JOHN BUCHAN

Witch Wood

Introduced by Allan Massie

First published in 1927 by Hodder & Stoughton
This edition published in Great Britain in 2018 by Polygon,
an imprint of Birlinn Ltd.

West Newington House
10 Newington Road
Edinburgh
EH9 1QS

www.polygonbooks.co.uk

ISBN 978 1 84697 456 4

British Library Cataloguing-in-Publication Data
A catalogue record for this book is available
on request from the British Library.

Typeset by Hewer Text UK Ltd, Edinburgh
Printed by Clays Ltd, St Ives Plc

Contents

To Walter Buchan

Introduction

The story of Major Weir is one of the most famous of Edinburgh tales. He was a soldier of the Covenant and a notably pious Calvinist. It was said that if three or four of the most extreme Presbyterians were gathered together, the Major was sure to be one of them. His power of extempore prayer filled all with admiration, even in that seventeenth century when ministers of the Kirk could call on the Almighty for an hour or more at a time. His conspicuous piety and eloquence caused him to be known as 'Angelical Thomas'. So there was consternation when, having fallen ill, he suddenly confessed to having had consort with the Devil and to other 'crimes of the most revolting nature', according to an account written by the Reverend Mr Fraser, minister of Wardlaw. Despite admitting his guilt, the Major refused to seek pardon, responding to every plea with the words 'Torment me no more, I am tormented enough already.' His confession seemed so improbable that the authorities at first refused to take him into custody, but eventually they did so, and he was tried and condemned for the sin of witchcraft. Sentenced to be burned in the Grassmarket, he refused the consolations of religion even to the end, crying out, 'Let me alone – I will not – *I* have lived as a beast, and I must die as a beast.' His sister, who confessed in like manner, was hanged. She had claimed that their mother had also been a witch.

Major Weir does not figure in Buchan's novel, which is set in Upper Tweeddale, not Edinburgh, and in 1645–6, some twenty years before the Major's confession and execution. But Buchan knew the story, and Weir's final cry is echoed in the fate that befalls the 'Heid Devil' of Woodilee last seen 'running demen-

ted on the hills, pursued by the dogs of his own terrors'. The
theme of the novel is perversion, a story as grotesque and
horrible as Weir's. The fanatical religiosity of seventeenth-
century Scotland, with its insistence on damnation from which
only the Elect were spared by God's Grace, could topple into a
species of insanity, a delusion which permitted members of the
Elect to persuade themselves that anything was permitted to
those assured of salvation. This of course is the theme of James
Hogg's masterpiece, *The Private Memoirs and Confessions of a
Justified Sinner*, a novel to which Buchan's may be regarded as a
companion piece.

Buchan was himself bred as a Calvinist, son of a Free Kirk
manse, and remained a Presbyterian all his life. But he was also
a humanist and a classicist; like his hero Montrose, who in
Witch Wood represents humanist reason and moderation, he
distrusted and rejected the extreme claims of the theocracy. In
his biography of Montrose he condemned the extreme Cove-
nanters:

> Their neurotic supernaturalism, which saw judgements
> and signs in the common incidents of life, weakened in
> the people the power of rational thought. If they gave
> manhood and liberty to Scotland, they did much to sap the
> first and shackle the second. Condemning natural plea-
> sures and affections, they drew a dark pall over the old
> merry Scottish world, the world of the ballads and the
> songs, of frolics and mummings and 'blithesome bridals,
> and, since human nature will not be denied, drove men
> and women to sinister and perverted outlets.

It is an old truth. As Buchan's beloved Horace put it: 'Naturam
expelle furca, tamen usque recurret' – 'You may drive nature out
with a pitchfork, but she will always return'.

This is the central argument of *Witch Wood*. The novel was
published in 1927, the biography of Montrose the following year
and the two books belong together. Buchan was at ease in the
seventeenth century, and of all his novels *Witch Wood* was the

most ambitious, the longest pondered, and, with the exception of *Sick Heart River*, written in the last months of his life, the most deeply felt.

It has never been as popular as the novels of adventure he threw off with such apparent ease, and which he described as 'shockers'. This is not surprising. Though the best of these go deeper than many of their early enthusiastic readers realised – something that Graham Greene was one of the first to remark on – *Witch Wood* is a very different and far more demanding piece of work. It has admittedly the narrative zest we associate with Buchan, and also that undercurrent of the uncanny which is to be found in novels like *The Three Hostages*, *The Dancing Floor* and, in a surprisingly macabre and sinister scene set in a French chateau, in *Mr Standfast*. It can be unnerving; when I read it first, at the age of fourteen or so, the chapter 'The Black Wood at Night' made the hairs on my neck stand on end. Buchan's evocation of the wilful surrender to the Powers of Darkness is effective because he recognises their attraction.

Yet here he makes demands on his readers as in no other novel. It is very completely set in time and place, and the political and theological questions he explores are distant from us. Certain passages are hard going for anyone ignorant of seventeenth-century Scottish history. Though some of its themes are for all time, nevertheless this is a novel that demonstrates the truth of L. P. Hartley's well known assertion: 'The Past is another country; they do things differently there.' They do indeed, and the concerns of what Christopher Harvie called 'the choric group of ministers' are remote from us.

So are the immediate political questions raised by the Civil Wars in Scotland and England. Yet Buchan's exploration of these, articulated by Montrose, has an enduring relevance. When he warns that 'if you upset the just proportion of the Law you will gain not liberty but confusion', and 'will have that anarchy which gives his chance to the spoiler, and out of anarchy will come some day a man of violence who will tyrannically make order again', and adds, 'it is the way of the world, my friend', one remembers that Buchan was writing a few years after the Bolshevik Revolution in Russia and shortly before Hitler established the tyrannical order of the Third Reich.

Stevenson, a powerful influence on Buchan, once described himself as 'Scotch, sir, very Scotch', and *Witch Wood* is in every way a very Scotch novel. The mature Buchan owed more to Walter Scott than to Stevenson, and *Witch Wood* may be read as a tribute to the author of *Waverley*. The central figure, the young minister, David Sempill, is, like so many Scott heroes, notably Henry Morton in *The Tale of Old Mortality*, a man-in-the-middle, a moderate caught up in, but rejecting, the fanaticism of his times. He is a classical scholar and a humanist, a zealous son of the Kirk and preacher of the Gospel, but repelled by extremism and all but powerless against its perverted certainties. He is also that characteristic figure of so much nineteenth-century Scottish fiction: the young minister at odds with the leading men in his parish.

Scott by his own account was no great hand at portraying young women, and nor is Buchan. Yet in this novel his usual inability to draw a convincing heroine matters little, for he sidesteps the problem. All the other characters are realistic, creatures of recognisable flesh-and-blood. But Katrine Yester, as Janet Adam Smith, Buchan's first (and best) biographer, realised, belongs to a different world – that of the Ballads. We see her almost entirely through David's eyes, and he sees her as ethereal. She is presented to us as a rare spirit because that is what she is to him.

It is a very Scotch novel, not only in setting, theme and argument, but also in language. In the introduction to his admirable anthology of Scots poetry, *The Northern Muse*, Buchan lamented the withering of the old rural Scots tongue, which he had learned to speak as a boy visiting his Masterton relations on their Tweeddale farm. But, he observed sadly, if he attended a sheep-sale there now and spoke as he had in his boyhood, he would find only a few old men to understand him. Much of the dialogue in *Witch Wood* is in that old Scots (though, like Scott, he has his hero and heroine, and also Montrose, speak in something close to standard, or genteel, English). The Scots of this novel is splendidly rich and racy – especially that spoken by Isobel Veitch, David's housekeeper, the other old women, and the farming folk; the chorus of ministers express themselves mostly in good Scots heavily laced with the language of the Old Testament, itself as unfamiliar to many readers today as Isobel's vernacular. The vigour and fecundity of the Scots is a delight. Nevertheless, as with the Scots of the Waverley novels, it poses problems for many now, even those who are Scots themselves, for much of the vocabulary is obsolete. It's probable that readers will find themselves turning often to the Glossary, though Scots ones at least will find that if they sound the words in their head, they will usually get the sense of a passage.

It is also a very Scotch novel in its moral seriousness. This remark requires qualification, for those who have claimed to incarnate moral seriousness in Scotland have often been the 'unco guid' mocked and satirised by Burns; hypocrites and Holy Willies who have perverted the gospel of Christ. Such are in truth the Pharisees of that gospel, the 'whited sepulchres', and they are here in strength in *Witch Wood*. David himself is a Christ-like figure, as Mark Kerr, the soldier-companion of Montrose, who emerges in the last pages of the book in the likeness of an avenging angel, tells the stunned congregation: 'A prophet came among you and you knew him not. For the sake of that witless thing that is now going four-foot among the braes you have condemned the innocent blood. He spent his strength for you and you rejected him, he yearned for you and you repelled him, he would have laid down his life for you and you scorned him. He is now beyond the reach of your ingratitude.' In their dream of being a people who have made a Covenant with God, the Kirk has worshipped the Old Testament and forgotten, even rejected, the New. Or, as Mark Kerr tells them, they have been 'muckle weans that played at being ancient Israelites'.

Critics tend to dwell on the themes of a novel, if only because they are its most discussible part. This is understandable, but it may lead them to forget that the themes underlying the narrative are not the immediately attractive or interesting elements of any fiction. Most of us read first for the story, and Buchan, here, as elsewhere, is a master of story-telling. Stevenson called this desire 'one of the natural appetites with which any lively literature has to count. The desire for knowledge, I had almost added the desire for meat, is not more deeply seated than this demand for fit and striking incident.' Buchan satisfies that appetite like few others, in his historical novels as surely as in his 'shockers'. There is incident aplenty in *Witch Wood* – one thinks of the disturbing visit of the 'witch-pricker', of the slaughter of camp-followers fleeing from the Battle of Philiphaugh, of the vivid account of the plague, of David's last dramatic conversation with Ephraim Caird, of Mark Kerr's superbly rhetorical appearance in the Kirk. This last strikes a characteristic note of Romance: it is highly improbable, yet absolutely convincing.

Buchan at his best, as he is here, always anchors his narrative in a particular place, which he evokes with the imaginative penetration that derives from knowledge. He knew that the incidents of a novel are made credible and persuasive if the setting is fully realised. Description of place is not mere decoration, not something added on, but integral to the character and atmosphere of the novel. Indeed one may say that in *Witch Wood* the landscape – country that Buchan had known since he was a child, hills that he had tramped over, woods he had explored – is so vividly brought before us as itself to be one of the principal characters in the novel.

If David Sempill is himself almost too good to be true and Katrine is, as I have suggested, a figure from the Ballads rather than real life, all the minor characters are among the most convincing that Buchan ever drew. He rarely failed when creating country women – one thinks of the admirable Phemie Morran in *Huntingtower* – but Isobel Veitch, loyal, sly, indignant, and quick-tongued, is wonderfully true to life. The novel sparkles whenever she opens her mouth. The group of ministers are subtly distinguished one from the other, and Buchan resists the temptation to make even the most objectionable of them appear as hypocrites. Mark Kerr may denounce them as such, but in truth they are sincere in their narrow interpretation of the Scriptures, while their unshakable conviction of self-righteousness is also something that is 'very Scotch'.

Indeed in his different way David Sempill is every bit as self-righteous as his adversaries. He draws his strength from the same sort of certainty, and this opens another aspect of the book. Good novels are always open to more than one interpretation, sometimes indeed, quite legitimately, to an interpretation beyond that intended by their author. So it is possible to question the indignation aroused in David by what he sees in the wood by night and to ask whether he is not perhaps in his own way as narrow-minded in his morality as those who will condemn him. For the devil-worship itself may be less awful than he supposes, more trivial and even silly, a mere excuse for sexual licence, for the release of those natural animal instincts which the severe rule of the Kirk has repressed. If legitimate joy in the body is denied, and carnality is condemned as shameful and sinful, then these instincts will seek an outlet, which may appear grotesque and repulsive as it does to David. A modern reader may well conclude that David should have made an effort to understand rather than rushing to condemn. But for Buchan to have had him doing so would have been grossly unhistorical; David may be a moderate among the ministers of the Kirk, more alert than his peers to the message of the New Testament; nevertheless he too is a Presbyterian of the seventeenth century, imbued with his creed's distrust of the flesh. Yet one may ask whether, in his final terrible dialogue with Ephraim Caird, it is not David who shows himself the neurotic. For all his genuine virtue and sweetness of character, he has not fully grasped the truth of Mark Kerr's warning that: 'The Kirk has made the yett of grace ower wide for sinful men, and all ither yetts ower narrow. It has banned innocence, and so made a calling of hypocrisy, for human nature is human nature, and if you tell a man that honest pleasure is a sin in God's sight he finds a way to get the pleasure, and yet keep the name for godliness.'

Buchan thought *Witch Wood* the best of his novels, and, though it has never been the most popular, he was right. It goes deeper than anything else he wrote. If it is first and foremost a historical novel, exploring in the manner of Scott and the mature Stevenson, a significant moment in Scottish history, and offering a study of Scottish society, and of the ideology which dominated that society and formed the historical character of the Scottish people, it is also a book which raises questions – disturbing questions – about human nature, about our capacity for self-deception, and about the consequences of repressing certain elements of that nature. Buchan's contemporary Ford Madox Ford held that the best imaginative literature has the power, denied in his view to other art forms, to make us think and feel at the same time. *Witch Wood* – more than anything else Buchan wrote – has that power. Like all great novels it makes a strong first impression, draws you to read it a second and third time, and reveals more at each subsequent reading.

Allan Massie
July 2008

Prologue

Time, my grandfather used to say, stood still in that glen of his. But the truth of the saying did not survive his death, and the first daisies had scarcely withered on his grave before a new world was knocking at the gate. That was thirty years ago, and today the revolution is complete. The parish name has been changed; the white box of a kirk which served the glen for more than two centuries has been rebuilt in red suburban gothic; a main railway line now runs down the Aller and the excellent summer service brings holiday-makers from a hundred miles distant: houses and shops have clustered under the Hill of Deer; there may be found a well-reputed boarding school for youth, two inns – both of them reformed – a garage, and a bank agent. The centre of importance has moved from the old village to the new town by the station, and even the old village is no more a clachan of thatched roofs straggling by a burnside. Some enemy of the human race has taught the burn to run straight like a sewer and has spanned it with a concrete bridge, while the thatch of the houses has been replaced by slates of a metallic green. Only the ruins of the old kirkton have not been meddled with; these stand as I remember them, knee-deep in docks and nettles, defended by a crumbling dry-stone dyke against inquisitive cattle from Crossbasket.

The old folk are gone, too, and their very names are passing from the countryside. Long before my day the Hawkshaws had disappeared from Calidon, but there was a respectable Edinburgh burgess family who had come there in the seventeenth century; now these have given place to a rawer burgess graft from the West. The farmers are mostly new men, and even the peasant, who should be the enduring stock, has shifted his slow bones. I learned from the postman that in Woodilee today there was no Monfries, no Sprot, but one Pennecuik, and only two bearers of the names of Ritchie and Shillinglaw, which had once been plentiful as ragwort. In such a renovated world it was idle to hope to find surviving the tales which had perplexed my childhood. No one could tell me when or why the kirk by the Crossbasket march became a ruin, and its gravestones lay buried in weeds. Most did not even know that it had been a kirk.

I was not greatly surprised at this, for the kirk of Woodilee had not been used for the better part of three centuries; and even as a child I could not find many to tell me of its last minister. The thing had sunk from a tale to an 'owercome,' a form of words which everyone knew but which few could interpret. It was Jess Blane, the grieve's daughter, who first stirred my curiosity. In a whirl of wrath at some of my doings she prayed that the fate of the minister of Woodilee might be mine – a fate which she expounded as to be 'claught by the Deil and awa' wi''. A little scared, I carried the affair to my nurse, who was gravely scandalised, and denounced Jess as a 'shamefu' tawpie, fyling the wean's mind wi' her black lees'. 'Dinna you be feared, dearie,' she reassured me. 'It wasna the Deil that cam for the Minister o' Woodilee. I've aye heard tell that he was a guid man and a kind man. It was the Fairies, hinny. And he leev'd happy wi' them and dee'd happy and never drank out o' an empty cup.' I took my information, I remember, to the clan of children who were my playmates, and they spread it among their households and came back with confirmation or contradiction. Some held for the Devil, some for the Fairies – a proof that tradition spoke with two voices. The Fairy school slightly out-numbered the others, and in a battle one April evening close to the ruined kirk we routed the diabolists and established our version as the canon. But save for the solitary fact – that the Minister of Woodilee had gone off with the Fairies – the canon remained bare.

Years later I got the tale out of many books and places; a folio in the library of a Dutch college, the muniment-room of a Catholic family in Lancashire, notes in a copy of the second

Latin edition of Wishart's *Montrose*, the diaries of a captain of Hebron's and of a London glove-maker, the exercise book of a seventeenth-century Welsh schoolgirl. I could piece the story together well enough, but at first I found it hard to fit it to the Woodilee that I knew – that decorous landscape, prim, determinate, without a hint of mystery; the bare hill-tops, bleak at seasons, but commonly of a friendly Pickwickian baldness, skirted with methodically-planned woods of selected conifers, and girdled with mathematical stone dykes; the even, ruled fields of the valley bottom; the studied moderation of the burns in a land meticulously drained; the dapper glass and stone and metal of the village. Two miles off, it was true, ran the noble untamed streams of Aller; beyond them the hills rose in dark fields to midsky, with the glen of the Rood making a sword-cut into their heart. But Woodilee itself – whither had fled the saviour? Once, I knew from the books, the great wood of Melanudrigill had descended from the heights and flowed in black waves to the village brink. But I could not re-create the picture out of glistening asphalted highway, singing telegraph wires, spruce dwellings, model pastures, and manicured woodlands.

Then one evening from the Hill of Deer I saw with other eyes. There was a curious leaden sky, with a blue break about sunset, so that the shadows lay oddly. My first thought, as I looked at the familiar scene, was that, had I been a general in a campaign, I should have taken special note of Woodilee, for it was a point of vantage. It lay right in the pass between the Scottish midlands and the south – the pass of road and water – yes, and – shall I say? – of spirit, for it was in the throat of the hills, on the march between the sown and the desert. I was looking east, and to my left and behind me the open downs, farmed to their last decimal of capacity, were the ancient land of Manann, the capital province of Pictdom. The colliery headgear on the horizon, the trivial moorish hill-tops, the dambrod-pattern fields, could never tame wholly for me that land's romance, and on this evening I seemed to be gazing at a thing antique and wolfish, tricked out for the moment with a sheep's coat. . . . To my right rose the huddle of great hills which cradle all our rivers. To them time and weather bring little change, yet in that eery light, which revealed in hard outline while it obscured in detail, they seemed too remote and awful to be the kindly giants with whose glens I daily conversed. . . . At my feet lay Woodilee, and a miracle had been wrought, for a gloom like the shadow of an eclipse seemed to have crept over the parish. I saw an illusion, which I knew to be such, but which my mind accepted, for it gave me the vision I had been seeking.

It was the Woodilee of three hundred years ago. And my mind, once given the cue, set out things not presented by the illuded eye. . . . There were no highways – only tracks, miry in the bogs and stony on the braes, which led to Edinburgh on one hand and to Carlisle on the other. I saw few houses, and these were brown as peat, but on the knowe of the old kirkton I saw the four grey walls of the kirk, and the manse beside it among elders and young ashes. Woodilee was not now a parish lying open to the eye of sun and wind. It was no more than a tiny jumble of crofts, bounded and pressed in upon by something vast and dark, which clothed the tops of all but the highest hills, muffled the ridges, choked the glens and overflowed almost to the edge of the waters – which lay on the landscape like a shaggy fur cast loosely down. My mouth shaped the word 'Melanu-drigill', and I knew that I saw Woodilee as no eye had seen it for three centuries, when, as its name tells, it still lay in the shadow of a remnant of the Wood of Caledon, that most ancient forest where once Merlin harped and Arthur mustered his men. . . .

An engine whistled in the valley, a signal-box sprang into light, and my vision passed. But as I picked my way down the hillside in the growing dusk I realised that all memory of the encircling forest had not gone from Woodilee in my childhood, though the name of Melanudrigill had been forgotten. I could hear old Jock Dodds, who had been keeper on Calidon for fifty years, telling tales for my delectation, as he sat and smoked on the big stone beside the smithy. He would speak of his father, and his father's father, and the latter had been a great hero with his flint-lock gun. 'He would lie in the moss or three on the winter mornin's, and him an auld man, and get the wild swans and the grey geese when they cam ower frae Clyde to Aller. Ay, and mony's the deer he would kill.' And when I pointed out that there were no deer in the countryside, Jock shook his head and said that in his grandfather's day the Black Wood was not all destroyed. 'There was a muckle lump on Windyways, and anither this side o' Reiverslaw.' But if I asked for more about the wood, Jock was vague. Some said it had been first set by the Romans, others by Auld Michael Scott himself. . . . 'A grand hidy-hole for beasts and an unco bit for warlocks.' . . . Its downfall had begun long ago in the Dear Years, and the last of it had been burnt for firewood in his father's day, in the winter of the Sixteen Drifty Days. . . .

I remembered, too, that there had been places still sacrosanct and feared. To Mary Cross, a shapeless stone in a field of bracken, no one would go in the spring or summer gloaming, but the girls decked it with wild flowers at high noon of Midsummer Day. There was a stretch of Woodilee burn, between the village and the now-drained Fennan Moss, where trout, it was believed, were never found. Above all, right in the heart of Reiverslaw's best field of turnips was a spring, which we children knew as Katie Thirsty, but which the old folk called the Minister's Well, and mentioned always with a shake of the head or a sigh, for it was there, they said, that the Minister of Woodilee had left the earth for Fairyland.

ONE

The Coming of the Minister

The Reverend David Sempill began his ministry in Woodilee on the twenty-sixth day of August in the year of grace sixteen hundred and forty-four. He was no stranger to the glen, for as a boy he had spent his holidays with his grandfather, who was the miller of Roodfoot. In that year when the horn of the Kirk was exalted the voice of a patron mattered less; Mr Sempill had been, as they said, 'popularly called', and so entered upon his office with the eager interest of the parish which had chosen him. A year before he had been licensed by the presbytery of Edinburgh; he was ordained in Woodilee in the present year on the last Sabbath of June, and 'preached in' on the third Sabbath of August by the weighty voice of Mungo Muirhead, the minister of Kirk Aller. His plenishing – chiefly books – had come from Edinburgh on eight pack-horses, and, having escaped the perils of Carnwath Moss, was now set out in an upper chamber of the little damp manse, which stood between the kirk and Woodilee burn. A decent widow woman, Isobel Veitch by name, had been found to keep his house, and David himself, now that all was ready, had ridden over on his grey cob from his cousin's at Newbiggin and taken seisin of his new home. He had sung as he came in sight of Woodilee; he had prayed with bowed head as he crossed the manse threshold; but as he sat in the closet which he named his 'study', and saw his precious books on the shelf and the table before him on which great works would be written, and outside the half-glazed window the goose-berry bushes of the garden and the silver links of the burn, he had almost wept with pure gratitude and content.

His first hour he had spent exploring his property. The manse was little and squat and gave lodging in its heather-thatched roof to more than one colony of bees. The front abutted on the kirkton road, save for a narrow strip of green edged with smooth white stones from the burn. The back looked on a garden, where stood a score of apple trees, the small wild fruit of which was scarcely worth the gathering. There was also a square of green for bleaching clothes, a gean tree, a plot of gillyflowers and monkshood, and another of precious herbs like clary, penny-royal, and marjoram. At one end of the manse stood a brewhouse and a granary or girnel, for the storing of the minister's stipend meal; at the other a stable for two beasts, a byre with three stalls, a hen-house of mud, and, in the angle of the dykes of the kirk loan, a midden among nettles.

Indoors the place was not commodious, and even on that warm August day a chill struck upward from the earthen floors. The low-ceiled lobby had no light but the open door. To the right of it was the living-room with a boarded ceiling, a wooden floor, and roughly plastered walls, where the minister's eight-day clock (by John Atchison, Leith, 1601) had now acclimatised itself. To the left lay Isobel's kitchen, with a door leading to the brew-house, and Isobel's press-bed at the back of it, and a small dog-hole of a cellar. The upper story was reached by a wooden staircase as steep as a ladder, which opened direct into the minister's bedroom – an apartment of luxury, for it had a fireplace. One door led from it to the solitary guest-chamber; another to a tiny hearthless room, which was his study or closet, and which at the moment ranked in his mind as the most miraculous of his possessions.

David ranged around like a boy back from school, and indeed with his thick sandy hair and ruddy countenance and slim straight back he seemed scarcely to have outgrown the school-boy. He spilt the browst in the brewhouse and made a spectacle of himself with pease-meal in the girnel. Isobel watched him anxiously out of doors, when he sampled the fruit of the apple trees, and with various rejected specimens took shots at a starling in the glebe. Then in response to his shouts she brought him a basin of water and he washed off the dust of his morning ride. The August sun fell warm on the little yard; the sound of the burn in the glen, the clack of the kirkton smithy, the sheep far off on Windyways, the bees in the clove gillyflowers, all melted into the soothing hum of a moorland noontide. The minister smiled as he scrubbed his cheeks, and Isobel's little old puckered apple-hued face smiled back. 'Ay, sir,' she said, 'our lines is fallen intil a goodly place and a pleasant habitation. The Lord be thankit.' And as he cried a fervent amen and tossed the towel back to her, a stir at the front door betokened his first visitors.

These were no less than three in number, neighbouring ministers who had ridden over on their garrons to bid the young man welcome to Woodilee. Presently stable and byre were crowded with their beasts, and the three brethren had bestowed themselves on the rough bench which adjoined the bleaching ground. They would have their dinner at the village ordinary – let not Mr Sempill put himself about – they would never have come thus unannounced if they had thought that they would be pressed to a meal. But they allowed themselves to be persuaded by the hospitable clamour of Isobel, who saw in such a function on her first day at the manse a social aggrandisement. 'Mr Sempill would think black burnin' shame if the gentlemen didna break breid. . . . There was walth o' provender in the house – this moment she had put a hen in the pot – she had a brace of muirfowl ready for brandering that had been sent from Chasehope that very morn. . . .' The three smiled tolerantly and hopefully. 'Ye've gotten a rare Abigail, Mr Sempill. A woman o' mense and sense – the manse o' Woodilee will be well guidit.'

The Reverend Mungo Muirhead had a vast shaven face set atop of a thick neck and a cumbrous body. He had a big thin-lipped mouth which shut tight like a lawyer's, a fleshy nose, and large grey eyes which at most times were ruminant as a cow's, but could on occasion kindle to shrewdness. His complexion was pale, and he was fast growing bald, so the impression at first sight was of a perfect mountain of countenance, a steep field of colourless skin. As minister of Kirk Aller he was the metropolitan of the company, and as became a townsman he wore decent black with bands, and boasted a hat. The Reverend Ebenezer Proudfoot from the moorland village of Bold was of a different cast. He wore the coarse grey homespun of the farmer, his head-covering was a blue bonnet, his shoes were thick brogues with leather ties, and he had donned a pair of ancient frieze leggings. A massive sinewy figure, there was in his narrow face and small blue eyes an air of rude power and fiery energy. The third, Mr James Fordyce from the neighbouring parish of Cauldshaw, was slight and thin, and pale either from ill-health or from much study. He was dressed in worn blue, and even in the August sun kept his plaid round his shoulders. In his face a fine brow was marred by the contraction of his lean jaws and a mouth puckered constantly as if in doubt or pain, but redeemed by brown eyes, as soft and wistful as a girl's.

At the hour of noon they sat down to meat. Mr Muirhead said a lengthy grace, which, since he sniffed the savour from the kitchen, he began appropriately with 'Bountiful Jehovah'. All the dishes were set out at once on the bare deal table – a bowl of barley kail, a boiled fowl, the two brandered grouse, and a platter of oatcakes. The merchant in the Pleasance of Edinburgh had given his son a better plenishing than fell to the usual lot of ministers, for there were pewter plates and a knife and a fork for each guest. The three stared at the splendour, and Mr Proudfoot, as if to testify against luxury, preferred to pick the bones with his hands. The homebrewed ale was good, and all except Mr Fordyce did full justice to it, so that the single tankard, passed from hand to hand, was often refilled by Isobel. 'Man, Mr David,' cried Mr Muirhead in high good-humour, 'this is a great differ from the days of your predecessor. Worthy Mr Macmichael had never muckle but bannocks to set before his friends. But you've made us a feast of fat things.'

David inquired about his predecessor, whom he remembered dimly from his boyhood as a man even then very old, who ambled about the parish on a white shelty.

'He was a pious and diligent minister,' said Mr Muirhead, 'but since ever I kenned him he was sore fallen in the vale of years. He would stick to the same "ordinary" till he had thrashed it into stour. I've heard that he preached for a year and sax months on Exodus fifteen and twenty-seven, the twelve wells of water and three score and ten palm trees of Elim, a Sabbath to ilka well and ilka tree. I've a notion that he was never very strong in the intellectuals.'

'He wrestled mightily in prayer,' said Mr Proudfoot, 'and he was great at fencing the Tables. Ay, sirs, he was a trumpet for the pure Gospel blast.'

'I doubt not he was a good man,' said Mr Fordyce, 'and is now gone to his reward. But he was ower auld and feeble for a sinful countryside. I fear that the parish was but ill guided, and, as ye ken, there was whiles talk of a Presbytery visitation.'

'I differ!' cried Mr Muirhead. 'I differ *in toto*. Woodilee has aye been famous for its godly elders. Has it not Ephraim Caird, who was a member of Assembly and had a hand in that precious work of grace done in the East Kirk of St. Giles's two years syne? Has it not Peter Pennecuik, who has a gift of supplication like Mr Rutherford himself? Ay, and in the Bishops' War you'll mind how Amos Ritchie was staunch to uphold the Covenant with the auld matchlock that had been his gudesire's. There's no lack of true religion in Woodilee.'

'There's no lack of carnal pride, Mr Mungo. The folk of Woodilee are ready enough for any stramash in kirk or state. But what of their perishing souls, I ask? Are they striving to get a grip of Christ, as a bird scrapes with its claws at a stone wall? And do they bring forth works meet for repentance?'

'There was no clash of cauld morality in worthy Mr Macmichael,' said Mr Proudfoot sourly.

'Is there the spirit of God in the people? That's what I want to ken. There's ill stories in the countryside anent Woodilee. The Black Wood could tell some tales if the trees could talk.'

Mr Muirhead, having finished his meal and said a second grace, was picking his teeth in great good-humour.

'Hoot toots, Mr James, you'll give our young brother a scunner of the place, to which it has pleased the Almighty to call him, before he has had a look at it himself. I'm not denying that the Wood is ower near Woodilee. It's a wanchancy thing for any parochine to have a muckle black forest flung around it like a maud. And no doubt the Devil walks about like a roaring lion in Woodilee as in other bits. But there's men of God here to resist him. I tell you, sirs, there have been more delations to the Presbytery for the sin of witchcraft in Woodilee than in any other parish on the water of Aller.'

'And what does that prove, Mr Mungo?'

'That there's wealth of prayerful and eident folk to confound the Adversary. This is no season to despair of Kirk and Covenant, when this day they hold the crown of the causeway. You'll no have heard of the astonishing mercy vouchsafed to us in England? A post came to Kirk Aller yestreen, and it seems that three weeks syne there was a great battle beside the city of York, where our Scots wrought mightily, and our own Davie Leslie gave the King's horsemen their kail through the reek. What does that portend?'

'It portends,' said Mr Proudfoot, whom food did not mellow, 'that our pure and reformed Kirk of Scotland is linked more than ever with sectaries and antinomians and those, like the bloody and deceitful Cromwell, that would defile the milk of the Word with the sour whey of their human inventions. What avails a triumphant Kirk if its doctrine be sullied?'

Mr Muirhead laughed. 'It portends nothing of the kind. The good work goes cannily on, and the noble task to which the Assembly of Divines at Westminster set itself is advanced by a long mile. Man, Eben, you folk at Bold live ower far from the world. It's the Kirk of Scotland that holds the balance today and can enforce its will on both King and sectaries. Two days back I had a letter from that gospel-loving nobleman, the Earl of Loudoun. . . .'

Mr Muirhead was mounted on his high horse. He lit his pipe and for the space of half an hour dealt comprehensively with politics, labouring to show the happy posture of affairs for what he called the 'good cause.' The Solemn League and Covenant bound all Scotland in a pact with the Lord, and presently all England would follow suit. There would be soon that comfortable sight which had been foretold by their godly fathers, a uniform Kirk and a pure Gospel established by law from London to the Orkneys, and a covenanted Sion to which all the peoples of the earth would go up. Mr Muirhead was eloquent, for he repeated a peroration which he had once used in the General Assembly.

'I have heard,' he concluded, 'that in Woodilee there was a signing of the Covenant by every soul that could make a scart with a pen. That for your encouragement, Mr David.'

Mr Fordyce shook his head. 'How many appended their names out of fear or from mere carnal policy? Mankind will run like jukes after a leader. I much misdoubt if there is any spiritual health to be got from following a multitude under duress. I would have left the choice to every man's conscience.'

'You're not sound,' cried Mr Muirhead. 'You're shaky on the fundamentals, Mr. James. I will confound you out of the Word. When King Josiah made a solemn covenant, did he leave it to ilka man's fancy to sign or no? Nay, he caused all – all, I say – in Jerusalem and Benjamin to stand to it. See Second Chronicles thirty-four and thirty-two.'

There was a touch of asperity in the one disputant and of recalcitrance in the other, so David for good-fellowship's sake suggested that he might show them the manse in its new guise. But at that moment Isobel appeared with word that Chasehope was at the door seeking speech with the minister of Kirk Aller. At her back appeared the fiery head of the visitor, who was that Ephraim Caird whom Mr Muirhead had already praised as a pillar of the Covenant and who farmed the biggest tack in the parish. He was a big fellow, red as a fox, with a white freckled face, no eyebrows and greenish blue eyes, a man of over forty, whose muscular frame was now somewhat overlaid by flesh. His mouth was small and generally puckered together, a habit which gave him an air of thought and gravity. He had been an opponent of David Sempill before the call, but had acquiesced in the majority vote and had welcomed the new minister at the 'preaching in' with a great show of goodwill. Today he was apologetic and affable. He asked pardon for his intrusion – he would take neither bite nor sup – he had heard that the ministers were at the manse and he begged a word with Mr Muirhead on Presbytery matters which would save him a journey to Kirk Aller, when he was busy with the bog hay. So David took the other two to his closet and left Chasehope and Mr Muirhead to their colloquy.

Mr Proudfoot eyed with disapproval the books in the little dark chamber. He was content, he said, with the Bible and the Institutes of John Calvin and old Robert Rollock's commentary on the Prophet Daniel. He read the lettering on one volume, *Sancti Clementi Opera*, and on another, a work by a Dutch theologian, *De Sancti Pauli Epistolis*. The word 'Saint' roused his ire. 'Rags of Popery,' he muttered, as he banged the books back on their shelves. 'What for "Saint" Paul and not "Saint" Moses or "Saint" Isaiah? It's a queer thing that Antichrist should set himself to miscall the godly Apostles of the New Testament and let the auld prophets alone. You're a young man, Mr Sempill, and, as is natural in youth, with but a small experience of religion. Take the advice of an older man, and no clog yourself on the road to Heaven with ower much printit lear, when ye can put the whole Word of God in your pouch.'

But Mr Fordyce looked at the shelves with greedy eyes. The moor-fowl at dinner had loosened a tooth, and now it came out in his hand and was wrapped carefully in his kerchief. 'I have kept ilka tooth I have ever cast,' he told the others, 'and they will go into my coffin with me that my bodily parts may be together at the Resurrection.' 'Would you shorten the arm of the Lord?' Mr Proudfoot had asked testily. 'Can He no gather your remnants from the uttermost parts of the earth?' 'True, true,' the other had answered gently, 'but it's just my fancy to keep all my dust in the one place.' This ceremony over, he flung himself on the books like a hungry man on food. He opened them lovingly, read their titles, fingered them as if he could scarcely bear to part with them. 'You're no half my age,' he told the owner, 'but you've twice as many books as there are in the Cauldshaw manse. You start well provided, Mr David.'

The theology he knew already and approved of, but there were other works over which he shook a moralising head. 'You've a hantle of Pagan writers, Mr David. I would counsel a young minister to apply himself rather to the Hebrew than to the Greek, for though the Greek was the tongue of the New Testament, it was also the tongue of lascivious poets and mocking philosophers, whereas the Hebrew was consecrate wholly to God. . . . But you have the Hebrew too, I see. Losh, here's the lexicon of Bamburgius, of which I have read but have never seen. We must consult, Mr David. I've a new theory of the Hebrew accents on which I would like your judgment.'

As he ran over the list he suddenly cried aloud with pleasure, and then checked himself almost shamefacedly. 'Preserve us, but here's Hieronymus Cardanus, and other astrologic works. Man, I've diverted myself whiles with the science of the stars, and can make a shape at calculating a nativity. I cannot see why the thing should not be turned to holy uses, as when the star guided the Wise Men of the East to Bethlehem. You and me must have long cracks some day. These books will be like the Pole Star to draw me to Woodilee, and I'm looking to see you soon at Cauldshaw. It's but a poor desert bit, but there have been precious occasions there and many an outpouring of grace. I'm sore troubled with the gravel, Mr David, and the goodwife has had a flux in the legs this twelvemonth back, but the Lord has showed me singular favour and my damps are lightened since a leech in Edinburgh prescribed a hyperion of bourtree and rue. . . . We're a childless household, for we had but the one bairn and sax year syne the Lord gathered her to Himself.'

Downstairs Mr Muirhead had finished his talk and the three ministers took their leave – they of Bold and Cauldshaw to jog the moorland miles to their homes, he of Kirk Aller to take his 'four-hours' with Chasehope at Lucky Weir's in the clachan. Each of the three kissed David on the cheek and blessed him after his fashion. 'May you live to be a pillar of the Kirk,' said Mr Muirhead. 'Keep a Gospel walk,' said Mr Proudfoot, 'on the narrow rigging of the truth.' But Mr Fordyce took the young man's hand, after saluting him and held it with a kind of wistful affection. 'I pray,' he said, 'that your windows may be ever open towards Jerusalem.'

When his guests had gone David Sempill explored once more his little domain, like a child who counts his treasures. Then, as the afternoon mellowed into evening, the slopes of the Hill of Deer, red with flowering heather, drew him for a walk. He wanted a wide prospect, to see his parish in its setting of hill and glen, and recall the landmarks now blurred in his childhood's memory. His black coat and breeches were of Edinburgh make and too fine for moorland work, but he had stout country shoes and hose of ram's wool, the gift of his cousin's wife at New-biggin, and he moved over the bent with the long stride of a shepherd. He crossed the burn of Mire, and saw below him the farm-town of Mirehope, with barley and nettles at strife in the infield, and the run-rigs of the outfield feathered with very green oats. Presently he was on the Hill of Deer, where the long stacks of peats were drying so well that every breath of air sent up from them a fine flurry of dust. The Mirehope cattle, wretched little black beasts, were grazing under the charge of a herd-boy, and the Mirehope sheep, their coats matted with tar till they looked like monstrous slugs, were picking up an uneasy livelihood among the heather bushes, leaving tufts of smelly wool behind them on the scraggy twigs which were still charred from the March moorburn. He reached the low summit, and flung himself down on a patch of thymy turf between the whinstone screes, with his face to the valley.

His holiday mood still held. The visit of his ministerial brethren had not dashed him, for he saw their prosiness through a golden haze. Mr Muirhead was a stout warder on the walls of Sion, Mr Proudfoot a guardian of the purity of the Temple, and Mr Fordyce beyond question a saint, with his haggard face and his wistful eyes. It was Mr Fordyce who stuck in his memory. A lovable saint, with his cast teeth saved up to make easy the business of a bodily resurrection, his love of the stars, his pathetic bookishness. David was full of the zest of his calling but for himself he was ready to circumscribe its duties. Not for him to uphold the Kirk against its ill-wishers in the State; in that cause he would do battle when the need arose, but not till then. He left to others the task of keeping the canon of truth pure from alloy: he accepted the Kirk's doctrine loyally, but let others do the dogmatising. The work for which he longed was to save and comfort human souls.

Seen on that hilltop the minister of Woodilee was a different figure from that beheld by his colleagues in the dim light of the manse. His active form, his colour, his tumbled hair, spoke of the boy, but his face was not boyish. In its young contours there were already thought and resolution and spiritual fineness, and there was a steady ardour in the eyes. If his chin was the fighter's, his mouth was the comforter's. Five years before he had been set on a scholar's life. At the college he had been a noted Grecian, and in Robert Bryson's bookshop at the Sign of the Prophet Jonah in the West Bow his verses, Latin and English, had been praised by the learned. When religion called him it was as a challenge not to renounce but to perfect his past. A happy preoccupation with his dream made him blind to the harshness and jealousies which beset the Kirk, and he saw only its shining mission. The beauty which is to be found in letters seemed in very truth a part of that profounder beauty which embraced all earth and Heaven in the revelation of God. He had not ceased to be the humanist in becoming the evangelist. Some had looked askance at him as too full of carnal learning for the sacred office, some as too cheerful for a shepherd of souls in a perishing world. But his critics as yet were few, for David carried with him a light and warmth which it was hard for the sourest to resist. 'He is a gracious youth,' an old minister had said at his ordination. 'May the Lord deal tenderly with him!'

David's eyes from his perch on the hilltop rested first on the kirkton of Woodilee. He saw the manse among its trees, and the church with its thatched roof – the roof had been lead till Morton the Regent stripped it and melted it down for bullets. He saw the little beehive cottages in the clachan with the taller gable-end of Lucky Weir's ale-house. He saw the adjoining farm-towns – the Mains, Chasehope, Nether Windyways, Crossbasket, the two Fennans, each with its patches of crops lifted well above the bogs of the glen. He saw the mill of Woodilee at present idle by the burn, and hay being cut on the side of Windyways hill, and what looked like the clipping of the miller's sheep. In the bright evening the scene was all of peace and pastoral and David's heart kindled. There dwelled his people, the little flock whom God had appointed him to feed. His heart yearned over them, and in a sudden glow of tenderness he felt that this sunset prospect of his parish was a new and more solemn ordination.

It was long before he lifted his eyes beyond the glen to the great encircling amphitheatre of the hills. At first he gazed at them in an abstraction, till childish memories came back to him and he began to name the summits to himself one by one. There was the bald top of the Lammerlaw, and the peak of the Green Dod, and far beyond the long line of the great Herstane Craig, which in that childhood had been the synonym for untravelled mystery. He saw the green cleft in the hills where the Aller came down from its distant wells, and the darker glen of the Rood where bent was exchanged for rock and heather. He saw the very patches of meadow by Roodside which he had made his boyish playground. Such a hilltop prospect he had never before known, for a child lives in a magnified world, and finds immensity in short vistas. One thing struck hard on his mind. Never before had he realised the extent of the forest ground. He remembered travelling to Roodfoot through trees, and all up the water of Rood there had been a drift of scrub. But it was the meadows and the open spaces that had been his kingdom, and his recollection was of a bare sunny land where whaup and peewit cried and the burns fell headlong from windy moors. But now, as he gazed, he realised that the countryside was mainly forest.

Everywhere, muffling the lower glen of the Woodilee burn and the immediate vale of the Aller, and climbing far up the hillside, was the gloom of trees. In the Rood glen there was darkness only at the foot, for higher up the woods thinned into scrub of oak and hazel, with the knees of the uplands showing through it. The sight powerfully impressed his fancy. Woodilee was a mere clearing in a forest. This was the *Silva Caledonis* of which old writers spoke, the wood which once covered all the land and in whose glades King Arthur had dwelt. He remembered doggerel Latin of Merlin the Bard and strange sayings of True Thomas – old wives' tales which concerned this sanctuary. He had grown up beside it and had not known of it, and now he had come back to a revelation. *Silva Caledonis!* Up the Rood water lay the house of Calidon. Were the names perhaps the same?

The young man's fancy was quick to kindle, and he looked with new eyes at the great cup of green, broken only at one spot by Aller side with the flash of water. At first in the soft evening light it had worn a gracious and homely air, even the darkness of the pines seemed luminous, and the feathery top of a patch of birches was like the smoke of household fires. . . . But as the sun sank behind the Rood hills a change seemed to come over the scene. The shade became gloom, a hostile impenetrable darkness. The birches were still like smoke, but a turbid smoke from some unhallowed altar. The distant shallows of Aller caught a ray of the dying sun and turned to blood. . . . The minister shivered and then laughed at himself for his folly.

The evening deepened in the hollows, though the hilltops were still faintly bright. The great wood seemed now to be a moving thing, a flood which lapped and surged and might at any

moment overflow the sandspit which was Woodilee. Again the
minister laughed at himself, but without conviction. It must be
an eery life under the shadow of that ancient formless thing.
Woodilee could not be quite as other parishes, or its folk like
other folk. The Wood, this hoary Wood of Caledon, must
dominate their thoughts and form their characters. . . . Had
not someone called it the Black Wood? – Yes, they had spoken of
it that afternoon. Mr Muirhead had admitted that it must be
queer to live so near it, and Mr Fordyce had shaken his head
solemnly and hinted at tales that could be told if the trees would
speak. . . . Did the Devil use the place as a stronghold and
seduce the foolish into its shadows? Could it be said of a lost
soul, *Itur in antiquam silvam?*

David was less superstitious than most men, but he had too
ready a fancy and a mind too well stored with learning to be easy
at the thought. Already he felt that he had found an antagonist.
Was Woodilee to prove a frontier-post for God's servant against
the horrid mysteries of heathendom? . . . He gave a sudden
start, for a voice had sounded behind him.

The voice was singing – a charm against bogles which he
remembered himself using as a child:

> Wearie, Ovie, gang awa,
> Haste ye furth o' house an' ha',
> Ower the muir and down the burn
> Wearie, Ovie, ne'er return.

A grotesque figure emerged from the dusk. It was a tall fellow,
who seemed to have been broken in the middle, for he walked
almost doubled up. His face, seen in the half-light, was that of a
man of thirty or so, with a full black beard and red protuberant
lips. His clothes were ruinous, an old leather jerkin which gaped
at every seam, ragged small-clothes of frieze, and for hosen a
wrapping of dirty clouts. There were no shoes on his feet, and
his unwashed face was dark as a berry. In his hand he had a long
ash pole, and on his head a blue cowl so tight that it was almost a
skull-cap.

David recognised the figure for Daft Gibbie, the village natural, who had greeted him with mewing and shouting at his ordination. In the clachan street he had seemed an ordinary deformed idiot – what was known locally as an 'object' – but up on this twilight hilltop he was like an uncouth *revenant* from an older world. The minister instinctively gripped his staff tighter, but Gibbie's intention was of the friendliest.

'A braw guid e'en to ye, Mr Sempill, sir. I saw ye tak' the hill and I bode to follow, for I was wantin' to bid ye welcome to Woodilee. Man, ye gang up the brae-face like a maukin. Ower fast, I says to mysel', ower fast for a man o' God, for what saith the Word, "He that believeth shall not make haste!"'

The creature spoke in a voice of great beauty and softness – the voice rather of a woman than of a man. And as he spoke he bowed, and patted the minister's arm, and peered into his face with bright wild eyes. Then he clutched David and forced him round till again he was looking over the Wood.

'The Hill o' Deer's a grand bit for a prospect, sir, for is it no like the Hill o'Pisgah from which ye can spy the Promised Land? Ye can lift up your eyes to the hills, and ye can feast them on the bonny haughs o' the Aller, or on the douce wee clachan o'Woodilee, wi' the cots sittin' as canty round the kirk as kittlins round an auld cat.'

'I was looking at the Wood,' said David.

The man laughed shrilly. 'And a braw sicht it is in the gloamin' frae the Hill o' Deer. For ye can see the size o' the muckle spider's wab, but doun in the glen ye're that clamjamphried wi' michty trees that your heid spins like a peery and your e'en are dozened. It's a unco thing the Wud, Mr Sempill, sir?'

'Do you know your ways in it, Gibbie?'

'Me! I daurna enter it. I keep the road, for I'm feared o' yon dark howes.' Then he laughed again, and put his mouth close to the minister's ear. 'Not but what I'll tak' the Wud at the proper season. Tak' the Wud, Mr Sempill, like other folk in Woodilee.'

He peered in the minister's face to see if he were understood. Satisfied that he was not, he laughed again.

'Tak' Gibbie's advice, sir, and no gang near the Wud. It's nae place for men o' God, like yoursel', sir, and puir Gibbie.'

'Do they call it the Black Wood?'

Gibbie spat. 'Incomin' bodies, nae doot,' he said in contempt. 'But ken ye the name that auld folk gie'd it?' He became confidential again. 'They ca'd it Melanudrigill,' he whispered.

David repeated the word. His mind had been running on heathen learning and he wondered if the name were Greek.

'That might mean the "place of dark waters",' he said.

'Na, na. Ye're wrong there, Mr Sempill. There's nae dark waters in Melanudrigill. There's the seven burns that rin south, but they're a' as clear as Aller. But dinna speak that name to ither folk, Mr Sempill, and dinna let on that Gibbie telled ye. It's a wanchancy name. Ye can cry it in a safe bit like the Hill o' Deer, but if ye was to breathe it in the Wud unco things might happen. I daurna speak my ain name among the trees.'

'Your name is Gibbie. Gibbie what?'

The man's face seemed to narrow in fear and then to expand in confidence. 'I can tell it to a minister o' the Word. It's Gilbert Niven. Ken ye where I got that name? In the Wud, sir. Ken ye wha gie'd it me? The Guid Folk. Ye'll no let on that I telled ye.'

The night was now fallen, and David turned for home, after one last look at the pit of blackness beneath him. The idiot hobbled beside him, covering the ground at a pace which tried even his young legs, and as he went he babbled.

'Tak' Gibbie's advice and keep far frae the Wud, Mr Sempill, and if ye're for Roodfoot or Calidon haud by the guid road. I've heard tell that in the auld days, when there was monks at the kirkton, they bode to gang out every year wi' bells and candles and bless the road to keep it free o' bogles. But they never ventured into the Wud, honest men. I'll no say but what a minister is mair powerfu' than a monk, but an eident body will run nae risks. Keep to fine caller bits like this Hill o' Deer, and if ye want to traivel gang west by Chasehope or east by Kirk Aller. There's nocht for a man o' God in the Wud.'

'Are there none of my folk there?'

For a second Gibbie stopped as if thunderstruck. 'Your folk!' he cried. 'In the Wud!' Then he perceived David's meaning. 'Na, na. There's nae dwallin' there. Nether Fennan is no far off and Reiverslaw is a bowshot from the trees, but to bide in the Wud! – Na, na, a man would be sair left to himsel' ere he ventured that! There's nae hoose biggit by human hand that wadna be clawed doun by bogles afore the wa' rase a span frae the grund.'

At the outfield of Mirehope Gibbie fled abruptly, chanting like a night bird.

TWO

The Road to Calidon

The minister sat at his supper of porridge and buttermilk when Isobel broke in on him, her apple-hued face solemn and tearful.

'There's ill news frae up the water, Mr Sempill. It's Marion Simpson, her that's wife to Richie Smail, the herd o' the Greenshiel. Marion, puir body, has been ill wi' a wastin' the past twalmonth, and now it seems she's near her release. Johnnie Dow, the packman, is ben the house, and he has brocht word that Richie is fair dementit, and that the wife is no like to last the nicht, and would the minister come up to the Greenshiel. They've nae bairns, the Lord be thankit; but Richie and Marion have aye been fell fond o' ither, and Richie's an auld exercised Christian and has been many times spoken o' for the eldership. I doot ye'll hae to tak' the road, sir.'

It was his first call to pastoral duty, and, though he had hoped to be at his books by candle-light, David responded gladly. He put his legs into boots, saddled his grey cob, flung his plaid round his shoulders, and in ten minutes was ready to start. Isobel watched him like a mother.

'I'll hae a cup o' burned yill waitin' for ye to fend off the cauld – no but what it's a fine lown nicht. Ye ken the road, sir? Up by Mirehope and round by the Back o' the Hill.'

'There's a quicker way by Roodfoot, and on this errand there's no time to lose.'

'But that's through the Wud,' Isobel gasped. 'It's no me that would go through the Wud in the dark, nor naebody in Woodilee. But a minister is different, nae doot.'

'The road is plain?' he asked.

'Aye, it's plain eneuch. There's naething wrong wi' the road. But it's an eerie bit when the sun's no shinin'. But gang your ways, sir, for a man o' God is no like common folk. Ye'll get a mune to licht ye back.'

David rode out of the kirkton, and past the saughs and elders which marked the farm of Crossbasket, till the path dipped into the glen of the Woodilee burn and the trees began. Before he knew he was among them, old gnarled firs standing sparsely among bracken. They were thin along the roadside, but on the hill to his right and down in the burn's hollow they made a cloud of darkness. The August night still had a faint reflected light, and the track, much ribbed by tree roots, showed white before him. The burn, small with the summer drought, made a faraway tinkling, the sweet scents of pine and fern were about him, the dense boskage where it met the sky had in the dark a sharp marmoreal outline. The world was fragrant and quiet; if this be the Black Wood, thought David, I have been in less happy places.

But suddenly at a turn of the hill the trees closed in. It was almost as if he had stripped and dived into a stagnant pool. The road now seemed to have no purpose of its own, but ran on sufferance, slinking furtively as the Wood gave it leave, with many meaningless twists, as if unseen hands had warded it off. His horse, which had gone easily enough so far, now needed his heel in its side and many an application of his staff. It shied at nothing visible, jibbed, reared, breathing all the while as if its wind were touched. Something cold seemed to have descended on David's spirits, which, as soon as he was aware of it, he tried to exorcise by whistling a bar or two, and then by speaking aloud. He recited a psalm, but his voice, for usual notably full and mellow, seemed not to carry a yard. It was forced back on him by the trees. He tried to shout with no better effect. There came an echo which surprised him till he perceived that it was an owl. Others answered and the place was filled with their eldritch cries. One flapped across the road not a yard from him, and in a second his beast was on its haunches.

He was now beyond the throat of the glen, and the Woodilee burn had left him, going its own way into the deeps of Fennan Moss, where the wood was thin. The road plucked up courage and for a little ran broad and straight through a covert of birches. Then the pines closed down again, this time with more insistence, so that the path was a mere ladder among gnarled roots. Here there were moths about – a queer thing, David thought – white glimmering creatures that brushed his face and made his horse half crazy. He had ridden at a slow jog, but the beast's neck and flanks were damp with sweat. Presently he had to dismount and lead it, testing every step with his foot, for there seemed to be ugly scaurs breaking away on his left. The owls kept up a continuous calling, and there was another bird with a note like a rusty saw. He tried to whistle, to shout, to laugh, but his voice seemed to come out of folds of cloth. He thought it was his plaid, but the plaid was about his chest and shoulders and far from his mouth . . . And then, at one step the Wood ceased and he was among meadows.

He knew the place, for after the darkness of the trees the land, though the moon had not risen, seemed almost light. There in front was the vale down which Aller flowed, and on the right was his own familiar glen of Rood. Now he could laugh at his oppression – now that he was among the pleasant fields where he had played as a boy. . . . Why had he forgotten about the Black Wood, for it had no part in his memories? True, he had come always to Roodfoot by the other road behind the Hill of Deer, but there were the dark pines not a mile off – he must have adventured many times within their fringes. He thought that it was because a child is shielded by innocence from ugliness. . . . And yet, even then, he had had many nightmares and fled from many bogles. But not from the Wood. . . . No doubt it was the growing corruption of a man's heart.

The mill at Roodfoot stood gaunt and tenantless, passing swiftly into decay. He could see that the mill-wheel had gone, and its supports stood up like broken teeth; the lade was choked with rushes; the line of a hill showed through the broken rigging.

He had known of this, but none the less the sight gave him a pang, for David was a jealous conserver of his past. . . . But as the path turned up the glen beside the brawling Rood he had a sudden uplifting of spirit. This could not change, this secret valley, whose every corner he had quartered, whose every nook was the home of a delightful memory. He felt again the old ardour, when, released from Edinburgh, he had first revisited his haunts, tearful with excited joy. The Wood was on him again, but a different wood, his own wood. The hazels snuggled close to the roadside, and the feathery birches and rowans made a canopy, not a shadow. The oaks were ancient friends, the alders old playmates. His horse had recovered its sanity, and David rode through the dew-dreched night in a happy rapture of remembrance.

He was riding up Rood – that had always been the thing he had hoped to do. He had never been even so far as Calidon before, for a boy's day's march is short. But he had promised himself that some day when he was a man he would have a horse and ride to the utmost springs – to Roodhopefoot, to the crinkle in Moss Fell where Rood was born. . . . 'Up the water' had always been like a spell in his ear. He remembered lying in bed at night and hearing a clamour at the mill door: it was men from up the water, drovers from Moffat, herds from the back of beyond, once a party of soldiers from the south. And up the water lay Calidon, that ancient castle. The Hawkshaws were a name in a dozen ballads, and the tales of them in every old wife's mouth. Once they had captained all the glens of Rood and Aller in raids to the Border, and when Musgrave and Salkeld had led a return foray it was the Hawkshaws that smote them mightily in the passes. He had never seen one of the race; the men were always at the wars or at the King's court; but they had filled his dreams. One fancy especially was of a little girl – a figure with gold hair like King Malcolm's daughter in the 'Red Etin of Ireland' tale – whom he rescued from some dire peril, winning the thanks of her tall mail-clad kin. In that dream he too had been mail-clad, and he laughed at the remembrance. It was a far cry from that to the sedate minister of Woodilee.

As he turned up the road to the Greenshiel he remembered
with compunction his errand. He had been amusing himself
with vain memories when he was on the way to comfort a bed of
death. Both horse and rider were in a sober mood when they
reached the sheiling, the horse from much stumbling in peat-
bogs, and the man from reflections on his unworthiness.

Rushlights burned in the single room, and the door and the one
window stood open. It was a miserable hut of unmortared stones
from the hill, the gaps stuffed with earth and turf, and the roof of
heather thatch. One glance showed him that he was too late. A
man sat on a stool by the dead peat-fire with his head in his hands.
A woman was moving beside the box bed and unfolding a piece of
coarse linen. The shepherd of the Greenshiel might be an old
exercised Christian, but there were things in that place which had
no warrant from the Bible. A platter full of coarse salt lay at the foot
of the bed, and at the top crossed twigs of ash.

The woman – she was a neighbouring shepherd's wife –
stilled her keening at the sound of David's feet.

'It's himsel',' she cried. 'Richie, it's the minister. Wae's me,
sir, but ye're ower late to speed puir Mirren. An hour syne she
gaed to her reward – just slipped awa' in a fit o' hoastin'. I've
strauchten'd the corp and am gettin' the deid claes ready –
Mirren was aye prood o' hers and keepit them fine and caller wi'
gall and rosmry. Come forrit, sir, and tak' a look on her that's
gane. There was nae deid-thraws wi' Mirren, and she's lyin' as
peacefu' as a bairn. Her face is sair faun in, but I mind when it
was the bonniest face in a' Roodwater.'

The dead woman lay with cheeks like wax, a coin on each eye
so that for the moment her face had the look of a skull. Disease
had sculptured it to an extreme fineness, and the nose, the jaw,
and the lines of the forehead seemed chiselled out of ivory.
David had rarely looked on death, and the sight gave him a sense
first of repulsion and then of an intolerable pathos. He scarcely
heard the clatter of the shepherd's wife.

'She's been deein' this mony a day and now she's gane
joyfully to meet her Lord. Eh, but she was blithe to gang in

the hinner end. There was a time when she was sweir to leave Richie. "Elspet," she says to me, "what will that puir man o' mine dae his lee lane?" and I aye says to her, "Mirren, my wumman, the Lord's a grand provider, and Richie will haud fast by Him. Are not twa sparrows," I says—'

David went over to the husband on the creepie by the fireside, and laid his hand on his shoulder. The man sat hunched in a stupor of misery.

'Richie,' he said, 'if I'm too late to pray with Marion, I can pray with you.'

He prayed, as he always prayed, not in a mosaic of Scripture texts, but in simple words; and as he spoke he felt the man's shoulder under his hand shake as with a sob. He prayed with a sincere emotion, for he had been riding through a living coloured world and now felt like an icy blast the chill and pallor of death. Also he felt the pity of this lifelong companionship broken, and the old man left solitary. When he had finished, Richie lifted his face from his hands, and into his eyes which had been blank as a wall came the wholesome dimness of tears.

'I'm no repinin',' he said. 'The Lord gave and the Lord has taken away, and I bless His name. What saith the Apostle – Mirren has gane to be with Christ, whilk is far better. There was mony a time when the meal-ark was toom, and the wind and weet cam in through the baulks, and the peats wadna kindle, and we were baith hungry and cauld. But Mirren's bye wi' a' that, for she's bielded in the everlasting arms and she's suppin' rich at the Lord's ain table. But eh, sir, I could wish it had been His will to hae ta'en me wi' her. I'm an auld man, and there's nae weans, and for the rest o' my days I'll be like a beast in an unco loan. God send they binna mony.'

'The purposes of the Lord are true and altogether righteous. If He spares you, Richie, it's because He has still work for you to do on this earth.'

'I kenna what it can be. My fit's beginnin' to lag on the hill, and ony way I'm guid for nocht but sheep. Lambin's and clippin's and spainin's is ower puir a wark for the Lord to fash wi'.'

'Whatever you put your hand to is the work of the Lord, if you keep His fear before you.'

'Maybe, sir.' The man rose from his stool and revealed a huge gaunt frame, much bowed at the shoulders. He peered in the rushlight at the minister's face.

'Ye're a young callant to be a minister. I was strong on your side, sir, when ye got the call, for your preachin' was like a rushin' michty wind. I mind I repeated the heids o' your sermon to Mirren. . . . Ye've done me guid, sir – I think it's maybe the young voice o' ye. Ye wad get the word from Johnnie Dow. Man, it was kind to mak siccan haste. I wish – I wish ye had seen Mirren in life. . . . Pit up anither petition, afore ye gang – for a blessin' on this stricken house and on an auld man who has his title sure in Christ but has an unco rebellious heart.'

It seemed to David as he turned from the door, where the shepherd stood with uplifted arm, that a benediction had been given, but not by him.

The moon had risen and the glen lay in a yellow light, with the high hills between Rood and Aller shrunk to mild ridges. The stream caught the glow and its shallows were like silver chased in amber. The young man's heart was full with the scene which he had left. Death was very near to men, jostling them at every corner, whispering in their ear at kirk and market, creeping between them and their firesides. Soon the shepherd of the Greenshiel would lie beside his wife; in a little, too, his own stout limbs would be a heap of dust. How small and frail seemed the life in that cottage, as contrasted with the rich pulsing world of the woods and hills and their serene continuance. But it was they that were the shadows in God's sight. The immortal thing was the broken human heart that could say in its frailty that its Redeemer liveth. 'Thou, Lord,' he repeated to himself, 'in the beginning hast laid the foundations of the earth, and the heavens are the work of Thy hands. They shall perish, but thou shalt endure; they all shall wax old as doth a garment, and as a vesture shalt Thou change them, and they shall be changed: but Thou art the same, and Thy years shall not fail.'

But as the road twined among the birches David's mood became insensibly more pagan. He could not resist the joy of the young life that ran in his members, and which seemed to be quickened by the glen of his childhood. Death was the portion of all, but youth was still far from death. . . . The dimness and delicacy of the landscape, the lines of hill melting into a haze under the moon, went to his head like wine. It was a world transfigured and spell-laden. On his left the dark blotch which was Melanudrigill lay like a spider over the hillsides and the mouths of the glens, but all in front and to his right was kindly and golden. He had come back to his own country and it held out its arms to him. 'Salve, O venusta Sirmio,' he cried, and an owl answered.

The glen road was reached, but he did not turn towards Roodfoot. He had now no dread of the wood of Melanudrigill, but he had a notion to stand beside Rood water, where it flowed in a ferny meadow which had been his favourite fishing-ground. So he pushed beyond the path into a maze of bracken and presently was at the stream's edge.

And then, as he guided his horse past a thicket of alders, he came full upon a little party of riders who had halted there.

There were three of them – troopers, they seemed, with buff caps and doublets and heavy cavalry swords, and besides their own scraggy horses there was a led beast. The three men were consulting when David stumbled on them, and at the sight of him they had sprung apart and laid hands on their swords. But a second glance had reassured them.

'Good e'en to you, friend,' said he who appeared to be the leader. 'You travel late.'

It was not an encounter which David would have sought, for wandering soldiery had a bad name in the land. Something of this may have been in the other's mind, for his next words were an explanation.

'You see three old soldiers of Leven's,' he said, 'on the way north after the late crowning mercy vouchsafed to us against the malignants. We be Angus men and have the general's leave to visit our homes. If you belong hereaways you can maybe help us with the road. Ken you a place of the name of Calidon?'

To their eyes David must have seemed a young farmer or a bonnet-laird late on the road from some errand of roystering or sweethearting.

'I lived here as a boy,' he said, 'and I'm but now returned. Yet I think I could put you on your way to Calidon. The moon's high.'

'It's a braw moon,' said the second trooper, 'and it lighted us fine down Aller, but the brawest moon will not discover you a dwelling in a muckle wood, if you kenna the road to it.'

The three had moved out from the shade of the alders and were now clear under the sky. Troopers, common troopers and shabby at that, riding weary ill-conditioned beasts. The nag which the third led was a mere rickle of bones. And yet to David's eye there was that about them which belied their apparent rank. They had spoken in the country way, but their tones were not those of countrymen. They had not the air of a gaunt Jock or a round-faced Tam from the ploughtail. All three were slim and the hands which grasped the bridles were notably fine. They held themselves straight like courtiers, and in their voices lurked a note as of men accustomed to command. The leader was a dark man with a weary thin face and great circles round his eyes; the second a tall fellow, with a tanned skin, a cast in his left eye and a restless dare-devil look; the third, who seemed to be their groom, had so far not spoken and had stood at the back with the led horse, but David had a glimpse above his ragged doublet of a neat small moustache and a delicate chin. 'Leven has good blood in his ranks,' he thought, 'for these three never came out of a but-and-ben.' Moreover, the ordinary trooper on his way home would not make Calidon a house of call.

He led them up to the glen road, intending to give them directions about their way, but there he found that his memory had betrayed him. He knew exactly in which nook of hill lay Calidon, but for the life of him he could not remember how the track ran to it.

'I'll have to be your guide, sirs,' he told them. 'I can take you to Calidon, but I cannot tell you how to get there.'

'We're beholden to you, sir, but it's a sore burden on your good-nature. Does your own road lie in the airt?'

The young man laughed. 'The night is fine and I'm in no haste to be in bed. I'll have you at Calidon door in half an hour.'

Presently he led them off the road across a patch of heather, forded Rood at a shallow, and entered a wood of birches. The going was bad and the groom with the led horse had the worst of it. The troopers were humane men, for they seemed to have a curious care of their servant. It was 'Canny now, James – there's bog on the left,' or 'Take tent of that howe'; and once or twice, when there was a difficult passage, one or the other would seize the bridle of the led horse till the groom had passed. David saw from the man's face that he was grey with fatigue.

'Get you on my beast,' he said, 'and I'll hold the bridle. I can find my way better on foot. And do you others each take a led horse. The road we're travelling is none so wide, and we'll make better speed that way.'

The troopers docilely did as they were bidden, and the weary groom was hoisted on David's grey gelding. The change seemed to ease him and he lost his air of heavy preoccupation and let his eyes wander. The birch wood gave place to a bare hillside, where even the grey slipped among the screes and the four horses behind sprawled and slithered. They crossed a burn, surmounted another ridge, and entered a thick wood of oak which David knew cloaked the environs of Calidon and which made dark travelling even in the strong moonlight. Great boulders were hidden in the moss, withered boughs hung low over the path, and now and then would come a patch of scrub so dense that it had to be laboriously circumvented. The groom on the grey was murmuring to himself, and to David's amazement it was Latin. 'Ibant obscuri sola sub nocte per umbram,' were the words he spoke.

David capped them:

> Perque domos Ditis vacuas et inania regna,
> Quale per incertam lunam. . . .

The man on the horse laughed, and David, looking up, had his first proper sight of his face. It was a long face, very pale, unshaven and dirty, but it was no face of a groom. The thin aquiline nose, the broad finely arched brow, were in themselves impressive, but the dominant feature was the eyes. They seemed to be grey – ardent, commanding, and yet brooding. David was so absorbed by this sudden vision that he tripped over a stone and almost pulled the horse down.

'I did not look,' said the rider, in a voice low-pitched and musical, 'I did not look to find a scholar in these hills.'

'Nor did I know,' said David, 'that Virgil was the common reading of Leven's men.'

They had reached a field of wild pasture studded with little thorns, in the middle of which stood a great stone dovecot. A burn falling in a deep ravine made a moat on one side of the tower of Calidon, which now rose white like marble in the moon. They crossed the ravine not without trouble, and joined the main road from the glen, which ended in a high-arched gate round which clustered half a dozen huts.

At the sound of their arrival men ran out of the huts and one seized the bridle of the leader. David and the groom had now fallen back, and it was the dark man who did the talking. These were strange troopers, for they sat their horses like princes, so that the hand laid on the bridle was promptly dropped.

'We would speak with the laird of Calidon,' the dark man said. 'Stay, carry this ring to him. He will know what it means.' It seemed curious to David that the signet given to the man was furnished by the groom.

In five minutes the servant returned. 'The laird waits on ye, sirs. I'll tak' the beasts, and your mails, if ye've ony. Through the muckle yett an it please ye.'

David turned to go. 'I've brought you to Calidon,' he said, 'and now I'll take my leave.'

'No, no,' cried the dark man. 'You'll come in and drink a cup after the noble convoy you've given us. Nicholas Hawkshaw will be blithe to welcome you.'

David would have refused, for the hour was already late and he was many miles from Woodilee, had not the groom laid his hand on his arm. 'Come,' he said. 'I would see my friend, the student of Virgil, in another light than the moon,' and to his amazement the young man found that it was a request which he could not deny. There was a compelling power in that quiet face, and he was strangely loth to part from it.

The four dismounted, the three troopers staggering with stiff bones. The dark man's limp did not change after the first steps, and David saw that he was crippled in the left leg. They passed through the gate into a courtyard, beyond which rose the square *massif* of the tower. In the low doorway a candle wavered, under a stone which bore the hawk in lure which was the badge of the house.

The three men bowed low to the candle, and David saw that it was held by a young girl.

THREE

Guests in Calidon Tower

'Will you enter, sirs?' said the girl. She was clad in some dark homespun stuff with a bright-coloured screen thrown over her head and shoulders. She held the light well in front of her, so that David could not see her face. He would fain have taken his leave, for it seemed strange to be entering Calidon thus late at e'en in the company of strangers, but the hand of the groom on his arm restrained him. 'You will drink a stirrup-cup, friend. The night is yet young and the moon is high.'

A steep stairway ran upward a yard or two from the doorway. Calidon was still a Border keep, where the ground-floor had once been used for byres and stables, and the inhabitants had dwelt in the upper stories. The girl moved ahead of them. 'Will you be pleased to follow me, sirs? My uncle awaits you above.'

They found themselves in a huge chamber which filled the width of the tower, and, but for a passage and a further staircase, its length. A dozen candles, which seemed to have been lit in haste, showed that it was raftered with dark oak beams, and that the walls were naked stone where they were not covered with a coarse arras. The floor, of a great age, was bare wood blackened with time and use, and covered with a motley of sheepskins and deerskins. Two long oak tables and a great oak bench made the chief furniture, but there were a multitude of stools of the same heavy ancient make, and by a big open fireplace two ancient chairs of stamped Spanish leather. A handful of peats smouldered on the hearth, and the thin blue smoke curled upward to add grime to an immense coat of arms carved in stone and surmounted by a forest of deer horns and a trophy of targes and spears.

David, accustomed only to the low-ceiled rooms of the Edinburgh closes, stared in amazement at the size of the place and felt abashed. The Hawkshaws had made too great a sound in his boyhood's world for him to enter their dwelling without a certain tremor of the blood. So absorbed was he in his surroundings that it was with a start that he saw the master of the house.

A man limped forward, gathered the leader of the party in his arms and kissed him on both cheeks.

'Will,' he said, 'Will, my old comrade! It's a kind wind that has blown you to Calidon this night. I havena clapped eyes on you these six year.'

The host was a man about middle life, with the shoulders of a bull and a massive shaggy head now in considerable disorder from the fact that a nightcap had just been removed from it. His clothes were of a comfortable undress, for the tags of his doublet and the points of his breeches were undone, and over all he wore an old plaid dressing-gown. He had been reading, for a pipe of tobacco marked his place in a folio, and David noted that it was Philemon Holland's version of the _Cyropaedia_. His eyes were blue and frosty, his cheeks ruddy, his beard an iron grey, and his voice as gusty as a hill wind. He limped heavily as he moved.

'Man Will,' he cried, 'it's a whipping up of cripples when you and me foregather. The Germany wars have made lameters of the both of us. And who are the lads you've brought with you?'

'Just like myself, Nick, poor soldiers of Leven's, on our way home to Angus.'

'Angus is it this time?' The host winked and then laughed boisterously.

'Angus it is, but their names and designations can wait till we have broken our fast. 'Faith, we've as wolfish a hunger as ever you and me tholed in Thuringia. And I've brought in an honest man that guided us through your bogs and well deserves bite and sup.'

Nicholas Hawkshaw peered for a moment at David. 'I cannot say I'm acquaint with the gentleman, but I've been that long away I've grown out of knowledge of my own countryside. But ye shallna lack for meat and drink, for when I got your token I bade Edom stir himself and make ready. There's a good browst of yill, and plenty of French cordial and my father's Canary sack. And there's a mutton ham, and the best part of a pie – I wouldna say just what's intil the pie, but at any rate there's blackcocks and snipes and leverets, for I had the shooting of them. Oh, and there's whatever more Edom can find in the house of Calidon. Here's back your ring, Will. When I read the cognisance I had a notion that I was about to entertain greater folk—'

'Than your auld friend Will Rollo and two poor troopers of Leven's. And yet we're maybe angels unawares.' He took the ring and handed it to the groom, who with David stood a little back from the others, while Nicholas Hawkshaw's eyes widened in a momentary surprise.

An ancient serving-man and a barefoot maid brought in the materials for supper, and the two troopers fell on the viands like famished crows. The groom ate little and drank less; though he was the slightest in build of the three travellers he seemed the most hardened to the business. The lame man, who was called Will Rollo, was presently satisfied, and deep in reminiscences with his host, but the other required greater sustenance for his long wiry body, and soon reduced the pie to a fragment. He pressed morsels upon the groom – a wing of grouse, a giblet of hare – but the latter smiled and waved the food away. A friendly service, Leven's, David thought, where a servant was thus tenderly considered.

'Yon were the brave days, when you and me served as ensigns of Meldrum's in the *Corpus Evangelicorum*. And yon was the lad to follow, for there never was the marrow of the great Gustavus for putting smeddum into troops that had as many tongues and creeds as the Tower of Babel. But you and me were ower late on the scene. We never saw Breitenfeld – just the calamitous day of Lutzen, and the blacker day of Nordlingen where Bernhard led us like sheep to the slaughter. That was the end of campaigning for you, Will. I mind leaving you on the ground for dead and kissing your cheek, the while I was near my own end with a musketoon ball in my ribs. Then I heard you were still in life and back in Scotland, but I was off with auld Wrangel to Pomerania and had to keep my mind on my own affairs.'

So the talk went on, memories of leaguers and forced marches and pitched battles, punctuated with the names of Leslies and Hamiltons and Kerrs and Lumsdens and a hundred Scots mercenaries. – 'I got my quietus a year syne serving with Torstensson and his Swedes – a pitiable small affair in Saxonia, where I had the misfortune to meet a round shot on the ricochet which cracked my shin-bone and has set me hirpling for the rest of my days. My Colonel was Sandy Leslie, a brother of Leslie of Balquhain, him that stuck Wallenstein at Eger, but a man of honester disposition and a good Protestant. He bade me go home, for I would never again be worth a soldier's hire, and faith! when the chirurgeon had finished with my leg I was of the same opinion. – So home you find me, Will, roosting in the cauld rickle of stones that was my forbears', while rumours of war blow like an east wind up the glens. I'm waiting for your news. I hear word that Davie Leslie. . . .'

'Our news can wait, Nick. We've a gentleman here to whose ears this babble of war must sound outlandish.' It seemed to David that some secret intelligence passed between the two and that a foot of one was pressed heavily on the other's toes.

'I am a man of peace,' David said, for the talk had stirred his fancy, 'but I too have word of a glorious victory in England won by the Covenant armies. If you have come straight from the south you can tell me more.'

'There was a victory beyond doubt,' said the tall man with the squint, 'and that is why we of Leven's are permitted to go home. We have gotten our pay, whilk is an uncommon happening for the poor soldier in this land.'

'I have heard,' said David, 'that the ranks of the Army of the Covenant fought for higher matters than filthy lucre.'

'For what, belike?'

'For the purity of their faith and the Crown honours of Christ.'

The other whistled gently through his teeth.

'No doubt. No doubt. There's a braw sough of the Gospel in Leven's ranks. But we must consider the loaves and fishes, good sir, as well as the preaching of the Word. Man canna live by bread alone, but he assuredly canna live without it, and to fill his belly he wants more than preaching. Lucre's none so filthy if it be honestly earned, and goes to keep a roof over the wife and bairns. I have served in many lands with a kennin' o' queer folk and, believe me, sir, the first thing a soldier thinks of is just his pay.'

'But he cannot fight unless he has a cause to fight for.'

'He'll make a very good shape at it if he has been learned his business by a heavy-handed sergeant. I have seen the riddlings of Europe stick fast as rocks before Wallenstein's horse, because they had been taught their trade and feared death less than their Colonel's tongue. And I have seen the flower of gentrice, proud as Lucifer and gallant as lions, and every one with a noble word on his lips, break like rotten twigs at the first musket volley. It's discipline that's the last word in war.'

'But if the discipline be there, will not a conviction of the right of his cause make a better soldier?'

'You have spoken a true word, and there's a man in England this day that knows it. That is what Cromwell has done. He has built up a body of horse that stand like an iron wall and move like a river in spate. They have the discipline of Gustavus's Swedes, and the fires of Hell in their hearts. I tell you, there is nothing in this land that can stand against them.'

'I have no love for sectaries,' said David. 'But cannot our Scots do likewise, with the Covenant to nerve them?'

The other shrugged his shoulders.

'The Covenant's but sour kail to the soldier. Davie Leslie has hammered his men into a wise-like army, because he learned his trade from Gustavus. But think you our bannockfed foot-sentinels care a doit for the black gowns at West-minster? A man will fight for his King and for his country and for liberty to worship God in his own way. But, unless he has a crack in his head, he will not fight for a fine point of church government.'

David was becoming ill at ease. He felt that it was his duty to testify, or otherwise he would be guilty of the sin of Meroz, the sin of apathy when his faith was challenged. But he was far from clear as to the exact nature of his faith. There was no blasphemy in questioning whether the Covenant were truly in the hearts of the people. Had not the minister of Cauldshaw that very afternoon expressed the same doubt?

Nicholas Hawkshaw was peering at him intently.

'I should ken you, friend, for they tell me you belong to this countryside. And your face sticks in my memory, but I canna put a name to it.'

'They call me David Sempill. I am the new ordained minister of Woodilee.'

Nicholas cried out. 'Auld Wat o' the Roodfoot's grandson. I heard of your coming, sir, and indeed I'm your chief heritor. I'll have your hand on that. Man, I kenned your gudesire well, and many a pouchful of groats I had from him when I was a laddie. You're back among kenned folk, Mr Sempill, and I wish you a long life in Woodilee.'

The troopers did not seem to share their host's geniality. Quick glances passed between them, and the tall man shifted his seat so that he came between David and the groom. This latter had taken no part in the conversation, indeed he had not spoken a word, but after his meal was finished had sat with his head on his breast as if sunk in meditation. Now he raised his eyes to David, and it was he who spoke.

'I am not less loyal to the Kirk of Scotland than you, Mr Sempill. You are a placed minister, and I am a humble elder of that kirk.'

'In what parish?' David asked eagerly.

'In my native parish benorth of Forth.'

The man's dress and station were forgotten by David when he looked at his face. Now that he saw clearly in the candle-light it was not the face of a common groom. Every feature spoke of race, the firm mouth of command, the brooding grey eyes of thought. The voice was sweet and musical, and the man's whole air had a gentle but imperious courtesy.

The movement of the tall trooper, while it had separated David from the groom, had brought the latter full into the view of Nicholas Hawkshaw. Now a strange thing happened. The host, after a long stare, during which amazement and recognition woke in his eyes, half rose from his seat and seemed on the verge of speaking. His gaze was fixed on the groom, and David read in it something at once deferential and exulting. Then the toe of the lame man's boot came down on his shin, and the lame man's hand was laid on his arm. The lame man too said something in a tongue which David could not understand. Nicholas subsided in his chair, but his face remained both puzzled and excited.

The groom spoke again.

'You are a scholar, and you are young, and you are full of the ardour of your calling. This parish is fortunate in its minister, and I would that all Scotland were as happily served. What is it that you and I seek alike? A pure doctrine, and a liberated Kirk? Is there no more?'

'I seek above all things to bring men and women to God's mercy-seat.'

'And I say Amen. That is more than any disputation about the forms of Presbytery. But you seek also, or I am mightily mistook in you, the freedom and well-being of this land of ours – that our Israel may have peace and prosperity in her borders.'

'If the first be won, all the rest will be added unto us.'

'Doubtless. But only if the first be truly won – if the Kirk attend to the work of salvation and does not expend her toil in barren fields. Her sovereign must be King Jesus. Take heed that instead it be not King Covenant.'

The words recalled to David Mr Fordyce's doubts, which had been so scornfully repelled by the ministers of Kirk Aller and Bold.

'Does it lie in the mouth of a minister or an elder of the Kirk to cavil at the Kirk's doings?' he asked, but without conviction in his tone.

The other smiled. 'You give due loyalty, as the Scripture enjoins, to the King, Mr Sempill?'

'I am faithful to his Majesty so long as his Majesty is faithful to law and religion.'

'Even so. It is my own creed. The King must respect the limits of his prerogative – it is the condition on which he rules in a free land. My loyalty to the Kirk is in the same case. I am loyal when she fulfils those duties which God has laid upon her – that duty above all of bringing mortal men to God. If she forget those duties and meddle arrogantly with civil matters that do not concern her, then I take leave to oppose her, as in a like case I would oppose his Majesty. For by such perversities both King and Kirk become tyrants, and tyranny is not to be endured by men who are called into the liberty of Christ.'

'Or by Scots,' added the tall trooper.

'I have no clearness on the point,' said David after a pause. 'I have not thought deeply on these matters, for I am but new to the ministry and my youth was filled with profane study.'

'Nevertheless, such study is a good foundation for a wise theology. I judge that you are a ripe Latinist – maybe also a Grecian. You have read your Aristotle? You are familiar with the history of the ancient world, which illumines all later ages? I would point my arguments from that armoury.'

'I cannot grant that the doings of ancient heathendom give any rule for a Christian state.'

'But, sir, the business of government is always the same. We have our Lord's warning that there are the things of Caesar and the things of God. The Roman was the great master of the arts of government, and he did not seek throughout his empire to . make a single religion. He was content to give it the peace of his law, and let each people go its own way in matters of worship. It was in that tolerant world which he created that our Christian faith found its opportunity.'

'Doubtless God so moved the Roman mind for His own purpose. But I join issue on your application. The Church of Christ is now in being, and the faith of Christ is the foundation of a Christian state. Civil law is an offence against God unless it be also Christian.'

The young man smiled. 'I do not deny it. This realm of ours is professedly a Christian realm – I would it were more truly so. But that does not exempt it from obedience to those laws of government without which no realm, Christian or pagan, may endure. If a man is so ill a smith that he cannot shoe my horse, I will be none the better served because he is a good Christian. If a land be ill governed, the disaster will be not the less great because the governors are men of God. If his Majesty – to take a pertinent example – override the law to the people's detriment, that tyranny will be not the less grievous because his Majesty believes in his heart that he is performing a duty towards the Almighty. Honest intention will not cure faulty practice, and the fool is the fool whether he be unbeliever or professor.'

David shook his head. 'Where does your argument tend? I fear to schism.'

'Not so. I am an orthodox son of the Kirk, a loyal servant of his Majesty, and a passionate Scot. Here, my friend, is my simple confession. There is but one master in the land and its name is Law – which is in itself a creation of a free people under the inspiration of the Almighty. That law may be changed by the people's will, but till it be so changed it is to be revered and obeyed. It has ordained the King's prerogative, the rights of the subject, and the rights and duties of the Kirk. The state is like the body, whose health is only to be maintained by a just proportion among its members. If a man's belly be his god his limbs will suffer, if he use only his legs his arms will dwindle. If therefore the King should intrude upon the subject's rights, or the subject whittle at the King's prerogative, or the Kirk set herself above the Crown, there will be a sick state and an ailing people.'

Nicholas Hawkshaw had been listening intently with a puzzled air, his eyes fixed on the groom's face, but the two troopers seemed ill at ease.

'Man, James,' said the tall man, 'you've mistook your calling. You should have been a regent in the college of St. Andrew's, and hammered sense into the thick heads of the bejaunts.'

Rollo, the lame man, shifted his seat and seemed inclined to turn the conversation.

'Patience, Mark,' said the groom. 'It's not often a poor soldier of Leven's gets a chance of a crack with a like-minded friend. For I'm certain that Mr Sempill is very near my way of thinking.'

'I do not quarrel with your premises,' said David, 'but I'm not clear about the conclusion.'

'It's writ large in this land today. There are those that would make the King a puppet and put all authority in parliaments, and there are those who would make the Kirk like Calvin's at Geneva, a ruler over both civil and religious matters. I say that both ways lie madness and grief. If you upset the just proportion of the law you will gain not liberty but confusion. You are a scholar, Mr Sempill, and have read the histories of Thucydides? Let me counsel you to read them again and consider the moral.'

'What side are you on?' David asked abruptly.

'I am on the side of the free people of Scotland. And you by your vows are on the same side, for your concern is to feed the flock of God which is among us. Think you, sir, if you depress the balance against the King, that thereby you will win more for the people? Nay, nay, what is lost to the prerogative will go, not to the people, but to those who prey on them. You will have that anarchy which gives his chance to the spoiler, and out of anarchy will come some day a man of violence who will tyrannically make order again. It is the way of the world, my friend.'

'Are you for the covenant?'

At the question the others started. 'Enough of politics,' cried Rollo. 'These are no matters to debate among weary folk.' But the groom raised his hand and they were silent.

'I am for the Covenant. Six years back I drew sword for it, and I did not sheathe that sword till we had established the liberties of this land. That was indeed a Covenant of Grace.'

'There is another and a later. What say you of that?'

'I say of that other that it is a Covenant of Works in which I have no part, nor any true lover of the Kirk. It is a stepping of the Kirk beyond the bounds prescribed by the law of God and the law of man, and it will mean a weakening of the Kirk in its proper duties. And that I need not tell you, as a minister of Christ, will be the starvation and oppression of Christ's simple folk. *Quicquid delirant reges, plectuntur Achivi.* Is it not more pleasing to God that His ministers should comfort the sick and the widow and the fatherless and guide souls to Heaven than that they should scrabble for civil pre-eminence?'

Into David's mind came two visions – that of the complacent ministers of Kirk Aller and Bold as they had discoursed at meat, and that of the old herd at the Greenshiel sitting by his dead wife. The pictures belonged to different worlds, and at the moment he felt that these worlds were eternally apart. He had the disquieting thought that the one had only the husks of faith and the other the grain. Dimly he heard the voice of the groom. 'I will give you a text, Mr Sempill. "The vineyard of the Lord of hosts is the house of Israel, and the men of Judah His pleasant plant; and He looked for judgment, but beheld oppression; for righteousness, but beheld a cry."'

He scarcely realised that the others had sprung to their feet, and it was only when Nicholas Hawkshaw exclaimed that he turned his head.

A girl stood before them, the girl who had opened the door, but whose face he had scarcely seen at the time in the poor light.

'Katrine, my dear, you've been long of coming.' It was Nicholas who spoke. 'I thought you had slipped off to your bed. This is my sister's child, sirs, who keeps me company in this auld barrack – Robert Yester's daughter, him that fell with Monro in the year 'thirty-four. You see three gentlemen-troopers of Leven's, my dear, and Mr Sempill, the new minister of Woodilee.'

The girl was dressed in a gown of blue velvet, the skirts of which were drawn back in front to show an embroidered petticoat of stiff yellow satin. It was cut low at the neck and shoulders, and round the top ran a broad edging of fine lace. Her dark hair was caught up in a knot behind, but allowed to fall in curls on each side of her face. That face, to David's startled eyes, was like none that he had ever seen before, certainly like none of the Edinburgh burger girls whom he had observed in their finery on the Saturday causeway. It was small and delicately featured, the cheeks flushed with youth and health, the eyes dark, brilliant, and mirthful. At another time he would have been shocked at her dress, for the fashion of a low bodice had not spread much beyond the Court, but now he did not take note of what she wore. He was gazing moonstruck upon a revelation.

She smiled on him – she smiled on them all. She curtsied lightly to her uncle, to Rollo, and to the dark man. But she did not curtsy to the minister. For suddenly, as she looked at the groom her composure deserted her. Her mouth moved as if she would have spoken, and then she checked herself, for David saw that the groom had put his finger to his lips. Instead she curtsied almost to the ground, a reverence far more deep than she had accorded to the others, and when he gave her his hand she bent her head as if her impulse was to kiss it.

All this David saw with a confused vision. He had scarcely spoken ten words in his life to a woman outside his own kin, and this bright apparition loosened his knees with nervousness. He stammered his farewells. He had already outstayed the bounds of decency, and he had a long ride home – he wished his friends a safe conclusion to their journey – in the course of his pastoral visitations he would have the chance of coming again to Calidon. ''Deed, sir, and you'll make sure of that,' said the hospitable Nicholas. 'There's aye a bite and a sup at Calidon for the minister of Woodilee.'

He bowed to the girl, and she looked at him for the first time, a quizzical appraising look, and gave him a fleeting smile. Five minutes later he was on his horse and fording Rood.

He took the long road by the back of the Hill of Deer, riding in bright moonshine up the benty slopes and past the hazel thickets. His mind was in a noble confusion, for on this, his first day in his parish, experiences had thronged on him too thick and fast. Out of the welter two faces stood clear, the groom's and the girl's. . . . He remembered the talk, and his conscience pricked him. Had he been faithful to his vows? Had he been guilty of the sin of Meroz? Had he listened to railing accusations and been silent?. . . . He did not know – in truth he did not care – for the sum of his recollection was not of an argument but of a person. The face of the young man had been more than his words, for it had been the face of a comrade, and an intimate friendliness had looked out of his eyes. He longed to see him again, to be with him, to follow him, to serve him – but he did not know his name, and they would doubtless never meet again. David was very young, and could have wept at the thought.

And the girl. . . .? The sight of her had been the coping-stone to a night of marvels. She was not like the groom – he had been glad to flee from her company, for she had no part in his world. But a marvel beyond doubt! The recollection of her made him a poet, and as he picked his way over the hill he was quoting to himself the lines in Homer where the old men of Troy see Helen approaching and wonder at her beauty. . . . *ου νεμεσις Τρωας* – how did it go? 'Small wonder that the Trojans and the mailed Greeks should endure pain through many years for such a woman. In face she is strangely like to some immortal.'

And then he felt compunction, for he remembered the worn face of the dead woman at the Greenshiel.

FOUR

The Faithful Servant

For two days the minister of Woodilee was a man unbalanced and distraught. He sat at his books without concentration, and he wandered on the hills without delight, while Isobel's face puckered in dismay as she removed his scarcely tasted meals. It was hot thundery weather, with storms that never broke in rain grumbling among the glens, and to this she set down his indisposition to eat. But David's trouble was not of the body. He had thought himself the mailed servant of God, single in purpose, armed securely against the world, and lo! in a single night he had been the sport of profane fancies and had rejoiced in vanities.

The girl he scarcely thought of – she had scared rather than enthralled him. But the Wood of Melanudrigill lay heavy on his conscience. Where was his Christian fortitude if a black forest at night could set him shivering like a lost child? David had all his life kept a tight hand on his courage; if he dreaded a thing, that was good reason why he should go out of his road to face it. His instinct was to return alone to Melanudrigill in the dark, penetrate its deepest recesses, and give the lie to its enchantments. . . . But a notion which he could not combat restrained him. That was what the Wood wanted, to draw him back to it through curiosity or fear. If he yielded to his impulse he would be acknowledging its power. It was the part of a minister of God to deny at the outset that the place was more than a common wilderness of rock and tree, to curb his fancies as things too vain for a grown man's idlest throught.

On this point he fixed his resolution and found some comfort. But the memory of Calidon and the troopers and the groom's words remained to trouble him. Had he not borne himself in their company as a Laodicean, assenting when he should have testified?. . . . He went over every detail of the talk, for it stuck firmly in his mind. They had decried the Solemn League and Covenant in the name of the Kirk, and he had not denounced them. . . . And yet they had spoken as Christian men and loyal sons of that Kirk. . . . What meant, too, the groom's disquisition on law and government? David found the argument hard to gainsay – it presented a doctrine of the state which commended itself to his reason. Yet it was in flat contradiction of the declared view of that Kirk which he was sworn to serve, and what then became of his ordination vows?. . . . But was it contrary to the teaching of the Word and the spirit of his faith? He searched his mind on this point and found that he had no clearness.

His duty, it seemed, was to go to some father-in-God, like the minister of Kirk Aller, and lay his doubts before him. But he found that course impossible. The pale fleshy face of Mr Muirhead rose before him, as light-giving as a peat-stack; he heard his complacent tones, saw the bland conceit in his ruminant eyes. Nor would he fare better with the militancy of his brother of Bold, who classed all mankind as Amalekites, save the chosen few who wore his own phylacteries. Mr Fordyce might give him comfort, and he was on the point many times of saddling his horse and riding to the manse of Cauldshaw. . . . But each time he found it impossible, and when he asked himself the cause he was amazed at the answer. Loyalty forbade him – loyalty to the young man, habited as a groom, who had spoken both as counsellor and comrade. That was the enduring spell of that strange night. David as a youth in Edinburgh had had few familiar friends, and none that could be called intimate. For the first time he had met one from whom had gone forth an influence that melted his heart. He recalled with a kind of aching affection the gentle, commanding courtesy, the kindly smile, the masterful and yet wistful grey eyes. 'I wonder,' he thought, 'if I was not meant to be a soldier. For I could follow yon man most joyfully to the cannon's mouth.'

On the third day peace returned to him, when he buried Marion of the Greenshiel. The parish coffin was not used, as was the custom for poor folk, since the farmer of Reiverslaw, Richie's master, paid the cost of a private one, and himself attended the 'chesting' the night before. On the day David walked the seven miles to the cottage, where Richie had set out a poor entertainment of ale and oatcakes for the mourners. It was not the fashion for the minister to pray at the house or at the grave, as savouring of Popish prayers for the dead, nor was it the custom for a widower to attend the funeral; but David took his own way, and prayed with the husband, the wailing women, and the half-dozen shepherds who had assembled for the last rites. The light coffin was carried by four young men, and David walked with them all the way to Woodilee. The farmer of Reiverslaw joined them at a turn of the road – his name was Andrew Shillinglaw, a morose dark man not over-well spoken of in the parish – and he and the minister finished the journey side by side. The bellman, Nehemiah Robb, who was also the gravedigger and the beadle, met them at the entrance to the kirkton, and with him a crowd of villagers. Preceded by the jangling of Robb's bell, the procession reached the shallow grave, the women remaining at the kirkyard gate. The coffin was lowered, the earth shovelled down, and the thing in five minutes was over. There was no 'dredgy' at the poor house of the Greenshiel to draw the mourners back upon the seven moorland miles. The men adjourned to Lucky Weir's, the kirk bell was restored to its tree, a woman or two sobbed, and the last of Marion Smail was a thin stream of figures vanishing in the haze of evening, one repeating to the other in funeral voices that 'puir Mirren had got weel awa'.'

Yet the occasion, austere and bare as poverty could make it, woke in David a mood of tenderness and peace. The lowering clouds had gone from the sky, all morning it had rained, and the afternoon had had a soft autumn freshness. He had prayed with

Richie, but his prayers had been also for himself, and as he walked behind the coffin on the path by the back of the Hill of Deer his petition seemed to have been answered. He had an assurance of his vocation. The crowd at the kirkyard, those toil-worn folk whose immortal souls had been given into his charge, moved him to a strong exultation. He saw his duty cleared from all doubts, and there must have been that in his face which told of his thoughts, for men greeted him and then passed on, as if unwilling to break in on his preoccupation. Only Reiverslaw, who was on his way to Lucky Weir's whence he would depart drunk in the small hours, was obtuse in his perceptions. He took the minister's hand and shook it as he would a drover's at a fair, seemed anxious to speak, found no words, and left with a grunted farewell.

It was a fine, long-drawn-out back-end, the best that had been known for twenty years. All September the sun shone like June, and it was well into October before the morning frosts began, and the third week of November before the snow came. The little crops – chiefly grey oats and barley, with an occasional rig of peas and flax – were well ripened and quickly reaped. The nettie-wives were busy all day in the fields, and the barefoot children made the leading in of the harvest a holiday, with straw whistles in their mouths and fantastic straw badges on their clothing. Then came the threshing with jointed flails, and the winnowing on barn roofs when the first east winds blew. There were no gleaners in the empty stubbles, for it was held a pious duty to leave something behind for the fowls of the air. Presently the scanty fruits of the earth were under cover, the bog hay in dwarfish ricks, the unthreshed oats and bear in the barns, the grain in the girnels, and soon the wheel of the Woodilee mill was clacking merrily to grind the winter's meal. In that parish the burden of the laird lay light. Nicholas Hawkshaw asked no more than his modest rental in kind, and did not exact his due in labour, but for a week the road by the back of the Hill of Deer saw a procession of horses carrying the 'kain' meal to the

Calidon granary. As the minister watched the sight one day, Ephraim Caird, the Chasehope tenant, stood beside him, looking gloomily at his own beasts returning. 'That's the way our puir crops are guided,' he said. 'As the auld folk used to say, "Ane part to saw, ane part to gnaw, and ane to pay the laird witha'".' His eyes showed that he had no love for Calidon.

Hallowmass that year was a cheerful season. The elders shook their heads at the Hallowe'en junketings, and the severe Chasehope was strong in his condemnation. But on the night of Hallowe'en, as David took a walk in the bright moonlight and saw the lights in the cottages and heard laughter and a jigging of fiddles, he did not find it in his heart to condemn the ancient fashions. Nor apparently did Chasehope himself, for David was much mistaken if it was not Ephraim's great shoulders and fiery head that he saw among the cabbage-stalks in Nance Kello's garden. He had been to Hallowe'en frolics himself in past days when he stayed with his cousin at Newbiggin, but it seemed to him that here in Woodilee there was something oppressed and furtive in the merriment. There was a secrecy about each lit dwelling, and no sign of young lads and lasses laughing on the roads. He noticed, too, that for the next few days many of the people had a look of profound weariness – pale faces, tired eyes, stealthy glances – as if behind the apparent decorum there had been revels that exhausted soul and body.

With the reaping of the harvest the ill-conditioned cattle were brought from the hills to the stubbles, and soon turned both outfield and infield into a miry wilderness. David, whose knowledge of farming was derived chiefly from the *Georgics*, had yet an eye in his head and a store of common sense, and he puzzled at the methods. The land at its best was ill-drained, and the trampling of beasts made a thousand hollows which would be puddles at the first rains and would further sour the rank soil. But when he spoke on the matter to the farmer of Mirehope, he was answered scornfully that that had been the 'auld way of the land,' and that those who were proud in their own conceit and had tried new-fangled methods – he had heard word of such in the West country – could not get two bolls from an acre where he had four. 'And Mirehope's but wersh land, sir, and not to be named wi' the Clyde howms.'

When the November snows came all live stock was gathered into the farm-towns. The cattle were penned in yards with thatched shelters, and soon turned them into seas of mud. The milking cows were in the byre; the sheep in paddocks near-by: the draught-oxen and the horses in miserable stables of mud and heather. It was the beginning of the winter hibernation, and the chief work of the farms was the feeding of the stock on their scanty winter rations. The hay – coarse bog grasses with little nutriment in them – went mainly to the sheep; horses and cattle had for fodder straw and messes of boiled chaff; while Crummie in the byre was sometimes regaled with the debris of the kailyard and the oddments left from the family meals. Winter each year was both for beast and man a struggle with famine, and each was rationed like the people of a besieged city. But if food was scarce at the best, Woodilee did not want for fuel. It had been a good year for peats, for they had ripened well on the hills, and the open autumn had made them easy to carry. Each cottage had its ample peat-stack, and when harvest was over there had been also a great gathering of windfalls from the woods, so that by every door stood a pile of kindlings.

Melanudrigill in the bright October days had lost its menace for David. He had no occasion to visit it by night, but more than once he rode through it by day on his pastoral visitations to Fennan or the Rood valley, and once in a flaming sunset he returned that way from Kirk Aller. The bracken was golden in decay, and the yellowing birches, the russet thorns, and the occasional scarlet of rowans made the sombre place almost cheerful. In his walks on the hill the great forest below him seemed to have grown thin and open, no longer a vast envelop-ing cloak, but a kindly covering for the ribs of earth. Some potency had gone from it with the summer, as if the tides of a fierce life had sunk back into the ground again. He had seen deer in the glades, and they looked innocent things . . . But he noticed as curious that none of the villagers in their quest for wood penetrated far into it, and that on its fringes they only gathered the windfalls. Up at the back of the Hill of Deer and in the Rood glen men were busy all day cutting birch and hazel billets, but no axe was laid to any tree in the Black Wood.

A week before Yule came the great snow. It began with a thin cold fog which muffled every fold of the hills. 'Rouk's snaw's wraith,' said the parish, and saw to its fuel-stacks and looked gloomily at its shivering beasts. The thick weather lasted for three days and three nights, weather so cold that it was pain to draw breath, and old folk at night in their box beds could not get warmth, and the Woodilee burn was frozen hard even in the linns. It was noted as a bad omen that deer from Melanudrigill were seen in the kirkton, and that at dawn when the Mirehope shepherd went out to his sheep he found half-frozen blue hares crouching among the flocks. On the fourth morning the snow began, and fell for three days in heavy flakes, so that it lay feet deep on the roads and fields. Then the wind rose and for six furious hours a blizzard raged, so that the day was like night, and few dared stir from their doors. David, setting out to visit Amos Ritchie's wife, who was sick of a congestion, took two hours over a quarter of mile of road, wandering through many kitchen middens, and had to postpone his return till the wind abated in the evening, while Isobel in the manse was demented with anxiety. The consequence was that the snow was swept bare from the knowes, but piled into twelve-foot drifts in the hollows. It was an ill time for the sheep in the paddocks, which were often one giant drift, where the presence of the flock could only be detected by the yellowish steaming snow. Chasehope lost a score of ewes, Mirehope half as many, and Nether Fennan, where the drifts were deep, the best part of his flock. To David it seemed that the farmers' ways were a tempting of Providence. Had the sheep been left on the hill they would have crowded in the snow to the bare places; here in the confined paddocks they were caught in a trap. Moreover, on the hill in open winter weather there was a better living to be picked up than that afforded by the narrow rations of sour bog hay. But when he spoke thus his hearers plainly thought him mad. Sheep would never face a winter on the hills – besides, the present practice was the 'auld way'.

The snow lay till the New Year was a week old, and when the thaw came and the roads ran in icy streams, David took to his bed for two days in utter exhaustion. All through the storm he had been on his legs, for there were sick folk and old folk in Woodilee who would perish miserably if left alone. The farm-towns could look after themselves, but in the scattered cottages of the kirkton there was no one to take command, and neigh-bourliness languished when each household was preoccupied with its own cares. Peter Pennecuik, a ruling elder, whose gift of prayer had been commended by Mr Muirhead, had lost a tup and had his byre roof crushed in by the drift, so he became a fatalist, holding that the Lord had prepared a visitation which it would be impiety to resist, and sat lugubriously by his fireside. David's fingers itched for his ears. From Amos Ritchie the blacksmith he got better assistance. Amos was a shaggy black-bearded man of thirty-five, a great fiddler and a mighty putter of the stone, whose godliness might have been suspect but for his behaviour in the Bishops' War. His wife was at death's door all through the storm, but he nevertheless constituted himself the minister's first lieutenant and wrought valiantly in the work of relief. There were old women too chilled and frail to kindle their fires in the morning and melt snow for water; there were households so ill provided that they existed largely on borrowed food; there were cots where the weather had broken roof or wall. Isobel in the manse kitchen was a busy woman and her girdle was never off the fire. David had looked forward to the winter snows as a season of peace, when he could sit indoors with his books; instead he found himself on his feet for fourteen hours out of the twenty-four, his hands and face chapped like a ploughman's, and so weary at night that he fell off his chair with sleep while Isobel fetched his supper.

Yet it was the storm which was David's true ordination to his duties, for it brought him close to his people, not in high sacramental things like death, but in their daily wrestling for life. He might visit their houses and catechise their families, but these were formal occasions, with all on their best behaviour, whereas in the intimate business of charity he saw them as they were.

The new minister was young and he was ardent, and his duties were still an adventure. His Sabbath sermons were diligently meditated. For his morning lecture he took the book of the prophet Amos, which, as the work of a herdsman, seemed fitting for a country parish. His two weekly discourses dealt laboriously with the fourfold state of man – his early state of innocence, his condition after the Fall, his state under grace, his condition in eternity. That winter David did not get beyond the state of innocence, and in discoursing on it he exhausted his ingenuity in piecing texts together from the Scriptures, and in such illustrations as he believed would awaken his hearers' minds. Profane learning openly used would have been resented, but he contrived to bring in much that did not belong to the divinity schools, and he escaped criticism, it may be, because his Kirk Session did not understand him. His elders were noted theologians, and what was strange to them, if it was weightily phrased, they took for theological profundity.

At ten o'clock each Sabbath morning Robb the beadle tinkled the first bell; at the second the congregation moved into the kirk, and Peter Pennecuik, who acted as precentor, led the opening psalm, reading each line before it was sung. When Robb jerked the third bell, David entered the pulpit and began with prayer. At one o'clock the people dispersed, those who came from a distance to Lucky Weir's ale-house; and at two fell the second service, which concluded at four with the coming of the dark. The kirk with its earthen floor was cold as a charnel-house, and the dimness of the light tried even David's young eyes. The people sat shivering on their little stools, each with the frozen decorum and strained attention which was their Sabbath ritual. To the minister it seemed often as if he were speaking to sheeted tombstones, he felt as if his hearers were at an infinite distance from him, and only on rare occasions, when some shining text of Scripture moved his soul and he spoke simply and with emotion, did he feel any contact with his flock.

But his sermons were approved. Peter Pennecuik gave it as his verdict that he was a 'deep' preacher and sound in the fundamentals. Others, remembering the thrill that sometimes came into his voice, called him an 'affectionate' preacher, and credited him with 'unction'. But there were many that longed for stronger fare, something more marrowy and awful, pictures of the hell of torment which awaited those who were not of the Elect. He had the 'sough', no doubt, but it was a gentle west wind, and not the stern Euroclydon which should call sinners to repentance. Their minister was a man of God, but he was young; years might add weight to him and give him the thunders of Sinai.

To David the Sabbath services were the least of his duties. He had come to Woodilee with his heart full of the mighty books which he would write in the solitude of his upper chamber. The chief was that work on the prophet Isaiah which should be for all time a repository of sacred learning so that Sempill on Isaiah would be quoted reverently like Luther on the Galatians or Calvin on the Romans. In the autumn evenings he had sketched the lines of his masterpiece, and before the great snow he had embarked on its prolegomena. But the storm made a breach in his studies. He felt himself called to more urgent duties, for he was a pastor of souls before he was a scholar. His visitations and catechisings among his flock were his chief care, and he began to win a name for diligence. On nights when even a shepherd would have kept the ingle side, David would arrive at a moorland cottage, and many a time Isobel had to welcome in the small hours a dripping or frozen master, thaw him by her kitchen fire, and feed him with hot ale and bannocks, while he recounted his adventures. He was strong and buoyant and he loved the life, which seemed to him to have the discipline of a soldier. His face high-coloured by weather, his cheerful eyes, and his boyish voice and laugh were soon popular in the length of the parish. 'He is a couthy lad,' said the old wives, 'and for a man o' God he's terrible like a plain body.'

Also he took charge of the children. In Woodilee there was no school or schoolmaster. There were three hundred communicants, but it was doubtful if more than a dozen could read a sentence or write their name. In the Kirk session itself there were only three. So David started a school, which met thrice a week of a morning in the manse kitchen. He sent to Edinburgh for horn-books, and with them and his big bible taught his class their rudiments. These were the pleasantest hours of the day for master and children, and weekly the gathering grew till there was not a child in the kirkton or in the farm-towns of Mirehope and Chasehope that would have missed them. When they arrived blue with cold and often breakfastless, Isobel would give each a bowl of broth, and while the lesson proceeded she would mend their ragged garments. Indeed more than one child emerged new clad, for the minister's second-best cloak and an old pair of breeches were cut up by Isobel – expostulating but not ill-pleased – for tattered little mortals.

David was more than a private almoner. He and his Session had the Poor Box to administer, the sole public means of relieving the parish's needs. Woodilee was better off than many places, in that it possessed a mortification of a thousand pounds Scots, bequeathed fifty years earlier by a certain Grizel Hawk-shaw for the comfort of the poor. Also there was the weekly collection at the kirk door, and there were the fines levied by the Session on evil-doers. In the winter the task of almoner was easier, for there were few beggars on the roads, and those that crossed the hills came as a rule only to die, when the single expense was the use of the parish coffin. Yet the administration of the scanty funds was a difficult business, and it led to David's first controversies with his Session. Each elder had his own favourites among the poor, and Chasehope and Mirehope and Nether Fennan wrangled over every grant. The minister, still new to the place, for the most part held his peace, but now and then, in cases which he knew of, he asserted his authority. There

was a woman, none too well reputed, who lived at Chasehope-
foot, with a buxom black-eyed daughter, and whose house,
though lamentably dirty and ill guided, seemed to lack nothing.
When he opposed Chasehope's demand that she should receive
a benefaction as a lone widow, he had a revelation of Chasehope's temper. The white face crimsoned, and the greenish eyes
looked for a moment as ugly as a snarling dog's. 'Worthy Mr
Macmichael. . . .' he began, but David cut him short. 'These
moneys are for the relief of the helpless poor,' he said, 'and they
are scant enough at the best. I should think shame to waste a
bodle except on a pitiful necessity. To him or her that hath shall
not be given, while I am the minister of this parish.' Chasehope
said nothing, and presently he mastered his annoyance, but the
farmer of Mirehope – Alexander Sprot was his name – muttered
something in an undertone to his neighbour, and there was
tension in the air till the laugh of the Woodilee miller broke it.
This man, one Spotswood, reckoned the richest in the parish
and the closest, had a jolly laugh which belied his reputation.
'Mr Sempill's in the right, Chasehope,' he cried. 'Jean o' the
Chasehopefit can manage fine wi' what her gudeman left her.
We daurna be lavish wi' ither folks' siller.' 'I am overruled,' said
Chasehope, and spoke no more.

Little news came in those days to Woodilee. In the open weather
before the storm the pack-horses of the carriers came as usual
from Edinburgh, and the drovers on the road to England brought
word of the doings in the capital. Johnnie Dow, the packman,
went his rounds till the snow stopped him, but in January when
the weather cleared he broke his leg in the Tarrit Moss and for six
weeks disappeared from the sight of men. But Johnnie at his best
brought only the clash of the farm-towns and the news of Kirk
Aller, and in the dead of the winter there was no chance of a post,
so that David was buried as deep as if he had been in an isle of the
Hebrides. It was only at presbytery meetings that he heard tidings
of the outer world, and these, passed through the minds of his
excited brethren, were all of monstrous portents.

The Presbytery meetings in Kirk Aller were at first to David a
welcome break in his quiet life. The one in November lasted two
days, and he, as the youngest member, opened the exercises and
discoursed with acceptance on a Scripture passage. The business was dull, being for the most part remits from the kirk
sessions of contumacious heritors and local scandals and re-
pairs to churches. The sederunt over, the brethren adjourned to
the Cross Keys Inn and dined off better fare than they were
accustomed to in their manses. It was then that Mr Muirhead in
awful whispers told of news he had had by special post from
Edinburgh. Malignancy had raised its head again, this time in
their own covenanted land. Montrose, the recusant, had made
his way north when he was least expected, and was now leading
a host of wild Irish to the slaughter of the godly. There had been
battles fought, some said near Perth, others as far off as
Aberdeen, and the victory had not been to the righteous.
Hideous tales were told of these Irish, led by a left-handed
Macdonald – savage as Amalekites, blind zealots of Rome,
burning and slaughtering and sparing neither sex nor age.
The trouble, no doubt, would be short-lived, for Leven's men
were marching from England, but it betokened some back-
sliding in God's people. The Presbytery held a special meeting
for prayer, when in lengthy supplications the Almighty was
besought to explain whether the sin for which this disaster was
the punishment lay with Parliament or Assembly, army or
people.

To David the tale was staggering. Montrose was to him only a
name, the name of a great noble who had at first served the
cause of Christ and then betrayed it. This Judas had not yet gone
to his account, was still permitted to trouble Israel, and now he
had crowned his misdeeds by leading savages against his own
kindly Scots. Like all his nation he had a horror of the Irish,
whose barbarity had become a legend, and of Rome, whom he
conceived as an unsleeping Anti-Christ, given a lease of the
world by God till the cup of her abomination was full. The news
shook him out of his political supineness, and for the moment

made him as ardent a Covenanter as Mr Muirhead himself. Then came the storm, when his head was filled with other concerns, and it was not till February that the Presbytery met again. This time the rumours were still darker. That very morning Mr Muirhead had had a post which spoke of Montrose ravaging the lands of that light of the Gospel, Argyll – of his fleeing north and, at the moment when his doom seemed assured, turning on the shore of a Highland sea-loch and scattering the Covenant army. It was the hour of peril, and the nation must humble itself before the Lord. A national fast had been decreed by Parliament, and it was resolved to set apart a day in each parish when some stout defender of the faith should call the people to examination and repentance. Mr Proudfoot of Bold was one of the chosen vessels, and it was agreed that he should take the sermon on the fast-day in Woodilee in the first week of March.

But David was now in a different mood from that of November. He repressed with horror an unregenerate admiration for this Montrose, who, it seemed, was still young, and with a handful of caterans had laid an iron hand on the north. He might be a fine soldier, but he was beyond doubt a son of Belial. The trouble with David was the state of his own parish, compared with which the sorrows of Argyll seemed dim and far-away.

January, after the snows melted, had been mild and open, with the burns running full and red, and the hills one vast plashing bog. With Candlemas came a black frost, which lasted the whole of February and the first half of March. The worst of the winter stringency was now approaching. The cattle in the yards and the sheep in the paddocks had become woefully lean, the meal in the girnels was running low, and everybody in the parish, except one or two of the farmers, had grown thin and pale-faced. Sickness was rife, and in one week the kirkyard saw six burials. . . . It was the season of births, too, as well as of deaths, and the howdie was never off the road.

Strange stories came to his ears. One-half of the births were out of lawful wedlock. . . . and most of the children were still-born. A young man is slow to awake to such a condition and it was only the miserable business of the stool of repentance which opened his eyes. Haggard girls occupied the stool and did penance for their sin, but in only one case did the male paramour appear. . . . He found his Session in a strange mood, for instead of being eager to enforce the law of the Kirk, they seemed to desire to hush up the scandals, as if the thing was an epidemic visitation which might spoil their own repute. He interrogated them and got dull replies; he lost his temper and they were silent. Where were the men who had betrayed these wretched girls? He repeated the question and found only sullen faces. One Sabbath he abandoned his ordinary routine and preached on the abominations of the heathen with a passion new to his hearers. His discourse was appreciated, and he was congratulated on it by Ephraim Caird; but there was no result, no confession, such as he had hoped for, from stricken sinners, no cracking of the wall of blank obstinate silence. . . . The thing was never out of his mind by day or night. What was betokened by so many infants born dead? He felt himself surrounded by a mystery of iniquity.

One night he spoke of it to Isobel, very shame-facedly, for it seemed an awful topic for a woman, however old. But Isobel was no more communicative than the rest. Even her honest eyes became shy and secretive. 'Dinna you fash yoursel', sir,' she said. 'The Deil's thrang in this parochine, and ye canna expect to get the upper hand o' him in sax months. But ye'll be even wi' him yet, Mr Sempill, wi' your graund Gospel preachin'.' And then she added that on which he pondered many times in the night watches. 'There will aye be trouble at this time o' year so long as the folk tak' the Wud at Beltane.'

The fast-day came and Mr Proudfoot preached a marrowy sermon. His subject was the everlasting fires of Hell, which awaited those who set their hand against a covenanted Kirk, and he exhausted himself in a minute description of the misery of an eternity of torment. 'They shall be crowded,' he said, 'like bricks in a fiery furnace. O what a bed is there! No feathers, but fire; no friends, but furies; no ease, but fetters; no daylight, but darkness; no clock to pass away the time, but endless eternity; fire eternal that ever burns and never dies away.' He excelled in his conclusion. 'Oh, my friends,' he cried, 'I have given you but a short touch of the torments of Hell. Think of a barn or some other great place filled up top-full with grains of corn; and think of a bird coming every thousand years and fetching away one of those grains of corn. In time there might be an end of all and the barn might be emptied, but the torments of Hell have no end. Ten thousand times ten millions of years doth not at all shorten the miseries of the damned.'

There was a hush like death in the crowded kirk. A woman screamed in hysterics and was carried out, and many sobbed. At the close the elders thronged around Mr Proudfoot and thanked him for a discourse so seasonable and inspired. But David spoke no word, for his heart had sickened. What meant these thunders against public sin when those who rejoiced in them were ready to condone a flagrant private iniquity? For a moment he felt that Montrose the apostate, doing evil with clean steel and shot, was less repugnant to God than his own Kirk Session.

The frost declined in mid-March, there was a fortnight of weeping thaw and a week of bitter east winds, and then in a single night came a south wind and Spring blew up the glens.

Isobel chased the minister from his books.

'Awa' to the hill like a man, and rax your legs. Ye've had a sair winter and your face is like a dish-clout. Awa' and snowk up the caller air.'

David went out to the moors, and on the summit of the Hill of Deer had a prospect of the countryside, the contours sharp in the clear April light, and colour stealing back after the grey of winter. The Wood of Melanudrigill seemed to have crowded together again, and to have regained its darkness, but there was as yet no mystery in its shadows. The hill itself was yellow like old velvet, but green was mantling beside the brimming streams. The birches were still only a pale vapour, but there were buds on the saughs and the hazels. Remnants of old drifts lay behind the dykes, and on the Lammer Law there was a great field of snow, but the breeze blew soft and the crying of curlews and plovers told of the spring. Up on Windyways and at the back of Reiverslaw the heather was burning, and spirals of blue smoke rose to the pale skies.

The sight was a revelation to a man to whom Spring had come hitherto in the narrow streets of Edinburgh. He had a fancy that life was beating furiously under the brown earth, and that he was in the presence of a miracle. His youth, long frosted by winter, seemed to return to him and his whole being to thaw. Almost shamefacedly he acknowledged an uplift of spirit. The smoke from the moorburn was like the smoke of sacrifice on ancient altars – innocent sacrifice from kindly altars.

That night in his study he found that he could not bring his mind to his commentary on the prophet Isaiah. His thoughts ranged on other things, and he would fain have opened his Virgil. But, since these evening hours were dedicate to theology, he compromised with Clement of Alexandria, and read again the passage where that father of the Church becomes a poet and strives to mingle the classic and the Christian. – '*This is the Mountain beloved of God, not a place of tragedies like Cithaeron, but consecrate to the dramas of truth, a mount of temperance shaded with the groves of purity. And there revel on it not the Maenads, sisters of Semele the thunderstruck, initiate in the impure feast of flesh, but God's daughters, fair Lambs who celebrate the holy rites of the Word, chanting soberly in chorus.*'

In these days his sermons changed. He no longer hammered subtle chains of doctrine, but forsook his 'ordinary', and preached to the hearts of the people. Woodilee was in turn mystified, impressed, and disquieted. One bright afternoon he discoursed on thankfulness and the praise due to God. 'Praise Him,' he cried, 'if you have no more, for this good day and sunshine to the lambs.'

'Heard ye ever the like?' said Mirehope at the kirk door. 'What concern has Jehovah wi' our lambin'?'

'He's an affectionate preacher,' said Chasehope, 'but he's no Boanerges, like Proudfoot o' Bold.'

The other agreed, and though the tone of the two men was regretful, their eyes were content, as if they had no wish for a Boanerges in Woodilee.

FIVE

The Black Wood by Day

On the 22nd day of April the minister went for a walk on the Hill of Deer. He had heard news from Isobel which had awakened his numbed memory. All the long dark winter Woodilee had been severed from the world, and David had also lived in the cage and had had no thoughts beyond the parish. Calidon and its people were as little in his mind as if they had been on another planet. But as Spring loosened the bonds word of the neighbourhood's doings was coming in.

'Johnnie Dow's ben the house,' Isobel had said as he sat at meat. 'He's come down the water frae Calidon, and it seems there's unco changes there. The laird is awa' to the wars again. . . . Na, Johnnie didna ken what airt he had ridden. He gaed off ae mornin' wi his man Tam Purves, baith o' them on muckle horses, and that's the last heard o' them. It seems that the laird's gude-sister, Mistress Saintserf frae Embro, cam oot a fortnight syne to tak' chairge o' Calidon and the young lassie – there's a lassie bides there, ye maun ken, sir, though nane o' the Woodilee folk ever cast een on her – and the puir body was like to be smoored in the Carnwath Moss. Johnnie says she's an auld wumman as straucht as a wand and wi' an unco ill tongue in her heid. She fleyed Johnnie awa' frae the door when he was for daffin' wi' the serving lasses.'

It was of Calidon that David thought as he took the hill. Nicholas Hawkshaw, lame as he was, had gone back to the wars. What wars? Remembering the talk of that autumn night he feared that it could not be a campaign of which a minister of the Kirk would approve. Was it possible that he had gone to join Montrose in his evil work? And the troopers and the groom?

Were they with Leven again under the Covenant's banner, or were they perilling their souls with the malignants? The latter most likely, and to his surprise he felt no desire to reprobate them. Spring was loosening other bonds than those of winter.

It was a bright warm day, which might have been borrowed from June, and the bursting leaves were stirred by a wandering west wind. David sat for a little on the crest of the hill, gazing at the high summits, which, in the April light, were clear in every nook and yet infinitely distant. The great Herstane Craig had old snowdrifts still in its ravines, and he had the fancy that it was really built of marble which shone in places through the brown husk. The Green Dod did not now belie its name; above the screes and heather of its flanks rose a cone of dazzling greenness. The upper Aller glen was filled with pure sunshine, the very quintessence of light, and the sword-cut of the Rood was for once free from gloom. There was no gold in the landscape, for the shallows, even when they caught the sun, were silver, the bent was flushing into the palest green, the skies above were an infinity of colourless light. And yet the riot of Spring was there. David felt it in his bones and in his heart.

The herd of Reiverslaw was busy with his late lambs. The man, Prentice by name, was a sour fellow whom an accident in childhood had deprived of a leg. In spite of his misfortune he could move about on a single crutch at a good pace, and had a voice and a tongue which the parish feared. He was a noted professor, with an uncanny gift of prayer, and his by-names in Woodilee were 'Hirplin' Rab' and the 'One Leggit Prophet'. But today even Prentice seemed mellowed by the Spring. He gave David a friendly good-day. 'The voice o' the turtle is heard on the yirth,' he announced, and as he hobbled over a patch of old moorburn, sending up clouds of grey dust, Prentice too became a figure of pastoral.

David had rarely felt a more benignant mood. The grimness of winter had gone clean out of his mind, and he had entered on a large and gracious world. He walked slowly like an epicure, drinking in the quintessential air of the hills, marking the strong blue swirl of the burns, the fresh green of the mosses, the buds on the hawthorns, the flash of the water-ouzels in the spray of the little falls. Curlews and peewits filled the moor with their crying, and as he began to descend into the Rood glen a lark – the first he had heard – rose to heaven with a flood of song.

His eyes had been so engaged with the foreground that he had not looked towards Melanudrigill. Now he saw it, dark and massy, the only opaque thing in a translucent world. But there was nothing oppressive in its shadows, for oppression could not exist in a scene so full of air and light and song. For a moment he had a mind to go boldly into its coverts by way of Reiverslaw and make for the lower course of the Woodilee burn. But the sight of the wild wood in the Rood glen detained him. It was a day not for the pines but for the hazels and birches, where in open glades a man would have always a view of the hills and the sky. So he slanted to his right through the open coppice, meaning to reach the valley floor near the foot of the path which led to the Greenshiel.

The coppice was thicker than he had imagined. This was no hillside scrub, but a forest, a greenwood, with its own glades and hollows, its own miniature glens and streams. He was in the midst of small birds who made a cheerful twittering from the greening boughs, cushats too were busy, and the thickets were full of friendly beasts. He saw the russet back of a deer as it broke cover, and the tawny streak of a hill-fox, and there was a perpetual scurrying of rabbits. Above all there was a glory of primroses. The pale blossoms starred the glades and the sides of the dells, clung to tree-roots, and climbed into crannies of the grey whinstone rock. So thick they were, that their paleness became golden, the first strong colour he had seen that day. David was young and his heart was light, so he gathered a great clump of blooms for his manse table, and set a bouquet in his coat and another in his bonnet. These latter would have to go before he reached the highway or the parish would think that its minister had gone daft. But here in the secret greenwood he could forget decorum and bedeck himself like a child.

Presently he had forgotten the route he had planned. He found himself in a shallow glade which ran to the left and away from the Greenshiel, and down which leaped a burn so entrancing in its madcap grace that he could not choose but follow it. Memory returned to him; this must be the burn which descended near the mill at Roodfoot; he knew well its lower course, for he had often guddled trout in its pools, but he had never explored its upper waters. Now he felt the excitement of a discoverer. . . . The ravine narrowed to a cleft where the stream fell in a white spout into a cauldron. David made the passage by slithering down the adjacent rocks and emerged wet to the knees. He was as amused as a boy playing truant from school, and when he found a water-ouzel's nest in the notch of a tree-root he felt that he had profit of his truancy. There came a more level stretch, which was a glory of primroses and wood anemones, then another linn, and then a cup of turf rimmed with hazels, where the water twined in placid shallows. . . . He looked up and saw on the opposite bank a regiment of dark pines.

He had come to the edge of Melanudrigill. The trees rose like a cloud above him, and after the open coppice of birch and hazel he seemed to be looking into deep water where things were seen darkly as through a dull glass. There were glades which ran into shadows, and fantastic rocks, and mounds of dead bracken which looked like tombs. Yet the place fascinated him. It, too, was under the spell of Spring, and he wondered how Spring walked in its recesses. He leapt the stream and scrambled up the bank with an odd feeling of expectation. He was called to adventure on this day of days.

The place was not dark but dim and very green. The ancient pines grew more sparsely than he had imagined, and beneath them were masses of sprouting ferns – primroses too, and violets which he had not found among the hazels. A scent of rooty dampness was about, of fresh-turned earth, and welling fountains. In every tree-root wood-sorrel clustered. But there were no small birds, only large things like cushats and hawks which made a movement in the high branches. A little further and he was in a glade, far more of a glade than the clearings in the hazels, for it was sharply defined by the walls of shade.

He stood and gazed, stuck silent by its beauty. Here in truth was a dancing-floor for wood nymphs, a playground for the Good Folk. It seemed strange that the place should be untenanted. . . . there was a rustling in the covert, and his heart beat. He was no longer the adventurous boy, but a young man with a fancy fed by knowledge. He felt that the glade was aware and not empty. Light feet had lately brushed its sward. . . . There was a rustling again, and a gleam of colour. He stood poised like a runner, his blood throbbing in a sudden rapture.

There was the gleam again and the rustle. He thought that at the far end of the glade behind the red bracken he saw a figure. In two steps he was certain. A green gown fluttered and at his third step broke cover. He saw the form of a girl – nymph, fairy, or mortal, he knew not which. He was no more the minister of Woodilee, but eternal wandering youth, and he gave chase.

The green gown wavered for a moment between two gnarled pines and then was lost in the dead fern. He saw it again in the cleft of a tiny rivulet which came down from a pile of rocks, but he missed it as he scrambled up the steep. It seemed that the gown played tricks with him and led him on, for, as he checked at fault, he had a glimpse of it lower down where an aisle in the trees gave a view of the bald top of a mountain. David was young and active, but the gown was swifter than he, for as he went down the slope in great leaps it vanished into the dusk of the pines. He had it again, lost it, found it suddenly high above him – always a glimmer of green with but a hint of a girl's form behind it. . . . David became wary. Nymph or human, it should not beat him at this sport of hide-and-seek. There was a line of low cliffs above, up which it could not go unless it took wings. David kept the lower ground, determined that he would drive that which he followed towards the cliff line. He succeeded, for after twice trying to break away, the gown fluttered into a tiny ravine, with thick scrub on both sides and the rock wall at the top. As David panted upward he saw in a mossy place below the crags a breathless girl trying to master her tumbling tresses.

He stopped short in a deep embarrassment. He had been pursuing a fairy, and had found a mortal – a mortal who looked down on him with a flushed face and angry eyes. He was furiously hot, and the pace and his amazement bereft him of speech. It was she who spoke first.

'What does the minister of Woodilee in the Wood – and bedecked with primroses?'

The voice was familiar, and as he brushed the sweat from his eyes the face too awoke recollection. She was far cooler than he, but her cheeks were flushed, and he had seen before those dark mirthful eyes. Mirthful they were, for her anger seemed to have gone, and she was looking down on him with a shy amusement. She had recognised him too, and had spoken his name. . . . He had it. It was the girl who had curtsied to Nicholas Hawkshaw's guests in the candle-light at Calidon. His abashment was increased.

'Madam,' he stammered, 'Madam, I thought you were a fairy.'

She laughed out loud with the abandonment of childhood. 'A fairy! And, pray, sir, is it part of the duties of a gospel minister to pursue fairies in the woods?'

'I am shamed,' he cried. 'You do well to upbraid me. But on this spring day I had forgot my sacred calling and dreamed I was a boy once more.'

'I do not upbraid you. Indeed I am glad that a minister can still be a boy. But folks do not come here, and I thought the wood my own, so when I saw you stumbling among the fern I had a notion to play a trick on you, and frighten you, as I have frightened intruders before. I thought you would run away. But you were too bold for me, and now you have discovered my secret. This wood is my playground where I can pick flowers and sing ballads and be happy with birds and beasts. . . . You were a man before you were a minister. What is your name?'

'They call me David Sempill. I lived as a child at the Mill of the Roodfoot.'

'Then you have seisin of this land. You too have played in the Wood?'

'Nay, madam, the Wood is strange to me. I have but ridden through it, and till today I have had some dread of it. This Melanudrigill is ill reputed.'

'Old wives' havers! It is a blessed and innocent place. But I do not like that name – Melanudrigill. There is dark magic there. Call it the Wood, and you will love it as I do. . . . See, I am coming down. Make room, please, and then I will take you to Paradise. You do not know Paradise? It is the shrine of this grove, and none but me can find the road.'

This was not the stately lady in the gown of yellow satin and blue velvet who had abashed him that night in Calidon tower. It was a slim laughing girl in green who presently stood beside him, her feet in stout country shoes, her hair bound only by a silk fillet and still unruly from the chase. He suddenly lost his embarrassment. His reason told him that this was Katrine Yester of Calidon, a daughter of a proud and contumacious house that was looked askance at by the godly, a woman, a beauty – commodities of which he knew nothing. But his reason was blinded and he saw only a girl on a spring holiday.

She led him down the hill, and as she went she chattered gaily, like a solitary child who has found a comrade.

'I saw you before you saw me, and I hoped you would follow when I ran away. I liked you that night at Calidon. They told me that ministers were all sour-faced and old, but you looked kind. And you are merry, too, I think – not sad, like most people in Scotland.'

'You have not been long in this land?' he asked.

'Since June of last year. This is my first Scottish spring, and it is different from France and England. In those lands summer comes with a rush on winter's heels, but here there is a long preparation, and flowers steal very softly back to the world. I have lived mostly in France since my father died.'

'That is why your speech is so strange to my ears.'

'And yours to mine,' she retorted. 'But Aunt Grizel is teaching me to be a good Scotswoman. I am made to spin till my arms are weary, and to make horrid brews of herbs, and to cook your strange dishes. "Kaatrine, ye daft quean, what for maun ye fill the hoose wi' floorish and nesty green busses? D'ye think we're nowt and the auld tower o' Calidon a byre?" That is Aunt Grizel. But she is like a good dog and barks but does not bite, though the serving-maids walk in terror. I play with her at the cartes, and she tells me tales, but not such good ones as Uncle Nick's. Heigho! I wish the wars were over and he were home again. . . . Now sir, what do you think of this? It is the gate of Paradise.'

She had led him into a part of the wood where the pines ceased and a green cleft was lined with bursting hazels and rowans and the tassels of birch. The place was rather hill than woodland, for the turf was as fine as on a mountain-side, and in the centre a bubbling spring sent out a rivulet, which twined among the flowers till it dropped in a long cascade to a lower shelf. Primroses, violets, and anemones made it as bright as a garden.

'I call this Paradise,' she said, 'because it is hard for mortals to find. You would not guess it was here till you stumbled on it.'

'It's away from the pines,' he said.

She nodded her head. 'I love the dark trees well enough and on a day like this I am happy among them. But they are moody things, and when there is no sun and the wind blows they make me sad. Here I am gay in any weather, for it is a kindly place. Confess, sir, that I have chosen well.'

'You have chosen well. It is what the poet wrote of – *Deus haec nobis otia fecit.*'

'La, la! That is Latin and I am not learned. But I can quote my own poets.' And in a voice like a bird's she trilled a stanza of which David comprehended no more than that it was a song of Spring and that it was Flora the goddess herself who sang it:

> O fontaine Bellerie,
> Belle fontaine chérie
> De nos Nymphes, quand ton eau
> Les cache au creux de ta source,
> Fuyantes le Satyreau
> Qui les pourchasse à la course
> Jusqu'au bord de ton ruisseau,
> Tu es la Nymphe éternelle
> De ma terre paternelle—

Some strange and cataclysmic transformation was going on in David's mind. He realised that a film had cleared from his sight and that he was looking with new eyes. This dancing creature had unlocked a door for him – whether for good or ill, he knew not, and did not care. He wanted the world to stand still and the scene to remain fixed for ever – the Spring glade and the dark-haired girl singing among the primroses. He had the courage now to call her by her name.

'You have a voice like a linnet, Mistress Katrine. Can you sing none of our country songs?'

'I am learning them from the serving-maids. I know "The Ewebuchts" and "The Yellow-hair'd Laddie" and – ah, this is the one for Paradise,' and she sang:

> The King's young dochter was sitting in her window,
>   Sewing at her silken seam;
> She lookt out o' a bow-window,
>   And she saw the leaves growing green, My luve;
>   And she saw the leaves growing green.

'But Jean, the goose-girl who taught it me, remembered just the one verse. I wish I was a poet to make others.'

Above the spring was one of those circles of green mounds which country people call fairy-rings. The girl seated herself in the centre and began to make posies of the flowers she had picked. David lay on the turf at her feet, watching the quick movement of her hands, his garlanded hat removed and the temperate sun warming his body. Never had he felt so bathed in happy peace.

The pixie seated above him spared time from her flowers to glance down at him, and found him regarding her with abstracted eyes. For he was trying to fit this bright creature into his scheme of things. Did the world of the two of them touch nowhere save in this woodland?

'Your uncle is the chief heritor in Woodilee parish,' he said, 'but you do not come to the kirk.'

'I was there no longer back than last Sunday—' she said.

'Sabbath,' he corrected.

'Sabbath, if you will have it so. Calidon is in Cauldshaw parish, and it was to Cauldshaw kirk we went. Four weary miles of jogging on a plough-horse, I riding pillion to Aunt Grizel. Before that the drifts were too deep to take the road. . . . I have heard many a sermon from Mr Fordyce.'

'He is a good man.'

'He is a dull man. Such a preachment on dismal texts. "Seventhly, my brethren, and in parenthesis –"' she mimicked. 'But he is beyond doubt good, and Aunt Grizel says she has benefitted from his words, and would fain repay him by healing his disorders. He has many bodily disorders, the poor man, and Aunt Grizel loves sermons much but her simples more.'

'You do not love sermons?'

She made a mouth.

'I do not think I follow them. You are learned theologians, you of Scotland, and I am still at the horn-book. But someday I will come to hear you, for *your* sermons I think I might understand.'

'I could not preach to you,' he said.

'And wherefore, sir? Are your discourses only for wrinkled carls and old rudas wives? Is there no place in your kirk for a girl?'

'You are not of our people. The seed can be sown only in a field prepared.'

'But that is heresy. Are not all souls alike?'

'True. But the voice of the preacher is heard only by open ears. I think you are too happy in your youth, mistress, for my solemnities.'

'You do me injustice,' she said, and her face was grave. 'I am young, and I think I have a cheerful heart, for I can exult in a Spring morning and I cannot be very long sad. But I have had sorrows – a father slain in the wars, a mother dead of grieving, a bundling about among kinsfolk who were not all gracious. I have often had sore need of comfort, sir.'

'You have found it – where?'

'In the resolve never to be a faintheart. That is my creed, though I fail often in the practice.'

To an ear accustomed to a formal piety the confession seemed almost a blasphemy. He shook a disapproving head.

'That is but a cold pagan philosophy,' he said.

'Yet I learned it from a sermon, and that little more than a year back.'

'Where was it preached?'

'In England, and in no kirk, but at the King's Court.'

'Was it by Mr Henderson?'

'It was by a Presbyterian – but he was no minister. Listen, and I will tell you the story. In March of last year I was taken to Oxford by my lady Grevel and was presented by her to the Queen, and her Majesty deigned to approve of me, so that I became a maid-of-honour and was lodged beside her in Merton College. There all day long was a coming and going of great men. There I saw' – she counted on her fingers – 'my lord of Hamilton – him I did not like – and my lord of Nithsdale, and my lord of Aboyne, and my lord Ogilvy, and that very grave person Sir Edward Hyde, and my lord Digby, and the wise Mr Endymion Porter. And all day long there were distracted counsels, and the King's servants plotting in side-chambers, and treason whispered, and nowhere a clear vision or a brave heart. Then there came among us a young man, who spoke simply. "If the King's cause go down in England," he said, "it may be saved in Scotland." When they asked him what he proposed, he said—"To raise the North for his Majesty." When they asked him by what means, he said—"By my own resolution." All doubted and many laughed, but that young man was not discouraged. "The arm of the Lord is not shortened," he said, "and they who trust in Him will not be dismayed. . . ." That was the sermon he preached, and there was silence among the doubters. Then said Mr Porter: "There is a certain faith that moves mountains and a certain spirit which may win against all odds. My voice is for the venture!". . . . And then the Queen my mistress kissed the young man, and the King made him his lieutenant-general. . . . I watched him ride out of the city two days later, attended by but one servant, on his mission to conquer Scotland, and I flung him a nosegay of early primroses. He caught it and set it in his breast, and he waved his hand to me as he passed through the north gate.'

'Who was this hero?' David asked eagerly, for the tale had fired him.

The girl's face was flushed and her eyes glistened.

'That was a year ago,' she went on. 'Today he has done his purpose. He has won Scotland for the King.'

David gasped.

'Montrose the malignant!' he cried.

'He is as good a Presbyterian as you, sir,' she replied gently. 'Do not call him malignant. He made his way north through his enemies as if God had sent His angel to guide him. And he is born to lead men to triumph. Did you not feel the compulsion of his greatness?'

'I?' David stammered.

'They told me that you had spoken with him and that he liked you well. Yon groom at Calidon was the Lord Marquis.'

SIX

The Black Wood by Night

Word came of a great revival in the parish of Bold. Men called it a 'work,' and spoke of it in hushed voices, attributing it to the zeal and gifts of Mr Ebenezer Proudfoot, the minister. For, after much preaching on fast-days in the shire, Mr Ebenezer had fallen into a rapture and had seen visions and spoken with strange voices. The terror of the unknown fell upon his people, fasting and prayer became the chief business of the parish, and the most careless were transformed into penitents. For a season there were no shortcomings in Bold; penny-bridals and fiddling and roystering at the change-houses were forgotten; even swearing and tippling were forsworn; the Sabbath was more strictly observed than by Israel in the Wilderness. To crown the Work a great field-preaching was ordained, when thousands assembled on Bold Moor and the sacrament was dispensed among scenes of wild emotion. In Bold there was a lonely field of thistles, known as Guidman's Croft, which had been held to be dedicate to the Evil One. The oxen of all the parish were yoked, and in an hour or two it was ploughed up and sown with bear for the use of the poor, as at once a thank-offering and a renunciation.

People in Woodilee talked much of the Work in Bold and the Session sighed for a like experience. 'Would but the wind blow frae that airt on our frostit lands!' was the aspiration of Peter Pennecuik. But David had no ears for these things, for he was engrossed with the conflict in his own soul.

Ever since that afternoon in Paradise he had walked like a man half asleep, his eyes turning inward. His first exhilaration had been succeeded by a black darkness of doubt. He had adventured into the Wood and found magic there, and the spell was tugging at his heartstrings. . . . Was the thing of Heaven or of Hell?. . . . Sometimes, when he remembered the girl's innocence and ardour, he thought of her as an angel. Surely no sin could dwell in so bright a presence. . . . But he remembered, too, how lightly she had held the things of the Kirk, how indeed she was vowed to the world against which the Kirk made war. Was she not a daughter of Heth, a fair Moabitish woman, with no part in the commonwealth of Israel? Her beauty was of the flesh, her graces were not those of the redeemed. And always came the conviction that nevertheless she had stolen his heart. 'Will I too be unregenerate?' he asked himself with terror.

The more he looked into his soul the more he was perplexed. He thought of the groom at Calidon, to whom had gone out from him a spark of such affection as no other had inspired. That face was little out of his memory, and he longed to look on it again as a lover longs for his mistress. . . . But the man was Montrose the recreant, who was even now troubling God's people, and who had been solemnly excommunicated by the very Kirk he was vowed to serve. . . . And yet, recreant or no, the man believed in God and had covenanted himself with the Almighty. . . . What were God's purposes, and who were God's people? Where in all the round earth should he find a solution of his doubts?

The study, now warm in the pleasant Spring gloamings, saw no longer the preparation of the great work on Isaiah. It had become a closet for prayer. David cast his perplexities on the Lord and waited feverishly for a sign. But no sign came. A horde of texts about Canaanitish garments and idol worship crowded into his mind, but he refused their application. A young man's face, a girl's eyes and voice, made folly of such easy formulas. . . . Yet there were moments when in sheer torment of soul David was minded to embrace them – to renounce what had charmed him as the Devil's temptation, and steel his heart against its glamour.

One day he rode over to Cauldshaw to see Mr Fordyce. He was in the mood for confession, but he found little encourage-

ment. Mr James was sick of a spring fever, and though he was
on his feet he had been better in bed, for his teeth chattered and
his hand trembled.

They spoke of the household at Calidon. 'Mistress Saint-serf
has beyond doubt her interest in Christ,' said the minister of
Cauldshaw. 'When I have gone to Calidon for the catechising I
have found her quick to apprehend the doctrines of the faith,
and her life is in all respects an ensample, save that she is
something of a libertine with her tongue. But the lassie – she's
but a young thing, and has sojourned long in popish and
prelatical lands. Yet I detect glimmerings of grace, Mr David,
and she has a heart that may well be attuned to God's work. My
wife pines for the sight of her like a sick man for the morning.
Maybe I fail in my duty towards her, for she is lamentably
ignorant, but I cannot find it in me to be harsh to so gracious a
bairn.'

David returned with his purpose unfulfilled but a certain
comfort in his soul. He would rather have Mr Fordyce's judgment than that of the Boanerges of Bold or the sleek minister of
Kirk Aller. His doubts were not resolved, but the very uncer-
tainty gave him ease. He was not yet called to renunciation, and
having reached this conclusion, he could let the memory of
Paradise sweep back into his mind in a delightful flood.

Yet youth cannot be happy in indecision. David longed for
some duty which would absorb the strong life that was in him.
Why, oh why was he not a soldier? He turned to his parish, and
tried to engross himself in its cares. It may have been that his
perception was sharpened by his own mental conflicts, but he
seemed to detect a strangeness in Woodilee.

It had been a fine Spring, with a dry seed-bed, and the sowing
of crops and the lambing had passed off well. The lean cattle had
staggered out of byres and closes to the young grass and their
ribs were now covered again. Up on the hills lambs no longer
tottered on weak legs. There was more food in the place, for
there had been feasts of braxy mutton, and the hens were laying
again, and there was milk in the cogies. The faces of the people

had lost their winter strain; the girls had washed theirs, and fresh cheeks and bright eyes were to be seen on the roads. Woodilee had revived with the Spring, but David as he went among the folk saw more than an increase in bodily well-being. . . . There was a queer under-current of excitement – or was it expectation? – and the thing was secret.

Everyone did not share this. There seemed to be an inner circle in the parish which was linked together by some private bond. He began to guess at its membership by the eyes. Some looked him frankly in the face, and these were not always the best reputed. Amos Ritchie, the blacksmith, for instance – he was a profane swearer, and was sometimes overtaken in drink – and the farmer of Reiverslaw had, in addition to the latter failing, a violent temper, which made him feared and hated. Yet these two faced him like free men. But there were others, whose speech was often the most devout, who seemed to have shutters drawn over their eyes and to move stealthily on tiptoe.

Woodilee was amazingly well-conducted, and the Poor Box received the scantiest revenue in penalties. Apart from the lawless births in the winter, there were few apparent back-slidings. David rarely met young lads and lasses at their hoy-denish courtings in the gloamings. Oaths were never heard, and if there was drunkenness it was done in secret. Not often was a Sabbath-breaker before the Session, and there were no fines for slack attendance at the kirk. But as David watched the people thronging to service on the Sabbath, the girls in their clean linen, walking barefoot and only putting on shoes at the kirk-yard gate, the men in decent homespun and broad bonnets, the old wives in their white mutches – as he looked down from the pulpit on the shoulders bent with toil, the heavy features hardened to a stiff decorum, the eyes fixed dully on his face – he had the sense that he was looking on masks. The real life of Woodilee was shut to him. 'Ye are my people,' he told himself bitterly, 'and I know ye not.'

This was not true of all. He knew the children, and there were certain of the older men and women in the parish who had

given him their friendship. Peter Pennecuik, his principal elder
and session-clerk, he felt that he knew to the bottom – what little
there was to know, for the man was a sanctimonious egotist.
With Amos Ritchie and Reiverslaw, too, he could stand as man
with man. . . . But with many of the others he fenced as with
aliens; the farmers, for example, Chasehope and Mirehope, and
Nether Fennan, and Spotswood the miller, and various elderly
herds and hinds, and the wives of them. Above all he was no
nearer the youth of the parish than when first he came. The
slouching hobbledehoy lads, the girls, some comely and high-
coloured, some waxen white – they were civil and decent, but
impenetrable. There were moments when he found himself
looking of a Sabbath at his sober respectable folk as a hostile
body, who watched him furtively lest he should learn too much
of them. . . . Woodilee had an ill name in the shire, Mr Fordyce
had told him the first day in the manse. For what? What was the
life from which he was so resolutely barred – he, their minister,
who should know every secret of their souls? What was behind
those shuttered eyes? Was it fear? He thought that there might
be fear in it, but that more than fear it was a wild and sinister
expectation.

On the last day of April he noted that Isobel was ill at ease. 'Ye'll
be for a daunder, sir,' she said after the midday meal. 'See and be
hame in gude time for your supper – I've a rale guid yowe-milk
kebbuck for ye and a new bakin' o' cakes – and I'll hae the can'les
lichtit in your chamber for you to get to your books.'

He smiled at his housekeeper. 'Why this carefulness?' he
said.

She laughed uneasily.

'Naething by ordinar. But this is the day they ca' the Rood-
Mass and the morn is the Beltane, and it behoves a' decent
bodies to be indoors at the darkenin' on Beltane's Eve. My
faither was a bauld man, but he wadna have stirred a fit over his
ain doorstep on the night o' Rood-Mass for a king's ransom.
There's anither Beltane on the aught day of May, and till that's
by we maun walk eidently.'

'Old wives' tales,' he said.

'But they're nane auld wives' tales. They're the tales o' wise men and bauld men.'

'I thought of walking in the Wood.'

'Mercy on us!' she cried. 'Ye'll no gang near the Wud. No on this day o' a' days. It's fou' o' bogles.'

Her insistence vexed him and he spoke to her sharply. The heavy preoccupation of his mind had put him out of patience with folly. 'Woman,' he cried, 'what concern has a servant of God with these heathen fables? Think shame to repeat such folly.'

But Isobel was not convinced. She retired in dudgeon to her kitchen, and watched his movements till he left the house as a mother watches a defiant child. 'Ye'll be hame in guid time?' she begged.

'I will be home when I choose,' he said, and to show his independence he put some cheese and bannocks in his pockets.

The afternoon was warm and bright with a thin haze on the highest hills. Spring had now fairly come; the yews in the kirkyard were russet with young shoots, the blossom was breaking on the hawthorn, and hazel and oak and ash were in leaf. His spirit was too laden to be sensible of the sweet influences of sky and moorland as on the walk which had first taken him to Paradise. But there was in him what had been lacking before – excitement, for he had tasted of magic and was in the constant expectation of finding it again. The land was not as it had once been, for it held somewhere enchantments – a girl's face and a girl's voice. From the summit of the Hill of Deer he looked towards Calidon hidden in the fold of the Rood hills. Was she there in the stone tower, or among the meadows whose green showed in the turn of the glen? Or was she in her old playground of the Wood?

He had resolved not to go near the place, so he set himself to walk in the opposite direction along the ridge of hill which made the northern wall of the Rood valley. As he strode over the short turf and scrambled through the patches of peat-bog his spirits rose. It was hard not to be light-hearted in that world of essential airs and fresh odours and nesting birds. Presently he was in view of Calidon tower, and then he was past it, and the Rood below him was creeping nearer to his level as its glen lifted towards its source. He strode along till he felt the sedentary humours leave his body and his limbs acquire the lightness which is the reward of the hill walker. He seemed, too, to gain a lightness of soul and a clearness of eye. In a world which God had made so fair and clean, there could be no sin in anything that was also fair and innocent.

The sun had set beyond Herstane Craig before he turned his steps. Now from the hilltops he had Melanudrigill before him, a distant shadow in the trough of the valley. Since that afternoon in Paradise awe of the Wood had left him. He had been among its pines and had found Katrine there. He watched the cloud of trees, growing nearer at each step, as earlier that day he had watched the environs of Calidon. It was her haunt; haply she might now be there, singing in the scented twilight?

When he stood above Reiverslaw the dusk was purple about him, and the moon, almost at her full, was climbing the sky. He longed to see how Paradise looked in this elfin light, for he had a premonition that the girl might have lingered there late and that he would meet her. There was no duty to take him home – nothing but Isobel's silly fables. But in deference to Isobel he took the omens. He sent his staff twirling into the air. If it fell with the crook towards him, he would go home. The thing lighted in a heather bush with the crook at the far end. So he plunged downhill among the hazels, making for the glade which slanted eastward towards the deserted mill.

He found it, and it was very dark in that narrow place. There was no light to see the flowers by, and there was no colour in it, only a dim purple gloom and the white of the falling stream, for the moon was still too low in the heavens to reach it.

In time he came to the high bank where the pines began. He was looking for Paradise, but he could not find it. It was not among the pines, he remembered, but among the oaks and hazels, but he had gone to it through the pines, led by a flitting girl. . . . He found the point where he had entered the darker Wood and resolved to try to retrace his former tracks.

The place was less murky than he had expected, for the moon was now well up the sky, so that every glade was a patch of white light. . . . This surely was the open space where he had first caught the glimmer of a green gown. . . . There were the rocks were she had stood at bay. . . . She had led him down the hill and then at a slant – but was it to right or left? Right, he thought, and plunged through a wilderness of fern. There had been briars, too, and this was surely the place where a vast uprooted trunk had forced them to make a detour.

Then he found a little stream which he fancied might be the outflow of the Paradise well. So he turned up hill again, and came into a jungle of scrub and boulder. There was in most places a dim light to move by, but a dim light in a broken wood is apt to confuse the mind. David had soon lost all sense of direction, save that of the upward and downward slopes. He did not know east or west, and he did not stop to think, for he was beginning to be mesmerised by the hour and the scene. Dew was in the air and an overpowering sweetness of fern and pine and mosses, and through the aisles of the high trees came a shimmer of palest gold, and in the open spaces the moon rode in the dusky blue heavens – not the mild moon of April but a fiery conquering goddess, driving her chariot among trampled stars.

It was clear to him that he would not find Paradise except by happy chance, since he was utterly out of his bearings. But he was content to be lost, for the whole place was Paradise. Never before had he felt so strong a natural magic. This woodland, which he had once shunned, had become a holy place, lit with heavenly lights and hallowed by some primordial peace. He had forgotten about the girl, forgotten his scruples. In that hour he had acquired a mood at once serene and gay: he had the light-heartedness of a boy and the ease of a wise philosopher; his body seemed as light as air, and, though he had already walked some twenty miles, he felt as if he had just risen from his bed. But there was no exuberance in him, and he had not the impulse to sing which usually attended his seasons of high spirits. . . . The silence struck upon him as something at once miraculous and just. There was not a sound in the Wood – not the lightest whisper of wind, though there had been a breeze on the hilltops at sundown – not the cry of a single bird – not a rustle in the undergrowth. The place was dumb – not dead, but sleeping.

Suddenly he came into a broad glade over which the moonshine flowed like a tide. It was all of soft mossy green, without pebble or bush to break its carpet, and in the centre stood a thing like an altar.

At first he thought it was only a boulder dropped from the hill. But as he neared it he saw that it was human handiwork. Masons centuries ago had wrought on it, for it was roughly squared, and firmly founded on a pediment. Weather had battered it, and one corner of the top had been broken by some old storm, but it still stood foursquare to the seasons. One side was very clear in the moon, and on it David thought he could detect a half-obliterated legend. He knelt down, and though the lower part was obscured beyond hope the upper letters stood out plain. I.O.M. – he read: 'Jovi Optimo Maximo.' This uncouth thing had once been an altar.

He tiptoed away from it with a sudden sense of awe. Others had known this wood – mailed Romans clanking up the long roads from the south, white-robed priests who had once sacrificed here to their dead gods. He was scholar enough to feel the magic of this sudden window opened into the past. But there was that in the discovery which disquieted as well as charmed him. The mysteries of the heathen had been here, and he felt the simplicity of the woodland violated and its peace ravished. Once there had been wild tongues in the air, and he almost seemed to hear their echo.

He hurried off into the dark undergrowth. . . . But now his mood had changed. He felt fatigue, his eyes were drowsy, and he thought of the anxious Isobel sitting up for him. He realised this was the night of Rood-Mass – pagan and papistical folly, but his reason could not altogether curb his fancy. The old folk said – folly, no doubt, but still – He had an overpowering desire to be safe in his bed at the manse. He would retrace his steps and strike the road from Reiverslaw. That would mean going west, and after a moment's puzzling he started to run in what he thought the right direction.

The Wood, or his own mind, had changed. The moonlight was no longer gracious and kind, but like the dead-fires which the old folk said burned in the kirkyard. Confusion on the old folk, for their tales were making him a bairn again! . . . But what now broke the stillness? for it seemed as if there were veritably tongues in the air – not honest things like birds and winds, but tongues. The place was still silent so far as earthly sounds went – he realised that, when he stopped to listen – but nevertheless he had an impression of movement everywhere, of rustling – yes, and of tongues.

Fortune was against him, for he reached a glade and saw that it was the one which he had left and which he thought he had avoided. . . . There was a change in it, for the altar in the centre was draped. At first he thought it only a freak of moonlight, till he forced himself to go nearer. Then he saw that it was a coarse white linen cloth, such as was used in the kirk at the seasons of sacrament.

The discovery affected him with a spasm of blind terror. All the tales of the Wood, all the shrinking he had once felt for it, rushed back on his mind. For the moment he was an infant again, lost and fluttering, assailed by the shapeless phantoms of the dark. He fled from the place as if from something accursed.

Uphill he ran, for he felt that safety was in the hills and that soon he might come to the clear spaces of the heather. But a wall of crag forced him back, and he ran as he thought westward towards the oaks and hazels, for there he deemed he would be free of the magic of the pines. He did not run wildly, but softly and furtively, keeping to the moss and the darker places, and avoiding any crackling of twigs, for he felt as if the Wood were full of watchers. At the back of his head was a stinging sense of shame – that he, a grown man and a minister of God, should be in such a pit of terror. But his instinct was stronger than his reason. He felt his heart crowding into his throat, and his legs so weak and uncontrollable that they seemed to be separate from his body. The boughs of the undergrowth whipped his face, and he knew that his cheeks were wet with blood, though he felt no pain.

The trees thinned and he saw light ahead – surely it was the glen which marked the division between pine and hazel. He quickened his speed and the curtain of his fear lifted ever so little. He heard sounds now – was it the wind which he had left on the hilltops? There was a piping note in it, something high and clear and shrill – and yet the Wood had been so airless that his body was damp with sweat. Now he was very near air and sanctuary.

His heart seemed to stop, and his legs wavered so that he sunk on his knees. For he was looking again on the accursed glade.

It was no longer empty. The draped altar was hidden by figures – human or infernal – moving round it in a slow dance. Beyond this circle sat another who played on some instrument. The moss stilled the noise of movement, and the only sound was the high mad piping.

A film cleared from his eyes, and something lost came back to him – manhood, conscience, courage. Awe still held him, but it was being overmastered by a human repulsion and anger. For as he watched the dance he saw that the figures were indeed human, men and women both – the women half-naked, but the men with strange headpieces like animals. What he had taken for demons from the Pit were masked mortals – one with the snout of a pig, one with a goat's horns, and the piper a gaping black hound. . . . As they passed, the altar was for a moment uncovered, and he saw that food and drink were set on it for some infernal sacrament.

The dance was slow and curiously arranged, for each woman was held close from behind by her partner. And they danced widdershins, against the sun. To one accustomed to the open movement of country jigs and reels the thing seemed the uttermost evil – the grinning masks, the white tranced female faces, the obscene postures, above all that witch-music as horrid as a moan of terror.

David, a great anger gathering in his heart, was on his feet now, and as he rose the piping changed. Its slow measure became a crazy lilt, quick and furious. The piper was capering; the dancers, still going widdershins, swung round and leaped forward, flinging their limbs as in some demented reel. . . . There were old women there, for he saw grey hair flying. And now came human cries to add to the din of the pipes – a crying and a sighing wrung out of maddened bodies.

To David it seemed a vision of the lost in Hell. The fury of an Israelitish prophet came upon him. He strode into the glade. Devils or no, he would put an end to this convention of the damned.

'In the name of God,' he cried, 'I forbid you. If you are mortal, I summon you to repent – if you are demons, I command you to return to him that sent you.'

He had a great voice but in that company there were no ears to hear. The pipe screeched and the dance went on.

Then the minister of Woodilee also went mad. A passion such as he had never known stiffened every nerve and sinew. He flung himself into the throng, into that reek of unclean bestial pelts and sweating bodies. He reached the altar, seized the cloth on it, and swept it and its contents to the ground. Then he broke out of the circle and made for the capering piper, who seemed to him the chief of the orgiasts.

In his flight through the wood David lost his staff, and had as weapon but his two hands. 'Aroynt you, Sathanas,' he cried, snatched the pipe from the dog-faced figure, and shivered it on his masked head.

With the pause in the music the dance stopped suddenly, and in an instant the whole flock were on him like a weasel pack. He saw long nailed claws stretched towards his face, he saw blank eyes suddenly fire into a lust of hate. But he had a second's start of them, and that second he gave to the piper. The man – for the thing was clearly human – had dealt a mighty buffet at his assailant's face, which missed it, and struck the point of the shoulder. David was whirled round, but, being young and nimble, he slipped in under the other's guard, and had his hands on the hound-mask. The man was very powerful, but the minister's knee was in his groin, and he toppled over, while David tore the covering of wood and skin from his head. It crumpled under his violent clutch like a wasps' nest, and he had a glimpse of red hair and a mottled face.

A glimpse and no more. For by this time the press was on him and fingers were at his throat, choking out his senses.

SEVEN

The First Blast

Late in the forenoon of the next day David awoke in his bed in the manse of Woodilee. He awoke to a multitude of small aches and one great one, for his forehead was banded with pain. The room was as bright with sunshine as the little window would permit, but it seemed to him a dusk shot by curious colours, with Isobel's head bobbing in it like a fish. Presently the face became clear and he saw it very near to him – a scared white face with red-rimmed eyes. Her voice penetrated the confused noises in his ears.

'The Lord be thankit, sir, the Lord be praised, Mr David, ye're comin' oot o' your dwam. Here's a fine het drink for ye. Get it doun like a man and syne ye'll maybe sleep. There's nae banes broke, and I've dressed your face wi' a sure salve. Dinna disturb the clouts, sir. Your skin's ower clean to beil, and ye'll mend quick if ye let the clouts bide a wee.'

Her arm raised his aching head, and he swallowed the gruel. It made him drowsy, and soon he was asleep again, a healthy natural sleep, so that when he awoke in the evening he was in comparative ease and his headache had gone. Gingerly he felt his body. There were bruises on his legs, and one huge one on his right thigh. His cheeks under the bandages felt raw and scarred, and there was a tenderness about his throat and the muscles of his neck, as if angry hands had throttled him. But apart from his stiffness he seemed to have suffered no great bodily hurt, and the effects of the slight concussion had passed.

With this assurance his mind came out of its torpor and he found himself in a misery of disquiet. The events of the night before returned to him only too clearly. He remembered his

exaltation in the Wood – the glade, the altar. He recalled with
abasement his panic and his flight. The glade again, the piping,
the obscene dance – and at that memory he had almost
staggered from his bed. He felt again the blind horror and
wrath which had hurled him into the infernal throng.

Isobel's anxious face appeared in the doorway.

'Ye've had a graund sleep, sir. And now ye'll be for a bite o'
meat?'

'I have slept and I am well enough in body. Sit you down,
Isobel Veitch, for I have much to say to you. How came I home
last night?'

The woman sat down on the edge of a chair, and even in the
twilight her nervousness was manifest.

'It wasna last nicht. It was aboot the hour o' three this
mornin', and sic a nicht as I had waitin' on ye! Oh, sir, what
garred ye no hearken to me and gang to the Wud on Rood-
Mass?'

'How do you know I was in the Wood?'

She did not answer.

'Tell me,' he said, 'how I came home?'

'I was ryngin' the hoose like a lost yowe, but I didna daur gang
outbye. At twal hours I took a look up the road and again when
the knock was chappin' twa. Syne I dozed off in my chair, till the
knock waukened me. That was at three hours, and as I waukened I heard steps outbye. I keekit oot o' the windy, but there
was naebody on the road, just the yellow mune. I prayed to the
Lord to strengthen me, and by and by I ventured out, but I fand
naething. Syne I took a thocht to try the back yaird, and my hert
gied a stound, for there was yoursel', Mr David, lyin' like a cauld
corp aneath the aipple tree. Blithe I was to find the breath still in
ye, but I had a sair job gettin' ye to your bed, sir, for ye're a weary
wecht for an auld wumman. The sun was up or I got your
wounds washed and salved, and syne I sat by the bed prayin' to
the Lord that ye suld wauken in your richt mind, for I saw fine
that the wounds o' your body would heal, but I feared that the
wits micht have clean gane frae ye. And now I am abundantly

answered, for ye're speakin' like yoursel', and your een's as I mind them, and the blood's back intil your cheeks. The Lord be thankit!'

But there was no jubilation in Isobel's voice. Her fingers twined confusedly and her eyes wandered.

'Do you know what befell me?' he asked.

'Eh, sirs, how suld I ken?'

'But what do you think? You find me in the small hours lying senseless at your door, with my face scarred and my body bruised. What do you think I had suffered?'

'I think ye were clawed by bogles, whilk a'body kens are gi'en a free dispensation on Rood-Mass E'en.'

'Woman, what is this talk of bogles from lips that have confessed Christ? I was assaulted by the Devil, but his emissaries were flesh and blood. I tell you it was women's nails that tore my face, and men's hands that clutched my throat. I walked in the Wood, for what has a minister of God to fear from trees and darkness? And as I walked I found in an open place a heathen altar and that altar was covered with a linen cloth, as if for a sacrament. I was afraid – I confess it with shame – but the Lord used my fear for His own purpose, and led me back in my flight to that very altar. And there I saw what may God in His mercy forbid that I should see again – a dance of devils to the Devil's piping. In my wrath I rushed among them, and tore the mask from the Devil's head, and then they overbore me and I lost my senses. When I wrestled with them I wrestled with flesh and blood – perishing men and women rapt in a lust of evil.'

He stopped, and Isobel's eyes did not meet his. 'Keep us a'!' she moaned.

'These men and women were, I firmly believe, my own parishioners.'

'It canna be,' the old woman croaked. 'Ye werena yoursel', Mr David, sir. . . . Ye were clean fey wi' the blackness o' the Wud and the mune and the wanchancy hour. Ye saw ferlies, but they werena flesh and bluid, sir. . . .'

'I saw the bodies of men and women in Woodilee who have sold their souls to damnation. Isobel Veitch, as your master and your minister, I charge you, as you will answer before the Judgment Seat, what know you of the accursed thing in this parish?'

'Me!' she cried. 'Me! I ken nocht. Me and my man aye keepit clear o' the Wud.'

'Which is to say that there were others in Woodilee who did not. Answer me, woman, as you hope for salvation. The sin of witchcraft is rampant here, and I will not rest till I have rooted it out. Who are those in Woodilee who keep tryst with the Devil?'

'How suld I ken? Oh, sir, I pray ye to speir nae mair questions. Woodilee as aye been kenned for a queer bit, lappit in the muckle Wud, but the guilty aye come by an ill end. There's been mair witches howkit out o' Woodilee and brunt than in ony ither parochine on the Water o' Aller. Trust to your graund Gospel preachin', Mr David, to wyse folk a better gait, for if ye start speirin' about the Wud ye'll stir up a byke that will sting ye sair. As my faither used to say, him that spits against the wind spits in his ain face. Trust to conviction o' sin bringin' evildoers to repentance, as honest Mr Macmichael did afore ye.'

'Did Mr Macmichael know of this wickedness?'

'I canna tell. Nae doot he had a glimmerin'. But he was a quiet body wha keepit to the roads and his ain fireside, and wasna like yoursel', aye ryngin' the country like a moss-trooper. . . . . Be content, sir, to let sleepin' tykes lie till ye can catch them rauvagin'. Ye've a congregation o' douce eident folk and I'se warrant ye'll lead them intil the straight and narrow way. Maybe the warst's no as ill as ye think. Maybe it' just a sma' backslidin' in them that's pilgrims to Sion. They're weel kenned to be sound in doctrine, and there was mair signed the Covenant—'

'Peace,' he cried. 'This is rank blasphemy, and a horrid hypocrisy. What care I for lip service when there are professors who are living a lie? Who is there I can trust? The man who is loudest in his profession may be exulting in secret and dreadful evil. He whom I think a saint may be the chief of sinners. Are there no true servants of Christ in Woodilee?'

'Plenty,' said Isobel.

'But who are they? I had thought Richie Smail at the Green-shiel a saint, but am I wrong?'

'Na, na. Ye're safe wi' Richie.'

'And yourself, Isobel?'

Colour came into her strained face. 'I'm but a broken vessel, but neither my man nor me had ever trokin's wi' the Enemy.'

'But there are those to your knowledge who have? I demand from you their names.'

She pursed her lips. 'Oh, sir, I ken nocht. What suld a widow-woman, thrang a' the day in your service, ken o' the doings in Woodilee?'

'Nevertheless you know something. You have heard rumours. Speak, I command you.'

Her face was drawn with fright, but her mouth was obstinate. 'Wha am I to bring a railin' accusation against anybody, when I have nae certainty of knowledge?'

'You are afraid. In God's name, what do you fear? There is but the one fear, and that is the vengeance of the Almighty, and your silence puts you in jeopardy of His wrath.'

Nevertheless there was no change in the woman's face. David saw that her recalcitrance could not be broken.

'Then listen to me, Isobel Veitch. I have had my eyes opened and I will not rest till I have rooted this evil thing from Woodilee. I will search out and denounce every malefactor, though he were in my own Kirk Session. I will bring against them the terror of God and the arm of the human law. I will lay bare the evil mysteries of the Wood, though I have to hew down every tree with my own hand. In the strength of the Lord I will thresh this parish as corn is threshed, till I have separated the grain from the chaff and given the chaff to the burning. Make you your market for that, Isobel Veitch, and mind that he that is not for me is against me, and that in the day of God's wrath the slack hand and the silent tongue will not be forgiven.'

The woman shivered and put a hand to her eyes.

'Will ye hae your bite o' meat, sir?' she quavered.

'I will not break bread till God has given me clearness,' he said sternly; and Isobel, who was in the habit of spinning out her talks with her master till she was driven out, slipped from the room like a discharged prisoner who fears that the Court may change its mind.

David rose next morning after a sleepless night, battered in body but with some peace of mind, and indeed a comfort which he scarcely dared to confess to himself. He had now a straight course before him. There was an evil thing in the place against which he had declared war, an omnipresent evil, for he did not know who were the guilty. The thing was like the Wood itself, an amorphous shadow clouding the daylight. Gone were the divided counsels, the scruples of conscience. What mattered his doubts about the policy of the Kirk at large when here before his eyes was a conflict of God and Belial? . . . For the first time, too, he could let his mind dwell without scruples upon the girl in the greenwood. The little glen that separated the pines from the oaks and the hazels had become for him the frontier between darkness and light – on the one side the innocency of the world which God had made, on the other the unclean haunts of devilry. . . . And yet he had first met Katrine among the pines. To his horror of the works of darkness was added a bitter sense of sacrilege – that obscence revelry should tread the very turf that her feet had trod.

That afternoon he set out for Chasehope. The matter should be without delay laid before his chief elder, and the monstrous suspicion which lurked at the back of his mind dispelled. He was aware that his face was a spectacle, but it should not be hidden, for it was a part of his testimony. But at Chasehope there was no Ephraim Caird. The slatternly wife who met him, old before her time, with a clan of ragged children at her heels, was profuse in regrets. She dusted a settle for him, and offered new milk and a taste of her cheese, but all the time with an obvious discomfort. To think that Ephraim should be away when the minister came up the hill! . . . He had had to ride off that morn to Kirk Aller upon a matter of a bull that Johnnie Davidson had brought from Carlisle – an English bull to improve the breed – and he would not be home till the darkening. The woman was voluble and hearty, but it seemed to David that she protested too much. . . . Was her husband all the while between the blankets in the press-bed?

On his way back, at the turn of the road from the kirkton, he encountered Daft Gibbie. The idiot had throughout the winter been a satellite of the minister, and had had many a meal in the manse kitchen. When they met it was 'Eh, my bonny Mr Sempill,' or 'my precious Mr David,' and then an outpouring of grotesque but complimentary texts. But now the first news he had of Gibbie was a small stone that whizzed past his ear, and when he turned he saw a threatening figure with a face twisted into a demoniac hate. A second stone followed, very wide of the mark, and when David threatened pursuit, the idiot shuffled off, shouting filth over his shoulder. A woman came out of a cottage, and said something to Gibbie which caused him to hold his peace and disappear into a kailyard. . . . But the woman did not look towards the minister, but hurried in again and closed the door. Was the whole parish, thought David, banded in a tacit conspiracy? Was this poor idiot one of the misbegotten things of the Wood?

The next Sabbath, which was the fifth of May, the kirk of Woodilee showed a full congregation. That day, save for infants in arms, there were few absentees. Never had the place been more hushed and expectant. David preached from the text, 'Enter into the rock, and hide thee in the dust for fear of the Lord,' and he delivered his soul with a freedom hitherto lacking in his carefully prepared discourses. Not the Boanerges of Bold could have outdone the fiery vigour with which he described how Israel went astray after forbidden gods and how the wrath of the Almighty smote her with death and exile. But when he came to the application, which should have been as a nail fastened in a sure place, he faltered. The faces below him, set, composed, awful in their decency, seemed like a stone wall against which he must beat with feeble hands.

'I have the sure knowledge,' he said, 'that there are altars set up to Baal in this very parish, and that this little Israel of ours has its own groves where it worships the gods of the heathen – ay, the very devils from the Pit. Be assured that I will riddle out this evil mystery and drag it into the light of day, and on the priests of Baal in Woodilee, be they libertines or professors, I will call down the terrors of the Most High. I summon now in this place all poor deluded sinners to confession and repentance, for in the strength of the Lord I will go forward, and woe be to those that harden their hearts.'

But his words seemed to be driven back upon him by the steely silence. He saw his elders – the heavy white face of Chasehope, the long sanctimonious jowl of Peter Pennecuik, the impish mouth of Spotswood the miller now composed in an alien gravity, the dark sullenness of Mirehope – they relished his vigour, but their eyes were hard as stones. And the folk behind them, men and women, old and young, were attentively apathetic. There was none of the crying and weeping and the spasms of conviction which had attended the fast-day service of the minister of Bold. Were they a congregation of innocents to whom his summons had no application? Or were they so thirled to their evil-doing that his appeals were no more than an idle wind?

His Session congratulated him on his discourse.

'Ye had a gale on your spirit this day, Mr Sempill,' said Chasehope. 'Yon was a fine waft o' the Word ye gie'd us, and it's to be hoped that it will be blessed to many.'

As David looked at the pale cheeks and the red hair of the man he had a sudden assurance. It was a mild day, but Ephraim Caird wore a strip of flannel as if he were nursing a cold. And was there not a discoloration of the skin around his fleshy jaw and a dark bruise below his left ear?

Next day David sought out Amos Ritchie, the smith. He learned that the man was on a job at Nether Windyways, and he watched for him on the hill-road as he returned in the evening. The big loose-limbed figure of Amos, striding down the twilit slopes with his bag of tools slung on his shoulder, was a pleasant sight to eyes that hungered for a friend. For with the smith David had advanced far in friendliness since their partnership in the winter snowstorm. The man was of a high spirit and a complete honesty, and his professions were well behind his practice. Rough of tongue and apt in a quarrel, he had a warmth of heart that did not fail even those he despised. He was no purveyor of edifying speech, but the milk of human kindness ran strong in him. It was a saying in the village that there was 'mair comfort in an aith from Amos than a prayer from Peter Pennecuik.'

But on this occasion the smith's straightforward friendliness seemed to have deserted him. When David appeared before him he looked as if he would fain have avoided the meeting. His eyes were troubled, and he increased the pace of his walk when the minister fell into step beside him.

'How's the wife?' David asked.

'Fine, sir. Her kist's stronger, and I'm hopin' the simmer will pit colour intil her cheek.' But as he spoke his eyes were on a distant hill.

'I want a word with you, Amos. You and I are, I believe, true friends, and I can speak to you as to a brother. I have become aware of a horrid evil in this parish. There is that in the Wood which tempts men and women to abominations. With these eyes of mine I saw it on Beltane's Eve.'

There was no answer.

'You were in the kirk yesterday, Amos, and you heard my sermon. The decision is on Woodilee to choose whom they will serve. You are my friend, and, apart from certain backslidings, a man of a Christian walk and conversation. I summon you to my aid, and conjure you by Christ Who died for you, to tell me what you know of this great sin and who are the sinners?'

Amos came to a standstill. He laid down his tools, and looked the minister in the face.

'Let it alane, sir. I rede ye, let it alane.'

'In the name of God, what folly is this?' David cried. 'Are you, too, my own familiar friend, entangled in this wickedness?'

The man's face crimsoned.

'Deil a haet! Na, na, I never could abide thae trokin's wi' the Wud. But oh, Mr Sempill, ye're but a callant, and ye kenna the wecht o' the principalities and poo'ers that are against ye. Hae patience, sir, and gang cannily. Trust in the Word, whilk it is your duty to preach, to bring conviction o' sin in the Lord's ain gude time, for if ye're ettlin' to use the arm o' flesh it will fail ye.'

It was the counsel which Isobel had given, and David's heart sank. What was it in Woodilee which made honest men silent and craven in the face of proved iniquity?

'Man Amos,' he cried, 'I never thought to get a coward's counsel from you. Am I to reckon you among my enemies, and among God's enemies? I tell you I see my duty as clear before me as the Hill of Deer. I must unveil this wickedness and blast its practisers into penitence or I fail in my first duty as the minister of this parish. And from you, my friend, I get only silence and contumacy, and what is worse, the advice of a Laodicean. Alas! that you who have fought stoutly in your country's battles should be such a poor soldier in God's battles.'

There was no answer. The two had resumed their walk, and the smith strode at a pace which was almost a run, his eyes steadily averted from his companion.

'This is my last word to you, Amos,' said David, as they reached the turn where the loan ran to the manse. 'Wednesday – the day after the morn – is the second Beltane, and I fear that that night there will be further evil in the Wood. I will go there and outface the Devil, but the flesh is weak, and I am one against many, and I would fain have a friend. Will you not bear me company?'

The smith stopped again. 'Deil hae me if I gang near the Wud! Na, na, I'll no pit my heid intil ony sic wull-cat's hole. And, Mr Sempill, be you guidit by an aulder man and bide at hame.'

'You are afraid!'

'Ay, I'm feared – but mair for you than for mysel'.'

'You're like the men of Israel that failed Gideon at the waterside,' David cried angrily as he turned away.

The next two days were spent by the minister in a strange restlessness. He walked each afternoon some violent miles on the hilltops, but for the rest he stayed in the manse, principally in his study. Isobel believed him to be at prayer, and indeed he prayed long and fervently, but he was also busied about other things. Among his belongings was a small-sword, for he had won some skill of fence in Edinburgh, and this he had out and saw to its point and edge. Also he read much in books which were not divinity, for he felt himself a soldier, and would brace his spirit with martial tales. With Isobel he exchanged no word save commonplaces, and the old woman, who had the air of a scolded child, showed no desire to talk. His meals were set before him in silence, and silently the table was cleared. Amos Ritchie came to the manse on some small repairing job, and he too seemed to be anxious to get his work done and leave. David saw him arrive as he set out for a walk, and when he returned, the shoulders of the smith were disappearing past the stable end.

Wednesday evening came, an evening of mellow light and a quiet sunset, and after his early supper David retired to his study to prepare himself for his task. He had already written out an account of what he had seen in the Wood and of what he proposed to do, and this he signed and directed under cover to Mr Fordyce at Cauldshaw. Whatever mischance befell him, he had left a record. He had also written a letter to his father, setting forth what, in the event of his death, was to be the destination of his worldly goods. Then on his knees he remained for a while in prayer.

The clock struck nine, and he arose to begin his journey, strapping the sword to his middle, and taking also a great stick which the shepherd of the Greenshiel had made for him. The moon would rise late and there was ample time.

But he found that the door of his study would not open. It had no lock, and had hung on a light hasp, but now it seemed to have bolts and bars. It was a massive thing of oak, and when he shook it it did not yield.

He shouted for Isobel, but there was no reply. Then he assaulted it furiously with knees and feet and shoulder, but it did not give. There was no hope from the window, which was a small square through which a child could not have crept.

Further attacks on the door followed, and futile shouting. By the time the late light had faded from the little window David had acknowledged the fact that he was imprisoned and his first fury had ebbed from sheer bodily fatigue. But the clock had struck one before he attempted to make a bed on the floor, with for pillow a bag of chaff which Isobel had placed there for a winter footstool, and the dawn was in the eastern sky before he slept.

He was awakened by Isobel in the doorway.

'Peety on us,' she wailed, 'that sic a thing suld hae come to this hoose! Hae ye spent the nicht in this cauld chamber and no in your bed? The wyte's on me, for I got Amos Ritchie yestereen to put a bar on the door for there's walth of guid books here and I wad like to steek the place when ye're awa' to the hills and me maybe in the kitchen. I maun hae steekit it to see if it wad wark, no kennin' ye were in inside. And syne I gaed doun to my gude-brither's to speir after his bairn, and I was late in getting back, and, thinks I, the minister will be in his bed and I'll awa' to mine. Puir man, ye'll be as stiff as a wand, and ye'll maybe hae got your death o' cauld. . . . See and I'll get ye a het drink, and your parritch's on the boil. . . . Wae's me that I didn' tak' a thocht . . .'

'Silence, woman, and do not cumber your soul with lies.' David's white face as he strode from the room did more than his words to cut short Isobel's laments.

EIGHT

The Second Blast

On the following Sabbath the minister's text was, 'When the light within you is darkness, how great is that darkness!' This time there was no faltering in the application. The congregation, men and women, were arraigned at the bar as sinners by deed or by connivance, and he had an audience hushed not in the ordinary Sabbath decorum, but in a fearful apprehension. Every moment he seemed to be about to name the sinner, and if he did not single out persons he made it blindingly clear that it was not for lack of knowledge. Never had he preached with greater freedom, never had passion so trembled in each sentence. Words seemed to be given him, stinging, unforgettable words that must flay the souls of the guilty. 'Blinded self-deceivers,' he cried, 'you think you can tamper with devilry and yet keep your interest in Christ. You are set up with covenants, public and private, but I tell you that your covenant is with Death and Hell. The man who believes he is elected into salvation, and thinks that thereby he has liberty to transgress and that his transgressions will be forgiven him, has sinned against the Holy Ghost – that sin for which there is no forgiveness.' He declared that till there was a general confession and repentance there would be no Communion in the parish of Woodilee, for those who sat down at the Lord's Table would be eating and drinking damnation to themselves. . . . But at the end he broke down. With tears in his eyes and a sob in his voice he besought a people whom he loved to abase themselves before the Mercy Seat. 'You poor folk,' he cried, 'with your little dark day of life, with your few years of toil and cold and hunger before the grave, what have you if you have not Christ?' He was moved with an ecstasy of pity, and told them, like the Apostle, that if he could but save their souls, he was willing that his own should be cast away.

Not the oldest remembered such a sermon in the kirk of Woodilee, and the fame of it was soon to go abroad in the countryside. The place emptied in a strange silence, as if the congregation went on tip-toe, and men and women did not look at each other till they were outside the kirkyard gates. The elders did not await the minister in the session-house, and as David walked the hundred yards to the manse he saw what looked like the back of Peter Pennecuik, crouching behind a turf dyke to avoid a meeting.

These were days of loneliness and misery for the minister of Woodilee. He saw himself solitary among enemies, for even those whom he thought his friends had failed him. It was clear that Amos Ritchie had conspired with Isobel to imprison him in his study on the eve of the second Beltane, and though their motive was doubtless affection it but emphasised the hopelessness of his task. He had to bring conviction of sin into a parish where even the innocent were ready to cumber his arm. These honest creatures feared for him – what? Anger would choke him at the thought of such contempt for his sacred mission, and then awe would take its place, awe at the immensity of the evil with which he fought. 'Principalities and powers,' Amos had said – yes, the Powers of the Air and the Principalities of Darkness. He had no doubt that the Devil and his myrmidons were present in the Wood in bodily form, mingling with the worshippers, and that the tongues which he had heard were in very truth mutterings of the lost. There were times when ordinary human fear loosened his knees, and he longed to flee from the parish as from a place accursed. But his courage would return, and his faith, for he knew that the armies of Heaven were on his side, and wrath would cast out fear, wrath and horror at the seducers of his flock. Nevertheless in these days his nerves were frayed, he lay awake of nights listening anxiously for noises without, and he would awake suddenly in the sweat of a nameless terror.

But his chief burden was that he did not know how to shape his course. The pulpit rang with his denunciations, but there was no response; no stricken Nicodemus came to him by night. On the roads and at the house-doors people avoided his eyes. There were no more stones from Daft Gibbie – indeed Gibbie had resumed his fawning friendliness – but none waited to speak a word with him. Isobel had recovered her cheerfulness, and sought to atone for past misconduct by an assiduous attention to his comforts, but Amos Ritchie shunned him. And the children, too, who had been his chief allies. Perhaps their parents had warned them, for a group would scatter when he came near, and once when, coming up behind him, he laid a kindly hand on a boy's head, the child burst into tears and fled. What was the *fama* of the minister which had been put about in Woodilee?

The worst of it was that he could contrive no plan of campaign. Evidence which was overwhelming to his own mind would not convince the Presbytery or the Sheriff. He could not bring a reasoned charge against any man or woman in the parish. As the days passed he began to sort out his flock in his mind as the guilty and the abettors. Some were innocent enough, save for the sin of apathy; but others he could believe to have shared in the midnight debauches – heavy-browed sensual youths, women with shifty eyes, girls high-coloured and over-blown, whose sidelong glances seemed to hint at secrets, old wives, too, whose wild laughter he heard at cottage doors. But of one, his first certainty was giving way to doubt. Ephraim Caird's white face had got a wholesome tan from the summer sun, and he alone in the parish seemed to seek out the minister. He gave him a cheerful greeting when they met, spoke wisely of parish matters, had a word of humble commendation for the Sabbath discourses. 'It's gaun to be a braw year for the aits,' he said, 'gin the weather hauds, and the lambs are the best I've yet seen on Chasehope hill. Let us hope, sir, that the guid seed ye've sown will come to as bountiful a hairvest.' The words were so simply spoken that they seemed no hypocrisy.

A plan of campaign! On that David could get no clearness, and the anxiety was with him at bed and board. He shrank from confessing himself to his brother-ministers, for what could they do to help him? Kirk Aller would pooh-pooh the whole thing, since Woodilee had been so forward in signing the Covenant. Bold would no doubt believe, but his remedy would be only a stiffer draught of doctrine. Even Mr Fordyce at Cauldshaw seemed a broken reed, for Mr Fordyce was an ailing saint, and this task was for the church militant. No, he must fight his battles alone, and trust to God to send him allies. He wanted men of violence, who would fight not with words but with deeds, Israelitish prophets who with their own hands cut down groves and uprooted altars and hewed Agag in pieces. And where would he find them in a countryside where the good were timid as sheep and their pastors like loud voices in a fog?

June was a month of hot suns and clear skies, when the hills were bone-dry and the deepest flowe-moss could be safely passed. It was weather for the high tops, and one afternoon David, walking off his restlessness on the Rood uplands, stumbled unexpectedly on a friend. For at the head of the glen where the drove-road crosses from Clyde to Aller, he fell in with the farmer of Reiverslaw leading his horse up a steep patch of screes.

This man, Andrew Shillinglaw, was something of a mystery both to parish and minister. He was a long lean fellow of some forty years, black-haired, black-bearded, whose sullen face was redeemed by a humorous mouth, so that the impression was of a genial ferocity. He was reputed the most skilful farmer in the place, and some held him a rival in worldly wealth to the miller, but beyond the fact that he had in Reiverslaw the best of the hill farms, there was no clue to his prosperity. He had the only good riding-horse in Woodilee and was a notable figure on the roads, for he travelled the country like a packman. For weeks on end he would be away from home, and he was heard of in Galloway and the west and as far south as the Border, so that speculation about his doings became a favourite pastime among his neighbours.

He neither sold nor bought in the parish, and he kept his own counsel, but his profession was clear enough had there been eyes to see. For he was dealer and middleman as well as farmer, and in a day when stock and produce scarcely moved beyond parish bounds, he sold and bought in outlying markets. In a district of home-keepers he was the sole traveller.

Few liked him, for there was always an undertone of satire in his speech. But all feared him, for his temper was on a hair-trigger. Drink made him quarrelsome, and the spence at Lucky Weir's had seen some ugly business, since with him blow followed fast on word. Three years before he had buried his wife, there were no children, and he lived at Reiverslaw with an aged cousin for housekeeper, who was half blind and wholly deaf. His attendance at kirk was far from exemplary; in winter there were the drifts and the full bogs to detain him and in summer he was often as not on his travels. The Session, who did not love him, had talked of citing him to appear before them, but in the end they seemed to shrink from belling so formidable a cat.

At the head of the little pass, which in that country is called a 'slack', he halted and let David approach him.

'A guid day to ye, sir,' he cried. 'We'll let Bess get her wind, for it's a lang gait frae Crawfordjohn. I rade ower yestereen to see the sma' Cumberland sheep that the Lowther herds are trying on yon hills. I hae nae great broo o' them. They'll maybe dae on yon green braes where the bite is short, but they're nae use for a heather country. . . . Sit ye doun, sir. What brings ye sae far ower the tops? Ye werena ettlin' to gie me a ca' in at Reiverslaw?'

David gladly stretched himself on the bent beside him. The man seemed willing to talk, and of late he had had little speech with his fellows.

'I came here for the caller air,' he said, 'and to drive ill humours from body and mind. There are whiles when I cannot draw breath in Woodilee.'

'Ay,' said the man. 'Ay! Just so.' He pursed his lips and looked at the minister under half-shut eyes.

'Were you born in this parish?' David asked.

'Na, na. Far frae that. I'm but an incomer, though I've had the tack o' Reiverslaw for a dizzen years. My father, honest man, was frae the Glenkens, and my mither cam frae the Cairn side. I was born at a bit they ca' Dunscore, but I was a stirrin' lad in my young days and I've traivelled the feck o' the Lawlands, frae the Forth to the Solway. But now I've got my hinderlands doun in Woodilee, and it's like I'll lay my banes here.'

The man spoke in a different voice from the people of the place, and to David he seemed as one detached from the countryside, sharing neither its interests nor affections. As he looked at him, sprawling in the heather bush with one foot on his horse's bridle, he had a sense of something assured and resolute and not unfriendly.

'Ye're an incomer like mysel', sir,' Reiverslaw said after a pause. 'What think ye o'Woodilee?'

'I think that the Devil has chosen this miserable parish for his own.'

'Ay. . . . Well, I wadna say ye were wrang. I jaloused frae your last discourse that ye were perplexed wi' the Enemy. And they tell me that ye've stirred up an unco byke against ye.'

'Are you one of them?' David asked.

'No me. If there's fechtin' to be done, I'm on your side. I aye likit a bauld man, and it's a question, sir, if ye ken yoursel' how bauld ye are when ye offer to drive the Devil frae Woodilee.'

David had got to his feet, for these were the first words of sympathy he had had.

'Andrew Shillinglaw, I command you to tell me if you have kept yourself clean from his mystery of evil which scourges the parish.'

The man still sprawled on the ground, and the face he turned to the minister was twisted in a grim humour.

'Ay. I'll swear ony aith ye like. I'll no deny my backslidin's, and, as ye may ken, my walk and conversation's no to boast o'. But as sure as God made me, I wad burn off my richt hand in the fire afore I wad file mysel' wi' the Babylonish abominations o' the Wud. I whiles drink a stoup ower muckle, and I whiles gie a maur straik than I ettle when my bluid's het, but these are honest stumblin's whilk I hope the Lord will forgie. But for yon—' and he spat viciously.

'Then, if you are yourself clean from this evil, tell me what you know of it and who are its chief professors?'

'That's easy speirin', but ill to answer. How suld I ken the covens that rampage in the Wud? I bide cheek by jowl wi' the muckle black thing, and often I wish it was a field o' strae in a dry back-end so that I could set fire to it and see it burn frae Reiverslaw to Windyways and frae Woodilee to the Aller side. But I've never entered the place in mirk or licht, for my wark's wi' sheep and the honest beasts will no gang near it.'

'But you must have heard . . .'

'I've heard nocht. I have maybe guessed, but it's no like I wad hear a cheep. I never gang near the clachan except to kirk or to Lucky Weir's, and the Woodilee folk are pawky bodies even when they're fou, and ony way I'm nae clatter-vengeance to be clypin' wi' auld wives at the roadside. But I've my ain notion o' what's gaun on, and I can tell ye, sir, it's gaun on in mony anither godly parochine in this kingdom o' Scotland, and it's been gaun on for hundreds o' years, long afore John Knox dang doun the Pape. But it's gotten a braw new tack in these days o' reformed and covenantit kirks. What do your Presbytries and Assemblies or your godly ministers ken o' the things that are done in the mirk? . . . What do they ken o' the corps in the kirkyairds buried o' their ain wull wi' their faces downwards? . . . They set up what they ca' their discipline and they lowse the terrors o' Hell in sma' fauts like an aith, or profane talk on the Sabbath, or giein' the kirk the go-by, and they hale to the cutty-stool ilka lass that's ower kind to her jo. And what's the upshot? They drive the folk to their auld ways and turn them intil hypocrites as weel as sinners.'

'Hush, man!' said the scandalised David. 'That is impious talk.'

'It's true a' the same, though it's maybe no for a minister's lugs. The Kirk is set against witchcraft and every wee while a daft auld wife is brunt. But, God help us, that's but the froth on the pat. Na, na, Mr Sempill. If you're lookin' to get to grips wi' the Adversary, it's no the feckless camsteery lad ye maun seek that likes a randan, or the bit lassie that's ower fond to wait for the Kirk's blessin', or the grannie that swears she rade to France on a kail-runt. It's the dacent body that sits and granes aneath the pu'pit and the fosy professor that wags his pow and deplores the wickedness o' the land. – Yon's the true warlocks. There's saunts in Scotland, the Lord kens and I ken mysel', but there's some that hae the name o' saunts that wad make the Devil spew.'

Reiverslaw had risen, and in his face was such a flame of fierce honesty that David's heart kindled. He had found an ally.

'Give me names,' he cried. 'I will denounce the sinner, though he were one of my own elders.'

'I speak nae names. I have nae proof. But ye've seen yoursel'. They tell me ye broke in on the Coven at their wark.'

'I had but a glinsk of them, before they beat the senses out of me. But I intend to go back to the Wood, and this time I shall not fail.'

'Ay. Ye've a stout heart, Mr Sempill.'

'But I must have help. Out of the mouths of witnesses I must establish the truth, and the innocent in Woodilee are very fearful. I have nowhere to look but to you. Will you come with me when I return to the Wood?'

'I'll no say that, for there's maybe better ways o' guidin' it. But this I will say – I'll stand by ye; for may the Deil flee awa' wi' me or I see a guid man beat. There's my hand on't. . . . And now I maun be takin' the road again. Come na near the Reiverslaw, sir, for that would set the bodies talkin'. If ye want word wi' me, tell Richie Smail at the Greenshiel.'

The knowledge that he had found a friend lightened David's heavy preoccupation of mind. Athanasius now was not alone against the world, and his path was not towards martyrdom but to victory. He walked with a more assured step and turned a bolder face to the furtive hostility of the parish. When he met Amos Ritchie he looked on him not in reproach but in defiance. His sermons were now less appeals than challenges, as of one whose course was proclaimed and whose loins were girded.

To his consternation he found that he now sat very loose in his devotion to the Kirk. The profession of religion was not the same thing as godliness, and he was coming to doubt whether the insistence upon minute conformities of outward conduct and the hair-splitting doctrines were not devices of Satan to entangle souls. The phrases of piety, unctuously delivered, made him shudder as at a blasphemy. The fact that his only supporter was one looked askance at by strict professors confirmed his shrinking. Had not Christ set the publican and the sinner above the Pharisee?

One consequence of his new mood was that his thoughts turned again to the girl in Paradise. In his season of desolation he had not dared to think of her; she belonged to a world of light and had no part in his perplexities. To let her image fill his memory seemed sacrilege, when that memory held so many foul shadows. But as the skies cleared for him her figure appeared again in the sunlight and he did not banish it, for it was she who was the extreme opposite of the horror of the Wood – she and her bright domain of oaks and hazels. He would go again to Paradise for his soul's comfort.

He chose a day when he was certain she would be there. There was a week of fiery weather – moist heat and heavy skies and flying thunderstorms, and after it came a spell of long bright days, when the sunshine had a dry tonic in it and the afternoons were mellow and golden. On one such afternoon he crossed the Hill of Deer and entered the glen which divided the pines from the hazels.

Midsummer had changed the place. The burn-side turf was all thyme and eyebright and milk-wort, with the stars of the grass of Parnassus in the wet places. The water was clear and small, and the cascades fell in a tinkling silver. He had no doubts as to his road now Paradise was among the hazels, but one could find it only by descending the glen to where the pines of the Wood began and then turning to the right towards the Greenshiel.

Presently the pines in a sombre regiment rose on the steep to the left. He looked at the beginning of the Wood with an awe which had now no fear in it. The place was hateful, but it could not daunt him. It was the battleground to which he was called. . . . On the edge of trees was a great mass of dark foxgloves, the colour of blood, and they seemed to make a blood-trail from the sunlight into the gloom.

He turned up the right bank, and through hazel copses and glades breast-high with bracken he made his way as if by instinct. He found the shallow cup lined with birches and the blossoming rowans, and as he brushed through the covert he saw the girl sitting on the greensward by the well.

Motionless he watched her for a little, while his heart played strange pranks. She had a basket beside her full of flowers, and she was reading in a book. . . . She laid down the book, and shook her curls and dabbled her fingers in the water. She sang as she dabbled, low and clear in snatches, a song which he was to remember to his dying-day:

> There's comfort for the comfortless,
>   And honey for the bee,
> And there's none for me but you, my love,
>   And there's none for you but me.

She crooned the verse twice, broke off to watch a ring-ouzel, and then sang again:

> It's love for love that I have got,
>   And love for love again,
> So turn your high horse heid about
> And we will ride for hame, my love,
>   And we will ride for hame.

He would fain have lingered and watched her, but he felt like an eavesdropper on her privacy. So 'Mistress Katrine,' he cried softly, and 'Mistress Katrine' a second time.

She sprang to the alert like a bird. Her face, when she saw him, showed no welcome.

'I give you good-day, sir,' she said. 'Have you maybe lost your road?'

'I am seeking Paradise,' he replied.

'It is the quest of all mortals, they tell me. But the ministers say it is not to be found on earth.'

'I was seeking the earthly one to which you yourself first led me.'

'You entered then by my invitation, but I do not think I bade you come again.'

'Then I beg for admission, mistress, for indeed I have sore need of Paradise.'

She looked at him curiously. 'You look older – and sadder. I have not been to your kirk, but they tell me that you are scorching the soul of your folk with your terrors.'

'Would to God I could scorch them into salvation! . . . I have been in dire straits, Mistress Katrine. For I came again to find Paradise and I found it not, but stumbled into Hell.'

The girl looked at him with compassionate eyes.

'You may sit down in Paradise,' she said. 'I permit you. And I will give you some of my wild strawberries. Tell me what has troubled you?'

He told her of the doings of Beltane Eve, stumblingly, with many omissions. He told her of his strife with his parishioners, of his loneliness, of the mission to which he was vowed. 'I am resolved,' he said, 'that though I go on alone I will not fail in courage. Your Montrose's comfort is mine – that the arm of the Lord is not shortened.'

The girl brooded.

'Did you come here to find me?'

'I had a conviction that you would be in Paradise. This is no tale for a maid's ear, but I came here to warn you, Mistress. The long glen that runs down to the Rood Mill is a frontier-line, which if you pass you are in the land of darkness. I found you first among the pines, and I beseech you go not again among them, though it were at high noon, for yon Wood is accursed.'

She nodded. 'I felt it too. When Spring was passing I felt a gloom come over me as I walked there, and one day a terror seized me and I ran and ran till I was among the hazels. I cannot bear even to be in sight of the dark trees. You say that there is witchcraft there.' She lowered her voice and her eyes were solemn. 'What is this witchcraft?'

'I cannot tell, save that it is the nethermost works of darkness and that it has seduced the hearts of my unhappy people. . . . God help me, but I have seen with my eyes what I cannot forget. . . . There is no smooth ministry for me, for now I am a soldier of Christ and must be fighting till I have got the victory.'

'And you are alone?'

'I have one who will stand by me.' And he told her of Reiverslaw.

'Nay, you have another,' she cried. 'You have me for a friend, and you have this greenwood for sanctuary. If I cannot fight by your side, you will know that I am here and that I am wishing you well. See, I make you free of Paradise. It is yours now, as well as mine.' She held out her hand.

He took off his hat.

'You were singing,' he said, 'and your song was true, for here's "comfort for the comfortless". You have put steel into my bones, Mistress Katrine. If I can come here and speak with you at times, it will be like the water beside the gate of Bethlehem to King David. . . . I will know when you are here without your sending me word.'

'Then there is witchcraft in the greenwood,' she said, smiling gravely, 'for I too knew that you were coming to-day before you came.'

NINE

Before Lammas

One day in July David saddled his horse and rode to Kirk Aller for a Presbytery meeting. He found a bewildered brotherhood. The usual 'exercises' were omitted, there was no prelection on a set doctrinal theme for the benefit of the younger ministers, the sittings in the kirk were occupied mainly with prayers for a humbled Sion and a distracted country, and the dinner thereafter in the Cross Keys was not notable for good-fellowship. But it was a crowded gathering, and among the lay members in the kirk was Ephraim Caird.

At the meal Mr Mungo Muirhead, primed with letters from Edinburgh, gave ill news of the war in the North. Montrose the recusant continued to win battles and was even now marching southward with his savage Irishry to strike at the citadel. 'What for does Davie Leslie no hasten,' he cried, 'and what profits it to have a covenanted State and a purified Kirk if a mailed Amalekite can hunt our sodgers from Dan to Beersheba? I tell you, sirs, this war which has hitherto been fought among Hieland glens will soon be at our ain doorcheeks, and our puir folk will be called to testify not with voice and word and the scart of a pen, but with sufferings and revilings and bloody murderings. Forth and Aller may yet run red, and the hand of death be on the Lowdon fields. Are we prepared, I ask, and I ask it yet again? Whatna gifts will we bring to the altar in the coming day of sacrifice?'

His fears had given dignity to the minister of Kirk Aller. The man was a fighter, for his mouth shut tight and there was a spark of fire in his heavy eyes. Nor was Mr Proudfoot of Bold less ready for the fray. He had got himself a pair of great boots, and looked a very Ironside as he expanded his big chest and groaned assent to his leader's warning.

'Let us see that there is no Canaanitish thing in our midst,' Mr Proudfoot cried, 'for the purge of the Lord is nigh. And let Israel dwell in unity, for a house divided shall not stand. These are the twin counsels for this day of wrath, a pure cause and a brotherly people. These, I say, are the dams with which to stem the tide of the heathen's rage.'

'And that's a word in season for you, Mr Sempill,' said Mr Muirhead. 'I hear ye've set the haill parish of Woodilee by the lugs with wanton accusations. You'll admit none to the Table, says you, till there is public confession of some unkenned iniquity. I applaud zeal in a young minister, but it seems you've fair got your leg ower the trams, and the serious folk of Woodilee are troubled to ken what ye mean. Have a care, Mr Sempill, lest this zeal of yours be but human impatience. This is no time to sow confusion among God's people.'

The minister of Kirk Aller had lost his air of rough good-humour. It was a hard face and an inquisitorial eye that he bent on David.

'I take my stand on the first of Mr Proudfoot's counsels,' said the latter. 'If the day of trial is coming, our cause must be pure, and there must be no Canaanitish thing in our midst. When I am clear about the sins of Woodilee, the Presbytery will have further news of me.'

The young man's speech was too assured to please Mr Muirhead. He drew down his eyebrows till they formed a straight line bisecting his huge expanse of face.

'Have a care, have a care, I counsel you,' he said crossly. 'I can tell you that there's many an auld exercised professor in Woodilee that's sore concerned about your doings.'

Mr Proudfoot added his reproof. 'When I mind on the precious work I witnessed in that very parish in the month of March, I will not believe that the Devil has got the master hand. Examine yourself, I rede you, Mr Sempill, and see if the beam be not in your own eye.'

David rode away from Kirk Aller in the company of Mr Fordyce of Cauldshaw, but they had not ridden a mile before there was a clatter of hoofs behind them and the minister of Bold joined himself to their company. His beast was fractious, having had an unaccustomed feed of oats in the Cross Keys stable, and Mr Proudfoot, since he was an awkward horseman, had to spend much of his energy in keeping it to the road. But what time he could spare from this task he devoted to catechising David, and for the three miles during which their course lay together his tongue never stopped.

'There's an ill *fama* of you gone abroad, Mr Sempill, and it is my duty as your elder in the Lord's service to satisfy myself thereanent. It is reported that you pervert the doctrine of election into grace, maintaining that this blessed estate may be forfeit by a failure in good works, as if the filthy rags of man's righteousness were mair than the bite of a flea in face of the eternal purposes of God.'

'I say that a man who believes that this redemption through Christ gives him a licence to sin is more doubly damned than if he had never had a glimpse of grace.'

'But ye maun distinguish. The point is far finer than that, sir. I will construe your words, for there is an interpretation of them which is rank heresy.'

The task of construing and distinguishing did not fare well, for every few minutes the teeth of Mr Proudfoot were shaken in his head by his horse's vagaries. He had just reached a point of inordinate subtlety, when the track to Bold branched off, and his animal, recognising at last the road home, darted down it at a rough gallop. The last seen of the minister of Bold was a massive figure swaying like a ship in a gale, and still, if one might trust the echoes the wind brought back, distinguishing and construing.

Even Mr Fordyce's grave face smiled as he watched the fleeing Boanerges.

'He is a wilful man, and he has a wilful beast. But what is this rumour in the countryside, Mr David? I fear that you are finding Woodilee a dour rig to plough.'

'What do they say in Cauldshaw?'

'I have been little about of late, for these last weeks I've been sore troubled with my bowels. I'm like the Psalmist – the Lord trieth my reins in the night watches – and I've never made out my visit to you to have a read of Cardanus. But I cannot but hear orra bits of news from the next parish, and the speak in the countryside is that you have uncovered the nakedness of Woodilee and preach siccan sermons that the een of the folk turn inward in their heads. What's the truth of it, Mr David? My heart yearns over you as if you were my own mother's son.'

'I have uncovered a great wickedness – but not yet all. I wait and watch, and when I have fuller knowledge I will know better how to act. You told me the first day we met that Woodilee had an ill reputation, and, sorrow on me! I have proved the justice of your words. And I greatly fear that it is the loudest professors that are deepest in the mire.'

'Man, David, that is a grievous business. Is it the Wood?'

'It is the Wood, and the blackest kind of witchcraft. Some old devilry of the heathen has lingered in that place, and the soul of my miserable parish is thirled to it. You will not find in Scotland a doucer bit, for there are no public sins and shortcomings. Man, there's times when Woodilee seems as quiet and dead as a kirkyard. But there's a mad life in its members, and at certain seasons it finds vent. In the deeps of night and in the heart of the Wood there are things done of which it is shameful even to speak.'

'What witness have you?'

'My own eyes. I stumbled upon one of their hellish Sabbaths.'

'God be kind to us! I have heard tell of siccan things and I have read of them in old books, but I never experienced them. I'm positive they're not in Cauldshaw, for the place is ower bare and bright and the wind blows ower clean on our braes. There's no cover for the abominations which must be done in darkness. But I have aye had a scunner of thon Wood. . . . It's a queer thing the heart of man, Mr David, and there's that in my own that whiles terrifies me. The work of redemption is done in an instant, but the job of regeneration is a lifetime's; and the holiest saint on his death-bed is but a bag of rottenness compared to the purity to which he shall yet attain. And at times I'm tempted to think that our way and the Kirk's way is not God's way, for we're apt to treat the natural man as altogether corrupt, and put him under over-strict pains and penalties, whereas there's matter in him that might be shaped to the purposes of grace. If there's original sin, there's likewise original innocence. When I hear the lassie Katrine Yester singing about the door at Calidon, I have an assurance of God's goodness as sharp as I ever got in prayer. If you ban this innocent joy it will curdle and sour, and the end will be sin. If young life may not caper on a Spring morn to the glory of God, it will dance in the mirk wood to the Devil's piping.'

Mr Fordyce stopped short with a rueful face. 'That's for your own ear, Mr David. If the bruit of what I have said came to the manse of Bold, Mr Ebenezer would be for delating me to the Presbytery. But if it's not orthodox it's good sense.'

'I doubt orthodoxy is no salve against sin,' said David. 'The devils, it is written, believe and tremble, and it's my surmise that the leader of the witches' Coven in Woodilee could stand his ground with Bold himself on matters of doctrine.'

'You have formidable foes.'

'I have a whole parish, for even those who are free of guilt are too timid to lift a hand. Likewise I have my Kirk Session.'

Mr Fordyce exclaimed.

'And it looks like I will have the Presbytery. I'm in ill odour with Mr Muirhead for dividing Israel and to Mr Proudfoot I smack of heresy.'

'You've aye gotten me on your side,' said Mr Fordyce. 'No that I'm much of a fighter, for my bowels melt and my speech sticks in my throat and I sit like a dumb ox, and syne mourn on my bed in the night watches that I have been found wanting. But my heart is with you, Mr David, and what voice my infirmities permit me, and you'll be never out of my prayers. . . . Come to

Cauldshaw whenever ye long for speech with a friend. I can aye give you sympathy if I canna give you counsel.'

But when David three days later turned his horse in the direction of Cauldshaw, it was not to the manse he went but to the tower of Calidon. For Katrine Yester had become for him the only light on his path. She personified the cause for which he fought, the fair world that stood in contrast to the obscene shades, and since their last meeting in paradise she was no longer a flitting wood-nymph, but a woman of flesh and blood and heart. He longed to see her in the house where she dwelt and among her own people.

But there was no Katrine in Calidon that afternoon, for she had gone to the greenwood. It was a still day of July in which no cloud tempered the heat of the sun, but the great upper chamber in the tower was cool and dusky. He asked for Mistress Saintserf and was received by that grim lady in state, for she kept him waiting while she donned a new toy and kerchief for the occasion. She spoke a Scots as broad as any shepherd's wife, but the sharp vowels of Edinburgh took the place of the softer Border tones. Large and gaunt and domineering, her high-nosed face and prim mouth were mellowed by an audacious humour. Katrine had clearly never spoken of him (at which he was glad), but she knew him by repute and by his connection with the miller of the Roodfoot. She entertained him with shortcake of her own baking and elder wine of her own brewing, and her tone mingled the deference of a good woman towards a spiritual guide and the freedom of an old woman towards a young man.

'That gilpie o' mine suld have been here, but she's awa' to the hill. As weel try to keep a young jeuk frae the water as Katrine frae stravaigin' the countryside. And her bred denty in France and England whaur there are nae hills! If she had a jo I wad say nocht, but she has nae jo but the whaups.'

He asked concerning Nicholas Hawkshaw.

'And that's speirin'' she cried. 'He's fechtin' and him a lamenter, but whaur he's fechtin' and in what cause the Lord alone kens! Since he gaed off wi' Tam Purves three months syne sorrow a word has come frae him. He's maybe in England and maybe in France, and maybe ryngin' with Montrose, and I'll wager wherever he is, him and his swird and Tam and his firelock are in the het o't. Ye'll no fetter a Hawkshaw, and they can nae mair bide in the ae place than a puddock on a brae, as my puir sister that was married on him kenned ower weel. And the same bluid's in Katrine, wha suld hae been a laddie, and a tinkler laddie, for it's no her that will mind her seam or watch the pot when the sun's shinin'. She's a fine lassie for a' that, but by ordinar' forgetfu'. I wish I saw her wed.'

Of Woodilee she had many questions to ask.

'It's a' Hawkshaw land, but I never likit the folk. There's a wheen fosy bodies yonder, wha pray mair with their tongues than their hearts, and they're as keen at a niffer as a Mussel-burgh wabster – aye wi' the puir face and the greetin' word when it comes to payin' siller. Auld Dobbie in Murchison's Close – he's our doer, ye maun ken, as his father was afore him – he has had mony a sair tuilzie for our bits o' rents. Now that Nicholas is at the wars it's my shoulther that has to carry the burden, and there's never a post frae Embro but brings me Dobbie's scribin'. Ye'll ken that the mailin' o' Crossbasket is to let, and whaur am I to get a guid tenant wi' the land in siccan a steer?'

David told her the news he had heard at Kirk Aller.

'Keep us a'!' she cried. 'God send Nicholas binna wi' Montrose or we'll hae him and Tam Purves here rauvagin' his ain lands, and if Argyll gets the upper hand they'll be glorifyin' God at the end o' a tow in the Grassmarket. Hech, sir, we're surely faun on the latter days when, it is written, confusion will be on the people. I'm for the Kirk, but they tell me Montrose is likewise for the Kirk as he conceives it, and between her twa well-wishers it's like our auld Sion will get uncoly mishandled. But I hae nae broo o' poalitics. My poalitics is just an auld wife's poalitics that wants to be left in peace by her fireside. . . . But ye say Montrose is mairchin' south? He'll be for England, and that means the road by Aller Water. I'll hae to kilt my coats and pit the tower o' Calidon in a state of defence against Nicholas or ony ither, for if I let the laird intil his ain house we'll hae to answer for't before the Privy Council.'

It was plain that Mistress Saintserf was not ill-pleased with David, for she talked freely and would hardly let him go.

'Ye're ower young for the sacred callin',' she told him when at last he took his leave. 'And ye're ower wise-like a man for a minister. Saunts suld hae weak stomachs, like our ain Mr Fordyce; it gars them sit loose to earthly affections.'

'I would put up with his affliction if I could get one-half of his goodness,' said David.

''Deed that's weel spoken. I'm sure o' Heaven if I can get haud o' the strings of Mr James's cloak. Never heed an auld wife's clavers. Come back and prie our grosarts when they're ripe, and if ye see thet lass o' mine on the hill tell her I'm waitin' for her wi' a besom.'

On his way home David had no sight of Katrine, but the next afternoon he met her in Paradise. She came to him smiling and friendly as a boy.

'You have been to Calidon and seen Aunt Grizel. I congratulate you on your conquest, sir, for my aunt is now your devout partisan and you have won another friend in this countryside. But what is this news of the Lord Marquis?'

They whiled away the summer afternoon with talk, rambling sometimes through the oak glades, but always returning to the nook by the spring, while David kept a jealous eye on the declining sun. The girl must be well on her way to Calidon before the first dusk began. When he came again they did not talk of his troubles, nor even of Montrose, but of little things, her childhood in France, her kin, the tales of the glen, his own youth at Edinburgh College. For she was not an ally so much as a refuge. When he was with her he was conscious that the world was still large and sunlit, the oppression lifted from his spirit, he saw himself not only victor in the quarrel but a messenger of God with a new gospel to perplexed mankind.

One evening, when he had seen the girl descend through the hazels to the Rood vale, and had turned back for the shoulder of the Hill of Deer, he saw a man's figure slanting across the hill as if coming from Melanudrigill. It was Reiverslaw, but though their paths all but intersected the farmer did not stop to talk. He waved a hand in greeting. 'Ye suld gie a look in at the Greenshiel,' he shouted. 'They tell me Richie Smail is in need of consolation.'

David took the hint, passed word to Richie, and the next evening met Reiverslaw in the herd's cottage. 'Tak' a look round the faulds, Richie,' said the master. 'Me and the minister has something to say to ither,' and the two were left alone in the dim sheiling.

'I've been spyin' oot the land,' said Reiverslaw, 'like the lads that Joshua sent afore him into Canaan. I canna say I likit the job, but I've been through the Wud east and west and I've found the bit whaur the Coven meets aside the auld altar. I think I could find the road till't on the blackest nicht. And I've been speirin' judeeciously in Woodilee.'

'But surely they did not answer?'

The dark face of the farmer had a crooked grin.

'Trust me, I was discreet. But I've a name for takin' a stoup ower muckle, and when the folk thocht I was fou, my lugs were as gleg as a maukin's. They're preparin' for another Sabbath, and it fa's on the Lammas Eve. On that nicht you and me maun tak' the Wud.'

David shivered, and the man saw it.

'The flesh is weak,' he said, 'and I'm feelin' like that mysel'. But you an' me are no the anes to pit our hand to the plew-stilts and turn back. Mr Sempill, are ye young enough to speel a tree?'

'I was a great climber as a laddie.'

'Weel, ye'll hae to be a laddie aince again. And I'll tell ye mair. Ye'll hae to leave this place afore the Lammas-tide. Is there ony bit ye can bide at, not abune twenty miles frae Woodilee?'

'There is my cousin at Newbiggin.'

'Weel, to Newbiggin ye gang, and your departure maun be public. Crack about it for days afore. Tell the auld wife at the manse and deave her wi' your preparation. For, if you're no oot o' the parish in guid time, ye'll be lockit in your chamber, as ye were on the second Beltane. And ye maun be in the Wud that nicht as a witness, for there's just us twasome, you and me, and we maun be witnesses that the Presbytery and the Sheriff and the Lords in Embro cannot deny.'

'I see that. But have you found out nothing more in Woodilee?'

'I've gotten a hantle o' suspeecions. Man, ye'd wonder to see how chief me and Chasehope are these days. I've been ower to see his English bull, and I've ta'en his advice about sheep, and I've sell't him a score o' gimmers at a price that made me voamit. He thinks I'm a dacent, saft, through-ither body, wi' his wits sair fuddled by strong drink, and has nae back-thichts o' ane that's just clay in his hands. . . . Ay, and I've been payin' muckle attention to his hen-house. His wife, ye maun ken, is a notable hen-wife, and she has a red cock that there's no the like o' in the countryside. I took Rab Prentice up wi' me to Chasehope toun, and I bade Rab tak' special note o' the red cock.'

'But I do not see the purpose . . .'

'Ye needna – yet. Ye'll be tell't in guid time. I'm thinkin' o' the process afore the Presbytery, and it's witnesses I'm seekin'. I hae twa honest men, my herds Richie Smail and Rab Prentice, but Richie's ower auld to tak' the Wud and Hirplin' Rab wad dee afore he would pit his neb inside it. So there's just you and me for the chief job, though the ither twa will hae their uses.'

The imminence of the trial made David's heart sick, for he had now brooded for three months on the mysteries of the Wood, whereas at Beltane he had stumbled upon them in hot blood unwittingly. He was confident in his cause, but he believed most firmly that the Devil in person would be his antagonist, and the cool tones of Reiverslaw struck him with admiration and awe.

'Man, you speak as calm as if you were making ready for a clipping. Is it that you do not believe in the power of Satan?'

'I believe in God,' said the man, 'and I've seen ower muckle o' the world no to believe in the Deil. But I'll no be feared o' a Deil that misguides auld wives and tak's up wi' rotten peats like Chasehope, and though he comes in a brimestane lowe I'll hae a nick at him.'

Then began for David a time of doubt and heart-searching. He could not share the robust confidence of Reiverslaw, for his memory of Beltane was too clear and he had lived too long under its shadows. His imagination, always quick and easily kindled, ran riot, and he saw the Wood as an abode of horrid mysteries, which spread into subtle ramifications of evil the more he pondered them. His secular learning was so much fuel to this fire. Courage did not fail him, but brightness died out of his world, and he knew himself condemned to tread a dark winepress alone.

It was the thought of Katrine that most disquieted him. The Wood, the whole parish, the very mission on which he was engaged, seemed to him one vast pollution, to be kept hidden for ever from youth and innocence. The girl must not be allowed to come within sight of the skirts of it. There could be no friendship between them, and it was his first duty to warn her.

So when they met in Paradise it was a shame-faced young man that stood before her, a young man with a white face who kept his eyes on the ground and spoke terrible things. Words came unreadily, but his broken speech was more moving than eloquence. He bade her keep to the clean precincts of Calidon and come not even near the greenwood. God's curse was on the parish, and in the judgment preparing innocent might share with guilty. As for himself, he was no friend for such as she.

'I am too heavily burdened,' he stammered. 'I must touch pitch and my hands will be defiled. I will blight your youth with my dark duties. . . . I will never come again to this place, and I plead with you to come no more, for it is too near the Enemy's country. . . . Go away now, I beg of you, and forget that you have ever seen me and called me friend. You will torture me if you bide . . . .'

There was more of the same sort, and then David stopped, confident that he had done his purpose, and that no proud girl would linger in the face of such a warning. He waited, very cold and lonely at heart, and he thought he heard her departing feet on the grass.

But when he raised his eyes, she had not moved, and her face was smiling.

TEN

What the Moon Saw

There was great heat at the end of July – sultry, thunderous weather when the hills drowsed under a haze and the sun's beams seemed to be the more torrid for the screen of vapours through which they fell. The heavens were banking up for the Lammas rains. But each evening the skies cleared, and the night was an amethyst dome sprinkled with stars.

David made a great to-do about his visit to Newbiggin. On the Monday morning he announced it to Isobel, and in an hour the word had gone through the village. His housekeeper seemed to receive the news with relief. 'Blithe I am to hear it, sir. Folk suld whiles change their ground like bestial, and ye've been ower lang tethered to this parochine. Newbiggin will be a caller bit in this lown weather, and while ye're awa' I'll get your chamber cleaned and the stairs washed doun. Dinna haste to come back, for I'll no look for ye or Setterday.'

He set off on the Tuesday after midday and there were many eyes in Woodilee to mark his going. That night he duly slept at Newbiggin, but the next day, which was Lammas Eve, he left his cousin's house and rode up Clyde water into the farthest moors. It was a wide circuit, which brought him in the afternoon to the uplands which separate Rood from Annan. All day he had been out of sight of human dwelling, and the first he saw was in the dusk when he descended upon the tower of Calidon by the glen of the Calidon burn. At Calidon he left his horse with the grieve, promising to return for it on the morrow, and with one look at the lit windows of the tower he set out on foot to ford the Rood. About nine o'clock in the mulberry gloaming he reached the cottage of the Greenshiel.

Three figures greeted him there. One was the herd of the outer hirsel, Richie Smail; another was Rab Prentice, the herd of the home hirsel, who sat on the turf deas at the cottage-end with his crutch beside him; the third was Reiverslaw himself, who was also seated, smoking a pipe of tobacco.

'Ye're in braw time, Mr Sempill,' said the last. 'Did ye pass ony folk on the road?'

'I have seen no man since the morning, except the Calidon grieve half an hour syne.'

'And that's just as weel. Richie, kindle the cruisie, for our job is better done indoors.'

The feeble light in the hut revealed a curious assembly. The two shepherds had faces of portentous gravity, and their twitching mouths and restless eyes were proof of an extreme discomfort. Reiverslaw wore his usual frieze small-clothes and boot-hose, but he had no coat, though he had slung on his arm what might have been that garment. He flung this on the settle. 'It's ower het to wear that muckle maud till the time comes. We maun get to business, Mr Sempill, for you should be on the road afore the moon rises. We're here to get our plan strauchtit oot and there's jimp time. Rab Prentice, ye've been twice wi' me to Chasehope in the last se'en days. Ye mind the braw red cock the wife has gotten?'

'Fine,' said the shepherd.

'There's no sic another fowl in the countryside?'

'That I'll engage.'

'Therefore if I show ye the morn a pluckin' o' red feathers, ye'll jalouse it's the Chasehope cock?'

'Ay. But I'm no gaun intil the Wud . . . not even in braid daylicht.'

'If I bid ye, ye wull gang, Rab Prentice, though I suld carry ye myself. . . . Now, secondly, as the ministers say. Do ye see this bottle? Smell it, a' three of ye. That's a smell ye never fand afore? It's what they call oil of hennyseed, and I got it frae a horse-doctor at Carlisle. I'll wager there's no anither phial o' the same between here and Embro. It's a smell ye'll no sune forget. Pit a dab on yer sleeves to remind ye o't. If the three o' us gangs to Chasehope the morn and finds Chasehope's breeks and Chasehope's sark stinkin' o' this oil, ye'll be able to swear to it, and to swear that I showed it you this verra nicht and that ye kenned the smell when ye fand it again.'

The two men agreed, sniffing the drop on their sleeve.

'Thirdly,' said Reiverslaw, 'I'm gaun to turn mysel' intil a guisard.'

He picked up the thing he had been carrying and revealed it as a cloak of deerskins which fitted like a loose jerkin. Over his head he drew a cap of skin with slits for his eyes, a roughly shaped nozzle like a deer's, and on the top the horns of a goat.

'Save us a'!' Richie cried, as he saw his master stand up, his lean, active body surmounted by a beast's head. 'Save us a', ye're no gaun to tamper wi' the accursed thing!'

'That's what I ettle, but the intention is guid, and it's by our intentions we'll be judged, as Mr Sempill will tell ye. Look at me, ye daft auld fules, for there's naething to be feared o'. I'm for the Wud the nicht, and it's my purpose to bide in cover till the folk are half dementit, and syne when their een are blind to join them. I've a notion that there will be some wark wi' the red cock, and I'd like a feather or twa as a keepsake. And I've a sort of notion that my auld friend Chasehope will be there! so as a token o' friendship I'll pit saut on his tail – whilk means that if I get the chance I'll anoint his dowp wi' the hennyseed. Now, you twa, take tent and listen to me. Ye will swear that I telled ye what I have telled ye, and that ye saw me at the Greenshiel dressed up like a merry-andrew. The horns suld hae been a stag's; but I was feared o' hankin' them in the busses, so the fine auld Reiverslaw billy-goat had to dee.'

He was a crazy sight with the goat's head on him, and a formidable sight without it, for as he stood in that dusk beside two men bent with labour, the one maimed and the other past the allotted span of human years, David had an impression of something desperate and fearless and light-hearted. The shepherds were clearly torn between loyalty and terror, and he himself, while firm enough in his resolve, had to keep his thoughts battened down to prevent his knees knocking. But Reiverslaw seemed to have no fears. He had set about the thing as cannily as if it were selling sheep at Lockerbie fair, and now, with a venture before him which not two other men in Scotland would have contemplated, he was notably the least embarrassed of the party.

'I saw three pyots flee intil the Wud this morning,' said Prentice, 'and but ane came back. That's an unco freit for the beginnin' o't!'

'Haud your tongue, ye auld wife,' said Reiverslaw. 'Freits fa' to them that fear them, and I'm no gaun to fash my heid about twa jauds o' birds . . . .'

'I had a vision yestereen,' Richie put it. 'I saw the haill land o' Scotland like a field of aits, white until the harvest, the haill land frae John o' Groats to Galloway, a' but the parish o' Woodilee, whilk was unplewed and rough wi' briars and thrissles. An' says I to myself, "Whatever place is yon?" and says a voice to me, "That's what we ca' the Deil's Baulk in the gospel field o' Scotland."'

'And a very true observe, for Deil's Baulk is just what the Wud is, and it's for us to pit a plew intil't and mak' a fire o' the wastry. Set bite and sup afore the minister, Richie.'

The shepherd produced some oatcakes, of which David ate only a mouthful, for though he had had no food since morning, his throat was dry and his tongue like a stick. He drank, however, a pint of buttermilk.

'Kirn-milk for you?' the host asked of Reiverslaw. 'I hae nae yill, but Rab has brocht a flask o' aquavitty ye gied him at the lambin'.'

'I'll hae spring water. Nae strong drink for me, for this nicht I'm like Jonadab the son of Rechab. . . . Are ye ready, Mr Sempill? Ye maun start first, for ye've a tree to speel. There's nae hurry for me till the Deil begins his pipin'.'

'You are either strong in the faith, or of a very stout heart,' said David admiringly.

'No as strong as I might be,' was the answer. 'Afore we part, wad it no be weel for you to pit up a prayer?'

The minister prayed – and it was as if he confessed alone to his God in his closet. He himself was strengthened by it, and the comfort of Richie and Rab was visibly enlarged. But Reiverslaw stood through the devotions in no very devout position, and from him came none of the responses which flowed from the others. Before the 'Amen' he had his goat-cap on, and was peering at the rising moon. He made his staff sing as he whirled it.

David took his strange confederate's hand, and his own shook. Reiverslaw noted his trepidation.

'Fear nocht, sir. It'll gang ill wi' the wirriecow gin we meet him. But what brocht a man o' peace like you into this tuilzie?'

'Jealousy for the honour of my God. And you? For it is less your quarrel than mine.'

The man grinned. 'Write it down that Andra Shillinglaw couldna see an honest man beat, and that he didna like kail-worms.'

David had many times gone over in his mind the route to the glade of the altar, and had compared notes with Reiverslaw that very night. The distance was less than three miles, and he had a couple of hours to reach the place and still be in position well before midnight. As on all the nights of the past week, the oppressive haze of the day had lifted, and the sky rose to an infinite height, thick studded with stars, for the moon was only new risen. David made his way to the dividing glen between the pines and the hazels in a miserable disquiet. He had lost the first fierce anger which had stiffened him for his frustrated expedition on the eve of the second Beltane, and his tacit ostracism all summer by the folk of Woodilee had engendered a profound self-distrust. Even the thought of Katrine Yester did not nerve him; she belonged to a world separated by impassable gulfs from that black necromancy which he warred against. Nor did the fact that he had an ally comfort him, for Reiverslaw, he greatly feared, fought in his own strength and not in that of the Lord, and in such a strife the arm of flesh could not avail them. As he stumbled through the dark undergrowth David's lips moved in anxious prayers.

He entered the pines, and, shaping his course by the low line of cliffs, came to the place where he had first met Katrine. Thus far he felt that he was not wholly outside the pale of kindly things. But after that he was in enemy country, and the moon was still too low to give him help. He wasted half an hour in the thickets, till by a strong effort of will he forced himself to take his bearings and remember Reiverslaw's instructions. He scrambled up hill again till he was in touch with the outcrop of rock, and then suddenly found himself looking down on the glade where stood the altar.

It was very dark, and the stone was only a ghostly blur. But the darkness was a blessing, for the place was not as he had seen it before, and the sight of it did not revive the terrors he had feared. It looked no more than a woodland glade, and the fact that a rabbit scurried from under his feet seemed a friendly omen. On the far side the trees grew thick, and he selected a gnarled Scots fir as his perch for the night. Its trunk, branchless for sixty feet, was too thick to climb, but he found a younger and slimmer tree, up which he could squirm and from its upper branches traverse to the other. He had not tried the game since he was a boy, and at first his legs and arms seemed too feeble; but the exercise warmed him, and after twice sliding back to the ground, he at last reached the umbrella-like spread of the crest. To gain the other tree proved more difficult than he had thought, and he was compelled to let his body swing and make a long stretch with his right arm. But the task was accomplished in the end, and he found himself on a platform of crooked fir boughs, hidden from everything but the stars, and with a view through the gaps of the branches to the glade below him.

He had now a clear sight of the sky. The moon was three-quarters up, and the whole of Melanudrigill with its slopes and valleys was washed in silver. He was in it and yet above it and outside it, like a man on a hillside looking into a cleft. He made his body comfortable in a crutch of the tree, and looked down on the stage beneath him. It was now lighting up, and the altar was whitened by a stray moonbeam. For the first time that night he felt his spirits returning. The oppression of the Wood was not realised on this outer shell of it, for here only winged things dwelt, and the unclean things of the dark had no wings.

In this happier mood his eyes sought the whereabouts of Calidon. It was ridden by a ridge, the ridge to the west where lay Paradise. The thought gave him an unreasoning pleasure. He was not cut off from the world of light, for, whatever befell on the earth beneath him, he had but to lift up his eyes and they rested on a happier country.

As the moon rose, the multitudinous little noises of a wood at night were hushed. There was a sleepy muttering of cushats to the south of him, and then, with a clatter which made him jump, the birds rose in a flock and flew across the valley. After that there was no sound until the music began.

There was no fixed moment for its beginning, for it seemed to steal insensibly into the air. And it was scarcely music, but rather a delicate babble of tongues which made a crooning like the low notes of a pipe. The sound was all beneath him near the ground, and gathering from different quarters to one centre. Suddenly in the midst of it came a sharp liquid note, several times repeated, a note with authority in it like a trumpet, and yet ineffably faint and distant as if it were the echo of an echo. It did not flutter David's heart, for there was no threat in it, but it made a strange effect upon his mind. For it seemed familiar, and there was that in him which answered it. He felt a boy again, for in the call there was the happy riot and the far horizons of childhood, and the noise of hill winds and burns, and the scent of heather and thyme, and all the unforgotten things of memory.

The silver trumpet did not speak again, but the soft babble was creeping nearer, and suddenly just beneath him it broadened and deepened into the sound of pipes. He looked down

and saw that the dance had begun. As before, the piper with his
hound mask sat cross-legged beyond the altar, and the dancers
revolved widdershins around him. . . .

To his amazement he found himself looking on not in terror,
but in curiosity. It was a graver dance than that of Beltane, not
the mad riot of the bursting life of Spring, but the more sober
march of summer and the hot suns bringing on the harvest. . . .
Seen from above, the figures were only puppets, moving at the
bidding of a lilt that rose and fell like a lost wind. The passion of
wrath with which he had watched the former Sabbath had
utterly gone from him. He felt a curious pity and friendliness,
for there was innocence here, misguided innocence.

'Will this be the way God looks down upon the follies of the
world?' he asked himself. What was it that Reiverslaw had said?
– If the Kirk confines human nature too strictly, it will break out
in secret ways, for men and women are born into a terrestrial
world, though they have hopes of Heaven. . . . That was
blasphemy, and he knew it, but he did not shudder at it.

How long these gentle dances continued he did not know, for
he was in a dream and under the spell of the piping. . . . Then
suddenly there came a change. The dancing-floor became dark,
and he saw that clouds were coming over the moon, and a chill
had crept into the air. Lights sprang up out of nowhere, and
though the wind had begun to sigh through the trees, he noted
that these lights did not flicker. . . . The music stopped, and the
dancers crowded together around the altar.

The hound-faced leader stood above them with something in
his hand. The mysterious light seemed to burn redly, and he
saw that the thing was a bird – a cock which was as scarlet as
blood. The altar top was bare, and something bright spurted into
the hollow of the stone. From the watchers came a cry which
chilled David's marrow, and he saw that they were on their
knees.

The leader was speaking in a high shrill voice like a sleep-
walker's, and David caught but the one word often repeated –
Abiron. Every time it was uttered the man dabbled his finger in

the blood on the altar and marked a forehead, and as each received the mark he or she fell prostrate on the ground. . . .

There was no innocence now in that spectacle of obscene abasement. Terror entered into David's soul, and his chief terror was that he had not been afraid before. He had come very near falling himself under the spell.

There followed what seemed to be a roll-call. The leader read names out of a book and the prostrate figures answered. The names seemed like an idiot's muttering, not good Scots words, but uncouth gutturals. And always like an undercurrent came the word Abiron.

Then with an unholy cry the whole Coven was on its feet. The pipes began again, and music other than pipes, which seemed to soak out of the ground and the adjacent coverts. Gone was every trace of gentleness and innocency. It was witch-music made by the Devil himself on the red-hot chanter-reeds of Hell, and the assembly capered as if their feet were on the lake of burning marl. The Israelitish prophet in David awoke, and he saw it all with clear eyes and horror-stricken soul.

If the Beltane dance had been hideous, this was the very heart of bestial lust. Round and round it swept, a fury and yet an ordered fury, in which madness and obscenity were mingled. He recognised the faces of women, old and young, who sat devoutly beneath him in kirk of a Sabbath. The men were all masked, but he knew that if he could tear off the beast coverings he would see features which were normally composed into a pious decency. Figure would clasp figure and then fling apart, but in each circuit he noted that the dancers kissed some part of the leader's body, nozzling him like dogs on the roadside.

Up in his treetop the minister had now an undivided mind. He had the names of several of the females of the Coven firm in his memory, and for the men he must trust to Reiverslaw. There were some of the dancers with goat-horns, but as the rout swung round it seemed to him that a new goat-mask had appeared, a taller wilder figure, who was specially devout in his obeisance before Houndface. Was it Reiverslaw with his aniseed?

The night had become very dark and the only light in the glade came from the candles which burned in its hidden hollows. And then suddenly a colder wind blew, and like the burst of a dam came a deluge of rain. The Lammas floods had broken, stealing upon the world, as is their fashion, out of a fair sky.

It seemed to David – and he held it part of the infernal miracle – that the torrent did not quench the lights. In a trice he himself was soaked to the skin, but the candles still burned, though the rain beat on the floor of the glade with a sound like a whip-lash. . . . But it ended the dance. The silver pipe sounded again, and as the wind rose higher and the falling water slanted under it to search out even the bield of the trees, he saw figures moving hurriedly off. The next time he looked down through the spears of rain – for the hidden moon still made a dim brightness in the world – the glade was empty. Above the noise of the storm he thought he heard the strange babble of tongues, but now it was departing to the far corners of the Wood.

He waited for a little and then tried to descend. But he found it harder to get down than to get up, for he could not find the branch by which he had swung himself from the lesser tree, and in the end had to drop a good twenty feet into the bracken, whence he rolled into the empty glade. . . . He scrambled to his feet and made haste to get out of it, but not before he had sniffed the odour of unclean pelts. – And yes – surely that was the stink of Reiverslaw's aniseed.

He had no difficulty about his homeward course. Most of the way he ran, but fear had completely left his heart. The rain in his face seemed to cleanse and invigorate him. He had looked upon great wickedness, but he had looked down on it, like the Almighty, from above, and it seemed a frail and pitiful thing – a canker to be rooted out, but a thing with no terror for a servant of God. The Devil was but a botcher after all. And then he remembered how the first notes of the music had melted him, and he felt humbled.

Reiverslaw had arrived at the Greenshiel before him. The place was filled with the reek of burning hides, and David saw that the goat-mask and cloak had been laid on the peats. His ally, a weird dripping figure, sat on a stool swilling the aqua vitae which Rab Prentice had brought with him. He, who had started the night's venture with such notable sangfroid, was now in a sweat of fright.

'Be thankit ye're safe,' he stuttered, while spirits spilled over his beard. 'I never thocht to see ye mair, for I never thocht to win out o' yon awesome place. My legs are a' gashed and scartit, for I cam here through stane and briar like a dementit staig. Oh, sir, siccan a sicht for mortal een!'

'Saw ye the Foul Thief?' asked the awed Prentice.

'I saw ane in his image, and I got a drap o' the red cock's bluid, and I loupit like the lave, but it wasna wi' their unholy glee. Sir, I was fair wud wi' terror – me that am no gien to fear muckle – for I got a cauld grue in my banes and my een turned back in their sockets. I tell ye, I forgot the errand I had come on, I forgot my name and my honest upbringing, and I was like a wean forwandered among bogles. . . . I've burnt thae skins, and when I get hame I'll burn every stitch o' cleading, for the reek o' the Pit is on it.'

'Did you recognise many?' David asked.

'No me. I had nae een to see wi'. I spun round like a teetotum and I wadna say but I let out skellochs wi' the best – may God forgie me!'

'But the oil – the aniseed?'

Reiverslaw held up something which David saw was an empty bottle.

'I didna fail ye there. For the ae man I kenned in the Coven was him that piped. When I cam near him I felt a stound o' black hate, and there's but the ae man on God's earth that can gar me scunner like yon. So when it was my turn to bow down afore him, he gat mair frae me than a kiss. Unless he burns his breeks this very nicht there'll be a queer savour aboot the toun o' Chasehope the morn.'

ELEVEN

The Minister Girds up his Loins

Next day David returned to the manse in time for the noontide meal. He was greeted by Isobel with a hospitable bustle, in which was apparent a certain relief. She had known of the Lammas festival; she guessed, no doubt, that David too was aware of it, and she evidently took his visit to Newbiggin as a sign that he had at last taken her prudent counsel. But from her master she got no response. When questioned as to the welfare of his kin at Newbiggin he answered in civil monosyllables, ate his dinner in silence, and thereafter secluded himself in his study.

That evening he walked to the Greenshiel, where Reiverslaw and Prentice met him. The former was in an excited state and had clearly been drinking – to the scandal of the two shepherds, who wore portentous faces. Richie Smail had the air of an honest man compelled to walk in abhorred paths; he had been reading his Bible before their arrival, and sat with a finger in the leaves, saying nothing, but now and then lifting puzzled eyes to his master. Prentice's hard jaw was set, and he swung his crutch as if it had been a pikestaff.

'We were at Chasehope by eleven hours this mornin',' Reiverslaw announced. 'I took Richie and Rab, as I forewarned Ephraim, to have a look at his new tups. But I needna tell you there was nae word of Ephraim. The wife said he was awa' to Kirk Aller, but she was like a hen on a het girdle a' the time, and I think we wad hae found him if we had ripit the press-beds. If he was lurking there he maun hae gotten a sair fricht, for I spak that loud ye could hae heard me on the tap o' Chasehope hill.'

'Did you find what you sought?' David asked.

'I fand eneuch.' He drew from a pocket a bunch of feathers. 'I got these last nicht in the Wud. Doubtless there'll be mair in the same place, if they havena been soopit up. But there's nae red cock the day in the toun o' Chasehope. I admired the wife's hens and speired what had become o' the cock, and was telled that it was deid – chokit last nicht on a grosart. I ken the kind o' grosart that ended the puir beast.'

'And the aniseed?'

Reiverslaw laughed tipsily.

'We were just in time, sir. The wife had a fire lowin' in the yaird. "What's burnin', mistress?" says I. "Just some auld clouts," says she. "There was a gangrel body sleepit ae nicht in the loft," says she, "and he left some duds ahint him, as fu' o' fleas as a cadger's bonnet. I'm haein' them brunt," says she, "for fear o' the weans." Weel, me and Richie and Rab stood aside the fire, and it loupit as if an oil can had been skailed on it, and the reek that rase frae it was just the reek o' my wee bottle. Mair nor that, there was a queer smell ayont the hallin – Richie and Rab fand it as weel as me. What name wad ye gie it, Rab?'

'It was the stink o' the stuff ye showed us in this house last nicht,' said Prentice solemnly.

'Sae muckle for that,' said Reiverslaw. 'We've proof that the lad in the dowg's cap was nae ither than him we ken o'. Na, na, I never let on to the wife. I was jokesome and daffin' wi' her, and made a great crack o' the tups, and praised a' I saw about the toun, and Rab and Richie were as wise as judges. I had a dram inside me, and was just my canty ordinar'. But my een and my nostrils werena idle, and I saw what I've telled ye. . . . My heid was in sic a thraw last nicht that I canna sweir wi' ony certainty to ither faces, though I hae my suspeecions about the weemen. But you, sir, sittin' aloft on the tree-tap, ye maun hae had a graund view, for there was licht eneuch to read prent.'

'I recognised certain women, to whom I can swear on my oath. About some I dare not be positive, but there were five of whom I have no doubt. There were Jean Morison and her daughter Jess.'

'The folk o' the Chasehopefit,' Reiverslaw cried. 'Ay, they wad be there. They've aye been ill-regarded.'

'And old Alison Geddie in the kirkton.'

'A daft auld wife, that skellochs like a sea-maw!'

'And Eppie Lauder from Mirehope road-end.'

Richie Smail groaned. 'The widow of a tried Christian, Mr Sempill. A dacenter body than Wattie Lauder never walked the roads. It's terrible to think o' the Deil's grip on the household o' faith.'

'And Bessie Tod from the Mains.'

'Peety on us, but I sat neist her at the March fast-day when Mr Proudfoot preached, and she was granin' and greetin' like a bairn. Ye surely maun be in error, sir. Bessie was never verra strong in the heid, and she hasna the wits for the Deil's wark!'

'Nevertheless she was there. I am as certain of that as that I was myself in the tree-top. Of others I have suspicions, but of these five I have certainty.'

Reiverslaw rubbed his great hands. 'Our business gangs cannily forward. We've gotten the names o' six o' the Coven and can guess at ithers. Man, we'll hae a riddlin' in Woodilee that will learn the folk no to be ill bairns. Ye'll be for namin' them frae the pu'pit, sir?'

'I must first bring the matter before the Presbytery. I will prepare my dittay, and bring it before Mr Muirhead of Kirk Aller as the Presbytery's Moderator, and I must be guided by him as to the next step. It is a matter for the courts of the Kirk and presently for the secular law.'

Reiverslaw cried out. 'What for maun ye gang near the Presbytery? If ye stir up yon byke ye'll hae commissioners of justiciary and prickers and the haill clamjamphrie, and in the lang end an auld kimmer or twa will suffer, and the big malefactors will gang scot frae. Chasehope's ower near the lug o' the law to tak' ony scaith, and yon's the kailworm I wad be at. Be guidit by me, Mr Sempill, and keep the thing inside the pairish. As the auld saying gangs, bleach your warst hanks in your ain yaird, for I tell ye if the Kirk and the Law hae the redding o't it's little justice will be done. Name and upbraid and denounce a' and sindry, but dinna delate to the Presbytery. A man may like the kirk weel eneuch, and no be aye ridin' on the riggin' o't. . . . I'll tell ye my way o't. Now that we ken some o' the Coven, the four o' us can keep our een open, and watch them as a dowg watches a ratton; and at their next Sabbath, as they ca' it, we'll be ready for them. I can get a wheen Moffat drovers that fear neither man nor deil, and aiblins some o' Laird Hawkshaw's folk frae Calidon, and we'll break in on their Coven and tear the masks frae the men, and rub their nebs in their ain mire, and dook the lot in the Water o' Aller. I'll wager that's the way to get rid o' witchcraft frae the parochine, for we'll mak' it an unco painfu' business to tak' the Wud. A witch or a warlock is a fearsome thing to the mind o' man, but they're bye wi't gin we mak' them gowks and laughing-stocks.'

The two shepherds stared at the speaker with upbraiding eyes, and David's face looked as if a blasphemy had been spoken.

'You would fight the Devil in your own carnal strength,' he said sadly. 'It's little you would make of it. You talk as if this wickedness of the Wood were but a natural human prank, when it is black sin that can only be combated by the spirit of God and such weapons as God has expressly ordained. Man, man, Reiverslaw, you've but a poor notion of the power of the Adversary. I tell you last night I was trembling like a weaned child before yon blast that blew out of Hell, and you yourself were no better when I found you here. I durstna have entered the Wood except as a soldier of the Lord.'

Reiverslaw laughed.

'I was sair fleyed, I'll no deny, but I got a juster view o' things wi' the daylicht.'

'It would appear that you got courage also from Lucky Weir.'

'True. I had my mornin' and my meridian and an orra stoup or twa sinsyne. I'm a man that's aye been used wi' a guid allowance o' liquor. But the drink, if so be ye're no fou, whiles gi'es ye a great clearness, and I counsel ye, sir, to keep wide o' the law, whether it be of the Kirk or the State. It's a kittle thing, and him that invokes it is like to get the redder's straik. It's like a horse that flings its heels when ye mount and dings out the rider's teeth. . . . But hae your ain way o't, and dinna blame me if it's a fashious way. There's me and Rab Prentice and Richie Smail waitin' to sweir to what's in our knowledge, and if there's mair speirin' to be done in the Wud, I'll no fail ye. But keep in mind, Mr Sempill, that I'm a thrang body, and maun be drawin' my crocks and sellin' my hog-lambs afore the back-end, and it's like I'll hae to traivel to Dumfries, and maybe to Carlisle. Richie will aye hae word o' my doings, and if ye want me it wad be wise to tell Richie a week afore.'

That night on his return David summoned Isobel to his presence. The housekeeper appeared with a more cheerful countenance than she had worn for weeks, but the minister's first words solemnised her.

'Isobel Veitch, I asked you a question after Beltane and you refused me an answer. I, your minister, besought your aid as a confessing Christian, and you denied it me. I told you that I would not rest until I had rooted the idolatry of the Wood from this parish. Since then I have not been idle, and I have found men who did not fail me. Three days back I rode to Newbiggin, as I told you, but I returned on Lammas Eve, and on Lammas Eve I was a witness a second time to the abominations of the heathen. Not only myself, but another with me, so that the thing is established out of the mouths of two witnesses, while Robert Prentice and Richard Smail can speak in part to confirm me. Now I have got my tale complete, and it is to the Presbtery that I shall tell it. Will you implement it with such knowledge as you possess, or do you continue stiff in your recusancy?'

The old woman's eyes opened like an owl's.

'Wha went with you – wha was sae left to himsel'?' she gasped.

'Andrew Shillinglaw in Reiverslaw. . . . One man and five women stand arraigned on our witness. I will speak their names, and I care not if you put it through the parish, for soon the names will be thundered from the pulpit. The man was Ephraim Caird.'

'I'll no believe it,' she cried. 'Chasehope's aye been a polished shaft in Christ's kirk. . . . He's o' your ain Session. . . . He cam' here, ye mind, when ye first broke bread in this house. Ay, and he was here when ye were awa at Newbiggin. I was seilin' the milk when I heard his voice at the door – cam' here wi' ane o' his wife's skim-milk kebbucks that she kens well how to mak', for she's frae the Wastlands – spoke sae kind and neeborlike, and was speirin' for the health o' the gude man my maister. . . . Tak' it back, sir, for ye maun be mistook. Ephraim's weel kenned for a fair Nathaniel.'

There was no doubt about her honesty, for the mention of Chasehope had staggered her.

'Nevertheless he is a whited sepulchre, painted without but inside full of bones and rottenness.'

'Oh, sir, bethink ye afore ye mak' this fearsome accusation. Your een may have played ye fause. And wha in their senses wad lippen to Reiverslaw? A muckle, black-avised, grippy incomer that nae man kens the get o' . . . sweirs like a dragon when the maut's abune the meal. Ye'll never gang to the Presbytery in siccan comany wi' siccan a tale! And Hirplin' Rab is a thrawn deevil, though I'll no deny he hae a gift o' prayer – and Richie Smail is sair failed in body and mind since last back-end when Mirren dee'd.'

'There are also five women,' David went on. 'There are Jean and Jess Morison from Chasehopefoot.'

'Sae that's where ye get your ill-will at Chasehope – because he's ower kind to turn twa randies intil the road! I hae nothing to say for the Morisons. They come oot o' a dirty nest, and they may ride on a saugh ilka nicht to Norroway for a' I ken.'

'There is Eppie Lauder at Mirehope.'

'Tut, man, as dacent a body as ever boiled sowens. And her man, Wattie, that dee'd in Aprile o' the year thretty-nine, was weel thocht o' by a' body. Ye've come till a frem'd toun wi' Eppie.'

'And Alison Geddie.'

'A tongue like a bell-clapper, but ettles nae hairm.'

'Likewise Bessie Tod of the Mains.'

'She's weak in her mind, sir. Lang syne she had a bairn to a sodger and it dee'd, and she never got ower it. Ye'll no convince me that there's ony ill in Bessie forbye the want o' sense.'

'I have evidence of ill. I accuse, I do not condemn. It is for others to do the judging.'

Isobel's timidity, which had been notable during the Beltane interview, seemed now to have left her. There was a sincere emotion in her voice.

'I plead wi' ye, sir, to halt while yet there's time, and if needs be content yoursel' wi' private examination. It's verra weel for Andrew Shillinglaw, that's but an incomer, and rakes the country gettin' as he gangs like a cadger's powny. But you're the minister o' Woodilee, and the fair fame o' the parochine suld be as dear to you as your ain. If ye tak' the gait ye speak o', ye'll mak' it a hissing and a reproach in a' the water of Aller. It's a quiet bien bit, wi' douce folk weel agreed, and ye wad mak' it a desolation, and a' because some daft lads and a wheen hellicat lassies dance their twasomes in the Wud. It's no as if they did ill things like garrin' the kye rin dry and the weans dwine.'

'Then you admit knowledge of the sin?'

'I admit nocht, for I ken nocht. Young folk will be young folk, peety though it be. . . . But for Chasehope and my auld gossip, Eppie Lauder, the man's gyte that wad chairge them wi' idolatry – and you can tell that to your drucken Reiverslaw.'

For the first time since he had known her Isobel flung out of the room in a temper.

Next day he sought out Chasehope, and found him alone on the hill. The man greeted him with effusion.

'The Lammas rains is weel-timed this year, Mr Sempill, nae ragin' flood but just eneuch to slocken the ground. I start cuttin' the bog hay the morn. I heard ye were at Newbiggin, sir, and I trust ye found your friends in guid health. A blaw on the hills yonder is fine for a body after the lown air o' Woodilee.'

'I returned home on the Lammas Eve. I ask you, Ephraim Caird, as you will answer to your God, where were you in the mirk of that night?'

The heavy face, now brick-red with summer suns, did not change.

'Where suld I be but in my bed? I gaed till't early, for I had a lang day wi' the hog-lambs.'

'You know that that is a lie. You were in the Wood, as you were in the Wood at Beltane, dancing away your miserable soul to the Devil's piping. With my own eyes I saw you.'

The astonishment of Chasehope was admirably simulated.

'Are ye daft, sir? Are ye gane clean gyte? Ye're no weel, Mr Sempill. Sit ye doun, and I'll fetch you some water in my bonnet. Ye've got a blaff o' the sun.'

'I am not mad nor am I sick. I have preached throughout the summer at the sin and the time has now come to get to grips with the sinner. This is your last chance, Ephraim Caird. Will you confess to me, who have been set in spiritual authority over you, or must confession be wrung from you by other means?'

It was a warning which David felt bound to give, but he was silent as to the rest of his purpose, for he had decided that the time had not yet come to show his hand. He looked sternly at Chasehope, and under his gaze the man's face seemed to whiten, and his odd greenish eyes to waver. But it might be in innocent amazement.

'I kenna what ye speak o', he stammered. 'What concern have I wi' the Wud? Ask the wife and she'll tell you that I sleepit the Lammas nicht in my bed. But oh – the thing fair coups the crans! . . . and me an elder thae ten year! Ye're no weel or ye're dementit to speak sic words to a man like me. Awa hame, sir, and humble yoursel' on your knees and pray that ye may be forgiven. . . . I may cry out in the words of the Psalmist, "They opened their mouth wide against me, and said Aha, our eye hath seen it." '

David's hand clenched on his staff. 'Before God,' he cried, 'I will strike you down if you utter another blasphemous word.

You neglect my warning? Then your punishment be on your own guilty head.'

He turned and strode away. Once he looked back, and saw Chasehope still staring, the very image of virtuous dismay.

There was no sermon in the kirk the next two Sabbaths. Robb the bellman had orders not to ring the bell, but few came to the kirkyard gate, for the rumour had spread that the minister would conduct no ordinances until he had taken counsel with the Presbytery. David waited, hoping for he knew not what – some thaw to melt this icy impenitence. At last on the sixteenth day of August he rode to Kirk Aller to visit Mr Muirhead.

He found the Moderator in his parlour in the little stone manse, which stood below the kirk on the knowe at the west gate above the brig of Aller. The room had few books, but a mass of papers, for Mr Muirhead was an active ecclesiastic and noted for his conduct of church business. Also, as if to meet the disturbed times in which he lived, a pair of spurred boots, still with the mud on them, stood beside the table, on it lay a brace of ancient pistols, and from the peg of the door hung a great horseman's cloak.

Mr Muirhead bent a preoccupied brow on David as he entered, but his face was well content. There were open letters before him, and it seemed that he had just been the recipient of welcome news.

'Come awa in, Mr David,' he cried. He saw his visitor's eye stray to the pistols. 'Ay, I've got me to the auld weapons. I had them with me at the memorable assembly in Glasgow in '38 when we dang down the Bishops. . . . I have a crow to pyke with you, but first I have some braw tidings for your ear. At the last Presbytery we met under the shadow of calamity, but the Lord has mercifully turned again the captivity of Sion. Yon devil's spawn, Montrose – alas that he should take his name from a burgh of which worthy Mr Saunders Linklater was so long the faithful minister! – yon Montrose, I say, approaches the end of his tether. It has been a long tether, and he has ravened like a hungry hound, but he will soon be back on his haunches with the rope tightening at his thrapple. The Almighty has wysed him with a sure hand intil the snare that was prepared for him.'

'Has he been defeated?' David asked.

'By this time there is good hope that he has been scattered to the four airts of Heaven. After his savageries in the north he marches south to rend the fair fields of Stirling and the Lennox, and summon the towns of Glasgow and Embro, whilk are the citadels of our faith. Like Jeshurun he has waxed fat and kicked, but his pride will have a fearful fall; for long ere he wins to Clyde the trap will be sprung. He is bye Perth and at this moment, I trow, at the skirts of the Ochills. Before him lie Argyll and Baillie with horse and foot, which are to his heathen hirelings as four men to one. The faithful folk of Fife are marching cannily against his left flank, and mustering from the Glasgow airt against his right are the braw lads of the West, led by those well-disposed noblemen, the Earl of Eglinton, the Earl of Cassilis, and the Earl of Glencairn. More – all the gentry of Clydesdale are on the road, commanded by the Earl of Lanark, and him and his Hamiltons are waiting to soop up the remnants of that which Argyll will shatter. Isna that a bonny tale, Mr Sempill? Isna that a joyful recalling of our bondage, even as streams of water in the south?'

David assented, but to his surprise his interest was faint. He had more pressing problems than the public captivity of Israel.

'And now for other matters,' said Mr Muirhead, setting his mouth again in severe lines. 'I have word of grave mishandling at Woodilee. You have created a stramash in the doucest and most God-regarding parish in the presbytery of Aller. You are sinning away your mercies, sir.'

'It is of that I came to speak,' said David. 'I have to submit to you, and through you to the Presbytery, proofs of a dreadful wickedness among professing Christians in that unhappy place. Will you be pleased to run your eye over these papers? You will see certain names subscribed as witnesses.'

Mr Muirhead began to read the depositions carelessly, as if he knew what to expect from them. Then his attention deepened and he wrinkled his forehead.

'Hoots! What's this?' he cried. 'Ye were in the Wood? Ye saw this and that? Mr Sempill, ye're not exempt from the charge of tampering with unlawful things.'

'I went there as God's servant.'

'Nevertheless—' He read on, and his brows darkened. He finished, flung the bundle on the table, and looked at David with a troubled and uncertain eye.

'Here's a bonny browst o' yill! You charge your chief elder with the sin of witchcraft – a man of noted godliness, as I myself can testify – and you conjoin in the libel five women who are unknown to me. What is your evidence, I ask? Your ain een, at a time when you were in no condition to see clear, and forbye you were on the top of a tree, and it was in the mid of the night. You have no corroboration. But I pretermit the women and come to Chasehope. You have cherished a suspicion of him since Beltane, says you, when you were present in the Wood. And what, I ask, did you there at that season, Mr Sempill? I opine that your ain conduct wants some explanation.'

'That I can give,' said David.

'You have further the evidence of the man Andrew Shilling-law, and the plot you prepared against Chasehope. Man, I see nothing in your red cock's feathers or your hennyseed, as you call it. The well is tainted, so how can you look for pure water? Your Reiverslaw is notoriously a wine-bibber and a ruffler and a despiser of ordinances. What hinders that he should be also a leear? The cock's feathers may all the time have been in his pouch, and he may have played some prank at Chasehope with the stinkin' oil. You have the witness of the herds, says you, but it's easy enough to begowk two landward simpletons. Your case will not hold water, sir, before any competent court, and Reiverslaw, your principal abettor, stands suspect. As the old owercome has it, he suld bide still that has riven breeks.'

Mr Muirhead spoke with a weighty assurance, and as David looked at his shrewd coarse face he felt a sudden helplessness. It would be hard to convince a tribunal so prejudiced – in whose ears, perhaps, Chasehope had already spoken.

'My advice to you,' the voice went on, 'is to get you home and let the steer settle. There's nothing in these papers that calls for action by the Presbytery – just hearsay and idle *fama*, the visions of an excited young man and the lees of a drucken reprobate. No doubt you mean well, but I will homologate no course which fastens evil on a man whose righteousness has been abundantly proven. Have mind of the virtue of charity, sir, which thinketh no evil. I opine that you're ower ready to think evil. Bring before me wise-like evidence and I will be prompt to act, but not these havers.'

So far he had spoken with a kind of rough good-humour, but now his voice became harsh.

'They tell me you have conducted no public worship these last two Sabbaths,' he said fiercely.

'I will not lead my folk into deeper hypocrisy,' said David. 'I will not preach or pray in the kirk till I also denounce the sinners, and that I purpose to do on the next Lord's day.'

'You will do no such thing,' said Mr Muirhead sternly. 'I, your elder, and father in God, forbid you.'

'I must follow my own conscience,' said David. 'I am as convinced of the abominations of the Wood and of the persons that partake in them as that I am sitting with you here in Kirk Aller this August morning.'

'You would add contumacy to your folly,' the other roared. 'You would sow dissension in the Kirk when it is necessary to set a stout front against the Kirk's oppressors.'

'That,' said David firmly, 'is mere carnal policy. In the name of God, whose purity is a flame of fire, would you let gross wickedness go unchecked because it may knock a splinter off the Kirk? I tell you it were better that the Kirk should be broken to dust and trampled underfoot than that it should be made a cloak for sin. I refuse to obey you, Mr Muirhead. Next Sabbath I will make every wall in Woodilee dirl under my accusation.'

The two men were on their feet, David white with wrath, and the face of the other mottled with a like passion. 'You rebellious schismatic,' the minister of Kirk Aller cried, when a knock at the door called both to a sense of the proprieties.

It was the minister's man, who entered with a letter held reverently with the tips of his fingers.

'A despatch, sir, from Embro. Brocht this moment by a mounted messenger, wha wouldna stay for meat, but maun post off down the water.'

When the man retired Mr Muirhead, still standing and puffing heavily, broke the seal. He seemed to have trouble with the contents, for he moved his spectacles, took them off and rubbed them, and then re-read the missive. His eyes stared, his face paled, and then at the last perusal reddened again. He turned to David in a flame of temper.

'The Kirk must suffer for you and your like,' he cried. 'The Lord had prepared an abundant mercy whilk has been denied us because of the hardness of our hearts. Wae's me, wae's me for the puir sheep that have sic faithless shepherds! The auld and the bauld and the leal-hearted must go down because of conceited halflings like you that are Achans in the camp.'

'You speak in riddles, sir,' said David, whose sudden anger had gone at the spectacle of this strange transformation.

'It's a riddle you'll read or you're a month older in letters of blood and fire. . . . Riddle, says you? The riddle is why the Almighty should give our convenanted Kirk sic a back-cast of His hand, and to that you maybe ken the answer. Our deliverance has most lamentably miscarried, and our bondage is waxed more grievous. Get out of my sight, for I must be about the Lord's business, and there will be no rest for Mungo Muirhead this many a day. You have defied me, but wait on and see if you can defy your Creator.'

'You have had bad tidings?'

'Bad, says you? Ay, bad for God's people and God's Kirk, but they're maybe blithe tidings for a schismatic like yourself. You'll maybe get Left-handed Coll and his Irishry to purge your parish and burn the honest folk with whilk you are unworthily blessed. Awa to Montrose, man, for yon's the lad for you!'

'Montrose!'

'Ay, Montrose. Know that yesterday at Kilsyth yon whelp of Satan was permitted to lay low the Covenant's banner, and rout the godly. This word I have gotten is a scribe from Argyll on his road to Berwick, written from a boat at the Queen's Ferry. This very day it's like that Antichrist will be hammering on the gates of Glasgow.'

TWELVE

The Man with the Squint

The sermon which was to indict by name the sinners was not preached to the kirk of Woodilee the next Sabbath.

For the day after his return from Kirk Aller a post reached the manse from the Pleasance of Edinburgh which in an hour set David on his horse riding hard for the capital. There was plague in the city and his father was sick of it. It was the plague in a new form, for death did not come quickly; the patient lay for days in a high fever, afflicted with violent headaches and shiverings and a contraction of muscles and nerves, and then, in nine cases out of ten, passed into a rigor which meant death. There was no eruption on the bodies, and the physicians were at a loss in the matter of treatment. But it was scarcely less deadly than the older visitations, and the dead-bell rang hourly and the dead-cart rumbled day and night on the cobbles.

David found the old man conscious, but very clear that he was near his end. The family doctor had bled him copiously, applied leeches to his head, and brought a horrid regiment of drugs and vomitories. The son pled with his father to receive them patiently. 'God works by means,' he told him, 'as Christ cured the blind man with clay and spittle, and what remedy could be more rude than these?'

'Aye, but it was the Lord that laid them on, Davie,' said the patient, 'and no an auld wife like McGlashan.' So he sent the physician packing, and engaged a new one, a certain young Crosbie from the Monk's Vennel, who had studied in France and had at least the merit of letting a sick man die in peace. Instead of smothering the patient under bedclothes, he kept him lightly covered, ordered the window to be open day and night, and let him drench his system with small ale. It is likely that under any treatment the old man would have died, for he was in his seventy-fourth year and had long been ailing, and the plague only speeded the decay of age. But under the new regimen his last days were less of a martyrdom. His head remained clear and he could speak with his son – chiefly of his mother and his childhood.

David lodged not in the city, but in the village of Liberton, and walked in daily to his father's bedside. He read the Scriptures to him and prayed with him, as his duty demanded, but he felt a certain shyness at inquiring into his father's state towards God. Nor was the old man communicative. 'I've made my peace lang syne,' he said, 'and I read my title clear, so there's no need of death-bed wark for me.' But he was full of anxiety for his son. 'You've chosen a holy calling, Davie lad, and I'm blithe to think you've got a downsetting in our calf-country. Man, there were Sempills in the mill o' the Roodfoot since the days of Robert Bruce. But the ministry in these days is a kittle job, for the preachers are ower crouse, and the Kirk has got its heid ower high. . . . What's come o' this Montrose they crack about? . . . Keep you humble before the Lord, my son, for Heaven's yett is a laigh yett.'

He died peacefully on the third day of September and David had a busy week settling his affairs – the sale of the business and the household effects and the payment of bequests to servants and distant kin. Hour after hour he sat with the lawyers, for there was a considerable estate, and to his surprise he found himself with worldly endowments such as few ministers of the Kirk possessed. There was money at the goldsmith's, and in his lawyer's boxes deeds and sasines and bonds on heritable property, and there would be more to come. His doer, a little old snuffy attorney of the name of Macphail, grew sententious as the business drew to its close. 'You've both the treasure on earth, Mr David, and the treasure in Heaven, and it's a pleasing thought that they's alike well-guided. Anent the latter, moth cannot corrupt, saith the Word, nor thieves break through and steal, and anent the former a moth will no do muckle ill to a wheen teugh sheepskins, and it would be a clever thief that got inside Georgie Gight's strong-room in the Canongate where your bonds are deposited. So you can keep an easy mind, Mr David, while you wrastle for souls in Woodilee.'

Those were strange days both for death in a bed and for conducting business, for the stricken city was the prey of wild fears. Scarcely a traveller entered her infected precincts, but rumour was as busy as the east wind in May. The battle of Kilsyth had worked a revolution in Scotland. Glasgow had surrendered and welcomed the conqueror, with enthusiasm for his person and largesse for his soldiers. The shires and the burghs were falling over each other in their haste to make submission. Edinburgh had been summoned, and a delegation of the town council had gone out beyond Corstorphine to capitulate to the young Master of Napier. The imprisoned Lords went free from the Tolbooth; David saw the sight – pallid men shivering with prison ague; only the Castle still held for the Covenant. Word came that the King had made Montrose Captain-general of all Scotland, and that soon the victorious army would move towards the Border; already, on the haugh of Bothwell by Clyde side, Sir Archibald Primrose had read the royal commission to the troops. A summons had gone out for a Parliament to be held presently in Glasgow – 'for settling religion and peace,' said the proclamation, 'and freeing the oppressed subjects of those insufferable burdens they have groaned under this time begone.'

The ministers who walked the Edinburgh causeway wore gloomy faces. David had a sight of Mr Muirhead, who sternly inquired of him what he did in the city. 'I have come to bury my father,' he replied. 'If he died in the hope and the promise,' was the answer, 'he has gotten a happy deliverance, for the vials of wrath are opened against this miserable land.' It was a phrase repeated like a pass-word by others of his ministerial brethren, and he replied with a becoming gravity, but he could not in his heart feel any great sorrow. For he remembered the face of the groom at Calidon, and he wondered how that face looked as a conqueror. Pride, he was assured, would not be in it. . . . News came that Montrose was at Cranstoun and moving by Fala Water to the Border. For a moment David had a crazy desire to follow him, to be in his presence, for he had a notion that if he could but have speech again with that young man the shadows and perplexities might lighten from his mind.

At last he set off homeward, and under the rowans at Carlops brig read a printed paper which had been circulated in the Edinburgh streets – torn across and cast away by many, but by others cherished and pondered. It was a manifesto of Montrose from the camp at Bothwell, and it set out his purpose. In it were the very words used by the groom that night at Calidon. The nobles had destroyed 'lawful authority and the liberty of the subject,' the Kirk had coerced men into a blind obedience worse than Popery. He took up arms, he said, for pure religion, 'the restoration of that which our first reformers had'; for the King, and the establishment of a central authority: for the plain people and the 'vindication of our nation from the base servitude of subjects.' He confuted the timorous souls 'who can commit nothing to God.' He repudiated the charge of blood-guiltiness, for he had never 'shed the blood of any but of such as were sent forth to shed our blood and to take our lives.' And he concluded by pointing to the miracles that faith had wrought: 'What is done in the land, it may sensibly seem to be our Lord's doing, in making a handful to overthrow multitudes.' The words came to David with a remembered sound, like the echo of a speaking voice. Could this man be the bloody Amalekite of the Kirk's denouncing? On which side, he asked his perplexed soul, did the God of Israel fight, for this man's faith was not less confident than that of the minister of Kirk Aller?

Isobel received him with the reverential gloom which the Scots peasantry wear on an occasion of death.

'So it's a' bye, sir. We got the word from the Embro carrier, but I wasna looking for ye yet awhile, for we heard ye were like to be thrang wi' the lawyer bodies. . . . He just slippit awa, for how could an auld man stand out against yon wanchancy pestilence? It's a gait we maun a' gang, and he would be weel prepared Godward, and at ease in his mind about warldly things, for they tell me he was brawly set up wi' gear. And there's just yoursel' to heir it, Mr David? . . . But shame fa' me to speak o' gear in this sorrowful dispensation, for a faither is a faither though he live ayont the threescore and ten years whilk is our allotted span.'

'He died as he lived, Isobel, a humble but confident Christian. I think he was pleased to know that I was settled in his forebears' countryside.'

'He wad be that, honest man. Fine I mind o' your gudesire, and mony a nievefu' o' meal I gat from him when I was a bairn. But I'm concerned for yoursel', Mr David, and fearfu' lest ye have got a smittal o' the pestilence. Ye're fine and ruddy, but there's may be fever in your veins. Drink off this wersh brew, sir – it was my mither's way to caller the blood – just kirnmilk boiled wi' soorocks.'

David asked concerning the parish.

'Woodilee!' Isobel cried. 'If Embro's a stricken bit, it's nae waur than this parochine. For the last se'en days it's been naething but wars and rumours o' war. Ye'll hae heard o' how Montrose has guidit our auld Sion, and now we've Antichrist himsel' on our waterside. Ay, he's no twenty miles across the hills, campin' with his Edomites somewhere on Yarrow, as welcome as snaw in hairst. The lads and lasses are a' fleyed out o' the sheilin's, for the Yerl o' Douglas – weary fa' him! – and his proud horsemen are drovin' ower frae Clyde like craws in the back-end. We canna move man nor bestial, and folk winna ride the roads except in a pack, and they tell me that Amos Ritchie wi' his auld firelock was sent for to convoy the minister o' Bold to Kirk Aller. The weans daurna keek past the doorstane, and Johnnie Dow winna gang his rounds, and he's been lyin' fou at Lucky Weir's thae three days. There's nae wark done in a' Woodilee, nor like to be done – it's a dowg's life we've gotten, muckle ease and muckle hunger.'

'But the place has suffered no harm?'

'No yet, forbye a wedder o' Richie Smail's that Douglas's dragoons brandered and ate yestreen at the Red Swire. But ony moment a vial may be opened. – What hinders Montrose to come rauvagin' this airt? for if it's meat and drink he's seeking for his sodgers, Woodilee is a bien bit aside yon bare Yarrow hills. Forbye Calidon's no that far, and they tell me that our auld hirplin' laird, wha suld rather be thinkin' o' his latter end, is high in the command o' the ungodly, and him and yon sweerin' Tam Purves will be rampin' like lions in their pride. Hech, sir, our kindly folk are in the het o' the furnace, in whilk they will either be brunt to an ass, or come out purified as fine gowd. . . . But what am I claverin' here for, when ye're wantin' your denner? It's little I hae for ye, for our meal ark is nigh toom, and there's no a kain hen left on the baulks.'

That night David sat long in his study. It was now the sixteenth day of September, and the sultry weather, which had fostered the plague, was sharpening towards autumn. He had returned from his father's death-bed in something of the mood in which he had first entered the manse. The confusion in the State was to him only a far-off rumour; he was not greatly concerned whether Covenant or King was a-top, for he had no assurance as to which had the right on its side. But he longed for peace, that he might be about his proper business, for the charge of Woodilee lay heavy on his soul. The wickedness against which he had raged seemed now to him as pitiful as it was terrible, a cruel seduction of Satan's against which he must contend, not without pity for the seduced. Charity filled him, and with his new tenderness came hope. He could not fail in the struggle before him – God would not permit his little ones to be destroyed.

Had he not forgotten the minister in the crusader? His books caught his eye – he had touched them little during the summer. What had become of that great work, Sempill on Isaiah? He pulled out his manuscript notes and for a little was happy in their contemplation. . . . The day's ride had been long and the sun had been hot. His head nodded, then dropped on his arm, and he fell asleep.

He awoke to a sound below the window. The manse stood at the extreme southern end of the kirkton, beyond the kirk, a long bowshot from the nearest dwelling, which was Robb the bellman's. To the west of it lay the broomy slopes of the Hill of Deer, to the east the glen of the burn and Windyways hill, and to the south the rough meadows through which the road dipped to the Wood. It was a lonely spot, as Isobel often testified, and after nightfall no soul came near it; even a traveller on the highway did not pass within half a mile.

His study window opened on the garden, and the sound seemed to come from someone knocking gently on the back door. David, still confused with sleep, took his candle, and descended the stairs. Isobel had heard nothing – for the muffled sound of her snores came from the press-bed behind the kitchen. . . . Again the soft knocking came, this time with a more insistent sound. In some trepidation David unbolted the door, telling himself that it might be a summons to attend a dying parishioner.

There was little moon and a thick autumn haze covered the ground. Rising out of it, like ships out of the water, were huge figures, and he saw that they were mounted men. One of them sat his horse, and held the other beasts; one was on his feet and supported a third who seemed very weary.

David raised hs candle, and saw the figure of the standing man. The face was dark with sun, but darker under the eyes with fatigue; the dress, once rich and splendid, was both mired and torn; and one hand was wrapped in a blood-stained kerchief.

'Do I speak with the minister of Woodilee?' the man asked, and at the first word David knew him. That voice had been echoing all the year in his chamber of memory.

'I am the minister,' was his reply. 'In what can I serve my Lord Marquis?'

The face relaxed into a smile, which made it for the moment gay in spite of the heavy eyes.

'You have not forgotten me? Nor have I forgotten you, and therefore I come to you in sore need to beg a charity. I do not doubt but you are of the opposite faction, but I know also that you are a faithful minister of Christ, whose custom was to do good to His enemies. Will you give shelter to this wounded comrade of mine, and thereby save the life of one whom you consorted with a year back in Calidon?'

'But this is but a poor manse, my lord. Why do you come here when Calidon is so nigh?'

'Alas! Calidon is no port for me or mine in this storm. Know, sir, that this day my army has been beaten on the Yarrow haughs and utterly scattered. Before morning Leslie's troopers will be knocking at Calidon door. I myself am a fugitive, and there is no safety till I cross the Highland line. But this comrade of mine has a broken leg, besides other hurts, and it is impossible that he should ride further. If he does, he will impede us and we shall be taken. But where can I leave him, for I am in an unfriendly country, and if he is captured it will be the gallows for an honest fellow? I bethought me that you were minister of this parish, and that your heart was not likely to be steeled to common humanity, and a manse is the one place that the pursuit will miss. Will you take him and let him lie hid till the hunt passes? After that he will fend for himself, for he is an old soldier of the German wars.'

'He has done no evil . . .?'

'None save what I have done myself. He has drawn the sword in a brave cause which this day has sorely miscarried. But, sir, it is not of politics I speak, but of charity. For the sake of Christ's mercy, I beseech you not to refuse.'

'It is a heavy charge, my lord, but I cannot say you nay.'

Montrose shifted the burden of the wounded man to David's arm. 'Farewell, Mark,' he whispered. 'The good cause is down but not dead, old friend. You know where to get news of me.' Then he kissed his cheek and gave his hand to David.

'May God bless and reward you, sir. I dare not linger. We will take the third horse with us, for it would be too kenspeckle in

your stable. Think kindly of me, whatever my fate, as I think
tenderly of you, and pray for a lonely man whose feet are set on a
long road.'

The next moment the riders had disappeared in the fog.
David stood in a dream, for he would have given worlds to recall
the speaker. His voice, the sight of his face, had brought back
tenfold the longing to be with him which had haunted him after
the Calidon meeting. The man had been a conqueror and was
now a fugitive, but earthly fortunes had no meaning for such an
one. Those calm eyes would look on triumph and disaster alike
unperturbed.

He was roused by the wounded man going limp in his arms,
and he saw that he had fainted. He carried him up the steep
stairs – Isobel's snoring still making a chorus in the background
– and laid him on the bedstead in the guest-room. The bed was
not made up, and it was clear that he must wake Isobel. As the
man's head dropped on the bolster David turned his candle on
it. The face was grimed and blood-stained, but there was no
mistaking the features: it was the tall trooper with the squint
whom he had once guided to Calidon.

David sought the kitchen and hammered at the door of the
press-bed. The snoring ceased and presently a scared and
muffled voice demanded what was the trouble.

'Get up, woman,' David ordered. 'There's a sick man here
that has need of you.'

Three minutes later Isobel appeared, shawled and night-
capped. 'Keep us, Mr David, is't yoursel' that's seeck?' she
wailed. 'I didna like the look o' ye the day and—'

He cut her short.

'A friend of mine has had a mischance. His leg is broken and
I think there is other trouble. Listen, Isobel. . . . The man is one
of Montrose's soldiers and Montrose's army has suffered defeat.
If he is found here by the pursuing troops, he will die. He is my
friend and I would save him. You and I must nurse him
between us, and no word of his presence must pass these
doors.'

'Mercy on us! A malignant!' the old woman exclaimed.

'And my friend,' said David curtly. 'If I think it consistent with Christian duty to save his life, so well may you. You and I have no quarrel with stricken men. I appeal to the kind heart that is in you and your regard for me, and I do not think I will appeal in vain.'

'Your wull be done,' said Isobel. 'Whaur is the body? See and I'll get blankets and pillows, for the bed hasna been made up this sax months.'

The sight of the figure on the bedspread, his quilted and brocade coat, his light cuirass, his long untanned boots much scratched and frayed, his feathered hat beside him on the floor, caused Isobel to shrink.

'A ramping Edomite,' she said. 'Look at the long hair and the murdering sword, stained nae doot with the bluid of the saints. Your friend, says you, sir? Weel, he's been walkin' ither than Gospel roads, I can see brawly, and gin he hadna been amang the craws he wadna hae been shot. . . . But the puir chield's in a dwam! Haste ye, sir, and help me off wi' thae Babylonish garments, and that westkit o' airn – what for sud folk gang to the smith for cleading and no to a wabster? And stap his swird aneath the bed, for I'm feared to look on't.'

The man half recovered consciousness as they stripped off his coat and cuirass, and when it came to the breeches he groaned aloud. So they left them on him and slit the boot on the broken leg. It was a clean break of the shin, and Isobel, who showed some skill in the business, set the leg, and bound it in firm splints made of the staves of an old cask. Then they searched for further damage and found that he was suffering from little except an extreme fatigue. There was a pike wound in his shoulder, which Isobel bathed and bandaged, and a pistol-ball had been turned by the mail he wore and had left a bruised rib. By the time the grime and blood were washed from his face he had got his senses sufficiently back to find his voice.

'You are the minister?' he asked. 'I am crippled, as you see, sir – an accursed fail-dyke on Minchmoor did it – and you'll not be wanting this kind of merchandise long on your hands. A drink and six hours' sleep will set me up, and I'll make shift to take the road. Let me bide here till the morn's night and you'll be rid of me.'

'You'll not be fit to move for a week. You can sleep here securely. You're in a friend's charge.'

The sick man was an old soldier who took life as it came. After he had drunk a bowl of gruel laced with usquebagh he turned on his side and fell asleep. David and Isobel went down to the kitchen and with the candle between them looked at each other with something like consternation.

'We must burn those clothes,' said David.

'Na, na. I'll make a bundle o' them and hide them in the cupples. It's braw raiment, gin it were cleaned. But, oh, sir, this is a bonny kettle of fish! Who wad hae thocht to see such wark in the manse of Woodilee?'

'It is a work of mercy.'

'There's some wad call it by anither name. There's some wad say it was a turnin' back from the gude fight and a faintin' and a backslidin' on the road. I'd be feared to think what yon thrawn minister o' Bold wad call it, but it wadna be mercy. He'd be for savin' the puir lad as Jael the wife of Heber the Kenite saved Sisera.'

'I will be party to no such wickedness, which would be an offence against human charity as well as against the law of Christ.'

'Ay, charity. I'm blithe to hear ye speak the word, sir.' Isobel's eyes had an inclination to twinkle.

'I must follow the guiding of my own conscience. But I would not constrain you. If the thing offends you, I will even now, before it is light, carry the man to the Greenshiel . . .'

'A bonny gait that wad be. The avenger of blood will be chappin' ony hour at Richie's door and there's nae space at the Greenshiel to hide a mouse. Na, na, I'm no denyin' your duty, Mr David. There never was woman yet, young or auld, that was ill-set to a sodger, forbye yon randy Jael, wha maun hae been an unco trial to her man. And the lad upbye seems a decent body, though he skellies sair wi' his left knee. I'se do your bidding, sir, and I hope it winna be accounted to me for sin.'

'Can we keep him here without anyone knowing of it?'

'Brawly. The folk o' Woodilee are sweir to come near the manse thae days. They're feared o' the glower they micht get from you.'

'But if Leslie's troopers arrive and offer to search—?'

'I'll search them! I'se warrant I'd be doun on them with my ten fingers like a gled on poutry. Isobel Veitch will learn the godless loons to mak' free with the house o' a man o' God. And mind, sir, if onybody speirs, ye maun brazen like a pack-man. Bleeze awa' about the needcessity o' speed in the guid cause and send them on their ways to Clyde, and maybe ye'll be spared the sin o' actual leein'.'

'If need be I will not shrink from the false word, which will be forgiven in the cause of mercy.'

'Fine, sir.' Isobel grinned appreciatively on him; for this confederacy seemed to have ended the estrangement between servant and master. 'There's a man ahint the minister in you, wilk is mair than ye can say for the feck o' the Presbytery.'

'And, meantime, I must be up and doing.'

'Ye'll awa' to your bed and sleep out your sleep. What's the need o' hurry when the body's leg is still to set. As my auld mither used to say, naething suld be done in haste but grippin' a flea. . . . But I'll look out some o' your auld garments, for our friend will hae to cast his braw coat and put on homespun or he wins forth o' Woodilee.'

THIRTEEN

White Magic

The man upstairs slept for a round of the clock and then awoke and clamoured for food. Isobel reported that he was cured of his weakness and that the pike wound in his shoulder was no more than a scratch. 'Forbye his leg, he's as weel as you or me, and he has the hunger o' a cadger's powny. It was an awesome sicht to see him rivin' my bannocks. He's speirin' to see ye, for nae doubt he has muckle on his mind.' The old woman was in the best of tempers, and her wizened face was puckered in a secret smile, for she and her master were now restored to friendship as partners in conspiracy.

David found his guest clad in one of his own bed-gowns, the hue of health once more on his unshaven cheeks. His first request was for a razor and for shears, and when Isobel had shorn his hair and he had got rid of a three-day's beard, it was a head of a notable power and dignity that rested on the pillow. The high-boned, weather-beaten face, the aquiline nose, the long pointed chin were no common trooper's, and the lines about mouth and eyes were like the pages of a book wherein the most casual could read of ripe experience. The brown eyes were dancing and mirthful, and the cast in the left one did not so much mar the expression as make it fantastically bold and daring. Here was one who had lived in strange places and was not used to fear.

'It's a sore burden I've brought on you, Mr Sempill,' he cried, 'and it's you that's the good Samaritan. It was my lord's notion that I should throw myself on your compassion, for it's a queer thing, I own, for a cavalier to be seeking a hiding-place in a manse, though Mark Kerr has had some unco ports in his day. I mind in Silesia – But there's no time for soldiers' tales. You'll be wanting me out of this as soon as I can put foot to ground, and it's blithe I'll be to humour you. My leg is setting brawly, says that auld wife who is my chirurgeon, and in less than a week I'll be fit to go hirpling on my road.'

'That will be to walk into the fire,' said David. 'If Montrose's army is scattered throughout the hills, there will be such a hunt cried as will leave no sheiling unsearched.'

'Just so. I'll not deny that this countryside is unhealthy for folk like me. You'll be well advised to bury or burn the clothes I had on last night, and if you can lend me a pair of grey breeks and an auld coat, I'll depart with a lighter mind.'

'You'll be for the sea and the abroad?'

'No me. It's at the coast that they'll be seeking me, and a wise man that's in trouble will go where he's no expected. I think I'll just bide hereaways. Put me in a frieze jacket and I'll defy Davy Leslie himself to see Mark Kerr, the gentleman-cavalier of Mackays, in the douce landward body that cracks of sheep and black nowt. You'll maybe have me in your congregation, Mr Sempill. I'm thinking of taking a tack of Crossbasket.'

David stared. 'Are you mad?' he asked.

'Not so – only politic, as is the way of us soldiers of the Low Germany. One of my profession must think well into the future if he's to keep his craig unraxed. I've had some such escapado in mind ever since I travelled north a year syne, and I've had a word on the matter with Nicholas Hawkshaw, so when the glee'd auld farmer body from Teviotside seeks the tack of Crossbasket the lawyer folk in Edinburgh will be prepared for him. Nicholas was like me – he kenned fine that our triumph in the North was fairy gold that is braw dollars one day and the next a nieve-full of bracken.'

'Where is the laird of Calidon?'

'By a merciful dispensation we left him sick at Linlithgow, and Nicholas, being an eident soul, had a boat trysted at the Borrowstounness and by this time doubtless will be beating down the Forth on his way to a kinder country. He'll be put to the horn, like many another honest gentleman, and his braw estates may be roupit. Thank the Lord, I have nothing to lose, for I'm a younger son that heired little but a sword.'

'A month ago,' said David, 'Montrose was lord of all Scotland. You tell me that everything has been lost in one battle, and that you and others were confident of its loss. Man, how did he succeed with such a rabble of the half-hearted behind him?'

'I wouldna just call it half-hearted. We won because James Graham is the greatest captain since Gustavus went to God at Lutzen, and because he has a spirit that burns like a pure flame. But he did not ken this land of Scotland as me and Nicholas kenned it. He had a year of miracles, for that happened which was clean beyond all sense and prevision, but miracles have an ugly trick of stopping just when they are sorest needed. . . . A year syne there were three men on Tayside, Montrose and Inchbrakie and me, and that was the King's army. By the mercy of Providence we fell in with Alastair Macdonald on the Atholl braes, and got a kind of muster at our back. . . . There's no Hieland blood in you, Mr Sempill? No? Well, it's a very good kind of blood in its way, but it's like yon Hieland burns, either dry as the causeway or a roaring spate. It's grand in a battle, but mortal uncertain in a campaign, if you follow me – and that James should have held it in leash till he had routed Argyll and Baillie and Hurry and brought the Kirk and Estates to their knees is a proof of a genius for war that Gustavus never bettered. But for conquering Scotland and keeping the conquest fixed – na, na! Hielands will never hold down Lowlands for long, and that Lowland support we reckoned on was but a rotten willow wand. My lord deceived himself, and it was not for me to enlighten him, me that had witnessed so many portents. So we kept our own thoughts – Nicholas and me – and indeed we had half a hope that a faith which had already set the hills louping might perchance remove the muckle mountains. But I tell you, sir, when we marched for the Borders I had a presage of calamity on me as black as a thundercloud.'

'But you had the army that won Kilsyth?'

'Not a third of it. Yonder on Bothwell haughs it melted away like a snow-wreath. Macdonald – he is Sir Alastair now and a Captain-general, and proud of it as an auld gander – must march off with the feck of his Irishry to Argyll to settle some private scores with Clan Diarmid. The Gordons took the dorts – a plague on their thrawn heids – and Aboyne and his horse went off in a tirrivee. James looked for a Lowland rising, for, says he, the poor folk for whom I fight are weary of the tyranny of greedy lairds and presumptuous ministers. If so, they are ower weary to show it. What can be done with lads that grovel before a Kirk that claims the key of Heaven and Hell? . . . If that sounds blasphemy, sir, you'll forgive a broken man that is unlocking his heart and cannot wale his words. . . . Forbye, the Irish were like a millstone round our necks, for what profit was it to plead that Munro used them in Ireland for an honest cause? To the Lowland herds and cotters they were murdering savages, and the man that had them on his side was condemned from the beginning. The sons of Zeruiah were too strong for us.'

'Is it true that they fight barbarously?' David asked.

'So, so. I'll not deny that they're wild folk, but they havena your Kirk's taste for murder in cold blood. There were waur things done in Methven Wood than were done at Aberdeen, and it's like that Davy Leslie is now giving shorter shrift to the poor creatures than ever they gave to the Campbells in Lorne and Lochaber. . . . We'll let that be, for there was never an army that did not accuse its enemies of barbarity, and the mere bruit of it on our side was enough to keep the Lowlands behind steekit doors. There were some of the nobles that we counted on – my Lord Home, and my cousin Roxburghe, and the sly tod Traquair. James was in good heart at their promises, but I mistrusted the gentry and I was most lamentably justified, for when we were on Teviotside, where were my lords but in Leslie's camp? – prisoners, they said – but willing refugees, as I kenned braw and well.'

'And the battle?'

A spasm of pain passed over the other's face.

'It was not, properly speaking, a battle, but more in the nature of a surprise and a rout. We were encamped on Yarrow at the gate of the hills, for the coming of Davy Leslie had altered our plans and we were about to march westward to the Douglas lands. We were deceived by false intelligence – it was Traquair's doing, for which some day he will get my steel in his wame – but I bitterly blame myself that an old soldier of the German wars was so readily outwitted and so remiss in the matter of outposts. . . . In the fog of the morning Davy was on us, and Douglas's plough-lads scattered like peesweeps. There were five hundred of O'Keen's Irish, and fivescore of Ogilvy's horse, and for three hours we held Davy's six thousand. These are odds that are just a wee bit beyond my liking, forbye that we had no meat in our bellies. Brawly they fought, the poor lads, fought as I never saw men fight in the big wars – but what would you have? . . . It's not tale for me to tell, though it will be in mind till my last breath.'

He sighed, and for a moment his face was worn and old.

'Well and on, sir,' he continued. 'The upshot is that the bravest of Scottish hearts is now, by God's grace, somewhere on the road to the Hielands, and the great venture is bye and done with, and here am I, a lamenter, seeking sanctuary of a merciful opponent. If to shelter me does violence to your conscience, sir, say the word and I'll hirple off as soon as the night falls. You've given me bite and sup, like a good Christian, and suffered me to get my sleep, and you've no call to do more for a broken malignant.'

'My conscience is at ease anent succouring the wounded and saving a man's life. And I have no clearness about this quarrel of Montrose and the Kirk, and would therefore give it the go-by. But I will exact the promise that, if you come off safe, you will fight no more in Scotland. In that much I am bound to serve my calling.'

'You shall have the promise. Mark Kerr is for beating his sword into a ploughshare. What says the Word? "His speech shall be of cattle" – though now I come to think of it, that's from

what you gentry call the Apocryphal books and think little of. . . .
I'm one that has no great love for idleness on the broad of his
back. Have you no a book to while away the hours? Anything but
divinity – I've lost conceit of divinity these last months when I've
been doing battle with the divines.'

David furnished his guest with reading which was approved,
and then went forth into Woodilee. The village made holiday,
and every wife was at her doorstep. A batch of troopers were
drinking a tankard at Lucky Weir's, and saluted him as he
passed. The people he met had an air of relief and good temper,
and looked with a friendly eye on the minister, forgetting
apparently the Lammas controversies and the shut kirk, for
he was a representative of the winning cause.

Peter Pennecuik, sitting on a big stone outside the smithy,
was the chief dispenser of tidings. His cheeks were swollen and
his voice faltered with pride.

'What for do ye bide in your tent, Mr Sempill, in this hour of our
deliverance? They tell me that Mr Ebenezer of Bold has mounted
his beast and ridden wi' the horsemen to harry the ungodly's
retreat. Ay, and baith Chasehope and Mirehope have ta'en the
road, for the haill land is fou' o' the wreckage of the wicked, as the
sands o' the Red Sea were strewed wi' the chariots o' Pharaoh. Our
General Leslie is no ane to weaken in the guid cause, for there's
word that his musketeers hae shot the Irish in rows on the Yarrow
haughs, ilk ane aside his howkit grave, and there's orders that
their women and bairns, whilk are now fleein' to the hills, are to be
seized by such as meet wi' them, as daughters of Heth and spawn
of Babylon, and be delivered up to instant judgment. Eh, sir, but
the Lord has been exceeding gracious us-ward, and our griefs are
maist marvellously avenged. . . . Nae doot ye'll be proclaimin' a
solemn fast for praise and prayer.'

David ate his dinner with a perturbed mind, for if the
countryside was being scoured for fugitives on this scale, it
was unlikely that the manse would remain long inviolate. But
Isobel reassured him. 'They wad never daur ripe the house, and
for the lave I can speak them fair in the gate.' In the afternoon

he set out to walk to the Greenshiel, since the road would give him a far-away glimpse of Calidon. Autumn was already chilling the air, and the horizon was a smoky purple, the heather was faded, the bracken yellowing, the rowan trees plumed with scarlet, the corn in the valley already more gold than green. To David, in whose ear was still the gloating voice of Peter Pennecuik, the place seemed to smell of death.

At the Greenshiel he found death in bodily form. On the plot of turf outside the cottage half a dozen troopers stared from their saddles at something that lay on the ground. The men were mostly a little drunk, and had the air of a pack of terriers who have chased a cat and found it at bay – an air that was puzzled, angry, and irresolute. David strode towards them, and they gave place to him, somewhat shamefacedly. On the turf lay a wretched draggle-tailed woman, her clothes almost torn off her back, her hair in elf-locks, her bare feet raw and bloody. Her face was emaciated and of an extreme pallor, her shrunken breast heaved convulsively, and there was blood on her neck. Richie Smail was on his knees attempting to force some milk between her teeth. But her lips shut and unshut with her panting and the milk was spilled. Then her mouth closed in that rigor from which there is no unloosing.

Richie lifted his head and saw the minister.

'She's bye wi't,' he said. 'Puir thing, puir thing! She ran in here like a hunted maukin.' Then to the soldiers: 'Ye had surely little to dae, lads, to mishandle a starvin' lassie.'

There was no sign of compunction on the coarse faces of the troopers.

'An Irish b-bitch,' one hiccoughed. 'What's the steer for a bawbee jo?'

'Tam Porteous kittled her wi' his sword-point,' said another. 'Just in the way o' daffin, ye ken. She let out a skelloch and ran like the wund.' The man put his hands to his sides and guffawed at the memory of it.

He did not laugh long, for David was on him like a tempest. The fuddled troopers heard a denunciation which did something to sober them by chilling their marrow. As men, as soldiers, as Christians, he left them no rag to cover them. 'You that fight in God's cause,' he cried, 'and are worse than brute beasts! Get back to your styes, you swine, and know that for every misdeed the Lord will exact punishment a thousand-fold.' He was carried out of himself in his wrath. 'I see each one of you writhing on a coming field of battle, waiting to change the torments of the flesh for the eternal agonies of Hell. You are the brave ones – your big odds gave you a chance victory over one that for a year hunted you and your like round the compass – and you purge your manhood by murdering frail women.'

It was not a discreet speech, and a sentence or two of it pierced through their befuddlement, but it sent them packing. They were too conscious of the power of a black gown in Leslie's army to dare to outface a minister. David marched homeward with his heart in a storm, to find an anxious Isobel.

'These are dreidfu' days,' she moaned. 'We were telled that Montrose's sodgers were sons of Belial, but if they were waur than yon Leslie's they maun be the black Deil himsel'. Wae's me, bluid is rinnin' like water on Aller side. There's awfu' tales comin' doun from the muirs o' wild riders and deid lasses – ay, and deid bairns – a' the puir clamjamphry that followed the Irish. It canna be richt, sir, to meet ae blood-guiltiness wi' anither and a waur. And yon thrawn ettercap frae Bold ridin' wi' the sodgers and praisin' the Lord when anither waefu' creature perishes! And Chasehope, they tell me – black be his fa' – guidin' the sodgers to the landward buts-and-bens like a dowg after rattons! Catch yon lad frontin' an armed man, but he's like Jehu the son of Nimshi afore defenceless women.'

David asked if anyone had been near the manse.

'That's what fickles me. There's been naebody at the door, but there's been plenty snowkin' round. There's a gey guid watch keepit. And waur than that, there's sodgers in the clachan – ten men and ane they ca' a sairgent at Lucky Weir's. I heard routin' as I gaed by the kirkton, and, judging by the aiths, there's sma'

differ between them that fechts for Montrose and them that
uphauds the Covenant.'

Next day the uneasiness of both increased. The place was
thronged with troopers, among them the men whom David had
denounced at the Greenshiel. It is probable that his hasty words
had been reported, for dark looks followed him as he passed the
ale-house. Moreover, Isobel had news in the village that Leslie's
main forces were even now moving towards Woodilee, and that
the triumphant general himself would lodge in the village.
Where would such lodging be found except in the manse? At
any moment the guest-room and its contents might lie bare to
hostile eyes.

By the afternoon David had come to a decision. The wounded
man must at all costs be moved. But where? Calidon would be as
public as the street, and besides he had heard that a picket had
been stationed there in case its laird came looking for shelter.
. . . The hills were too open and bare. Reiverslaw would be
suspect – in any case its tenant babbled in his cups. . . . Then he
had an inspiration. Why not Melanudrigill, for its repute would
at ordinary times make it the perfect sanctuary? He would be a
bold man, it was true, who sought a lair in its haunted recesses,
but this Mark Kerr did not lack for stoutness of heart. He found
him yawning and extracting indifferent entertainment from a
folio of Thuanus.

Kerr only grinned when he heard of the danger.

'I might have guessed that the place would soon be hotching
with Davy's troops. And maybe I'm to have Davy in bed aside
me? Faith, I fear we wouldna agree, though I'll no deny that the
man has a very respectable gift in war. . . . I must shift, you say,
and indeed that is the truth of it, but hostelries are no that plenty
in this countryside for one like me that's so highly thought of by
his unfriends.'

Melanudrigill was set before him, and he approved.

'The big wood. Tales of it have come down the water, but I've
never paid much attention to clavering auld wives. . . . There's
black witchcraft, you say – you've seen it yourself? I care not a

doit. There's just the one kind of warlock that frichts me, and that's a file of Davy Leslie's men. Find me a bed in a hidy-hole and some means of getting bite and sup till I can fend for myself, and I'll sit snug in Melanudrigill, though every witch coven in Scotland sat girning round me with the Deil playing the bagpipes.'

David was clear that he must be moved that night, but he was far from clear as to how it was to be done. He did not dare to take any other into the secret, not even Reiverslaw or Amos Ritchie, for hatred of Montrose was universal among the Lowland folk. He and Isobel might make shift to get him to the Wood, for Isobel was a muscular old woman, but there was much to do besides that – a bed to be found, food transported, some plan made for a daily visit. There was no help to be found in Woodilee.

And then he remembered Katrine Yester.

For a long time he would not admit the thought. He would not have the girl enter a place of such defilements. The notion sickened him and he put it angrily from him. . . . But he found that a new idea was growing in his mind. The Wood had been a nursery of evil, but might it not be purified and its sorceries annulled if it were used for an honest purpose? The thought of Mark Kerr, with his hard wholesome face and his mirthful eye, eating and sleeping in what had been consecrated to midnight infamies, seemed to strip from the place its malign *aura*. . . . To his surprise, when he thought of Mark in the wood, he found that he could think of Katrine there also, without a conscious-ness of sacrilege. The man was her uncle's comrade-in-arms – he was of the cause to which she herself was vowed – she was a woman and merciful – she was his only refuge. . . . Before the dusk fell he was on the road to Calidon.

He had expected to find a house garrisoned and dragooned, and had invented an errand of ministerial duty to explain his presence. He found instead a normal Calidon – the evening bustle about the gates, an open door, and Katrine herself taking the air in the pleasance beside the dovecot. She came towards him with bright inquiring eyes.

'You have soldiers here?' he asked breathlessly.

She nodded to a corner of the house, which had been the shell of the old peel tower.

'They are there – three of them – since last night. They arrived drunk – with two wretched women tied to their stirrups. . . . We were most courteous to them, and they were not courteous to us. So Jock Dodds wiled them into the place we call the Howlet's Nest and gave them usquebagh and strong ale till they dropped on the floor. They are prisoners and woke up an hour ago, but they may roar long and loud before a cheep is heard outside the Howlet's Nest, and the door is stout enough to defy an army.'

'But Leslie himself will be here. Other soldiers will come, and how will you explain your prisoners?'

The girl laughed merrily. 'Trust Aunt Grizel. Two lone women – violent and drunken banditti – locking them up the only way – and then a spate of texts and a fine passage about soldiers of the good cause setting an ensample. I will wager my best hawk that Aunt Grizel will talk down General Leslie and every minister in his train. . . . The women are safe in the garret, less hurt than frightened. The poor things talk only the Erse, and there's none about the town to crack with them.'

He told her of the midnight visit to the manse and the lame man left on his hands.

'You saw him? she whispered. ''You saw the Lord Marquis. How did he look? Was he very weary and sorrowful?''

'He was weary enough, but you face does not show sorrow. There's an ardour in it that burns up all weakness. He would continue to hope manfully though his neck were on the block.'

'Indeed that is true, and that is why I will not despair. When I heard the news of disaster I did not shed a single tear. . . . Whom did he leave behind?'

'The tall man – Mark Kerr is his name – who was in this house of yours a year back. Him that has a cast in his eye.'

'But that is the Lord Marquis's most familiar friend,' she cried. 'The occasion must be desperate which parts them.'

'The occasion grows more desperate,' he said, and told her of the need for instant removal. When he spoke of the Wood she showed no surprise.

'Where else so secret?' she said.

'Dare you go into it?' he asked. 'For unless I have your help the business is like to prove too hard for me. I will confess that it sticks in my throat to stir one step myself into the gloom of the pines, when I ken what has been transacted there, and it sticks sorer to have you in that unholy place. But if this Kerr is to be saved, there's need of us both. The man will have to be fed, and that would be done more easily from Calidon than from the manse.'

'Why, so it must be. I have been pining for some stirring task and here it is to my hand. I will be your fellow-labourer, Mr David, and we begin this very night. For a mercy there is a small moon. . . . No, Aunt Grizel shall not hear of it. I have the keys and can leave and enter the house as I choose. When the dusk comes and our guests in the Howlet's Nest are quiet from hoarseness, I will bid Jock Dodds carry certain plenishing to Paradise.'

A little before midnight, when even the clamour of Lucky Weir's was still, three figures stole from the manse, after David by many reconnaissances had assured himself that the coast was clear. Montrose's erstwhile captain was dressed like a small farmer, in David's breeches and a coat that had once belonged to Isobel's goodman. He had a rude crutch with which he managed to keep up a good pace, having learnt the art, he said, during an escape from a patrol of Wallenstein's, which for greater security had manacled the prisoners in pairs leg to leg. Isobel prospected the road before him like a faithful dog, while David steadied him with his arm. In such fashion they crossed the Hill of Deer, and in a darkness lit only by the stars came to the glade called Paradise. There they found awaiting them a glimmering girl, at the sight of whom Isobel's fears broke loose, for she prayed in words not sanctioned by any kirk, and her prayer was for mercy from the Good Folk.

Kerr made an attempt at a bow. 'Mistress Yester, it is not the first time I have come for succour to women of your house. They say I must take to the shaws like Robin Hood, but the wildwood will be a palace if you are among its visitors.'

'Yester,' Isobel muttered to herself. 'The young leddy o' Calidon! Wha wad have thocht that the minister was acquaint there? Certes, she's the bonny ane,' and she bobbed curtsies.

Katrine was the general. 'These bundles are bedding and food. Up with them, sir, and I will guide Captain Kerr. I have also brought a covered lantern, which will light us through the pines better than your candle, Mr David. La, this is a merry venture.'

The sense of company, the presence of Katrine and the soldier, the nature of the errand, above all the preposterous figure of Isobel, whose terrors of the Wood were scarcely outweighed by her loyalty to her master and her curiosity about the girl, took from the occasion for David all sense of awe, and even endowed it with a spice of fun and holiday. The mood lasted till they had crossed the boundary glen and entered the pines; it endured even when, feeling their way along the foot of the low cliffs, they looked downward and saw by the lantern light an eery white stone in a dim glade. The girl guided them to a dry hollow where an arch of rock made a kind of roof and where a yard off a spring bubbled among the stones. It was she and not Isobel who made a couch of branches and fir boughs on which she laid the deerskins and plaids she had brought. It was she and not David who gathered dry sticks against the morning fire and saw that Kerr had flint and steel and tinder. It was she, too, who made a larder of a shelf in the rock, where she stored the food, and fixed certain hours of the day for further provisioning, and enjoined a variation of routes to prevent suspicion. It was she finally who presented Kerr with a pistol, shot, and powder – belonging, it is to be feared, to one of the imprisoned troopers – and who saw him to bed like a nurse with a child.

'I'm as snug here as a winter badger,' said Kerr contentedly. 'I lack nought but a pipe of tobacco, and that I must whistle for,

seeing that I left my spleuchan at Philiphaugh. . . . Mistress,
you've the knack of an old campaigner. You might have been at
the wars.'

'The men of my race have always been at the wars and the
women have always dreamed of them,' she said, and on his
forehead she kissed him good night.

David Leslie came to Woodilee in the morning, but did not halt,
pushing on to Lanark in the afternoon. His army was in less of a
hurry, and three troop-captains made their beds in the manse,
while the minister slept on his study floor. They were civil enough,
cadets of small houses in Fife, who had had their training to arms
abroad, and cared as little for the cause they fought for as any
mercenary of Tilly's. Within two days the neighbourhood was
clear of soldiery, save for the garrisons left as earth-stoppers at
houses like Calidon, which might be the refuge of malignants.

For a week Mark Kerr lay in the recesses of Melanudrigill, and
for David the days passed like a seraphic vision. Every night
after the darkening he met Katrine in Paradise and the two
carried to the refugee his daily provender – eggs and milk, ale
from the Calidon buttery, cakes which were Mistress Grizel's,
cheese which was Isobel's. For David the spell of the Wood had
gone. He looked on it now as a man does at his familiar
bedroom when he wakes from a nightmare, unable to recon-
struct the scene of his terrors. His crusading fury, too, had
sensibly abated, for part of his wrath against witchcraft had been
due to his own awe of the Wood and his disgust at such awe.
Now the place was a shelter for a friend, and a meeting-ground
with one he loved, and the cloud which had weighed on him
since he first saw it from the Hill of Deer gave place to clear sky.
Men might frequent Melanudrigill for hideous purposes, but
the place itself was innocent, and he wondered with shame how
he came ever to think that honest wood and water and stone
could have intrinsic evil.

Nightly, in the light mists of the late September, when pine
trees stood up out of vapour like mountains, and the smell of

woodland ripeness was not yet tinged with decay, David and
Katrine threaded the aisles and clambered among the long
bracken, till a pinpoint of light showed from beside a rock
and was presently revealed as Kerr's bivouac. They would sit late
with him, listening to his tales and giving him the news of the
glens, while owls hooted in the boughs and from the higher
levels came the faint crying of curlews. There was much
business to be done between Mark and Calidon – business
of Nicholas Hawkshaw's, who had been duly put to the horn,
and over whose goods, by the intrigues of Mistress Grizel, a
friendly curator had been appointed, and business of his own
anent the tack of Crossbasket – and Katrine carried daily
messages by letter and by word of mouth. When his leg was
healed there was a certain polish to be given to his appearance,
and the ladies of Calidon were busy with their needles. When he
left his lair at last it was just before dawn – on foot, with a blue
coat instead of the hodden grey of Isobel's goodman, and four
miles on the Edinburgh road Jock Dodds from Calidon waited
with a horse for him.

David would fain have had the leg prove troublesome that the
time of hiding in the Wood might be prolonged, for that season
passed for him with the speed of a too happy dream. To be with
Katrine was at all times bliss, but to be her partner on these dark
journeys and in these midnight conclaves was a rapture of
happiness. If he had lost his awe of the Wood, he had lost also
the sense that in letting his heart dwell on the girl he was falling
away from duty. The standards of the Kirk meant the less to him
since he was in declared controversy with its representatives,
and a succourer by stealth of its enemies. His canons of conduct
were dissolving, and in their confusion he was willing to
surrender himself to more ancient instincts. The minister
was being forgotten in the man and the lover.

The lover – though no word of love was spoken between the
two. They were comrades only, truant children, boy and girl on a
Saturday holiday. It was a close companionship, yet as unem-
barrassed as that of sister and brother. In her presence David

caught her mood, and laughed with it, but when absent from her he was in a passion of worship. The slim green-gowned figure danced through his waking hours and haunted his dreams. He made no plans, forecast no future; he was in that happy first stage of love which is content to live with a horizon bounded by the next meeting.

In such a frame of mind he may have grown careless, for he did not see what Isobel saw. His housekeeper, brisk with the consciousness of a partnership with her master in things unlawful and perilous, and under the glamour of Katrine's gentrice and beauty, was as unquiet as a hen with a brood of young ducks on the pond's edge. She clucked and fussed, and waited for David's return in an anxious tempest. 'There's queer ongaein's in this bit,' she told him. 'When I hearken in the sma' hours I hear feet trailin' as saft as a tod's, and whiles a hoast or a gant which never cam frae a tod's mouth. And yestreen when ye set out, sir, there was something slipped atween the birks and the wa' and followed. I wish it mayna be your deid wraith.' He pooh-poohed her fears, but on the last night, when he parted from Katrine in Paradise, and according to his custom watched her figure as, faint in the moonlight, it crossed a field of bracken above Rood, he saw something move parallel to her in the fern. On his way home, too, as he passed the kirkton road in the first light, there was a rustling among the elders and a divot fell mysteriously from the turf dyke.

FOURTEEN

The Counterblast

He dreamed that night that he was being spied upon, and next day – with no more meetings with Katrine before him to fire his fancy – his cold reason justified the fear. The conviction was presently confirmed by a discovery of Isobel's. Mark Kerr's cast clothes had been hidden at first in the gloom of the rafters in David's camceiled bedroom, but the coming of Leslie's troops compelled her to change its place of disposal to the stable, where in the space between the wall and the thatch she bestowed them, wrapped stoutly in sacking. She kept an eye on the bundle, and one morning it had disappeared. More, it had clearly been stolen and hurriedly opened, for the sacking and a tarry rope which bound it were found among the nettles beyond the kirkyard wall. Compromising goods indeed to come forth of a minister's house!

That same day Isobel returned from a visit to her cousin with a queer tale.

'Something's gotten out, sir. The wives in the kirkton are clatterin' like daws. "What's this they tell me, gossip," says one, "about Babylonish garments found in the manse?" "Faith, I kenna," says I. "They're nane o' my findin', but wi' roarin' sodgers quartered in ilka chamber ye'll no surprise me if some unco gear were left behind." "But it's nae honest gear o' Davy Leslie's lads," she says, "but the laced coats and plumit hats o' the malignants. And there's a report that ithers hae sleepit in the manse this past se'nnight than our ain Covenant sodgers." "Wha tell't ye that, my wumman," I says, "was a black leear, and a thief forbye. I'd like brawly to ken wha has been snowkin' round our doors and carryin' awa leein' tales and maybe some o'

our plenishin'. Tell me the names, and man or wumman, I'll
hae my fingers at their lugs." It was Jean of the Chasehope that
spoke to me, and she got mair frae me than she expeckit. There
wasna ane o' her auld misdaein's I didna fling in her teeth.'

The name of the woman disquieted David and he asked what
she had answered.

'Her! She took my flytin' wi' downcast een, and that angered
me sae that I had muckle ado to keep my hands frae her face. Syne
she says, quiet-like, "Ye needna get in a steer, Isobel Veitch. If Mr
Sempill's an honest man, he'll get his chance to redd up the
fama." *Fama*, says she, whatever yon may mean – there's a reek o'
Chasehope about the word. And she went on wi' her saft een and
her mim mou'. – "There's waur nor that, Isobel wumman," she
says. "Our minister, that's sae fierce against warlocks, has been
walkin' a queer gait. There's them that hae seen him in the Wud,
and wha do you think he met wi' there? It's no a name that I daur
speak, but folk hae brunt for less than sic a randyvoo." Ye may
fancy, sir, what a stound I got, but I just spoke the kimmer civil
and speired for mair. She wasna laith to tell. "There's them," says
she, "that saw the green gown o' the Queen of Elfhame, and the
mune shinin' through her hair, and saw her gie a kiss to the
minister." Ye never kissed the leddy, sir?'

'God forbid,' cried David, startled as if at an impiety.

'I thocht ye werena just as far forrit as that. . . . Weel, that's
the tale they've gotten, and may it stick in their thrapples! I'm no
feared for their blethers about fairies, but we'll need some
stench lees to get the sodger's claes blawn over. I wish I kenned
wha was the thief. I'll threip that they were left by Leslie's folk
and that ye kenned nocht about them.'

'For me,' said David, 'I shall tell the plain truth, save in the
mentioning of names. I command you, Isobel, to do likewise.
The man is by now out of danger, and a falsehood, which may
be pardoned if it is to save another, is black sin if used by a
coward to save himself.'

Isobel looked at him uneasily. 'There will be an awfu' speak in
the parish, sir. Bethink ye, is it wise to gie such a handle to them

that wad bring ye doun? . . . But I see your mind is made up and
nae words o' mine will turn ye. We maun hope that the question
will never be speired, and I daur ony man or wumman in the
place to get sae far wi *me* as the speirin'.'

During David's absence in Edinburgh Mr Fordyce, by the
command of the Presbytery, had preached in the afternoon in
the Woodilee kirk – to but scanty audiences, for the news of
Montrose's advance had inclined the people to keep inside their
doors. On the first Sabbath after his return, when there were
still troops in the place, the pulpit had been occupied by one of
Leslie's chaplains, a stalwart member of the Church militant,
who hailed from the Mearns and whose speech was conse-
quently understood with difficulty in the Border parish. But on
the next, when Mark Kerr had gone from his refuge in the
Wood, David changed his mind, and himself filled the pulpit. At
the news a great congregation assembled, for in that joyous day
of delivery it was believed that the sins of the parish would be
left on one side, and that the service, as in the other kirks in the
land, would be one of thanksgiving and exultation. To the
surprise of most of his hearers – and to the satisfaction of
the suspicious – there was no word of the recent crowning
mercies, save a perfunctory mention in the opening prayer.

David, as befitted one who had just buried his father, discoursed on death. He was in a mood which puzzled himself, for
gentleness seemed to have come upon him and driven out his
jealous wrath. He had seen the righteous die, the man who had
begot him, the last near kin he possessed, and memories of
childhood and something of the wistfulness of the child had
flooded in on his soul. He had seen, too, the downfall of human
pride, the descent of greatness to dust, and yet in that dust a
more compelling greatness. Above all, his love for Katrine had
mellowed and lit the world for him; it had revealed depths of joy
and beauty which he had never known, but the beauty and joy
were solemn things, and of a terrible fragility. He felt anew the
dependence of all things upon God and the need of walking
humbly in His sight. So he preached not like an Old Testament

prophet confident in his cause and eager to gather the spoil, but as one who saw from a high mountain the littleness of life against the vast background of eternity. He spoke of the futility of mortal hopes, the fallibility of man, the certainty of death. In a passion of tenderness he pled for charity and holiness as the only candles to light the short dark day of life – candles which, lit by a heavenly hand, would some day wax into the bright ever-lasting day of the New Jerusalem.

There were those among his hearers who were moved by his words, but to most they were meaningless and to many they were an offence. Peter Pennecuik was darkly critical. 'The man is unsound as a peat,' he declared. 'Whaur's the iron o' doctrine and the fire o' judgment in sic a bairnly screed? There's an ill sough there, sirs – he's ower fond o' warks and the rags o' our ain righteousness. Worthy Mr Proudfoot will be garrin' the stour fly the day denouncin' the Laodiceans that wad be luke-warm in cuttin' off the horns o' the wicked. Is there ony such goodly zeal in our man? Whaur's the denunciation o' the sins o' Montrose and his covenant-breakers? It seems that he's mair convinced o' his ain sins.'

'He has maybe cause,' Chasehope observed drily.

It had been David's intention to visit the manse of Kirk Aller and obtain the answer of the Presbytery's moderator to the charges he had formulated. This was a duty which could not be shirked, since he had put his hand to it, but at the moment the fire of battle had died in him and he had no zest in the task. He found himself longing to take Isobel's view and believe that his senses had played him false, that the events of the Beltane and Lammas nights were no more than illu-sions. So he had delayed journeying to Kirk Aller, hoping that his mood would change and that that which was now a cold duty would revive as a burning mission. . . . Suddenly a post brought him a summons from Mr Muirhead to wait upon him without delay.

He rode down the riverside in a day of October glooms and shadows. Sometimes a wall of haze would drop from the hills so

that the water ran wan as in the ballads, and the withering fern
and blanching heath had the tints of December. Then a light
wind would furl the shrouded sky into fantastic towers and
battlements, through long corridors of which the blue heavens
would shine like April at an infinite distance, and the bald
mountain-tops, lit by sun-gleams, would be revealed. When he
rode over the crook-backed bridge of Aller past the burgh
gallows he saw that the doomster had been busy at his work.
Three ragged scarecrows hung in chains, the flesh already gone
from their limbs, and a covey of obscene birds rose at his
approach. Stragglers of Montrose, he guessed, and he wondered
how many gallows-hills in Scotland showed the same grim
harvest. The thought, and the fantastic October weather, deepened the gloom which all morning had been growing on him.

He found a new man in the minister's chair. The victory of
his cause seemed to have expanded Mr Muirhead's person, so
that he loomed across the oaken table like a judge in his robes.
Pride pursed his lips and authority sat on his forehead. Gone
were the airs of tolerant good-humour, the assumption of
meekness, the homeliness which had a greeting and a joke
for all. This man sat in the seats of the mighty and shared in the
burden of government, and his brow was heavy with the weight
of it. He met David with a cold inquisitorial eye, and greeted
him with a formal civility.

'I sent for you, Mr Sempill,' he said, 'anent the charge which
you have set out in these papers and on which you have already
conferred with me. There has been no meeting of Presbytery,
owing to the disturbances in public affairs, but I have shown the
papers to certain of my brethren and obtained their mind on
them. I have likewise had the privilege of the counsel of the
godly laird of Wariston, who, as you no doubt ken, is learned
alike in the law of God and the law of man. I have therefore
taken it upon myself to convey to you our decision, whilk you
may take to be the decision of the courts of the Kirk, and that
decision is that there is no substance in your case. You are upset
on the relevancy, sir. There is nothing here,' and he tapped the

papers, 'which would warrant me in occupying the time of folk who have many greater matters in hand.'

'I did not ask for a judgment, but for an inquiry, and that I must continue to demand.'

'Ay, but you must first show a *prima facie* case, and that you have failed to do. You have brought grievous charges against one noted servant of God, and sundry women, of whom it can at least be said that they bear a good repute. Your evidence – well, what is your evidence? You say that you yourself have seen this and heard that, but you are a tainted witness – a matter to which I shall presently revert. . . . You have the man Andrew Shillinglaw in Reiverslaw, who, in the bit of precognition with which you have furnished me, tells a daft tale of dressing himself up like a mountebank, visiting the wood of Melanudrigill, and sharing in certain unlawful doings. I ask you, sir, what credence can be given to such evidence? *Imprimis*, he was himself engaged in wrong-doing, and so is justly suspect. *Item*, he is a notorious wine-bibber, and when the maut is in, the wits are out. Whatna condition was he in to observe justly in the mirk of the night in the Black Wood, where by his own account he was capering like a puddock and was all the time in a grue of terror? He claims on that occasion to have laid a trap for the accused and to have informed two men of undoubted Christian conversation of his purpose, and he claims that on the next day the same witnesses at the toun of Chasehope were cognisant of the success of his trap. As I live by bread and by the hope of salvation, this is the daftest tale that ever came to my ears. A smell of burning duds, and a missing hen! The veriest cateran that ever reived in the Hielands would be assoilzied on such a plea. There is not evidence here to hang a messan dog. Away with you, man, and let's hear no more of what I can only judge to have been a drunken cantrip.'

'I demand that Ephraim Caird be interrogated by the Presbytery and confronted with me and my witnesses.'

'You must first prove a *prima facie* case, as I say, for otherwise honest men might lose time and siller in being set to answer malicious libels. That is the law of Scotland, sir, and it is the law of every Christian land, and you have lamentably failed in that prior duty.'

'There is my own evidence – the evidence of an eye-witness. You may account for Reiverslaw, but you have still to account for me.'

'Just so.' A grim humour seemed to lurk at the corner of Mr Muirhead's mouth. 'We have to account for you, Mr Sempill, and it seems it will be a sore business. For I have here' – he tapped a paper – 'another dittay in which you yourself are named. It is painful for me even to give ear to accusations against a brother on whose head my own hands have been laid in holy ordination. But I have my solemn duty to perform and must consider the complaints of a kirk session against a minister as carefully and prayerfully as those of a minister against a kirk session.'

The effect on David was of a sudden clearing of the air and a bracing of nerve. This was, then, to be no one-sided war, for his enemies had declared themselves, and met attack by counter-attack. He smiled at the portentous solemnity of Mr Muirhead's face.

'I can guess one of the names appended to the charge,' he said. 'It is that of Chasehope.'

Mr Muirhead turned over the paper. 'Ephraim Caird is there, and others no less weighty. There is Peter Pennecuik . . . and Alexander Sprot in Mirehope . . . and Thomas Spotswood in the mill of Woodilee. If godly elders are constrained to delate him who has been set over them in spiritual affairs, it's scarcely a thing to be met with a smirk and a grin.'

'I am waiting to hear the charge.'

'It is twofold. The complainants allege that you have had trokings with the Wood and the evil of the Wood – and indeed on your own confession we know that you have frequented it when decent folk were in their beds. There are witnesses to depone to following you to the edge of the thing, as you made your way stealthily at dead of night. On what errand, Mr Sempill? And in what company?'

'That is what I would like fine to know,' said David.

'You were seen to meet a woman. They were simple folk who saw you and not free from superstition, so they jumped to the conclusion that the woman was no mortal but the Queen of the Fairies. That's as it may be. You and me are not bairns to believe in fays and bogles. But the fact that emerges is that you were in the Wood at night, not once but many times, and that you were seen in a woman's company. That is a fine report on a minister of God, and it will want some redding up, Mr Sempill.'

'My movements were wholly innocent, and can be simply explained,' said David. But the charge maddened him, he blushed deep, and he had much ado to keep his tongue from stammering. He wrestled with a pagan desire to buffet Mr Muirhead violently in his large authoritative face.

'But can you explain *this*?' the latter cried, for he was not unconscious of David's confusion. 'There is a second charge and its gravamen is the heavier, seeing that it alleges an offence both against the will of God and the governance of this land. On the 26th day of the month of September in this year of grace there was found in the appurtenances of the manse of Woodilee – to wit in the baulks of the stable atween the thatch and the wall – a bundle of garments, including a laced coat such as is worn by malignants, and sundry other habiliments strange to the countryside but well kenned in the array of caterans whereof Montrose was the late leader. It is argued therefore that shelter was given in the manse to a fugitive, and that a minister of the Kirk connived at the escape from justice of one of the Kirk's oppressors. What say to that, sir?'

'I say that it is true.'

David was not prepared for the consternation in the other's face. Mr Muirhead sat erect in his chair, his head was poked forward from between his shoulders like that of a tortoise from its shell, colour surged over cheeks and forehead and his bald crown, and his voice, when he found utterance, was of an unnatural smallness. His careful speech broke down into country dialect.

'Ye admit it! God peety you, ye do not blench to admit this awful sin! Have ye no shame, man, that ye sit there snug and canty and confess to a treason against Christ and His Kirk.'

There was more in the man's face than anger and incredulous horror; there was pity, regret, a sense of an unspeakable sacrilege done to all that he held most dear. David saw that the minister of Kirk Aller, though he might have little love for himself, would have given much had this confession been unsaid – that he felt that shame had been cast upon his calling and even upon his own self-respect. So he answered gently:

'A wounded man came to my door. I fed him and nursed him, and he is now, I trust, in health and safety. I would do the same thing again for any distressed mortal.'

Mr Muirhead's eyes goggled.

'Have you no notion – have you no glimmering of what you have done? I speak patiently, for I'm driven to think you're not right in the mind. You have loosed on the world a malefactor, a slayer and despoiler of God's people.'

'I have his word that he will not again take up arms in Scotland. He was a soldier of the great Gustavus.'

'What's the word of a malignant to lippen to? Man, you're easy begowked. When the Lord's command anent our enemy is Smite and spare not, you, an ordained minister, connive at his escape. . . . Ay, and there's more to it. I have news that you molested Leslie's troops in their pursuit of a light woman that followed Montrose's camp, and that you took the name of the Lord in vain in interdicting them from their manifest duty. Have you not heard that at the brig of Linlithgow the wantons were drowned in scores by the command of the worthy General, whilk was a notable warning to sinners and an encouragement to God's people? Are there not Commissions of the Estates and of the Kirk appointed to judge the captured malefactors in Edinburgh and St Andrews, and gallows set on every burgh knowe besouth of Forth? And you dare help to cheat the wuddy of one who was no doubt the blackest of them? There's no a presbytery in the land but has sent in a memorial to encourage those in authority in their righteous work. For shame, man! Even in your own parish you have Chasehope lending a hand and riding the hills like a moss-trooper – the very man you would delate for sin.'

'I obey God's word and my own conscience. I can imagine no blacker sin than cruelty to the defenceless.'

'God's word!' cried Mr Muirhead. 'You've been lamentably ill-instructed. What did Joshua to the people of Jericho, but utterly destroy them, both man and woman, young and old? What did Gideon to the kings Zeba and Zalmunna? What was the command of the Lord to Saul when he went out against Agag king of the Amalekites but to slay both man and woman, infant and suckling, and when Saul would have saved Agag, what said Samuel to him? – "Rebellion is as the sin of witchcraft and stubbornness is as iniquity and idolatry." Your eyes are full of fatness if you canna see the Lord's will. And your conscience! You would set up your own fallible judgment against God's plain command and the resolved opinion of the haill Kirk.'

'I am a minister of Christ first and of the Kirk second. If the Kirk forgets its Master's teaching, we part company.'

'And what's that teaching, prithee?'

'To have mercy and not sacrifice.'

The minister of Kirk Aller closed his eyes as if in pain.

'You're deep deep in the mire of your carnal conceits,' he said. 'I thought you were only wayward and mistaken, but I see you're firm on the rock of your impenitence. Troth, Mr Ebenezer of Bold was in the right – you've heresy in you as well as recalcitrance. This is Presbytery business, sir – ay, and maybe matter for the General Assembly. I would be a faithless guardian of the sheepfold if I didna probe it to its bottom. This complaint must go forward. – Meantime, till the Presbytery has adjudged it, I forbid you to conduct the ordinances in the kirk of Woodilee. I will appoint some worthier person, lest the pure gospel milk on your lips be turned to poison.'

'I refuse to obey you,' said David, 'for you have no power to command. I stand on my rights to continue my ministrations till such time as the lawful authority sets me aside. Meantime I require that my charge against Chasehope go to the Presbytery equally with his charge against me.'

Mr Muirhead was on his feet, with the famous glower on his face which had aforetime awed timid brethren. It did not awe David, who gave him back stare for stare with a resolution to which he was little accustomed. Indeed the vigorous youth of his antagonist and something in the set jaw made the elder man pause. He shuffled off as if to end the interview, and David strode from the house with unseeing eyes and a burning heart.

All the way home his head was filled with a confusion of angry thoughts. He saw himself caught in toils at once absurd and perilous. He could imagine the prejudice which his shelter-ing of the fugitive would raise against him; he saw his indict-ment of Chasehope nullified by this legend of his own visits to the Wood; above all the bringing in of Katrine made him clench his hands with a sense of furious sacrilege. In that moment he seemed to himself like a child without friends battering at a wall as broad as the earth and as high as the heavens. . . . But the consequent feeling was not of hopelessness but of a tight-lipped rage. He longed to be in a world where blows could be struck swift and clean, and where hazards were tangible things like steel and powder. Not for the first time in his life he wished that he had been a soldier. He was striving against folly and ignorance, blind prejudice, false conventions, narrow cove-nants. How much better to be fighting with armed men?

Isobel met him at the manse door with a portentous face.

'There's a new man come to Crossbasket,' she announced. 'His plenishin' cam up the water this mornin' – four horseloads – and the drovers are bringin' his sheep and kye. I saw the body himsel' in the kirkton an hour syne. He's the rale down-the-water fairmer breed, verra weel set up and no that auld, and he wears a maud like a herd. But Mr David, sir,' – she lowered her voice – 'guess ye wha he is? I couldna be mistook, and when he cried me guid day I saw brawly that he kenned me and kenned that I kenned him. He ca's himsel' Mark Riddel, but it's the glee'd sodger man that lay in our best bed.'

FIFTEEN

Hallowmass

Ill news travels fast, and by noon next day word of the complaint against their minister, of Mr Muirhead's suspension of him from the pulpit, and of David's defiance was in the mouth of every parishioner in Woodilee. David was aware of curious eyes following him as he went about the place, and of a new constraint on the part of most of his Kirk Session. Peter Pennecuik fled his approach and could be seen hobbling into the nearest kail-yard, while Mirehope, when he met him, gave him greeting with averted face. But he noted, too, a certain sympathy in others. Women, who had formerly avoided him, had now a friendly word, especially the young ones, and Alison Geddie – whose name had appeared in his charge – was overheard, as he passed, to comment in her pea-hen voice to her gossip: 'Peety for sae wise-like a lad, and him aye with the kind word and the open hand to puir folk.'

Isobel, whose face was now always heavy with unspoken news, he kept at a distance, for in these days he was trying to make peace with his soul. By day and by night, on the hills and in his closet, he examined himself to find in his conscience cause of offence. He went over every step in his past course and could discover no other way than that he had followed. He could not see matter for blame in an act of common charity, though Old Testament precedents might be quoted against it; nor could he blame himself for his war against the things of the Wood. If he read his duty more by the dispensation of Christ than of Moses, it was Christ whom he had been ordained to preach. . . .
Of Katrine he scarcely suffered himself to think. She was a thing too fine and gracious to be touched with such doleful cares. Yet

it was the thought of her which kept youth alive in him, and in his dreariest moments gave him a lift of the heart. When he looked down from the Hill of Deer on the dark shroud of Melanudrigill and beside it the shaws of birch and hazel which stretched towards Calidon, he saw his strife as a thing natural and predestined, and he himself as only a puppet in the grip of primordial powers. The thought gave him the confidence which springs from humility.

On the Sabbath he preached from a text in Ecclesiastes: 'So I returned, and considered all the oppressions that are done under the sun: and behold the tears of such as were oppressed, and they had no comforter; and on the side of their oppressors there was power; but they had no comforter.' His hearers looked no doubt for some topical word, but they did not find it; few realised the meaning of a discourse which David preached rather to himself than to others. It was a confession of faith, a plea for personal religion, and an anathema against shibbo- leths and formulas which did not dwell in the heart. So long as religion is a pawn in a game of politics – the argument ran – so long will there be oppressors and oppressed, with truth the perquisite of neither side, and therefore comfort to none. . . . The congregation was notably reduced, for the five elders and their families were absent. But there was one new figure who sat modestly in the back parts of the kirk. It was that of a man of middle age, dressed like the other farmers in homespun, but holding himself with a spruceness rare in a place where men and women were soon bowed in the shoulders by unremitting toil. His cheeks were shaven, so that he stood out from the others, since, besides the minister, only Chasehope was un- bearded. His skin was as brown as a hazel-nut, and though the face was composed to a decent gravity, there was a vigour in the lines of it which spoke of a life not always grave. The man had a blue bonnet of a pattern common nearer the Border – smaller than the ordinary type which came from the Westlands – and after the fashion of Cheviot and Liddesdale he had a checked plaid of the kind called a shepherds' tartan. But in the cast in the left eye, shown by a sudden lifting of the face, he revealed his identity.

The stranger did not wait to speak to the minister, but David found Amos Ritchie at the kirkyard gate, and asked concerning him. 'It's the new man that has ta'en the tack o' Crossbasket,' was the answer. 'He's frae the far Borders – Jeddart way, they tell me – and it's no easy to understand the wild hill tongue o' him. But he's a decent fairmer and a graund judge o' sheep. He has stockit his mailin' weel, and has a full hirsel on Windyways. . . . Na, he's a single man and hauds to himsel', though he has a name for a guid neebor.'

Amos accompanied the minister to the manse, and there was a shy friendliness in his air, as if he regretted the estrangement of the summer. He spoke only of weather and crops, but his manner suggested a desire to say something by way of encouragement. Only at the manse gate, however, did he find utterance. 'If there's deep waters to be crossed, sir, I'll ride the ford wi' ye,' he muttered as he turned away.

Presently it was apparent that a change had come over the parish. David's doings in the summer had puzzled and alarmed it; even those with a clear conscience had thought of him as a danger to their peace and good repute. But now that he was himself in dire trouble and indicted before the Presbytery, there was a revulsion in his favour; his friendliness was remembered, his kindness in the winter storms, his good looks and his youth. He had his own party in the place, a party composed of strange elements. There were in it noted professors like Richie Smail and Rab Prentice; Isobel and her kin were hot on his side; Reiverslaw, of course, many of the frequenters of Lucky Weir's ale-house, and all who from poverty or misdeeds were a little blown upon. If the Pharisees and Scribes were against him, he had the publicans and sinners. Also he had the children. By some secret channel the word had gone round in the circles of childhood that their friend was in trouble, and in queer ways they showed their affection. The girls would bring him posies; bowls of wild rasps and blaeberries would be left at the manse;

and often on the doorstep Isobel found an offering of guddled trout neatly strung on rushes. Daft Gibbie, too, had become a partisan. He would dog David's footsteps, and when spoken to would only reply with friendly pawings and incoherent gabble. He would swing his stick as if it were a flail. 'Sned them, sir,' he would cry, 'sned them like thristles.'

But the comfort of the atmosphere in which he now moved was marred for David by the conduct of Reiverslaw. That worthy had been absent in Nithsdale when Philiphaugh was fought and did not return till the week after the battle. It would seem that the general loss of stock due to the disturbances had benefited his pocket; he had sold his hog-lambs to advantage and had had a prosperous deal in black cattle with Leslie's quartermaster. By the middle of October the work on the hill farms was all but over for the year, and Reiverslaw was a leisured man. Whether the cause was the new access of wealth or the excitements of Lammas, he fell into evil courses. There was word of brawls in ale-houses as far apart as Lanark and Kirk Aller, and he would lie for days in Lucky Weir's, sleeping off potations, only to renew them in the morning. His language coarsened, his tongue grew more unbridled, his aptitude for quarrels increased till he became a nuisance in the village and a public scandal. 'A bonny friend ye've gotten in Andra Shillinglaw,' Isobel said bitterly. 'For three days he has been as fou as the Baltic and cursin' like a cornet o' horse.' David made several attempts to reason with him, penetrating to the back parts of the ale-house, but got no reply but tipsy laughter and owlish admonitions. It looked ill for the credit of his principal witness.

The call of Calidon was always in his ears, but he did not yield to it. October brought a fortnight of drenching rains, and Katrine came no more to Paradise. He could not bring himself to seek her in her home, for he dared not compromise her. Already a nameless woman appeared in the tales against him, and he would have died sooner than let the woman's identity be revealed. From her he had had kindness and comradeship, but these things were not love, and how could he ask for love when every man's hand was against him and he could offer nothing but company in disrepute? . . . But loneliness weighed on him, and he longed to talk with two especially – the minister of Cauldshaw and the new tenant of Crossbasket. But when he rode one afternoon to Cauldshaw, it was not only the minister's self that drew him there, but the remembrance that the Calidon household were among his parishioners.

Mr Fordyce was scarcely recovered of an autumn ague, and his little bookroom was as bleak and damp as a grave. He sat in a wooden armchair propped up with pillows, nightcap on head, a coarse drugget dressing-gown round his shoulders, and two pairs of stockings on his thin shanks. His wife was sick a-bed, outside the rain dripped steadily, there was no fireplace in the chamber, and gloom muffled it like a shroud. Yet Mr James was casting a horoscope, and mild and patient as ever.

'Tell me the whole story, Mr David, for I've heard naught but rumour. They say you've fallen out sorely with Mr Mungo at Kirk Aller.'

David recounted the events of the past months, beginning with Lammastide in the Wood and ending with his last visit to Mr Muirhead. The other heard him out with many sighs and exclamations, and mused for a little when he had finished.

'You havena been over-gentle with the Moderator,' he said. 'Far be it from me, that am so imperfect, to impute error to a brother, but you canna deny that you took a high line with Mr Mungo.'

'I was within my rights in refusing to obey his suspension. He had no resolution of the Presbytery behind him.'

'Maybe no. But was there no excess of vehemence, Mr David, in defying one who is your elder? Would not the soft word have availed better? You seem to have spoken to him like a dominie to a school bairn.'

'Oh, I do not deny that I was in a temper, but if I was angry it was surely with a righteous anger. Would you have me let that black business of the Wood be smothered just because Chase-hope with his sleek face and his cunning tongue has imposed on the Presbytery? And for the charge against myself, would you, I ask you, have refused succour to any poor soul that came seeking it, though his sins were scarlet on him?'

'I'll not say. I'm a timid man by nature, and I'm so deeply concerned with my own state towards God that I'm apt to give other duties the go-by – the more shame to me! In the matter of the Wood, I think you have done honestly and bravely, and I doubt I wouldna have had the courage to do likewise myself. The Lord be thankit that such a perplexity never came my way! . . . As for Montrose's man, what am I to say? Mr Mungo will quote Scripture against you, and it's not for me to deny the plenary inspiration of the whole Word, though I whiles think the Kirk in Scotland founds a wee thing over much on the Old Testament and forgets the New. But I can see great trouble for you there, Mr David, for the view of Kirk Aller will be the view of the Presbytery – and the General Assembly, if the thing ever wins that far.'

'But what would you yourself have done in like case? Would you have turned the suppliant from your doors?'

'I do not know. To be honest with you, I do not know. I am a weak vessel and very fearful. But in such a case I should pray – ay, I should pray to be given strength – to do as you did, Mr David.'

The young man smiled. 'I've got the comfort I wanted. I'm content to be judged by you, for you are nearer the Throne than the whole Presbytery of Aller and the Merse.'

'No, no. Dinna say that. I'm the feeblest and poorest of God's servants, and at the moment I'm weakening on what I said and doubting whether a man should not bow to lawful authority and cultivate a humble spirit as the first of the Christian graces. What for did our Lord found the Kirk if it wasna to be obeyed?'

'Bide where you were, Mr James. What kind of a Presbyterian would you make yourself out? By your way we should be still under the bondage of Rome, because Rome was once the lawful authority. A bonny Covenanter, you! If the Kirk constrains conscience unduly and makes a tyranny out of Christian freedom, then the Kirk is no more to be respected than the mass the old priests mumbled in Woodilee.'

Mr Fordyce smiled wanly. 'I daresay you're in the right. But what a tangle for an honest man! You've taken the high road, Mr David, and I must keep jogging along the low road, for there's but the two of them. A man must either jouk and let the jaw go bye, as the owercome says, or he must ride the whirlwind. I have been given the lown downsetting, where I can nourish my own soul and preach Christ to the best of my power, and let the great matters of Kirk and State pass me, as a man hears the blast when he sits by his fireside. It is for stronger spirits like you to set your face to the storm. Alack and alas, I'm no fierce Elijah to break down the temples of Baal, and I'm no John Knox to purge the commonwealth of Israel. If you go forward in God's name, my dear young man, you'll have a hard road to travel, but you'll have the everlasting arms to support you. . . . But, oh, sir, see that you fight in the Lord's strength, and not in your own. Cultivate a meek and contrite spirit, for I suspect that there is a good leaven of the old Adam in your heart.'

'That's a true word. There's an unregenerate heat of temper in me at which I often tremble.'

'And you must keep your walk and conversation most pure and circumspect. Let there be no cause of reproach against you save what comes from following your duty.' Mr Fordyce hesitated a little. 'There was word of another count in Mr Mungo's complaint anent you. . . . Wasna there some tale of a woman?'

David laughed.

'The Queen of the Fairies, Mr Muirhead says, though he does not believe in her. . . . I have a confession to make to you, Mr James, which I would make to no other ear. I have met with a lady in the Wood, for indeed she was engaged with me in the same errand of mercy. I had met with her before that, and I count the days till I may meet with her again. It is one whom you know – Katrine Yester.'

'Mistress Katrine!' Mr Fordyce cried out. 'The young lassie from Calidon. Mr David, Mr David, is this not a queer business for a minister of the Kirk? Forbye that she is of a house that is none too friendly to our calling – though far be it for me to deny her Christian graces – forbye that, I say, she is of the high gentrice. What kind of wife would she be for a poor Gospel preacher?'

'Oh, man, there's no question of wife. You make me blush to hear you. The lady would never think of me any more than an eagle would mate with a throstle. But a minister is a man like the lave, and this one is most deeply in love, though he has not the thousandth part of a hope. There's no shame in an honest love, which was a blessing given to man by God's own self in Eden.'

'It's a matter I ken little of,' said Mr Fordyce shyly. 'Me and Annie have been that long wedded that we've forgot what our wooing was like. She wasna by-ordinar in looks, I mind, but she had a bonny voice, and she had mense and sense and a fine hand for making apple jeely. . . . Mistress Katrine! You fly high, David, but I wouldna say – I wouldna say . . . Anyway you've a well-wisher in me. . . . But Katrine Yester!'

David left the minister of Cauldshaw ingeminating that name, and in a blink of fine weather set out on his way home. He was on foot and beyond Reiverslaw, where the road first runs out of the birks to the Hill of Deer, when he was overtaken by a horseman. The mount was no farmer's shelty or minister's garron, but a mettled chestnut mare, with marks of breeding in head and paces, and he who rode her was the new tacksman of Crossbasket.

In that open bright place there could be no eavesdropper. The rider dismounted and flung his arms round the minister.

'I pay my debt,' he cried, 'by becoming your dutiful parishioner, your next-door neighbour, and your faithful hearer ilka Sabbath. . . . Danger, you say. Man, the darkest hidy-hole is just under the light, and the best sanctuary for a hunted man is where he is not expected. They're riping the ports for Mark Kerr, once captain of Mackay's and till late a brigadier under the King's Captain-general, but they'll no trouble about honest

Mark Riddel, a plain farmer-body from Teviotside, that comes up Aller seeking a better tack and has mair knowledge of sheep than any herd on the hills. And Mark will pay his way with good white siller and will be a kind neighbour at kirk and market. My Roxburghe kin are buried deep, but there's folk in Woodilee already that mind of my great-aunt that was married into Annandale, and my cousin once removed that was a herd in Megget. Trust an old soldier for making a fine palisado around him of credible lees. I run no risk save the new ones that I make for myself, and I'm in no mind for that, for a peaceful year or two will be good for my soul, till I see whatna way the cat jumps. Montrose must get him abroad, and if I'm to bide quiet let it be in my own countryside and not in a stinking foreign city. . . . But for yourself, Mr David? From all I hear you've been making an ill bed to lie on.'

They sat down in the roadside heather and David brought up to date the tale which he had first told him in the deeps of the Wood. To unburden himself to this man was a greater comfort than his talk at Cauldshaw, for this was one accustomed to desperate straits and chances and of a spirit more akin to his own. The soldier whistled and looked grave.

'Faith, you've stirred up the hornets, and it's not easy to see where you will get the sulphur to smoor them. There's much in common between you and my Lord Marquis. You see the ills of the land and make haste to redd them, but you have no great notion of what is possible.'

'You would not have had me do otherwise?'

'No, no. I like your spirit fine, and beyond doubt you've taken the honest road. But we live in a pitiful world, where honesty is an ill-requited trade; and you've let yourself be forced into defence, whilk is an unpleasant position for a campaigner. . . . Count me on your side, but let me take my own gait. It widna do for you and me to appear to be chief in public. I'll make haste to conciliate the mammon of unrighteousness – whilk I take to be Chasehope – so dinna wonder if you hear that the two of us are like brothers. But it's the Kirk I fear, your own sacred calling, Mr David. One shilpit body in bands and a Geneva gown, the way things are guided now, is more powerful than a troop of horse and less easy to get upsides with. . . . Still and on, I'm at hand across the glebe, and we'll no be beat for lack of good contriving. The night's the time, when we can step across and collogue at our ease.'

To have the soldier at Crossbasket gave a lift to David's spirits. But at first he saw him rarely, for it was wise to let the man settle down in the place before appearing in his company, lest people should suspect a previous friendship. Mark Riddel appeared to be for ever on the move, and the minister met him oftenest on the Rood road – generally in the early darkness. It pleased him to think that his neighbour was visiting Calidon, for it seemed to bring Katrine nearer. But he made no effort to see the girl himself. With the fall of the leaf the season for Paradise had gone, and he could not seek her at home till he had unravelled the tangle of his own perplexities.

The chief of them was the approach of Hallowmass. He was determined not for one moment to forgo his charge against Chasehope and his Coven, whatever the counter-charge against himself might be, and if necessary to go in person again to the Wood. But his chief ally Reiverslaw spent his days drinking soddenly in the clachan, and when he sought him out at the ale-house he got nothing but fuddled laughter. Then one morning he found him on the hill, and apparently in a better mind.

'My randan is bye,' said Reiverslaw sullenly. 'Ye've cause to upbraid me, sir, and no words o' yours can be waur than what I gie mysel'. It's apt to take me that way at this time o' year, and I think black burnin' shame that I should be sae thirled to the fauts o' the flesh – drinking like a swine in a stye among folk that, when sober, I wadna touch wi' a grape's end. I'm no better than the beasts that perish. But I've found out ae thing in these humblin' days. There'll be nae Wud at Hallowmass. The folk we ken o' dinna fancy the Wud aince the Lammas is bye, and it's the clachan itsel' that will see their next cantrips.'

'But there is no place that could contain them—' David began.

'I ken, but they maybe follow some ither gait. I'll be in the kirkton that nicht – na, na, ye needna fear for me, I'll no gang near the hostler-wife – the verra thocht o' yill and usquebagh staws me. But I'll be there, and you maun be in the manse, and we'll guide our gait according to what the nicht brings forth. I'll wager Chasehope will no be long out o' my sicht, and if he meddles wi' me he'll find me waur than the Deil's oxter. . . . Keep a watch on yoursel' that day, sir, for there's mony will wish ye out o' the clachan.'

The last day of October came and David rose to find that the rain had gone, and that over the drenched hills had dawned a morning as bright as April. He spent the forenoon in distracted study, striving to keep his mind on printed pages, but his restlessness was such that after dinner it sent him to the moors. He took his old road for the Rood tops, and by three o'clock had reached the pass from Clyde, where in July he had had his talk with Reiverslaw.

The earth was soaked with the October rains, and as the sun's power declined in the afternoon a mist began to creep out of the glens. Insensibly the horizon shortened, the bold summit of Herstane Craig became a blur and then was hidden in clouds, the light wind of the morning died away, and over the land crept a blind eery stillness. David turned for home, and long before he had reached the crest above Reiverslaw the fog was down on him. It was still a gossamer covering through which it was possible to see a hundred yards ahead, but objects stood up in it in unfamiliar outlines – a sheepfold like a city wall, a scrag of rowan like a forest tree.

A monstrous figure appeared in the dimness which presently revealed itself as a man on horseback. David saw that it was Mark on his chestnut.

'Well met,' the man cried. 'I'm pushing for home, for I'm getting the yowes to the infield, but I saw you before the mist dropped and I guessed I would find you here. There's a friend of

yours up bye that would be blithe to see you – up the rig from
the auld aik on the road to the Greenshiel.' With no further
word Mark touched his mare and went off at a canter.

The friend, thought David, would be Richie Smail, who might
have some message to him from Reiverslaw. So he turned as
directed past the root of oak towards the ridge of the hill. In
twenty yards a figure loomed before him, a figure on a horse.
He fancied it was Mark returning, till as he drew nearer he saw
that it was no man that sat the black gelding and peered into the
thick weather.

It flashed through his mind that Mark had sent him here on
purpose. And then something came into his soul which he had
never known before, a reckless boldness, a wild joy which
caught at his heart. The girl was looking away from him and
did not turn her head till he was close on her and had spoken.

'Mistress Katrine,' he cried breathlessly.

She looked down on him, her face rosy, her hair bedabbled
with the mist jewels. She did not start at his approach. Was it
possible that she was expecting him?

'What does the minister on the hill?' she asked.

'What does Mistress Katrine? It will be a thick night and you
are still far from Calidon.'

She was dressed all in green, with a kirtle which scarcely
reached her ankles and left her foot in the stirrup clear. The
feather from her green hat hung low over her curls. David had
never seen a woman gloved and booted for the hunt, and in that
hour and in that wild place the apparition was as strange and as
beautiful as a dream.

'I took out the hawks this morning with Edie the falconer, for
the mallards were flighting over from Clyde. Edie went back an
hour ago with the birds, and I lingered to watch the mist creep
up. Maybe I have lingered too long.'

'That was good fortune for me,' he said. 'I have not dared to
come seeking you, but now that we are met I will convoy you to
Calidon. Presently the world will be like the inside of a feather
bed.'

She made no protest, when he laid his hand on her bridle to turn her horse, and as he stole a look at her he saw that she was smiling. That smile sent a tremor through him so that he forgot every care and duty. He and she were enclosed in a magical world – together and alone as they had never been before. . . . He felt that he could bring her safely through raging rivers and across mountains of stone, that for her he could scale the air and plough the hills, that nothing was impossible which she commanded. They two could make of the world a song and a rapture. So deep was his transport that he scarcely heard her voice when she spoke.

'I have been hearing of your troubles, Mr David. He whom we must call Mark Riddel has told me.'

'I have no troubles,' he cried. 'Now that I see you the world is altogether good.'

'Will you tell that to the Presbytery?' she asked, laughing.

'I will tell it to the broad earth – if you give me leave.'

A momentary confusion came over her. She slightly checked her horse, and as the ground shelved the beast stumbled. The slip brought her in contact with David's shoulder, and before she knew his hand was laid on hers.

'Oh, my dear, my dear,' he cried. 'Katrine, I must say it . . . I am daft for love of you. . . . Since I first saw you down in the greenwood your two eyes have been sun and moon to me. Your face – God forgive me – comes between me and the Word. There are times when I cannot pray for thinking of you. . . . It's nothing I ask of you, Katrine, but just leave to tell you. What was it your song said? – "There's none for me but you, my love" – and oh! it's the gospel truth.'

She did not reply, but her hand did not move under his. They were descending the hill towards Rood, and the fog had grown so thick that each to the other was only a shadow. Before it had enclosed them in a visible encirclement; now it seemed to have crept so near that it dislimned the outlines of horse and rider. He held her by touch and by sight, and this disembodiment seemed to give him courage.

'I seek nothing,' he said, 'but that you should know my love. I am perplexed with coming battles, but so long as you're in life there's nothing can daunt me. I would not have you smirched with the stour of them, but if you'll let me think of you and mind of you and whiles see you I'll be as strong as Samson. The papist cries on his saints, and you are the saint whose name is written on my heart.'

Still she did not speak, and he cried out in alarm.

'Have I angered you? Forgive me – forgive me – but I had to speak. Not one other word more will I say till we are at Calidon door.'

Her answer, when it came, was strange, for it was a song crooned very softly:

> It's love for love that I have got,
> And love for love again.

A great awe came over David and checked his breath – the awe of one who sees and yet does not believe, the answer to a hopeless prayer. His hand tightened on hers, but she slipped it away. 'So turn,' she sang:

> So turn your high horse heid about
> And we will ride for hame, my love,
> And we will ride for hame.

The hand which had moved from under his was laid on his head. Suddenly a face bent down towards him and a kiss as light as a bird's wing brushed his forehead. He caught her to him from the saddle.

SIXTEEN

The Witch Hunt

David awoke next morning to a world which had been suddenly re-created. That Katrine should return his love upheaved for him the foundations of the globe. Nothing could be the same again, in face of this tremendous fact; his troubles lifted like mist in the sun, for what ill could befall one whom Katrine loved? Even the incubus of sin in Woodilee seemed to lighten, for evil could not prevail with such a lady walking the earth. He felt that he had come anew into the land of the living, and every fibre of him sang praises.

His new fortitude was proof against even the news which Reiverslaw brought. That worthy arrived at the manse with a long face. The Coven in Woodilee had held their Hallowmass rites and to the best of his belief they had held them in the kirk. . . . He had lost sight of Chasehope early in the evening, and had gone to Mirehope on a false scent. . . . They had been watching the manse and knew that the minister was from home. . . . He had hastened up the road seeking David and had been overtaken by the fog, and when he got back to Woodilee the place had been under a blanket. Doubtless the Devil was protecting his own. . . . There had been no cruisies lit in the cottages, even of those who were known to be of the Coven. But, as luck would have it, he had entered the kirkyard and had seen a speck of light in the kirk. The door was locked, but he was clear that there were folk inside. . . . He had roused Robb to get the key, but no key was to be found. He had gone for Amos Ritchie to break open the door, and though Amos had refused to stir, he had borrowed a mell and a crowbar; but when he reached the kirk, the place was quiet and dark again, and the keys were lying on Robb's doorstep.

The man was really shocked, for this was a superfluity of naughtiness for which he had not been prepared. To David, with a memory of his Kirk Session, the sacrilege was less of a surprise; if men and women could defy their Maker by sitting at the communion table and by taking in vain the Gospel words, they would not shrink from polluting God's house. But it proved the boldness and security of the evil-doers. It was Chasehope of whom he chiefly thought, Chasehope, that darling of the Presbytery, the ally of the Kirk in hunting down malignants, the one in all the parish who flaunted most his piety. The man grew in stature as he contemplated him. Here was no feeble sinner, but a very provost in his craft, who turned all the uses of religion to his foul purposes. And at the thought David, fired by his new happiness, almost rejoiced; he was fighting not with human frailty, but against a resolute will to damnation.

That day he received a summons to attend on the following Monday upon a special meeting of Presbytery at Kirk Aller for a preliminary examination. The thing seemed to him now to have lost all terrors. He had no anger against his accusers, for were they not dull old men who knew nothing of the ravishing world that had been opened to him? He would be very meek with them, for he pitied them; if they chose to censure and degrade him he would bear it patiently. His extreme happiness made him feel more than ever in the hands of the Almighty and disposed to walk softly before Him. He had given many hostages to fortune, but he had won something which could never be taken away. Thankful and humble he felt, in love with life and with all humanity, and notably less bellicose. His path of duty was clear, but he would not court antagonisms. He owed much to the less fortunate, he who daily met Katrine in the greenwood or on the hill in the soft noons which make a false summer at autumn's end.

So on the Sabbath he preached a sermon which was long spoken of in Woodilee. He discoursed of charity – a topic not popular in the Kirk, and commonly left to such as Mr Fordyce who were afflicted with ill-health. For a young minister, his face ruddy with the hill winds and his figure as well set up as a dragoon's, to expand on such a matter seemed a mere waste of precious time, when so many more marrowy subjects lay to his hand. Yet there was that in David's earnestness which impressed his audience almost as much as if his sermon had been on death and judgment. He had a new hearer. A man sat beneath the pulpit whose eyes never moved from the minister's face – a mere lath of a man, thin to emaciation, with a narrow head and a much-freckled face, a ragged beard, and eyes with red lights in them like a ferret's. David noticed that as the kirk emptied the others seemed to shun the new-comer's proximity. As he moved to the door, there was a drift away from him, like sheep from a collie.

That night Isobel gave him news of the stranger.

'The pricker has come,' she announced in a solemn voice. 'He arrived yestreen and is bidin' wi' Chasehope. Yon was him in the kirk the day, yon body wi' the fernietickles and the bleary een. They ca' him Kincaid – John Kincaid, and he's frae Newbottle way – anither than a guid ane, if a' tales be true. Eh, sir, this is a shamefu' business, routin' out puir auld bodies and garrin' them gie daft answers, and syne delatin' them on what they ca' their confessions. There's naebody safe that hasna a power o' keepin' a calm sough and giein' back word for word. I wadna be feared mysel' o' ony Kincaid, but if you was to cross-speir me, Mr David, wi' your searchin' een, I daresay ye could get me to own up to any daftness ye liked to pit to me. I dinna haud wi' this prickin' o' witches, and I can find nae warrant for it in the Word. Belike it's some device that thae weary Embro lawyers hae howkit out o' their rotten herts.'

As he rode to Kirk Aller next day David reflected much on Isobel's tale. Who could have brought a pricker to Woodilee – and lodged him with Chasehope? Was it the work of the Presbytery? Was it a plan to cover up the major sin by hunting out minor sinners? He knew of the pricker class as of the worst repute, knaves and quacks who stirred up popular superstition and were responsible often for hideous brutalities. Even the Law

looked askance at them. He did not like to be absent from his
parish when such a creature was let loose in it.

The examination of the Presbytery lasted for two days. He had
gone lightly to face it, but he found it a formidable affair.
Business began with long prayers and prelections delivered
to his address. The Moderator constituted the court with the
formality of a Lord of Session and the solemnity of a minister
fencing the tables at the Communion season. He announced
that the matter for examination would be limited to the charge
of assisting the Kirk's enemies. The prior charge of witchcraft
preferred by the minister of Woodilee against certain parishioners would be relegated to a later day, since the Privy Council
on his motion had issued a commission to inquire into the
machinations of the Devil in that parish, naming as its members himself, the minister of Bold, and the Laird of Killiquhair.
This, thought David, explains the pricker. Mr Muirhead added
that he had moved in the matter at the request of a godly elder,
known to all of them, Ephraim Caird in Chasehope.

The court was composed of the two score of ministers in the
Presbytery, and only Mr Fordyce was lacking, for he was once
more stretched upon a bed of sickness. As it was only a
preliminary examination there were no witnesses, since the
object was to give the accused a chance of stating his case and so
narrow the issue to be ultimately tried. The Moderator read
aloud sworn statements, to which no names were appended, the
names, as he explained, being reserved for the time when the
complainants should appear in person. To David it was obvious
that, though one of the statements was by a soldier of Leslie's,
the others must come from members of his own flock. There
was nothing new in the details – the finding of the cavalier's
clothes in the manse outhouse, the interference with the
troopers at the Greenshiel, and certain words spoken on that
occasion; but what surprised him was the fact that the avowal
which he had made to Mr Muirhead was not set down. It was
clear from the Moderator's manner that he proposed to forget
that episode, and was willing that David should deny any and

every charge in the libel. Indeed he seemed to encourage such a course. 'The Court will be glad,' he said, 'if our young brother can blow away these most momentous charges. Everybody kens that among wars and rumours of war daft tales spring up, and that things are done in the confusion without ill intent, whilk are not defensible. It is the desire of all his brethren that Mr Sempill shall go forth assoilzied of these charges, which are maybe to be explained by the carelessness of a domestic and the thoughtless words of a young man carried for a moment out of himself, and no doubt incorrectly reported.'

But David did not take the hint. He avowed frankly that he had entertained a fugitive of Montrose at the manse, and had assisted him to escape. Asked for the name, he refused to give it. He also confessed that he had endeavoured too late to protect an Irishwoman at the Greenshiel and had spoken with candour his opinion of her persecutors.

'It is alleged,' said a heavy man, the minister of Westerton, 'that you promised these poor soldiers eternal torments, and them but doing their Christian duty, and that you mocked at them as inferior in valour to the reprobate Montrose.'

'No doubt a false report, Mr Archibald,' said the Moderator. 'It's like that the worthy sodgers had been looking at the wine when it was red and werena that clear in their understanding.'

'I cannot charge my memory with what I said,' David replied, 'but it may well have been as set forth. That, at any rate, was what I had it in my mind to say.'

A sigh of reprobation rose from the Court, and the Moderator shook his head. He honestly desired to give David a way of escape, not from any love he bore him, but for the credit of the Kirk. This, too, was the general feeling. As David looked over the ranks of his judges he saw stupidity, arrogance, confusion, writ on many faces, but on none malevolence. This Court would deal mildly with him, if he gave them the chance, for the sake of the repute of their common calling.

He laboured to be meek, but no answers, however soft, could disguise the fact that he and they looked upon things from

Witch Wood

standpoints eternally conflicting. It was suggested to him again and again that the stranger at the manse had been entertained by his housekeeper, an ignorant woman and therefore the less reprehensible, for had she not rolled up the clothes and hidden them in the byre, as the accused admitted? But David refused to shelter behind any misapprehension. He had admitted the man, what was done had been by his orders, and – this in reply to a question by the minister of Bold – what he had done he was prepared to do again. The close of the first day's sederunt found the charges proven in substance by the admission, indeed by the vehement proclamation, of the accused.

For David there was no share in the clerical supper at the Cross Keys. He lay at a smaller inn in the Northgate, a resort of drovers and packmen, and spent such time as remained before bed in walking by Aller side, under the little hill crowned with kirk and castle, watching the salmon leap as they passed the cauld. Next day, the facts having been ascertained by admission, the Presbytery debated on principles. David was summoned to justify his conduct, and – with prayer that he might be given humility – complied. With every sentence he rode deeper into the disapprobation of his hearers. He claimed that the cause of the helpless, however guilty, was the cause of Christ. Should a starving enemy be turned from the door, even though it was an enemy of the Kirk's?

'Man, can ye no distinguish?' thundered the minister of Bold. 'Have you no logic in your head?' And he quoted a dozen savage Scriptural precedents against him.

Was the Court, David asked, in a time of civil strife and war between brothers, clear that the precedent of Israel and the tribes of Canaan held? The men they fought against were professing Christians, indeed professed Presbyterians. Granted that they were in error, was it an error which could only be extirpated in blood?

It was an unlucky plea, for it brought forth a frenzied torrent of denials. The appeal of his opponents was not only to Scripture, but to the decisions of the Kirk. Was there not here,

one cried, that rebellion which was as the sin of witchcraft?
What became, cried another, of the deference which a young
man was bound to show to the authority of his fathers in God?
'Are we to be like Rehoboam, who hearkened to callow and
inexperienced youth, and not to those elders who partook of the
wisdom of his father Solomon?'

Presently David was silent. He remembered that meekness
became him, and he had a sharp sense of the futility of
argument. Respectfully he bowed his head to the blast, while
a dozen of his brethren delivered extracts from their recent
sermons. The Moderator confirmed the sense of the Court.

'Our young brother is lamentably estranged from Christ,' he
said in a voice which was charged with regret as well as with
indignation. 'He is like the Church of Laodicea of whom it was
written "Because thou art lukewarm, and neither cold nor hot, I
will spue thee out of my mouth." I tell you, sir, he that is not
with us is against us, and that in the day of the Lord's judgments
there can be no halting between two opinions. It is the duty of
the Kirk to follow His plain commandment and to rest not till
the evil thing be utterly destroyed from our midst, even as Barak
pursued after the chariots to Harosheth of the Gentiles, and all
the host of Sisera fell upon the edge of the sword, and not a man
was left. You are besotted in your error, and till you repent you
have no part in the commonwealth of Israel, for you are like Lot
and have taken up your dwelling in the Cities of the Plain and
have pitched your tents towards Sodom, whereas the Kirk, like
Abram, dwelleth in the plain of Mamre which is in Hebron, and
hath built there an altar to the Lord.'

The Presbytery refrained from any judgment on the case, that
being deferred till a later meeting, when, if necessary, evidence
could be called; but in view of the fact that the minister of
Woodilee had acknowledged his fault and exhibited contumacy
thereanent, he was by a unanimous decision suspended from
occupying the pulpit and dispensing the Sacrament in the
parish, and from all other pastoral rights and duties. As the
winter was close on hand, when evil roads lessened church

attendance, it was agreed that spiritual needs would be met if
Mr Fordyce were enjoined to conduct public worship alternately
in Woodilee and Cauldshaw.

David rode home in a frame of mind which was neither sad
nor glad. He felt no shame at his suspension, but he recognised
with a pang the breadth of the gulf which separated him from
his brethren and the ruin of those high hopes with which a year
ago he had begun his ministry. He realised that he was but a
poor ecclesiastic, for he could not feel that loyalty which others
felt to a Kirk which was mainly the work of men's hands. 'They
have lamentably perverted reason and justice' – he remembered
Montrose's words, and yet most of them were honest men and
pious men, and maybe their good on a wide computation was
greater than their ill. It was his unhappy portion to have
encountered the ill. But if the Kirk cast him off he had Christ
– 'Other sheep I have which are not of this fold,' was Christ's
word – and he must follow with all humility the light that was
given to him. When the main trial came on he would not relent
in his denunciation of the Wood, and his loss would be well
repaid if, like Samson, he could bring down with him the pillars
of Gaza. . . . He consoled himself thus, but he knew in his heart
that he had no need of consolation, for the thought of Katrine
was there like a live coal.

He came to the manse in the gloaming to find Isobel waiting
for him in the road.

'Heaven save us a'!' she said, 'but there's an awfu' thing come
to Woodilee. They've prickit a witch, and it's nane ither than
puir Bessie Todd o' the Mains. Guid kens what they did till her,
but a' night the clachan rang wi' her skirlin'. The pricker fand
the Deil's mark on her back, and stappit a preen intil it up to the
head and nae bluid came, and they burnt her feet wi' lichtit
candles, and hung her by the thumbs frae the cupples till they
garred her own to awesome deeds. I canna believe it, the puir
doited body, but if the ae half is true she's far ben wi' the
Adversary, and oh, sir, it's fearsome to think what wickedness
can be hidden in the hert o' man. She said the Deil gie'd her a

new name, whilk she wadna tell, and she owned that ilka Lord's
Day when she sat under ye on the pu'pit stair she prayed to him
– "Our Father, which wert in Heaven." But whatever her faut it
canna be richt the way they guidit her, lickin' her wi' a bull's
pizzle and burnin' the gums o' her till she yammers like a bitted
powny. If she maun dee, let death come quick. For the Lord's
sake, Mr David, get her down to the Kirk Aller tolbooth, for the
Shirra is kinder than you red brock o' a pricker. The verra sicht
o' his wild een sends a grue to my banes – and Chasehope
standin' by him and speakin' saft and wicked and smilin' like a
cat wi' a mouse.'

David's heart sickened with disgust. Chasehope had turned
the tables on him; he had diverted suspicion from himself by
sacrificing a half-witted woman. And yet this Bessie Todd had
been a member of the Coven – he had seen her grey locks flying
in the Wood. Chasehope was presiding at the examination and
torture; he would no doubt take good care that no word of the
truth came out in her delirium. And Isobel, who had denied
with violence his own charges against this very woman, seemed
to believe her confession. She was revolted by the cruelty, but
convinced of the sin. That would no doubt be the feeling of the
parish, for who could disbelieve avowals which must send the
avower to a shameful death?

'Where is the wretched woman?' he asked.

'They have her lockit up in Peter Pennecuik's girnel. . . .
They've gotten a' they want, and they say that the Shirra has
been sent for to carry her to the Kirk Aller steeple, whaur they
confine the warlocks. . . . They're in the girnel now, and the feck
o' Woodilee is waitin' at the door. Will you stop for a bite? . . .'

David waited only to stable his horse, and to buckle on the
sword with which he had girt himself on the night of the second
Beltane. He ran so fast towards the clachan that he was at Peter
Pennecuik's house before Isobel, labouring in his wake, had
turned the corner of the manse loan.

The night had fallen dark, but from inside the girnel came a
flicker of light. David had once before seen a witch hunt – in

Liberton as a boy – and then there had been a furious and noisy crowd surging round the change-house where the accused was imprisoned. But the Woodilee mob was not like that. It was silent, almost furtive. The granary was a large building, for it had once been the barn of the Mains farm; it was built of unmasoned stone cemented with mud, and had a deep roof of thatch; through the chinks of both walls and roof came thin streams of light. The spectators did not press on the door, but stood in groups some paces back, as hushed as in the kirk of a Sabbath. The light was too dim for David to recognize faces, but he saw that one man stood at the door as keeper, and knew him for Reiverslaw.

He had been drinking, and greeted the minister hilariously.

'We've gotten ane o' the Coven,' he whispered, thickly, 'ane you saw yoursel' in the Wud.'

'But Chasehope is among her accusers.'

'I ken, but we'll get that kail-worm too, in the Lord's guid time. At ony rate we're sure o' ane o' the deevils.'

'You fool, this is a trick of Chasehope's to divert attention from the Wood. This miserable woman has only confessed bairnly faults, and on that he'll ride off scot free.'

The truth penetrated slowly to Reiverslaw's foggy brain, but in the end he saw it.

'God's curse on him, but ye're maybe right. What are ye ettlin', sir? Gie me the word and I'll come in by and wring the truth out o' him wi' my hands at his gutsy thrapple.'

'Bide where you are, and let none leave this place unless I bid you. I will see if I can get justice done.'

But when Reiverslaw opened the heavy door to let him enter, the first glance told David that he had come too late. The great empty place had straw piled at one end, and on a barrel in the centre a flickering lantern. By it, on an upturned barrow, sat the pricker, a paper in his hand and an inkhorn slung round his neck, his face wearing a smirking satisfaction. He had once been a schoolmaster, and at this moment he looked the part again. Behind him, sitting on kegs or squatted on the floor, were a dozen men – Chasehope at his elbow, Mirehope, the miller, Peter Pennecuik, Nether Fennan – David saw only a few faces in the dim light. Daft Gibbie by some means or other had gained entrance, and had perched himself in a crevice of the wall, whence his long shoeless legs dangled over Chasehope's head.

On the straw behind the lantern lay the witch. Her grey hair had fallen round her naked shoulders, and that and a ragged petticoat seemed her only garments. Even in the mirk David could see the cruel consequences of torture. Her feet were black and swollen, and her hands with dislocated thumbs were splayed out on the straw as if they were no longer parts of her body. Her white face was hideously discoloured in patches, and her mouth was wide open, as if there were a tormenting fire within. She seemed delirious, for she gabbled and slavered uncouthly to herself, scarcely moving her lips. Every now and then her thin breast was shaken with a frenzied shivering.

At the sight something gave in David's head. He felt the blood rush above his eyebrows, and a choking at the back of his throat. Always a hater of cruelty, he had rarely seen its more monstrous forms, and the spectacle of this broken woman awoke in him a fury of remonstrance. He strode to the lantern and looked down on her, and then turned away, for he sickened. He saw the gimlet eyes of the pricker – red like a broody hen's – and behind him the sullen secret face of Chasehope.

'What devil's prank have you been at?' he cried. 'Answer me, Ephraim Caird. Who is this mountebank, and what have you done to this unhappy woman?'

'All has been done decently and in order,' said Chasehope. 'The Presbytery is resolved to free this parochine of the sin of witchcraft, and this worthy man, who has skill in siccan matters, has been sent to guide us. There is a commission issued frae the Privy Council, as ye may have heard, to try those that are accused, but the first needcessity is to find the witches and exhort them to confession. This woman, Elspeth Todd, is convict out o' her ain mouth, and we've gotten a memorial o' the ill deeds she owns to. Word has been despatched to the

Shirra, and the morn nae doot he'll send and shift her to Kirk
Aller.'

The man spoke smoothly and not discourteously, but David
would have preferred oaths and shouting. He put a great
restraint on his temper.

'How did you extort the confession? Answer me that. You
have tortured her body and driven her demented, and suffering
flesh and crazed wits will avow any foolishness.'

'We followed the means sanctioned by ilka presbytery in this
land. It's weel kenned that flesh sell't to the Devil is no like
common flesh, and the evil spirit will no speak without some
sort o' compulsion.'

David snatched the paper from the pricker and held it to the
lantern. It was written clearly in a schoolmaster's hand, and
though oddly and elliptically worded he made out the sum of it.
As he read, there was silence in the place, except for the
babbling of the woman and the mowing of Daft Gibbie from
his perch.

It seemed to him a bedlamite chronicle. The accused confessed that she had been guilty of charming, and had cured a
cow on the Mains by taking live trouts from its belly. She had
'overlooked' a boy, Hobbie Simson, at Nether Fennan, and he
had sickened and lain for three months on his back. She had
made a clay figure of one of the ewe-milkers at Mirehope and
stuck pins into it, and the girl had suffered from pains and
dizziness all summer. She had shot cattle with elf-bolts and had
cursed a field on Windyways by driving round it a team of
puddocks. The Devil had trysted with her on a rig of Mirehope's,
and had given her a name which she would not reveal, and on
the rig there had been ever since an intractable crop of thistles.
Her master visited her in the likeness of a black cat, and she
herself had often taken the same likeness, and had travelled the
country at night sitting on the crupper of one of the Devil's
mares. By means of the charm of the seven south-flowing
streams and the nine rowan berries she had kept her meal-
ark full in the winter famine. She confessed to having ridden

John Humbie, a ploughman of Chasehope's, night after night to a witch-gathering at Charlie's Moss, so that John was done with weariness the next day and unfit for work. The said John declared that he woke with the cry of 'Up horsie' in his ear. At these gatherings she admitted to having baked and eaten the witch-cake – a food made of grey bear and a black toad's blood and basked in the light of the moon, and at the eating had sung this spell:

> Some lass maun gang wi' a kilted sark;
> Some priest maun preach in a thackless kirk;
> Thread maun be spun for a dead man's sark;
> A'maun be done ere the sang o' the lark.

She admitted that she had taken the pains of childbirth from women – but what women she would not say – and that then the child had been born dead, and had so become a 'kain bairn' for the Devil. Last, and most damning, she had between her shoulders the Devil's secret mark.

Some sentences from the document David read aloud, and in his voice there was bitter scorn. He believed most devoutly in the menace of witchcraft and in a Devil who could take bodily form and divert the course of nature to seduce human souls, but this catalogue of sins seemed to him too childish for credence. It was what any woman crazed with pain might confess in the hope of winning respite. Most of the details he remembered from his boyhood as common talk; the witch-cake rhyme he had sung himself; the charm to fill Bessie's meal-ark during the winter he knew to be false, for she had nearly died of want, and he had fed her from the manse kitchen. . . . He had seen her in the Wood, and yet there was no mention of the Wood. Chasehope had been present at the torture, and doubtless his fell influence had kept her rhapsody away from the point of danger. The poor soul was guilty, but not of this childishness.

He looked at her as she lay, mindless, racked, dying perhaps, and an awful conviction entered his mind. She was a human sacrifice made by the Coven to their master. . . . He had read of such things, he half-remembered tales of them. . . . Perhaps she was a willing victim – he had heard of such – coming forward with a perverted joy to confess her shame. The torture – that would be to stimulate her imagination. Isobel had always said she was weak in her mind. . . . She might have been chosen by lot in the kirk on Hallowmass-e'en. . . . Chasehope was not her inquisitor, but the dark priest who conducted the ritual.

His anger and disgust rose to a fury. He tore the paper into little pieces and flung them in the pricker's face.

'What doubly damned crime have you committed?' he cried. 'You have tortured a wretched weak woman and taken down her ravings for truth. You have maybe killed her, murderer that you be! Your sins cry out to God, and yours above all, Ephraim Caird, whose hands I have myself seen dipped in the blackest witchcraft.'

Chasehope's face was smiling blandly.

'I kenna what right ye have to meddle, sir,' he said. 'The paper ye've torn is but a copy. The memorial itsel' will be in safe hands this night. Wad ye set yoursel' up against the Presbytery and the law o' the land, you that have been suspended this day, as is weel kenned, frae your rights as minister o' this parish? Ye'd best gang hame to your bed, sir, and pray that ye may be delivered frae the sin o' presumption. This woman will bide the nicht in this place under lock and key, till the Shirra sends for her.'

'She will go with me to the manse this night – and, please God, I will nurse her back into life.'

There could be no question of the consternation of the audience – it almost equalled his own. Chasehope alone kept his composure; the others stared in horror and growing anger.

'That will no be permitted,' came from the lowering Mirehope, and 'A bonny minister,' cried another, 'to file his house wi' a dirty witch. He maun himsel' be ower great wi' the Deil.' The pricker twisted and grinned, and his eyes watched approvingly the spasms of the woman on the straw.

David was carried out of himself, and before he was aware of it had drawn his sword.

'She goes to the manse. I will suffer no let or hindrance in this plain duty. Whoever opposes me will rue it.'

'Wad ye deforce the session?' Mirehope shouted in a voice like a bull and got to his feet. From the idiot on his perch came an unexpected encouragement. 'Fine, sir. Fine, my bonny Mr David,' cried Gibbie. 'Stap your sword in his wame. I'll uphaud ye wi' my staff, for the puir kimmer was ill-guidit. I couldna sleep a wink a' nicht for her skellochs.'

A voice broke in on the storm, and David saw that it was the new tenant of Crossbasket.

'Put up your blade, sir,' he said. 'There's no need for fighting among Christian folk. These honest men have been following the light vouchsafed to them, and if there's blame to be cast it's on this pricker chiel that comes from I know not where.'

There was something in the quiet tones which fell like oil on yeasty water. David settled back his sword into its sheath, Mirehope sat down again on his keg, Chasehope turned his head to the speaker with the first sign of discomposure he had yet shown.

'Ye'll forgive me, neighbours,' Mark continued, 'since I'm but new come to the parish, but I've seen a hantle o' the world and I would be wae to see honest men run their heids against a stone wall. The woman may be a' you say and waur, but it looks as if her handlin' had been ower sair, and I'm muckle mista'en if she'll no be a corp ere morning. Consider, friends. – This is no a court constituted by a Privy Council commission; it's nae mair than a private gathering o' well-wishers to the Kirk and the Law. In my time I've meddled ower much wi' the Law for my comfort, and I ken something about the jaud. The Law has no cognisance of a pricker or onything like him, and if well-meaning folk under his guiding compass the death of a man or woman that has not been duly tried and sentenced, the Law will uphaud it to be murder, just as muckle as if a caird had cut a throat at a dyke-side. I greatly fear ye've brought yourselves into its danger by this day's work.'

Mark spoke with an air of anxious and friendly candour that called for no opposition. Indeed it was plain that more than one of his hearers had similar doubts of their own.

'The wife's weel eneuch,' said Mirehope. 'Ye'll no kill a tough auld greyhen like that wi' a raxed thumb or brunt taes.'

'I hope you're right, neighbour,' said Mark. 'But if she suld dee, what will ye say to the Shirra – and what to the Court o' Justiciar? Ye've taken doun frae her mouth a long screed o' crimes, but I'm of the minister's opinion, that they're what any distrackit body wad admit that wasna verra strong in the intellectuals and fand her paiks ower sair for her. Lord bless me, but they're maist o' them owercomes I heard at my grannie's knee. I counsel ye in all friendliness to let the minister do his best to keep her in life, or it sticks in my mind that Woodilee will mak' an ill showing when the King's judges redd up the business.'

Chasehope angrily dissented, but he had few supporters. Most of the others wore an anxious air.

'I come to the matter of the pricker.' Mark's homely wheed-ling tones were like those of a packman in an alehouse kitchen. 'I ken nocht about him, but I canna say I like the looks o' him. I doubt if I was strapped up by the thumbs and had yon luntin' een glowering at me I wad speak wi' strange tongues mysel'. It's no that difficult for a pawky body to gar a weaker vessel obey his will. . . . Get up off that barry,' he said sharply. 'Stand ayont the licht till I have a look at ye.'

The words came out like a crack of a whip-lash. The atmo-sphere of the place had suddenly changed, the woman's mut-terings had ceased, and, as David stood back from the lantern, he saw that Mark had moved forward and was beside the pricker, a yard from him, with the light between them, and the faces of both in full view of the rest. The one shambled to his feet and set his hand to his head as if to avert a blow, while the other, his dark face like a thundercloud, stood menacingly over against him.

'Look at me,' Mark cried. 'Look me in the een if there's that muckle smeddum in your breast.'

The eyes of the pricker were like small dark points in his dead-white eyeballs.

'Ye're one Kincaid, but ye've gone by many names. Ye've been a dominie and a stickit minister, a thief and a thief-taker, a spy and a witch-finder, and ye'd fain be a warlock if the Deil thocht your soul worth half a bodle. . . . Turn your een to the licht, and keep them there. . . . Answer me ere the Pit open for ye. Was there ever a word in your mouth that wasna as false as hell? Say "I am a liar, like my father the Devil afore me".'

'I am a liar,' the man croaked.

Mark stretched out one hand and passed it over the pricker's brow.

'What's aneath here?' he asked. 'Honest banes? Na, na, rottenness like peat.' To the horrified spectators he seemed to pass his hand backwards and forwards through the man's head as if a knife had gone through a pat of butter.

'What's in your een? he cried, leaning forward. 'I see the fires of hell and the worm that dieth not. God! the bleeze o' them is keekin' through!'

For a moment it seemed to all that a ruddy glow of flame leaped to the roof, and Daft Gibbie in his agitation fell from his seat and rushed to the door. The idiot flung it open and screamed beyond Reiverslaw to the waiting crowd. 'Come inbye, every soul o' ye. The pricker that tormented puir Bessie is getting his paiks, and Glee'd Mark is drawin' hell fire out o' him. Come inbye and see the bonny sicht.'

Reiverslaw and a dozen others entered the granary; the door remained half open and the night wind swept up the dust and chaff of the floor and made the red light seem a monstrous wavering cloud that hung like an infernal aureole over the wretched man.

Mark had him by the shoulder. 'And what's this?' he cried, tearing his doublet aside and showing his bare throat. 'As I live by bread, it's a Deil's pap!' Certainly to the audience it seemed that above the breast grew a small black teat.

The creature was in an extremity of terror. Fear had so drained the blood from his eyeballs that the pupils seemed to burn with an uncanny brightness, even after the red had gone out of the light.

'There's nae bull's pizzle needit to make this wauf body confess.' Mark's iron grip was still on his shoulder. 'If ony neighbour has ony misdeed in his mind, I'll warrant to wring it oot o' the pricker as glib as a bairn's schule-lesson. I'll mak' him own to the Black Mass in the Kirk on Hallowe'en. . . . There's nane speaks? Weel, we'll leave the dott'rel to his own conscience.'

He relaxed his grip and the man dropped gibbering and half-senseless on the floor.

'There's your bonny pricker,' said Mark to Chasehope. 'There's your chosen instrument for getting truth out o' auld wives. Do as you like wi' him, but I counsel ye to get him furth o' the parish if he be a friend o' yours, or the folk will hae him in the deepest hole in Woodilee burn.'

Chasehope, white and stammering, found himself deserted by his allies, but he still showed fight.

'I protest,' he cried. 'I kenna what hellish tricks ye've played on a worthy man—'

'Just the same tricks as he played on the auld wife – a wee bit o' speirin'.'

'It's no my blame,' said Chasehope, changing his ground, 'if I have leaned on a broken reed. The man was sent here by folk that vouched for his worth. And nevertheless, whatever the weakness o' the instrument, the Lord was wrocht through him to produce a confession—'

'Ay. Just so,' said Mark dryly. 'But what kind o' instrument is yon to procure the truth? Will ye get caller water out o' a foul pipe?'

'The Lord works—' Chasehope began, but Mark broke in on him. His dark mocking face, in which the squint of the left eye was now most noticeable and formidable, was thrust close to the other's.

'See here, my bonny man. – Ye can get any mortal daftness out o' man or woman if ye first put fear on them. Ye've seen the auld wife and ye've seen the pricker. Do *you* come forrit forenent the licht. Ye're a buirdly chiel, and weel spoken o' for canniness. Ye can keep your thumbs unraxed and your hide unscorched for me, but by the God abune us I'll warrant that in ten minutes by the knock I'll hae ye confessin' fauts that will keep the haill parish waukrife till Yule. . . . Will ye thole the trial?'

The big man shrank back. 'Na, na. I kenna what spell the Deil has gien ye, but ye'll no lay it on me.'

'So muckle the better for yoursel'.' Mark turned to the others. 'Ye've a' seen, neighbours, that my spell, as he ca's it, was nae mair than just an honest speirin'. I'm loth to think that this clachan should suffer for what has been done this day, so the sooner we get the wife to bed and weel-tended the better for us a'.'

'She shall go the manse at once,' said David. He had been examining the tortured woman, who had passed into unconsciousness, and it seemed to him that her heart beat very faintly.

'That will be wisest, no doubt,' said Mark, but at this point Chasehope found support in his protest. Mirehope, Nether Fennan, and the miller exchanged anxious looks.

'Take her to Alison Geddie,' they cried. 'She has a toom bed, and it's near by.'

'She will go to my own house,' said David, 'and be nursed by my own hand. I trust no man or woman of you after to-day's devilry.'

The place had filled up and it seemed to him that the better part of the parish were now onlookers. It was clear that a considerable number were on Chasehope's side, for the mention of the manse had wakened a curious disquiet in many faces. David solved the problem by dragging out from the back of the granary a wooden sledge used for drawing peats. He covered it with straw and laid the woman on it.

'Reiverslaw!' he cried. 'You take the one end and I'll take the other.'

The farmer advanced, and for a second it looked as if he might be prevented by force. He turned fierce eyes on the crowd. 'Ay, sir. I'll dae your bidding. . . . And if ony man lifts his hand to prevent me, he'll get a sarkfu' o' broken banes.'

The strange cortège moved out into the darkness, without opposition. It may have been the honest feeling of the majority that let it go; it may have been the truculent Reiverslaw, or David with his white face and the sword bobbing at his belt: but most likely it was the fact that Mark Riddel walked by the minister's side.

Bessie Todd died just before morning. Isobel received her old gossip with tears and lamentations, laid her in the best bed, washed and salved her wounds, and strove to revive her with cordials. But the trial had been too hard for a frail woman far down in the vale of years. David watched all night by her bedside, and though at the end she became conscious, her mind was hopelessly unhinged, and she babbled nonsense and scraps of childish rhymes. If he could not pray with her, he prayed by her, pleading passionately for the departing soul.

As Isobel straightened the body and closed the eyes, she asked anxiously if there had been any space given for repentance.

David shook his head.

'Puir thing, she got the Devil's fee and bountith, and muckle guid it did her. Let's hope, sir, that afore her mind left her she had grace given her to renounce him and creep to the Mercy Seat. . . . We'll gar some folks in Woodilee look gash for this. There was a time, Mr David, when I wad have held ye back, but my word now is Gang forrit, till ye rive this parish wi' the fear o' God, and sinners we ken o' will howl on their knees for as quiet a death-bed as Bessie's.'

SEVENTEEN

Woodilee and Calidon

The pricker disappeared from the parish in the night. The dead woman was buried decently in the kirkyard, and her male kin attended the funeral as if there had never been a word against her fair fame. There was indeed a certain revulsion of feeling among plain people in Woodilee. Bessie had been liked; she was regretted and pitied; the downfall of the pricker seemed to invalidate her confession. But there was a party – Chasehope was the leader – who held that solemn things had been trifled with and that the minister had gone far to bring God's curse on the parish. He had laid his hand to his sword like a malignant, and had made light of an awful confession before the pricker had been discredited. Bessie might have been innocent of witchcraft, but in his plea for her he had shown a discreditable leniency towards the sin. Women might be old and frail, but if they were leagued with Satan it was enough to put them beyond the pale of Christian sympathy. The minister was patently rebellious and self-willed, a scorner of the yoke of Kirk and Word.

But the night's events caused a notable increase in one reputation. The new tenant of Crossbasket had shown himself an ill man to counter. He had the interests of the parish at heart and had given wise advice, and he had confounded the pricker with a terrible ease. Clearly a man with power; nor was there reason to think that the power was not given him from on high. A hard man to gainsay, as even Chasehope had found. His friendliness had made him popular, and folk were slipping into neighbourly ways with him. Soon he would have been 'Mark' to most, and 'Glee'd Mark' behind his back. But from that night

formality and decorum invested him; he was 'Crossbasket' even
to the children, and the humbler doffed their bonnets when he
drew near.

He came to David one evening when the candle was lit in the
study.

'What arts were yon,' the minister asked, 'that turned the
pricker from a man into a jelly?'

Mark had sat himself in a deep armchair covered with black
leather, which had been David's father's and had come to the
manse from the Pleasance after the roup. He had crossed his
legs and let his head lie back while he puffed his tobacco-pipe.
He laughed as he answered:

'A simple divertisement, but good enough for such a caddis-
worm. A pinch of Greek powder in the lantern, and for the rest a
device I learned among the tinklers in Hungary when some of
us gentleman-cavaliers had to take to the hills and forests for a
season. But the body was easy game. The sight of my een was
enough to melt his wits. . . . Chasehope's another kind of lad –
there's metal there, though it's maybe of the Devil's forging. . . .
But for the moment we've fairly houghed his shelty.

'You saw how distraught he was,' Mark continued, 'ay, and
others beside him, when you offered to carry the wife to the
manse. The reason wasna ill to seek. When she was being
tortured to confession, Chasehope was beside her and mastered
her with his een. . . . She was one of the Coven, you tell me. But
once in your hands he was feared she would tell things of more
moment than the blethers they wrung out of her. . . . She didna
speak? Ay, I thought she was ower far gone. It was maybe as well
that the puir thing died, for after the handling she got there was
small bodily comfort left for her.'

'By her death her tormentors are guilty in God's sight of
murder,' said David.

'No doubt. And maybe also in the sight of the Law. That's why
I say we have houghed Chasehope's mare for him. He canna
ride off on a pretended zeal for witch-hunts, for this one has
notably miscarried. This pricker business is looked askance at

by those that ken best, and it's certain it has no countenance frae
the Justiciar. They've killed the wife with it, and their pricker
will not show face again in this countryside. What becomes,
think you, of the braw commission of the Privy Council that
Chasehope had the procuring of? The thing is begowked before
it is begun. The ministers of Kirk Aller and Bold and yon knock-
kneed haverel, the laird of Killiquhair, will e'en hae to content
themselves at home, and Chasehope, in place of hiding his sins
behind his zeal for burning witches, is left with his repute a wee
thing touched, like a bad egg. There's folk in the parish
beginning to speir questions that never speired them before.'

'I am convinced that the woman Bessie Todd was a human
sacrifice, decided on by the Coven, and maybe accepted of her
free-will. I have heard that every now and then they must pay
such a teind to Hell. . . . She was weak in the mind, remember.'

'I had the same notion myself. No, I wasna there when the
pricker was busy, but them that were tell me that he put the feck
of the words intil her mouth. That would consort with what I've
heard of the black business elsewhere. She was doomed to die,
as surely as if she had stood in the doomster's cart. . . . But I
have found out another thing. Our neighbour Chasehope is a
King-Deil.'

'What in Heaven's name is that?'

'You may well speir. He is the priest of the Coven, but he is
more, for he is a kind of Deil on his own account. That is why
you saw them in the Wood bowing before him and nozzling
him like dogs. There's been King-Deils before this in Scotland.
Francie Stuart was one – him that was Earl of Bothwell in the
days of James the Saxt, and he had a braw Coven down by
Dunbar and the Bass.'

'And the man an elder of the kirk!' David exclaimed. 'The
words of Scripture are never off his lips, and more than once he
has reproved me for sin.'

'That's the lad. There's a holy pleasure to be gotten out of
hypocrisy. And yet – and yet! I'll wager that Chasehope has no
doubt but that he is a redeemed soul and will get an abundant

entrance at the hinder end. That Kirk of yours has so cunningly twisted religion that a man can grow fat in his own sins and yet spend his time denouncing the faults of others, for he is elected into grace, as they call it, and has got some kind of a title to Heaven. I'm a plain body that canna see how God and the Devil can be served at the one time, but there's many a chiel makes a trade of it. They've gotten one creel that holds their treasure in Heaven and the one full of the lusts of the flesh, and though they ettle to coup the latter before the day of death, they are confident that it winna canker what's in the other creel. It's queer doctrine, and maybe I havena riddled it out right, for I'm loth to believe that an honest man could uphold it, though I've heard it often propounded with an unction that made my flesh creep.'

'You speak not of the Christian doctrine of election, but of its perversion,' said David solemnly.

'Weel, it's the perversion that has gotten the upper hand these days. The Kirk has made the yett of grace ower wide for sinful men, and all ither yetts ower narrow. It has banned innocence and so made a calling of hypocrisy, for human nature is human nature, and if you tell a man that ilka honest pleasure is a sin in God's sight he finds a way to get the pleasure and yet keep the name for godliness. And mind you, the pleasures he enjoys with a doubtful conscience will no long be honest. There will be a drop of black ink in the spring water that makes it drumly, and ere he kens he'll be seeing a stronger brew. The upshot will be that folk who sit under you in the kirk will dance in the Wood on the auld heathen holy-days, and the man whose word gangs furthest with the Presbytery will be hugging lusts to his bosom that would make a common foot-sentinel spew. For they've all their sure title, as they call it – they're all elected into grace, so what for should they fash themselves?'

Mark's face was smiling, but his voice had a note in it which was not humour.

'You laugh,' David cried, 'but I'm nearer weeping.'

'I laugh, but it's to prevent me cursing.' The other's jaw had set and there was a smouldering fire in his eyes. 'I tell you the

Cities of the Plain were less an offence to Almighty God than this demented twist of John Calvin that blasts and rots a man's heart. For if it makes here and there a saint, it is like a dung-heap to hatch out sinners.'

David was suspended from officiating in the kirk, but he was still a placed minister and there was no embargo upon his utterances elsewhere. So while every alternate Sabbath Mr Fordyce came over from Cauldshaw to occupy the pulpit, and in defiance of the Presbytery ate his dinner at the manse, on the others David preached in the kirkyard. Twenty years later these sermons in the open air were remembered, when Mr Fordyce, then far advanced in age, was driven from Cauldshaw to hold preachings in the Deer Syke . . .

There was a novelty in the practice which brought many the first day; and on later Sabbaths the audience increased, for David had never delivered such discourses in the Woodilee pulpit. One famous sermon was on the peril of trifling with salvation. A soul was not saved by an easy miracle, but must mount hardly and painfully to eternal life; to accept grace lightly was to cast scorn upon the atonement of the Cross. But doctrine figured little, nor were there any of the forecasts of hell and judgment which were the common proof of an earnest minister. 'He is a guid dowg,' Richie Smail was reported to have said: 'he wad wyse folk gently to Christ.' Something of the joy in his own heart revealed itself in a peculiar tenderness; often there were wet eyes among his hearers, and the children, squatted on the grass or on the flat gravestones, forbore to whisper and fidget and listened with a grave attention. His elders did not attend; indeed, with the exception of Peter Pennecuik, they forbore even to grace the orthodox ministrations of Mr Fordyce. Chasehope and his friends walked the five moorland miles to Bold to sup on the strong fare of Mr Ebenezer till such time – early in the New Year, it was believed – as the Presbytery pronounced final judgment on their minister.

Woodilee had split into two factions. There was the party of the Session, who held David to be a malignant, or at best a Laodicean, one who gave a doubtful sound of doctrine, a rebel, a despiser of authority, a preacher of a cold morality. To this side belonged many of undoubted piety who had been shocked by his defiance and gave ready ear to whispered scandal. Of David's party were respected professors like Richie Smail and Rab Prentice, several godly women, a decent hind or two, and a tail which was neither godly nor respected. Among his supporters were some whom he suspected of dealings with the Wood, and in general he had with him all that was least esteemed in the parish. To have Reiverslaw – who was again drinking hard – as his prophet, and Daft Gibbie as his fugleman, did not enhance the credit of his cause. Between the Jews and the Samaritans there were no dealings. Isobel, now a hot partisan, had quarrelled on this score with her nearest and dearest, and, encountering Jean of Chasehope-foot in the clachan and being goaded by her tongue, fell on her tooth and nail and chased her into Peter Pennecuik's kail-yard. Amos Ritchie, too, had declared his colours, and woe be to the man who in his presence spoke ill of the minister. He was no longer employed by the farmers around the kirkton, so the smithy fire was mostly unlit, while the smith did odd jobs at Reiverslaw and Calidon. Only the new tenant of Crossbasket mixed amicably with all. On the road he had the same greeting for Chasehope as for the minister, and he would drink a stoup at Lucky Weir's with Amos or Mirehope, Reiverslaw or the miller, in all good-fellowship. But this popularity rested more perhaps on fear than on affection. Dark whisperings began to spread. 'What ken we o' Crossbasket?' said one. 'Nae doot he's frae Teviotside, but whaur was he afore that? He never learned that glower on Jed Water.' 'He's a pawky carle,' said another, 'and ye canna get far ben wi' him. There's mair in his heid than the Word ever learned him. I wadna wonder some fine day to see him gang off in a fuff and a lowe. Ye say he has the speech o' a guid Christian? Weel-a-weel, a soo may whistle, though it has an ill mouth for it.'

By late November winter should have closed in upon the glen with an iron hand. The first frosts should have stripped the trees, and the first snows lain at the dyke-back. But that year it seemed as if the seasons had gone widdershins. November was bright and calm, and the harvest, delayed by October rains, was soon gathered. Oats and bear, flax and rye – the little crops were housed within a week, and, since the snows tarried, it was the middle of December before the cattle were in the byres and yards and the sheep brought down to the infields. The country-side presented a strange spectacle. Heather lingered in bloom, and the leaves were on the ashes and hazels till long after Hallowmass. When they did fall there were no frosts to crumble them, and they lay in great drifts in the woods and by the roadside, and children dived and scrambled among them. There were swallows still in the thatch in November, and Amos Ritchie, when he went out to the moss to intercept the travelling skeins of wild geese, found that the curlews and plovers had not yet flitted to the seashore and that there were no wildfowl to be seen in all the blue heavens. Morning after morning the sun rose clear as in June, the nights were mild and starlit, herbs which should have been snug below the earth sprouted prematurely, the hedgehog and the badger had forgotten to go to sleep, and only the short hours of light showed that it was mid-winter. Reiverslaw, always a scorner of precedents, kept his sheep on the hills, where the pasture was as rich as in summer-time.

But the old and the wise frowned and shook their heads. One said it was such a year as '71, of which his grandsire had told, when winter did not begin till February and did not end till June. Another recalled 'sixteen fifteen, named the Lown Year, when there was nae frost, and a blight o' worms and cawterpillars and hairy objects fell on the land.' And every wife in the parish, when at Christmas the grass was still rank and high and hips and haws still hung on the bushes, quoted dolefully the saw that 'a green Yule makes a fat kirkyard.'

But if there was a presage of calamity in it for the thoughtful, it was weather of a rare beauty for those who had the heart to enjoy it. There was no sickness in the parish and as yet no hunger, so David's pastoral duties were light. He was on the uplands most of the day, and now his feet took him away from the Hill of Deer and the north ridge of Rood and across the glen to the hills between Calidon and Aller, for there he could meet Katrine with no fear of interfering parishioners. The garrison had been withdrawn from Calidon, since Nicholas was known to be out of the country and Mistress Saintserf was regarded as well affected, but David did not go there. So long as the short afternoons were crystal under a canopy of blue and the sun set behind Herstane Craig in gold and crimson, the place for lovers was the hill, for there the world was narrowed to themselves.

But the minister's conscience smote him at last, and on New Year's morning he presented himself at Calidon door. By arrangement Katrine was not there, and from her aunt he got the tempestuous welcome which custom ordained as appropriate to the season.

'Sit ye down, sir, and prie our shortcake and October. Yours is the first stranger foot that has crossed this threshold, and it's surely propitious that it should be a minister's. Our ain Mr James is lyin' again, for this lown weather doesna' 'gree wi' him, though it's hard to say what 'grees wi' him, for the creature's body is sair failed. . . . It's mony a day since we cast een on ye here, Mr David, and siccan days as they've been for me and mine.'

She descanted on the troubles of the autumn, her success in saving Calidon from being sequestered – 'Peter Dobbie, him that's our doer, is far ben wi' Wariston, ye maun ken, and worthy Mr Rintoul in the West Kirk said a word in the right lug' – on the difficulty in getting funds to Nicholas Hawkshaw at Utrecht, on the garrisoning of Calidon. 'They punished our yill, but they fashed us little, for they were sair hadden down by Katrine.' But she said nothing of Mark, though in the end she had been made privy to that business, and she did not hint at the trouble in Woodilee which was the talk of the country. Behind all her garrulity lurked a certain embarrassment, and it did not make David's task the easier.

At last he took his courage in both hands.

'I came here this morn for a purpose,' he said, and with halting voice and a fiery face he made his confession. The old woman regarded him with eyes that strove to express amazement and failed; it was clear that she had had her suspicions.

But her words when she spoke were those of one who had been startled out of all propriety.

'Heard ye ever the like?' she cried. 'Man, d'ye ken of whom ye speak? Katrine is a leddy born – there's nae aulder or prouder stock in the land – and ye're the oy o' the miller o' the Roodfoot, and ye seek to make her your marrow. We ken that the warld is coupit upside-down these days, but this fair cowes a'. Guid faith, ye're no blate.'

David held his peace, for he had no answer. He felt in the pith of his bones his immense audacity.

'How would the lassie set wi' a manse, think ye?' she continued. 'She's been brocht up amang papists and prelatists, and though she's had mony a swatch o' the Gospel frae honest Mr James, she's no muckle wiser than a babe. Forbye, she's a daft quean that wad never mak' a 'sponsible minister's wife. Think ye that the King's court and dancin' and glee-singin' and ridin' on a horse is a guid preparation for a moorland parish and a fower-room house? How will ane that's been used to velvet and pearlins tak' wi' linsey-wolsey and drugget?'

'That is for Katrine to decide,' he said humbly. 'I have heard that true love can glorify a cot-house.'

'Havers!' she cried. 'There's a decency in a' things and ye canna mate a blood-horse wi' a cadger's powny. Wedlock, as I weel ken, is nae business o' kissin' and rhymin', but a sober contrack, and if twa folks are gaun to live cantily thegither, they maun see that mair than their hearts are weel agreed. There maun be a guid chance – there's nae certainty in this perishin' world – o' a bien doun-settin', and a sufficiency o' gear, and a life that will be guid for baith. What say ye to that? A minister's wife! Guidsakes, the Session wad think her a randy, for she'd lauch at their solemnities, and your brither ministers, wha are maistly cotters' sons, wad be fleyed by her gentrice, and the folk

wad be as feared o' her as a chuckie o' a pyot. Ye're a man o'
sense, Mr David. Ye canna deny that the thing is past a' reason.'

'Oh, Mistress,' said the unhappy David. 'There's truth in what
you say – I cannot gainsay it. But I plead that true hearts may
break down every obstacle, and Katrine's and mine are as true to
each other as the dial to the sun. There was a time when you
were young yourself, Mistress – you mind that then there was
no rule for lovers but their love.'

'I mind weel,' she said more gently, 'but it's for auld folk to be
eident and save the young frae folly. . . . I'll no deny that I would
be blithe to see Katrine provided for. She's a fine lassie but
forbye mysel' she has nae near kin to mind her, now that
Nicholas is put to the horn and hidin' amang the Hollanders.
Fine I wad like to see her in safe hands. . . . But what can ye
offer, Mr David? It's no as if ye were on firm ground yoursel'.
They tell me ye're cast out wi' your Session and are bickerin' wi'
the Presbytery, and ony day may be turned out o' Woodilee and
maybe excommunicat by the Kirk. That's the braw prospect for a
wife. Wad ye have Katrine tak' a creel on her back, like a tinkler
quean, her that has in her the bluid o' the Black Douglas and the
auld kings o' Scots? Ye've made a bonny hash o' things, for ane
that's ettlin' to be a bridegroom.'

'I am set about with perplexities, and the hands of many are
against me. But I have Katrine on my side – and I was in hopes
that I might have you, Mistress.'

'I'm no against ye,' she said, and there was kindness in her
eye. 'Never think that. I've heard the clash o' the country and
I've riddled it out, and by my way o't ye've taken the richt road. I
ken nocht about the Wud, but I ken something o' the tods and
foumarts o' Woodilee, and for the business o' glee'd Mark Kerr
it's no a Hawkshaw or a Yester or a Saintserf would cast a stone
at ye. But it's solemn truth that ye've gotten on the wrang side o'
the Kirk, and the Kirk is your calling, Mr David. . . . Ye maun
ken that I've had mony a crack wi' our Mr James anent ye, and if
it's the pure Gospel word I'm seekin' it's to him I'll gang and no
to Kirk Aller. I'll tell ye what he said. "Mr David," says he, "has

his plew on the wrang rig. He wad hae made a grand sodger, and if he had been a papist he wad hae made a guid monk. He has the makings o' a saint and he has the makings o' a warrior, but a manse is no the place for him. For," says Mr James, "he canna like me withdraw himsel' into his closet – he is ower hale o' body and het in spirit for that – and he canna walk doucely as the Kirk ordains. For, if he sees wrang he maun set it richt, though the Kirk tells him to bide still, and he'll no put his conscience in the keeping o' any Presbytery. He's ower staunch a Presbyterian," says he, "for the Kirk of Scotland as at present guidit, whilk is a kind o' Papery wi' fifty Papes instead o' ane." '

'Maybe that's the truth,' said David.

'Ay, it's the truth, and I'm blithe to hear ye acknowledge it. . . . But we'll hae the lassie in, for this crack concerns her maist. The cunnin' limmer to keep sae mum and begowk her auld auntie!'

When Katrine appeared, her cheeks a little flushed and her eye bright, she was greeted by Mistress Grizel with surprising gentleness.

'What's this I hear o' ye, lassie? Ye've gotten a jo and never telled me! . . . Na, na, my lamb, dinna be feared that I'll flyte on ye. It's a road we maun a' travel, and nae doubt wedlock is a holy and blessed state and a hantle better than spinsterhood, for a woman maun either be guidit by a husband or be subject to a' and sindry. But it's a serious step, and wants carefu' and prayerfu' thocht. I've had a word wi' Davie – for I tak' the liberty to ca' him Davie as if he were my ain son – and as in duty bound I've set forth the difficulties. I say naething against ye as a man, Davie. Ye're wise-like and weel-spoken, and ye've gentle ways, if ye hae na gentle bluid. But I say muckle against ye as a minister, and I canna picture Katrine as the leddy o' a manse. Forbye there's the solemn fact that ye've made Woodilee ower het a bit to bide in, and what ye've done there ye'll dae in ony ither parochine in the land. . . . Sae hearken to me, sir. Ye've mista'en your trade, like mony anither honest lad, but the faut can be mended. Ye're young eneuch to start in a better.'

Katrine had moved to David's side and laid her hand on his shoulder. 'Aunt Grizel would have you forsake the Kirk for the world,' she laughed.

'But I am solemnly vowed to God's service,' he said.

'Nae doot,' said Mistress Grizel. 'But a man serves his Maker as weel in buckskin as in a Geneva gown – better, if a' tales be true. This is the counsel of ane that wishes ye weel, you and that denty lass at your elbuck. Mak' your peace wi' the Kirk – submit yoursel' to the Presbytery – ye need gie up nane o' your views, but submit yoursel' to the lawfu' authority. Tell them that ye'll be guidit in your public doings by them that has been set ower ye. . . . Troth, they'll no be sweir to mak' a brig for ye, for they dinna want a scandal in the Kirk. They'll censure ye lichtly for a thochtless callant and the thing will drap. By that course ye'll dae nae violence to your conscience – ye'll just be humblin' yoursel' before your elders in the Lord, as we're commanded.'

'But what of the witchcraft in Woodilee?' he asked.

'Let it gang by the board. It's no you or ten like you will clean out that dirty nest. Leave it to the Almighty, whose judgments are slow and siccar.'

'You would have me sit silent in Woodilee in the midst of that iniquity?'

'Na, na. I would have ye get out o' Woodilee as fast as a bird when the thack's burnin'. We've Mr James's opinion, whilk ye canna controvert, that ye were never meant for a minister. I'se warrant it will be made easy for ye – the Presbytery will no object, and Calidon's the chief heritor, and I'll get a word spoken to Mr Rintoul. Ye'll leave wi' a guid name, at peace wi' God and man, and there's a' braid Scotland for ye to find a habitation. . . . Peter Dobbie tells me that your father, honest man, made a hantle o' siller and that ye've heired the haill o't. Gang down the water to the auld Yester lands, and buy a bit estate and set up Katrine in her forebears' countryside. Ye're young and yauld and there's muckle guid work to be done in Scotland by ane that lives in the fear o' God, be he laird or minister.'

David turned to Katrine, but her face was impassive. From her he would get no guidance. Like her aunt, she awaited his answer.

For a moment he wavered. On one side he saw peace, comfort, a new life with his beloved in a new place, the cutting of a tangle which constricted his youth; on the other – a thankless fight, where victory was wellnigh impossible, a sordid struggle which would darken the sunlight for both and taint all the springs of joy. He dropped his head on his breast and suffered for an instant the anguish of indecision. Then he spoke and his eyes were on Katrine.

'I cannot. I would be going back upon my vows – I would be false to my faith – I would deserve to be cried out upon as a coward – I would be making terms with the Devil.'

'Thank God,' said the girl, and her arms were round his neck.

The old woman stared at him, coughed dryly, and then very deliberately took her seat in the big armchair which had been Nicholas Hawkshaw's. The two stood before her like prisoners brought to judgment.

'Ye'll tak' that puir lassie and expose her to the ill-will o' the Kirk and the countryside. – Ye'll set her up as a mark for clash and scandal. – Ye'll condemn her to a wearifu' battalation that can have but the one end, for those that are against ye are mair than those that are for ye. A man may fecht stoutly his lee lane, but he is sair trauchled by a wife.'

'I will reply,' Katrine cried. 'I am a Yester. What cognisance does Yester bear, Aunt Grizel?'

'Azure a chevron or between three garbs of the same, and for badge a lion guardant, wi' the ditton "Thole feud." '

'My motto is my answer. Would you have me shame my kin and run from a challenge?'

'But what kind o' challenge, my lamb? Ye'll be nae Black Agnes o' Dunbar – but a minister's wife, fechtin' against lees and clypes and fause tongues and ignorance – the cauld law o' the land and the caulder laws o' the Kirk. Ye'll hae to thole and thole wi' never a back-straik o' your ain, and keep a smilin' face

and a high heid when your heart is sick. Ye maun bow to them
ye scorn and bend the knee to them that your guidsire would
have refused for horse-boys, and be servant to the silliest body
that summons ye in the name o'Christ. Have ye made your
market for that, my doo? There never was Yester – or Hawkshaw
neither – that feared feud, but can ye thole sic dreidfu' servitude,
day in day out, in a wee house in a dreich parochine wi' nae
company but hinds and wabsters?'

The girl looked at David and there was that in her eyes which
made him both exultant and very humble, so that he longed at
once to sing and to weep. She turned to the Bible which lay on
the great table, ran a finger over its pages and read, and the
words were those which Ruth spoke to Naomi:

> Intreat me not to leave thee, or to return from following
> after thee: for whither thou goest, I will go; and where
> thou lodgest, I will lodge: thy people shall be my people,
> and thy God my God: where thou diest, will I die, and
> there will I be buried: the Lord do so to me, and more also,
> if ought but death part thee and me.

'So that's the way o't,' said the old woman. 'Weel, I've said my
say. Ye're a pair o' fules, but there's maybe waur things than
fules in God's sicht. . . . Davie, lad, get down on your hunkers
and I'll gie ye my blessing – the blessing o' a wardly auld wife
that yet has orra glints o' better things. . . . Man, I kenna where
ye got it, but there's gentle bluid in ye. Your common body
would have chosen the saft seat.'

EIGHTEEN

The Plague

In the first week of the New Year the miraculous weather
showed no sign of breaking. The sun from rising to setting
shone temperately in a clear sky, the nights were little less warm
than May, and even the old folk cast the blankets from them and
opened the doors of their press-beds; the peat-stacks and the
fuel-stacks were scarcely touched, and the fires smouldered only
for cooking; the burns were shrunken to summer size, and the
spawning fish could not pass the shallows of Rood. But a change
had come over the mind of the parish. Men no longer called
down blessings on the fine open winter, for such weather
seemed in defiance of nature, and an uneasy anticipation of
portents weighed on their spirits. The sun did not warm, the
unclouded skies did not cheer, the hard roads did not invite to
movement. A curious languor fell upon Woodilee.

It seemed as if the same apprehension were felt by the natural
world. The cattle and sheep, in spite of the good pasture, grew
thinner than in the rigours of winter. The packman's pony
turned away from the rich bite by the roadside. Though the air
was cool and tonic, beast and man sweated with the smallest
exertion. David, tramping the high moors, found that he was
more weary after five miles than after twenty in the summer
heats. The deer from Melanudrigill had none of their winter
boldness, and indeed all wild animals had become shyer of the
presence of man than the oldest inhabitant remembered. But all
were aware and restless; there were more worm-casts on the turf
than in spring, and migrant birds, which usually tarried long in
the sheltered glen, now passed high in air for the south. David
saw many a drove as he opened his window in the morning.

Even the fieldfares, which Amos Ritchie used to snare in the
Mirehope fields, did not come within sight of his bird-lime. . . .
A brooding strangeness had come into the air, and apathy
silenced the very tykes in the village street. Neighbours rarely
gathered at Lucky Weir's for a mutchkin, though it was thirsty
weather; men seemed to be afraid lest what they saw in
another's eye might give substance to their own fears.

Peter Pennecuik, sitting on the stone by the smithy door and
mopping a wet forehead, watched Amos drop his tools heavily
as he returned from a job at Reiverslaw.

'What mak' ye o' the weather?' he asked.

Amos straightened his back.

'I dinna like it. The gillyflowers in my yaird are ettlin' to
bloom. My grannie had a verse o' auld Thomas the Rhymer –
what was it?—:

> A Yule wi'out snaws,
> A Januar' wi' haws,
> Bring the deid thraws.

'There's a judgment preparin',' said Peter, 'but whatna kind o'
judgment I daurna guess. Certes, it's no canny.'

'I've heard o' nane ailin', but there's seeckness comin'. I can
smell it in the air, and the brute beasts can smell it, for they're
sweir to come near Woodilee. There's no a tod or a maukin on a'
the Hill o' Deer. D'ye no find a queer savour in the countryside,
Peter? There's wind enough to shake the saughs, but the warld
smells like the inside o' a press-bed when the door's steekit. Oh
for a snell, dirlin' blast! There's something rotten and stawsome
and unearthly about the blue lift and the saft air. It's like
withered floo'ers on a midden. . . . If there's nae seeckness
yet, there's seeckness on the road. I maun awa in and see to
Ailie, for this morn she was complaining o'a sair heid.'

Two days later the child of a cotter at Mirehope returned from
school in the manse kitchen and to his mother's amazement
beat his head against the door. He fell asleep on the wedder's
skin beside the fire, and when he was awakened for his supper

his cheeks were flaming and he seemed to have difficulty with his speech. He was put with the rest into the box which was the children's bed, and all night filled it with his cries, so that the others sought peace on the floor. In the morning his face and throat were swollen, his eyes were sightless, and he struggled terribly for breath. Before noon he was dead.

In this way came the plague to Woodilee.

Its coming was realised in an instant, for the sinister weather had prepared the people for calamity. Before the dark the rumour of the breaking out of the pest was in the uttermost sheilings. With it went the word that Peter Pennecuik had sickened, and that another child at Mirehope and one of the Chasehope ewe-milkers were down with it. . . . Next day the place was a beleaguered city. Johnnie Dow, the packman, hearing the news at Cauldshaw, diverted his round to Kirk Aller, though thirty pounds Scots were owing to him in Woodilee. The roads were blocked as if Montrose's kerns commanded them. As it was winter-time there was little work on hand, and even that little was not done. A Sabbath hush fell on the glen, people shut their doors and sat within at their prayers, and that best seeding-ground for plague, a lively terror, was amply prepared.

Peter Pennecuik died in eight hours. There was no heart in the man, and in sickness his command of pious phrases fell away from him, and he passed out of life in a whimpering misery. It was not an edifying death-bed for one who had been a notable professor. But very soon Peter was forgotten – for he was an old man and ripe for his end – as the young and strong were, one by one, struck down. Amos Ritchie's wife, Ailie, followed – the less to be wondered at, for she had always been frail. But when Jess Morison at Chasehope-foot, dark-browed, high-coloured, and not yet twenty, swooned as she drew water at the well, and died in delirium before evening, fear in the parish became panic. The young herd at Windyways, the trimmest lad in the glen, and the miller's man, who looked as gnarled as an oak and as strong as a mill-wheel, followed. But the tragedy was the children. Two of them were struck down for each grown-up person, and perished with the speed of plucked flowers. . . . It was another kind of peril from that which old folk remembered in the year '10, for no pox attended it nor any of the usual sores. The ordinary first symptom was a blinding headache and a high fever; then came a swelling of the throat and glands and a quick delirium. But in many cases there was no outward swelling; the mischief seemed to descend straightway to the lungs and produce a severe haemorrhage. In such cases there was no final delirium; the patient died with clear mind and little bodily pain in an extreme languor. The first type commonly seized the young and full-bodied; children and old folk followed, as a rule, the second course. But both were fatal: in a week out of fifty-nine smitten, fifty-nine were dead.

There was no doctor to be had in all the countryside. The leech at Kirk Aller, sent for by David, refused to come within a mile of Woodilee, and the old women, the usual medical authorities of the village, had nothing but senseless concoctions and – in secret – more senseless charms. Presently even these were forgotten and the place lay in a stupor of fear under a visitation from Heaven. Cottages which the pest had entered were by popular consent shut to the world, so that they became a hot-bed of infection for the other inmates. A man who had sickness in his dwelling dare not show his face in the street except under cover of night. There was no neighbourly assistance asked or given. The members of a stricken family had to conduct their life in a dreadful isolation, till they too sickened; there were shuttered dwellings where life was slowly blotted out, and the village only learned that the end had come for all by the fact that the chimney ceased to smoke. . . . At first an attempt was made to bury the dead decently, the remaining members of a household under-taking the task, but the spread of the pestilence soon made this impossible. The dead were laid in byre and stable beside the startled beasts, sometimes by the poorer households in the kailyard, and David more than once found a staring unshrouded corpse in the nettles of the manse loan. There were cottages

where all the inmates were dead and unburied, with a lean cat
mewing round the barred doors. . . . And all the while the soft
blue weather continued, and the wind came balmy from the hills
over those silent fields of death.

At first the stupor of Woodilee was shot with an awful
apprehension of divine wrath, and the people sought to pro-
pitiate their Maker by humbling themselves before Him, and –
even the least devout – by constant prayer and the reading of
Scripture. But this mood did not long survive. The fury of the
blast which smote them drove all religion out of their minds,
and left them stark and numb with mortal fear. To begin with,
David was welcomed in the house of death, he was summoned
in haste, his coming was watched for; even if his ministrations
did no good to the unconscious sufferers they seemed to
comfort the others. But presently he found himself an unre-
garded intruder. Whenever he knew of a case he hastened to it,
but the panic-stricken eyes of the living looked at him as blindly
as the glazing eyes of the dying. His prayers even to himself
seemed idle; at any rate they fell upon dulled ears. What contact
could he establish with the sick in the delirium or languor of
death, and with those who waited on the same fate with the wild
despair of beasts in a trap? What use to point to God when God
over-shadowed them as a merciless tormentor? And all the
while he was in a fever of anxiety. More than one of the dead
were among those whom he had remarked in the Wood. Men
and women were hastening to judgment with their sins heavy
on them – sins unrepented and for ever unrepentable. He, their
minister, had to stand feebly by and see souls descending into
damnation.

The thought drove him frantic, but it alone gave him power to
continue in his fruitless duties, for in this trial he found the
flesh very weak. It was not that he feared death, even death by
plague, but that a horror of Woodilee had fallen on his spirit.
His shrinking from the Wood, his hatred of the sins of the
Wood, his quarrel with the Session, the distrust in which he was
held by many of his congregation, the episode of the pricker and

Bessie Todd's death – all combined to make the place reek for him of ugliness and decay. The pest seemed merely to add rotting carcases to rotting souls. . . . Then the pity of it would overcome him, when he thought of children whom he had taught and honest folk who had been kind to him, now cold in death. He was helpless to cure either body or spirit. He had no leechcraft – what would it have availed if he had, for he remembered the Edinburgh doctor by his father's bed? – and his spiritual ministrations were as idle as wind. . . . Above all he felt himself a prisoner shut into a noisome cage from which there was no escape. None dare leave or enter Woodilee. One afternoon in a mood of despair he climbed the Hill of Deer for a glimpse of the outer world. There lay Calidon on its windy braes, but Calidon was now as distant for him as the moon. There lay the hills in whose spacious wildernesses no pest lurked, for there were no unclean mortals to harbour it, and beyond them was the world where men might live in daylight and honour. As he looked down on Woodilee a haze seemed to lie over it. Was it the effluvia of the plague, a miasma which walled it round more impenetrably than stone walls and iron shutters? . . . He struggled to conquer his shrinking. 'Faithless servant,' he told himself, 'faithless even over a few things! David Sempill, you rebel against the Lord's will not because of the sufferings of your poor folk, but because of your own pitiable discomfort. Think shame, man, to be such a whingeing bairn.' For he had realised that the root of his trouble was that he was severed from Katrine.

But that evening Katrine came to him.

While he sat for a little in his study before starting on his melancholy visits, he heard Isobel's voice below high-pitched in excitement. Then he heard another voice which took him down the stairs three steps at a time. The girl, booted as he had seen her in the mist on the eve of Hallowmass, stood in the light of Isobel's candle, one gloved hand raised in protest and with an embarrassed smile at her lips and eyes. To David it seemed the first smile that he had seen for an eternity.

'Awa' hame wi' ye, my leddy,' Isobel cried. 'Ye canna come here, for the pest's in ilka bite we eat and sowp we drink and breath we draw. Awa' wi' ye, an' keep your mouth tight steekit till ye're ower the Hill o' Deer. Oh, haste ye, or ye'll be smitten like the lave, and ye're ower young and bonny to dee.'

'Katrine, Katrine,' David exclaimed in agony. 'What madness brought you here? Have you not heard that half the parish is sick or dead? There is poison in the very air. Oh, my dear, come not near me. Wrap a fold of your cloak over your mouth and never slacken rein till you are back in Calidon.'

The girl drew off her gloves. Her eyes were on Isobel.

'I am his promised wife,' she said. 'Where should I be if not by his side?'

The news left Isobel staring. 'His promised wife,' she stammered. 'Heard ye ever the like – the manse o' Woodilee to seek a mistress from Calidon! . . . But the mair reason why ye suld tak' tent. There's nae place for a bonny doo like yersel' in this stricken parish – ye canna help ithers and ye may get your ain death. Awa' hame, my braw leddy, for the minister has eneuch to trouble him without concern for his jo.'

The girl walked to David's side and put her hand in his arm.

'You will not forbid me,' she said, and her face was still smiling. 'I do not fear the plague, and I do not think it will harm me, for it smites those who live in foul hovels and I am always about the hills. But I do fear this loneliness. I have not seen you for two weeks, David, and I have been imagining terrible things. I have come to help you, for I have known the pest before – many times in France, and in Oxford too. I know what precautions to take, for I have heard wise men discuss them, but you in Woodilee from all I hear are no better than frightened bairns.'

'But your aunt – Mistress Saintserf—'

'Aunt Grizel knows of my coming. She has given me this pomander of spices.' She touched a trinket which hung from her neck by a gold chain.

David struggled to salve his conscience by energy in dissuasion, and though his heart cried for her presence it was torn too by fear for her safety. He commanded, pled, expostulated, but she only turned a smiling face. She sat down before the peat fire and stretched out her feet to the hot ashes.

'You will not drive me away, David,' she said. 'Would you forbid me from a work of necessity and mercy – and you a minister?'

In the end he gave up the task, for here was a resolution stiffer than his own, and his strongest arguments faltered when he saw her smile, which was like sunlight in a world of darkness and grim faces. He found himself telling her how the plague had begun and of the nature of its course – the lack of leeches and medicines, the dearth of helpers, the households perishing silently indoors. She listened calmly, and did not blanch even at the tale of the shuttered cottages and the unburied dead.

'A pretty mess your folk have made of it,' she said. 'You have turned Woodilee into a lazar-house and given the pest a rare breeding-ground. Never mind your spiritual consolations, David. Let the miserable bodies come before the soul. You say you have no leech to cure the sick, and that maybe is as well, for I never yet heard of leech that could master the plague. But if you cannot cure, you may prevent its spread. Our first task is to safeguard those who are not yet smitten. If you shut up a cottage where there is one sick man, you condemn every member to death. That must be stopped without delay – and for God's sake let us bury the dead – bury or burn.'

'Burn?' he cried out aghast.

'Burn,' she nodded. 'Fire is the best purifier.'

'But we shall rouse the place to madness.'

'Better that than death. But we want helpers – bold men who fear neither the pest nor an angry people.'

He shook his head. 'There are none such in Woodilee. The bones of all are turned to water.'

'Then we must stiffen them. . . . There is the one whom we now call Mark Riddel. It was he who told me of your trouble, for he was at Calidon yesterday on his way back from Annandale.

There is the black-avised man, too, at Reiverslaw. . . . Are there none more?'

The girl's briskness was rousing David's mind from its torpor.

'Amos Ritchie, maybe.'

'That gives us three – four with yourself – and four resolved men can do wonders. Others will fall in once the drum is beaten. Rouse yourself, David, and be as eager to save bodies as you ever were to save souls. And do not forget to pray for a change in this lamentable weather. A ringing frost would do more to stay the pest than all the leeches in Scotland. . . . .'

She departed as suddenly as she had come. 'I dare not come by day,' she told him, 'for if Woodilee heard of a stranger its panic would be worse. We have to do with terrified bairns. But I will be here at the same hour tomorrow night, and by that time you must have gathered your helpers.'

David did not return from his visitations till the small hours, but he brought back the first piece of good news. One of the hinds at the Mains, after lying for two days in delirium, was now quit of the fever and in a wholesome sweat – sleeping, too, a natural sleep. It was the first case of a possible recovery, and he was aware how much a single life saved would do to quiet the broken nerves of the parish. Also Katrine's advent had lifted him out of the slough of despond in which he had been sunk for weeks. She had spurred him to action, and shown him a duty which he had been too blind to see. He fiercely repressed the anxiety with which the mere thought of her presence in that tainted place filled him. He dare not forbid the exercise of courage in another – even in one who was dearer to him than life.

Next morning he went to Reiverslaw, but got no comfort. Andrew Shillinglaw met him out of doors, and made it very clear that he had no desire to come too near him. The conversation was conducted at a distance of a dozen yards.

'Na, na,' he cried. 'I'm off this verra day to Moffat, and I'll no set foot in Woodilee till the pest has gane. Ye ask ower muckle,

Mr Sempill. It's maybe *your* duty to gang among them – though you ken as weel as me that the haill parochine is no worth the life o' a tinkler's messan – but it's no duty o' Andra Shillinglaw's. I never could abide the reek o' the folk, and they have doubtless gotten what they deserved.'

'Ay, I'm feared,' he admitted in answer to David's appeals. 'Ilka body has something that puts the grue on him, and with me it's aye been the pest. I'll face steel and pouther, angry men and angry beasts, but I'll no face what gars a man dee like a ratton in a hole. And what for should I face it for folk that are no a drap bluid's kin to me?'

The man spoke loudly and violently, as if a little ashamed of himself, and went into the house, where David could hear the bar falling.

From Amos Ritchie he had a different answer. Amos since his wife's death had gone about with bent shoulders and a grey face and had sat for long hours in his smithy beside a dead fire. There David found him and propounded his request.

'I'll do your will, sir,' was the answer. 'I've sae little left to live for that I've the less to fear. But there'll be need o' mair than you and me, for the parish is dementit, and daft folk are ill to guide. The first thing is to get the deid buried. For God's sake dinna speak of burnin', for though the body is but our earthly tenement, burnin' is ower like the Deil's wark.'

That night Katrine came again, and with her Mark Riddel. The soldier had lost something of his bluff composure, and a troubled eye met David's.

'I have been listening to a sermon on courage,' he said ruefully.

Katrine pointed a mocking finger at him.

'He would run away,' she said, 'he the old soldier of a hundred battles.'

''Deed and I would. A hundred battles, nor a thousand battles, wouldna reconcile me to the pest. I could name you many a bold captain who at the rumour of pestilence shifted his leaguer, though he would have held his ground before all the

Emperor's armies. But it seems I must take my orders from this child, when I hoped to slip off cannily to a cleaner countryside. . . . Ugh, Katrine, my dear, I wish you had set me an easier task than to sweep the midden of Woodilee and turn sexton.'

'It's an armed and mailed sexton you must be,' she said. 'You may have to put reason into the folk with the flat of your sword. Comfort yourself, Mr Mark, this task is not so much unlike that you were bred to.'

The soldier grew visibly more cheerful when he heard that there were only three volunteers for the business. 'There's trouble brewing, then,' he said, 'and it's God's mercy that I've won a certain respect in the parish, for it looks as if more persuasion would be needed than a good word and a clap on the back. When do we start our dowie job, for I confess I would sooner be at it than thinking of it?'

'A lean man like you, all bone and whipcord, need not fear,' said David.

'Tut, man,' said Mark impatiently, 'fear is not in the question. My trouble is that I've a nice stomach and a fastidious nose. Death, whether it comes by pest or steel, is the same to me, and that's a thing worth less than a strae. . . . God's curse on this weather! . . . To work, Mr David, or I'll be rueing my bargain.'

For three days and nights the three men wrought at their repulsive task with niggardly intervals for food and sleep. They made a list of the stricken houses and forced their way into them, even when the doors were bolted. The dead were buried – some in the kirkyard, some in near-by fields, and this duty fell especially on Amos Ritchie, who performed it with dogged fidelity. Now and then there was trouble – a crazed wife or mother would refuse to part with the body of a husband or child, and in some cases the minister had to intervene with stern appeals. More difficult was the business of keeping houses, where the sick lay, open to the air and light. David and Mark had to drive cowering sons out of doors with threats of violence, and in some cases with violence itself. One obstinate household had their door smashed by Amos's axe; another was turned neck and crop into the byre that a sick woman might have peace and air. The three men constituted themselves a relieving force, and had often to do the fetching of food and water. Terrible were the sights revealed behind many of those bolted doors and windows, and, though Amos seemed unaffected, the other two had often to rush to the air to check their nausea. Thanks they got none, rarely even curses; the miserable folk were too sunk in despair for either. Yet it is likely they would have failed, had not the news of recoveries got about. Besides the hind at the Mains, two children had now weathered the storm and were reported to be mending fast. The communal mind of Woodilee, which up to then had been blank fatalism and lethargy, was now shot with gleams of hope. The pest might have worked itself out and be on the decline: the corridor was still long and black but there was a pinprick of light at the end of it. . . . Also Mark Riddel in himself was a cogent persuasion. The dark keen face and the reputation of mystery and command which he had won at the witchpricking were arguments sufficiently potent, apart from the long sword which he wore at his side. For in this work the douce tacksman of Crossbasket had disappeared: it was the captain of Mackay's who gave orders and saw that they were obeyed.

By Candlemas it was clear that the tide had turned, for there were more on the way to recovery than dying. Well it was that the change had come, for the weather now broke – not, as David had prayed, in wholesome frost, but in perpetual drenching rains. The downpour had come in an instant; within half an hour during the night the wind had shifted, the sky had clouded, and the fall had begun. It was the night, the eve of Candlemas, which the three men had chosen for their work of burning. Now that people were beginning to move about the streets again, it was essential to get rid of centres of infection, and two of the worst were cottages in the clachan where all the inmates had died. Such houses could only be purified by burning, and about ten that night fire was put to them. Dry as tinder, they blazed furiously to heaven, and there were those in the parish, dabblers in witchcraft, who must have turned scared eyes to the glow which was fiercer than any that the altar in the Wood had known. . . . But in an hour came the rain, and the murky smoke-wreaths were turned to steaming embers.

It was a proof of the returning strength of the parish that the burning of the cots started it out of apathy. Woodilee feebly and confusedly began to take stock of things, and tongues started to wag again. The numbness of loss, the langour of fear, gave place to recrimination. Who was responsible for the calamity of the pest? It must be a mark of the Lord's displeasure, but against whom? They remembered that their minister lay under the ban of the Kirk – had been forbidden to conduct ordinances – was convicted of malignancy and suspected of worse. In their search for a scapegoat many fastened upon David. Practical folk said that he had been in Edinburgh in the time of plague, and had maybe brought back the seeds of it. The devout averred that the uncanny weather had followed upon his public sins, and that the pest had come close on the heels of the Presbytery's condemnation. Was there not the hand of God in this, a manifest judgment? The ways of the Almighty were mysterious and He might ordain that the people should die for the sins of one man. Even those who had been on David's side were shaken in their confidence.

To crown all, came the events of the past week. To his critics there was no reason in his doings: they believed the pestilence to be a visitation of Heaven, to be stayed not by the arm of flesh, but by fasting and prayer. He had been assiduous in his futile visiting, it was true, and he had buried the dead; but he had broken in on their suffering with violent hands, and had herded men and women like brute beasts. Doors and windows, open to the February rains, attested his methods; by his act two cottages, once snug and canty, were now grey ashes. . . . Amos Ritchie in such matters was but a tool; Mark Riddel was too much feared to be the mark of censorious tongues; but David, still their titular minister, was a predestined target.

And as the village crept back to life, and those who had escaped took heart to do a little work again, and the convalescent staggered to their doors and looked on the world, there arose stranger rumours. The minister was all day out and about – praying on occasion, but more often engaged in homely tasks like cleaning up a kitchen and boiling water for those who were too frail to help themselves. Dark looks and ugly mutterings often followed him, but he was too intent upon his work to take heed of them. The general sullenness he set down to the dregs of grief and terror. That was for the daylight hours, but – it was whispered – after nightfall he had a companion. There were stories of a woman, a creature beautiful and young, who sang in a honeyed voice, and appeared especially at the bedsides of the children. At first few credited the talk, but presently came ample confirmation. She had been seen at three houses in the clachan, at the Mirehope herd's, at the Mains; with her had been the minister; and the bairns to whom she had spoken cried for her return. . . . The old and wise shook their heads. There was no such woman in the parish or in all the countryside. And some remembered that the minister in the back end had been observed to meet with a woman in the Wood, and that she had seemed to those who saw her to be no mortal, but the Queen of Elfhame.

The truth was that no commands of Mark, no protestations of David, could keep Katrine out of the village. She saw the reason for not appearing in the daylight, for a stranger in Woodilee – above all such a stranger as she – would have been too much for the brittle nerves of the parish. But after nightfall the case was different, and when with David she had once stood by the bed of a sick child, nothing could prevent her making a nightly duty of it. Into those sodden woeful households she entered like a spring wind; the people may have marvelled, but they were still too apathetic to ask questions, and they felt dumbly her curative power. Among unkempt pallid men and frowsy wild-eyed women the face bright with the weather, the curls dabbled with rain, the cool firm arm, the alert figure, worked a miracle, as if an angel had troubled the stagnant waters of their life. Her hand on a child's hot brow sent it into a peaceful sleep; her presence gave to the sick the will to live and to the fearful a gleam of courage. What they thought and said when she had gone will never be known, but for certain they longed for her coming again.

On the 18th day of February the pestilence took its last victim – an old woman, the mother of the Windyways herd, and the earth was still fresh on her grave when the rain ceased. The wind swung to the north-east, and the black frost for which David had longed settled on the land. It put an end to the pest, but it bore hard on the convalescent, and the older and feebler died under its rigour. In the pure cold air the taint seemed to pass from the land, and the problem of David and his helpers was now a straightforward fight with normal ailments and the normal winter poverty. Stock during the visitation had been scarcely tended, and the byres and infields were full of dead beasts; while in the general terror the customary frugality of the parish had been forgotten and many a meal-ark was empty. There was need of clothing and food, of fuel and cordials, and it did not appear where they were to come from.

There was no help to be looked for from outside, for to the neighbourhood Woodilee was like a leper settlement; none would have dared to enter the place, and had a Woodilee man shown his face in another parish he would have been driven back with stones. Mr Fordyce managed to send to David more than one distressful letter, lamenting that for the sake of his own people he could not lend his brother a helping hand; but save for that, from the 8th day of January to the 15th day of March, there was no communication with the outer world. In this crisis Mark Riddel wrought mightily. He had ways and means of getting supplies from distant places, and his pack-horses, guided by himself or Amos Ritchie, brought meal and homespun blankets from quarters which no man knew of. David exhausted the manse stores, and Isobel kilted her coats and, with a charity seasoned by maledictions, kept her pot or girdle continually on the fire. But it was the house of Calidon that provided the main necessaries. Its brew-house and its

girnel, its still-room and its cellars, not to speak of Mistress
Grizel's private cordials, were plundered for the sake of the
parish which Mistress Grizel could not refer to without a sour
grimace. When Katrine rode to the manse of a night she would
bring with her usually a laden shelty.

The end of the plague was for David a harder season even
than its height. For with convalescence Woodilee seemed to
lose its wits. Before it had sat dazed and broken under the rod;
now it woke to an ardour of self-preservation. At the beginning
the people seemed to be careless of infection; now the survivors
were possessed with a craze to live and fought like terrified
animals to get out of danger. They could not leave the parish
bounds, but those that were able fled from the village. The leaky
sheilings on the hills, occupied by the ewe-milkers during the
height of summer, gave lodging to many, and several died there
of the violence of the frost. The outlying farms were believed to
be the safer, so Mirehope and Nether Fennan had many
undesired tenants in their out-houses. The result was that,
in a season of convalescence, when nursing was especially
needed, the bed-ridden were often left deserted. David tried to
enlist men and women who had either escaped the plague or
had been for some weeks recovered, but he got only fierce
denials or an obstinate silence. The place had become brutish,
and the selfishness of the beasts seemed to have become the
rule of life.

The one exception was Chasehope. During the worst weeks
the clachan had had no news of him, but it was rumoured that
he had made a fortress of his farm-town, and had assiduously
tended his own people. At any rate at Chasehope there had been
only one death. Now he appeared in the street, and to David's
amazement it was clear that he came on an errand of mercy. His
house seemed still to be well provided, and he brought with him
a certain amount of provender. This he did not bestow indis-
criminately but only on certain families, which David guessed to
contain members of the Coven. To these he spoke with authority, and he used his power to put reason into the distracted.

He alone in the place seemed to have no fear of infection – to be careless of the risk which had sent panic abroad among the others. He passed the minister with a grave salutation, and showed no wish to give or ask for help; he had some business afoot which was his private concern. But the fact stood out that this man, alone in Woodilee, had mastered fear.

Once in a cottage where a child was recovering he came upon David and Katrine. The girl was sitting on a stool by the bed making a toy out of reeds for the child's amusement, and singing a French nursery song about Cadet Roussel and his three houses. David lifted his eyes from admiring the grace and swiftness of her hands to see Chasehope's heavy white face in the glow of the firelight. The latter doffed his bonnet at the sight of Katrine, and murmured some civility. Clearly he knew her, for he picked up a reed from the floor. 'Frae the Calidon mill-dam, belike,' he said.

'You are the one man in Woodilee who has courage,' David said. 'You are no friend of mine, Ephraim Caird, but I give you the praise of a stout heart.'

'Why should I be feared?' the other asked. 'Why should I dread to walk even in the valley of death if His rod and staff are there to comfort me?'

'Why should you! But many professors are of a different mind.'

'They are but poor professors, then. I fear no ill, for I am in the Lord's hand till His appointed time.'

'But many who do not fear death fear to die by the pest.'

'Ay, but I have my assurance. I have the Lord's own promise, Mr Sempill. I ken as weel that no pest can touch me as that my name is Ephraim Caird and my habitation is Chasehope. It's the lack o' sound doctrine that gars folk turn cowards – they dinna lippen enough to the Lord – they havena a firm enough grip o' their calling and election. I have my compact sure, and I ken that the Lord will no gie me a back-cast. I can rejoice even in this sore affliction, for He hath demanded a sacrifice, and what is man to question His will? Dear in His sight is the death of His saints – ay, and of sinners, too, for His judgments are not exhausted. There's mair to come, Mr Sempill – take tent o' that, sir – the conviction is heavy on me that the wind o' His displeasure has still a blast to blaw.'

The pale eyes had almost the green of a cat's in the dim light, and the bald brows above gave the whole face the air of a mask, which at any moment might slip and reveal nightmare lineaments. The child in the bed looked up as he spoke, saw his face and screamed in terror, and Katrine, after one glance behind her, was busied in crooning consolations. . . . In that moment David had a revelation. This man, secure in his election to grace, secure against common fear, was likewise secure against common reason. He was no hypocrite. To him the foulest sin would be no sin – its indulgence would be part of his prerogative, its blotting out an incident in his compact with the Almighty. He could lead the Coven in the Wood and wallow in the lusts of the flesh, and his crimes would be but the greater vindication of God's omnipotence. . . . In that illuminating instant madness had looked out of his eyes.

NINETEEN

The Sacrifice

As March drew to its close the wheels of life began once again to run creakingly in Woodilee. The frost disappeared under a week of south-westerly gales, and then the wind moved to the east and blew dry and blighting, so that the lean beasts shivered in the infields. The gross unseasonable herbage of the winter had gone, and it promised to be a backward spring. The men went out feebly to the farm-work, and the ploughing began, though the draught-oxen were so poor in condition that the work moved slowly. The siege, too, was raised. Johnnie Dow once again showed his cautious face in the clachan and brought news of the outer world; the pack-horses again struggled through Carnwath Moss; and there came word from Kirk Aller that the meeting of the Presbytery to adjudicate on David's case was fixed for a day in April. Mr James rode over from Cauldshaw and the kirk was opened, but David did not renew his preachings at the kirkyard gate.

The truth is that he was weary to the bone. Mark Riddel met him one morning on the road and drew rein sharply at the sight of his face.

'Man David, you're like a ghost. You've worked your body ower sore these last months, and if you dinna take care you'll be on your back. You and Katrine are two inconsiderate bairns. You've both of you done the work of ten men, and you'll no listen to wiser folk. Take my advice and get furth of this woeful parish till your body is rested and your mind quieter.'

'I am summoned to my trial at Kirk Aller in a week's time.'

'And that's the crown of it! That's what you get for wearing yourself to skin and bone for a thankless folk. There are times

when I scunner at my native land. There's a rumour that
Montrose has escaped abroad and is now at the Emperor's
court, and if it werena for you and Katrine I could find it in me
to join him. There's a blight on the country which affects even a
brisk heart like mine, and I'm getting mortal sick of the eternal
crack of nowt and wedders.'

But though Mark came to the manse every evening and would
have nursed him like a mother, David could not relax the
tension of body and spirit. He slept badly, and in spite of
Isobel's coaxing ate little; his nights were filled with wild
dreams, and, worse, these dreams seemed to pursue him in
his waking hours. He felt no special ailment of body to which he
could attribute his distress, beyond an extreme fatigue. He
would take long walks by day and night, but though he returned
from them very stiff and weary, they did not bring him healthful
sleep. He tried to master himself, to laugh at himself, but the
malaise would not be expelled. . . . He was the prey of childish
fears, looking nervously for something malign to come out of
the dark or round the corner. And presently the barrier of the
real seemed to crumble. He saw faces where there were none,
he listened to voices in the deepest silence. Once, coming at
night up the manse loan, he heard footsteps on the dry earth
approaching him. They grew louder, passed and died away
behind him, and he realised that the footsteps were his own.

A word of Chasehope's stuck evilly in his memory. The Lord
had demanded a sacrifice, but the sacrifice was not yet complete, the man had said. The word tortured him and could get no
relief from thinking, for the thing was beyond thought. An
oppression of coming disaster weighed on him. He told himself
that his enemy had meant no more than the Presbytery trial, but
he could not lay the ghost. Something darker, more terrible,
hung on the skirts of his imagination. Chasehope was no doubt
mad, but truth might lurk in madness; a maniac saw that which
was hidden from others. It was for Katrine that he feared, and
what he feared he could not give a shape to – there lay the agony
of it.

Presently his old dread of the Wood returned – that dread which he thought he had exorcised for ever. He had defied it, but what if it should prove too strong for him? In his distraught thoughts the pestilence seemed to have come out of it – Chasehope had moved unscathed through the weeks of plague – Chasehope and the devils he served were the plague's masters. Was there some other terror still in its depths waiting to be loosed on him? He had moments of clear-sightedness, when he despised himself for his folly, and realised that to be thus faint of heart was to acknowledge defeat and to abase himself before his enemy. But the conviction returned, stronger than will or reason, and David would walk the hill with clenched hands and muttering lips, or in his closet struggle in blind prayer for a comfort that would not come.

After Katrine's nightly visits to Woodilee had ceased the minister had meant to go daily to Calidon. But with this new mood of terror upon him he was ashamed to face the girl; and he had sufficient manhood to put restraint upon his longings. The time came, however, when anxiety conquered scruples. He rode to Calidon with a fluttering heart, an excitement rather of fear than of joy.

Mistress Saintserf faced him grimly.

'What have ye done wi' my bairn?' she demanded. 'She is fair broke wi' ridin' the roads and tendin' the riff-raff o' Woodilee – and the haill parochine no worth a hair o' her heid. Christian charity, says you – but there's bounds to Christian charity! Ye're a bonny lad to tak' so little care o' your jo.'

Presently she condescended to details. 'She has nae strength, the puir thing – clean worn out like an auld bauchle. Yestreen I garred her tak' to her bed, and she's lyin' as biddable as a wean, and her for ordinar' sae sweir to bide still. . . . Na, ye canna see her. But dinna fash yoursel', my man. She's no sick – just weary wi' ower heavy a task. A long lie in her bed will put her richt, and a change in this dowie weather. Pray for a bit blink o' sun. . . . Ye're lookin' gey gash yoursel'. Ye'd be nane the waur o' a week on your back.'

As David rode homeward he remembered the last words and laughed at their irony. A week in bed, when he could scarcely endure three hours in a night! Mistress Saintserf's news had put him into an agony of apprehension. He stabled his horse and set out to work off his anxiety by bodily fatigue, but it grew with every mile he walked. Weariness, he told himself, was only natural after such a winter's toil; was not he himself worn out, and did not even Mark Riddel confess to a great fatigue? But he could not console himself with such thoughts. At any moment she might fall into a fever, and then – he remembered with dreadful distinctness the stages of the malady. Was this the last lingering effort of the pest? – he had heard of such cases coming weeks after the thing seemed to have been stayed. And always there rose in his mind Chasehope's prophecy of a sacrifice still to come.

He would fain have gone back to Calidon and waited for news. Instead he sent Isobel with a message to Mistress Grizel. His housekeeper was noted as a skilful nurse and an amateur leech, and he begged that she should be allowed to help in waiting upon Katrine. The sending of her did something to ease his mind, for it was a direct piece of service to his beloved; moreover, if Isobel was in Calidon he could go there as often as he wished and have speech with her, for he was a little ashamed to reveal to Mistress Grizel his lack of fortitude. Meantime he could fend for himself, and cook what food he needed.

The time passed on leaden feet and the hours of darkness were one long sleepless nightmare. Next day he was early at Calidon and found Isobel with a composed face. 'Ye needna tak' it sae sair, Mr David,' she assured him. 'The leddy's no that bad. Nae doot she's sair weary, but the fleck o' the time she sleeps like a bairn, and there's nae fever. There's strong bluid in her that will no be lang ere it conquers the weakness. But losh, sir, ye've the face o' a bogle. Awa' hame wi' ye and lie doun, or I'll no bide anither hour in Calidon. Are ye takin' your meat? Dinna look at me like a glum wean, but do as I tell ye.'

David returned to the manse, and under the influence of Isobel's cheerfulness fell asleep in his chair and slept till the late afternoon. He awoke freshened in body, but with a new alarm at his heart. Isobel had said there was no fever, but that meant that she dreaded fever. . . . By this time it might have come. Even now Katrine might be delirious. . . . He realised how swiftly during the pest fever had succeeded listlessness.

Nevertheless the hours of sleep had given him a greater power of self-control, and he curbed his instinct to ride forthwith to Calidon. He wandered through the house and out into the glebe, striving to fix his mind on small and homely things. It was the third day of April, but there was no sign of spring. The dislocation of the seasons had given the earth an autumnal air, for the shoals of fallen leaves lay as if it were November, and the frosts had not bleached the herbage. He remembered how a year ago at this time he had wandered on the hills and felt with joy the stirrings of new life. To-day the world was still clamped in bonds, and death was in the bare trees and the leaden sky. What had become of his high hopes? All gone save one – and that the dearest. A year ago he had had no thought of Katrine and had been happy in other things. Now these had been turned into ashes, but he had got Katrine in their stead. If she were to go—? The thought so chilled his heart that he fled indoors, as if in the house he could barricade himself against it.

In his study he turned over his books. He tried to pray, but set prayer was idle, for every breath he drew had become an impassioned supplication. He had out his notes on Isaiah and the prolegomena which he had completed, but his eyes could scarcely read them. How small and remote these labours seemed! Every now and then a quotation from the prophet stood out in his manuscript, and these were as ominous as a raven's croaking. *Burning instead of beauty . . . Their faces shall be as flames . . . Through the wrath of the Lord of hosts is the land darkened, and the people shall be as the fuel of the fire . . . This is the rest wherewith ye may cause the weary to rest.*

He turned from his notes in awe and took up his secular books. One he opened at random and saw that it was the *Aeneid*, and the words which caught his eyes were 'manibus date lilia plenis.' Small wonder that the book had opened there, for it was a well-thumbed passage; but he shuddered as if he had cast the *sortes Virgilianae* and had got a doleful answer.

In the evening he found himself some food, and since the dark was full of ghosts for him he lit many candles and banked up the peats on the fire. He was in a strange mood, rapt out of himself, suffering not so much pain in his thoughts as a fever of expectation. His fingers drummed ceaselessly on his knees; as he looked into the glowing peats he saw forms and figures that seemed to mock him; to his unquiet ears a wind was blowing round the house – a wind that talked – though the night was very still. And always there was in his head, like the refrain of a ballad, the words 'Burning instead of beauty.'

He did not see Mark Riddel till the man was beside him and had touched his shoulder. Then he started up with a cry and encountered a grave perturbed face.

'You had better come to Calidon,' Mark said. 'Katrine . . . she has taken a turn for the worse. She has been in a fever since midday.'

It was the news he had been expecting, and David rose obediently.

'I'll go on foot,' he said. 'I can run faster than any horse.'

Mark looked at him anxiously. 'You'll do no such thing. You'd faint or ye were across the Hill o' Deer. Bide where you are and I'll saddle your beast.'

The two set off at a gallop, but in the rough parts of the road Mark slackened and took David's bridle. 'Hold up,' he cried. 'It'll no mend matters if you break your neck.'

David asked only one question. 'Have you got a leech?' he said.

'I'll have no leeches. Your country botcher would only bleed her, and she hasna the strength for that. Grizel and yon wife Isobel are all the leeches that are needed, and I'm not without skill myself. Keep up your heart, David. All is no tint yet, and it's a young life.'

At Calidon gate David spoke again. 'Is it the pest?'

'I canna tell, for the pest has many shapes to it. Weakness and fever – there's no other signs, though God kens that's bad enough.'

He was taken straight to her chamber by Isobel, and found there Mistress Grizel, a silent, stern-faced guardian. Katrine lay tossing in high delirium, moaning a little, and moving her arms feebly on the coverlet. A bandage of wet cloths was on her brow, and, as David laid his hand on it, he felt the pulse of the fever beneath. Her long dark lashes lay on her flushed cheeks, but every now and then her eyes would open in a glassy stare. He took her hand and it was dry and burning.

'We maun let the fever rin its course,' said Mistress Grizel. 'She maun fecht her ain battle without the help o' man. God be kind to my bairn,' and she kissed the hot lips.

'Ye'll be putting up a prayer?' she turned to David.

'I cannot pray . . . I can only watch. . . . I beg you to let me watch here beside her.'

'Have your way. There's little need o' speech if there be prayer in the heart. Isobel will get ready your chamber, for ye canna leave this house.'

Presently David was in the sick-room alone, and if he could not pray he spent the hours on his knees. Isobel and Mistress Grizel returned from time to time; once Mark came and put his hand on the girl's brow. The night passed and the dawn came, but still David knelt at a chair by the bedside, his head sometimes in his hands and sometimes lifted to gaze at the face on the pillow. He was tortured with the sense of his frailty. A sacrifice, another sacrifice, was required, and for what sins but his own? He had been lacking – oh, he had been lacking in every Christian grace. In those black moments he saw himself as the chief of sinners, his struggles to rise foiled by a dragging weight of self, his ardours half-hearted, the fruits he brought forth but poor pithless stalks, his errors dark and monstrous like birds of night. He was not conscious of any special sin – only of a deep unworthiness which made him unfit to touch the hem of her garment. . . . Had ever anyone so made music in the world by merely passing through it? And now – burning instead of beauty. . . .

Mr Fordyce came over from Cauldshaw in the evening. He spoke to David but got no answer – it may be doubted if his words were understood. But an invitation to follow him in prayer was rejected, so Mr James prayed alone – 'for Thy hand-maiden who is in the pangs of a great sickness – and for him Thy servant to whom her welfare is especially dear.' The prayer seemed to David to make an enclave for Katrine and himself apart from the world. . . .

Mark took him to his room and made him lie down on his bed. He gave him a bowl of spiced ale which David drank greedily, for he was very thirsty. Maybe the posset contained some innocent drug, for he slipped into dreams. They were pleasant dreams, shapeless and aimless, but with a sense of well-being in them which soothed him, so that he woke to Mark's pressure on his arm with a vacant smile. But one glimpse of the real world – the corner of a four-post bed, torn arras, and the skirts of Mark's frieze coat – brought down on him the dark battalion of his cares. He had no need to wait for the spoken word; Mark's eyes were message enough.

'Come! The fever has abated,' were the words.

David's brain was sluggish: the words seemed to be at variance with the speaker's face; for a moment he had a bewildered spasm of comfort.

'She is recovered?'

'She is dying,' said Mark. 'It is now the afternoon. She is going out with the daylight.'

The small lozenged windows, though there were two of them, lit the room faintly, for the sky was lowering and grey. Mr Fordyce had returned, and poured out his soul at the bed-foot, but presently he grew silent like the others, for there was a hush in the room which made even the words of prayer a sacrilege. . . .

The flush had gone from the girl's face, and the waxen cheeks and the blanched lips told of a mortal weakness. Her hand was in David's, as passive as a plucked flower. The lashes were quiet on her cheeks, and her faint difficult breathing scarcely stirred the coverlet.

In that final hour peace of a kind entered into David's soul. He was truly humble at last, for all the flickerings and unrest of human desires were stilled. The joy which he had scarcely dared to hope for, the possession of that bright and rare thing, was now confirmed to him. Katrine was securely his for ever. . . At the very end her eyes opened, and if they looked a little blindly at the others they seemed to enfold him in a passion of love. There was even the glimmer of a smile. And then the gloaming crept round them, and, as Mark had foretold, she went out with the daylight.

The quiet was broken by the loud wailing of the two women, for the composure of even the iron-lipped Mistress Grizel now failed her. Mr Fordyce stilled it with an uplifted hand. 'The lamb is safe folded,' he said.

Mistress Grizel, after the fashion of her kind, must speak. 'She was a kind lassie and had nae thochts but guid thochts, and if she was maybe no that weel instructed in sound doctrine, it was nae faut in her . . . she was aye blithe to hearken to Mr James—' She stopped short at the sight of David's face.

'She is now at the right hand of the Throne,' he said, 'and I say that in the face of every minister that ever perverted the Word. She was made in the image of her Lord, and she has gone to meet Him.'

Later in the evening the mind of the practical Mistress Grizel turned to the dismal apparatus of death. 'She'll better lie in Cauldshaw in the Hawkshaw buryin' ground. There's room in the auld vault, the mair as it's no likely Nicholas will lay his banes there.'

'Nay, but she will not lie in Cauldshaw.' David's face had a strange calm in it and his voice was toneless and steady. 'She will lie in the part of the greenwood which was her own, in the place she called Paradise. I know her wishes as if she had told them to me. I will not have her laid in any kirkyard vault. . . . She is too young. . . . She is not dead but sleeping.'

Mistress Grizel protested, but half-heartedly. Mr Fordyce had little objection to raise. 'It is not the way of our Kirk,' he said, 'to consecrate ground for the dead. All earth is hallowed which receives Christian dust. But lest the graves of the departed be forgotten, it has been the custom to gather them together in some spot under the kirk's shadow. In a wild wood among bracken and stones it will be ill to keep mind of a place of sepulchre.'

'I will not forget it.'

'But when you yourself are dead and gone . . .?'

'What matters it then?' He could have laughed at the meaninglessness of human fashions. He felt that Katrine and he were in a sphere of their own, safe for ever from intrusion, a sphere independent of time and space, even of life and death. But Paradise had been the spot where their love had first been born; it had become in the mind a symbol and a mystery; let Paradise therefore receive the earthly covering of the blessed spirit, for even the blessed have their terrestrial shrines.

So it came about that by night – for Mistress Grizel would not permit a ceremony so unconventional in daylight – and by the light of the torches of Jock Dodds and Edie the falconer, the girl was buried near the spring in Paradise, with David and Mr Fordyce at the grave's head and foot.

To the former it was all a waking dream. The solid earth had become for him bodiless; the sun's progress, human speech, rain, wind, the ritual of daily life, no more than a phantasmagoria: reality lay only in that inner world where Katrine still lived for him. He abode solitary in the manse, and refused to let Isobel return. Indeed he begged Mistress Saintserf to keep her and be kind to her.

' 'Deed I will do that, and be glad to do it, for she's a skilly auld body and a great stand-by in the house. But, Davie my man, what is to come o' you? I was lookin' to get ye as a guid-son, and the Lord kens Calidon needs a man about the place – what wi' the forty thousand merks to be paid for Nicholas's fine. . . .'

But she saw that her words fell on unheeding ears. David's eyes seemed to be looking beyond her to an infinite distance.

TWENTY

The Judgment

David rode to Kirk Aller to face the Presbytery in a blustering day of April rains. The wind blew high from the south-west in the leafless branches, and tossed the rotting leaves which should long ago have been powdered by frosts and snows. Aller was red with spate and in the haughs the flood-water lay in leaden shallows. The birds, who should have been riotous in the bent, were few and silent; scarcely a plover or a curlew piped; only from the gnarled firs of the Wood came the croak of a nesting raven. It was a day to deaden a man's spirits, but David regarded it not. He was still in his secluded world, a chamber barred to all memories but one. He had no clear vision of the home of the blessed dead, and what he had would have been held unorthodox by the Kirk. Now he thought of her in a Platonic mood as inhabiting all things lovely and pure, a spirit as rare as the lingering light of sunset. But more often he pictured her as an embodied saint admitted into the fellowship of Christ, wrapped round with a richer love than mortals but reaching out warm hands to his loneliness. And the words that came to his tongue were the lines of Peter Abelard:

> O quanta qualia sunt illa sabbata
> Quae semper celebrat superna Curia;

but the sabbaths he dreamed of were not the sabbaths of the Kirk.

The world, the tangible world, was broken for him in fragments. His chamber was not only shut to its winds, but it seemed set in a high tower from which common realities showed infinitely small and distant. The Presbytery – the

General Assembly – the Kirk – seemed tiny things vanishing down the perspective of an inverted spy-glass. He was armoured against censure, for it was idle to censure one who was over-whelmed by his own unworthiness and who at the same time saw all human authorities diminished to cockle-shells. He had no fears and no hates: God had smitten him, and, humble under that awful rod, he could view with indifference the little whips of his fellows. He did not blame them – why should dust accuse dust?

In his detachment only one thought affected him with any passion. He retained his horror of the Wood. If he were to fall he would fain have brought down with him that unholy temple. For Chasehope he felt no hatred except as its high-priest; the man himself, with his crazy twisted soul, was rather a mark for pity. But he would fain have rid Woodilee of that incubus. . . . He had failed, and Chasehope was the victor – Chasehope and the Wood. For a moment his mind returned to realities, and he questioned himself if he had left anything undone. This day his original libel would come before the Presbytery, and he had the right to call his witnesses. But where were they? Reiverslaw had been absent two months from the parish and had not yet returned, and without his testimony Richie Smail and Rab Prentice were meaningless voices. He could give his own witness, but that the Presbytery had already officially rejected. Let it go – the Almighty in His own time would be his vindication – he who was filthy let him be filthy still. . . .:

> Ubi molestiis finitis omnibus
> Securi cantica Sion cantabimus.

But even in his secret world regret penetrated and irked him, for Melanudrigill was nigh to the greenwood and to Paradise.

The old kirk on the brae above the Aller bridge was crowded to its full. Never had been so large a meeting of Presbytery, both lay and clerical, for the case of the minister of Woodilee had made a great talk all winter in the glens. Woodilee itself, now purged of its taint, was strongly represented by four members of

Session, and in a prominent place at the Moderator's elbow sat
Ephraim Caird. As David entered heads were averted, but as he
advanced to the seat prescribed for him he found that Mr
Fordyce was his neighbour – Mr Fordyce heavily muffled in
his ancient plaid, and with a face whose ordinary sick pallor
seemed to be flushed with a timid excitement. He seized
David's hand, and his own was hot and nervous, and his lips
moved as if he were praying under his breath.

The forty-third Psalm was sung, there were two lengthy
readings of Scripture, and then Mr Muirhead, the Moderator,
constituted the Court and prayed for guidance. David's attention wandered, though he tried to supplement the public
supplication with his own. . . . His eyes seemed to have
become distorted and the whole assembly had gone crooked.
The fathers and brethren were no more than a gathering of
death's heads, their voices were like the creaking of wheels
and the scraping of boughs and the grinding of stones. The
Moderator's massive visage was the mask behind which his
brain ticked small and foolish like a clock. The minister of
Bold was only a child, a petted, noisy child. The grave
countenance around him seemed shot with fear and confusion: almost it seemed he could look into their hearts and see
terrors and jealousies writhing like coils of worms. . . . He
rubbed his eyes and forced himself to attention. The Moderator was speaking of the charge against Chasehope and
others anent the Wood.

'We have your written libel, Mr Sempill,' he said. 'It is your
right to implement it by the calling of witnesses. Have you them
here?'

'My principal witness, Andrew Shillinglaw in Reiverslaw, has
left the parish because of the pest and is not yet returned.
Without him I can do nothing.' David's voice, to his own
surprise, came out full and clear.

'Do you seek a postponement?'

David shook his head. 'What boots it? The Lord will judge the
wickedness in His own time and in His own way. But I would

ask that the matter be put to him whom I have accused as principal, and that he deny or affirm it on his solemn oath.'

'You hear that, Ephraim,' said Mr Muirhead. 'I'm loath to put such a task on one of your noted godly walk, but it would maybe conduce to the satisfaction of the Court if you would formally and finally give these monstrous charges a solemn denial.'

Chasehope rose and called his Maker to witness that there was no word of truth in the accusation. His voice was steady, his expression of a decent gravity. He looked towards David, and there was not a quiver in the large placidity of his face.

'The Court is content,' said Mr Muirhead. 'Have you anything to add, Mr Sempill?'

'The Lord will yet judge between us,' said David.

'That matter can therefore be dismissed,' said the Moderator, in a voice in which solemnity wrestled with satisfaction. 'We proceed to the charges against our unhappy brother.'

He set forth – not unfairly – the counts against David. The principal was that abetting of malignancy with which the Court was already familiar, and which David had admitted and justified. But he added new matter.

'It has come to my knowledge,' he said, 'through the praiseworthy vigilance of our friend Chasehope, that there is further incriminating evidence on this score. In the recent melancholy visitation at Woodilee, our brother was guilty of strange deeds and in strange company. It seems that he harled the poor folk out of their bits of dwellings, on the plea that when they crept together they fomented the pest. Thereby it is alleged he spread the taint of the malady, and sorely troubled many a death-bed. Further, he violently and wrongfully broke open doors that were barred to him and set fire to cot-houses where the sick had lain, thereby destroying gear which was not his and depriving the folk of their lawful habitations. I have here an attested statement setting forth the wrongs complained of. What answer do you make to that, Mr Sempill?'

'I admit the acts, and reply that by their means and by God's mercy the pest was stayed.'

There was a murmur of disapproval throughout the gathering, and Mr Muirhead cast up his eyes to Heaven.

'More of this sinful pride! As if the hand of the Lord was stayed by breaking in the doors and burning the thatch of honest folks' houses! But these are matters which are properly for the civil courts and do not come within the cognisance of this Presbytery. What deeply concerns us is the company in which it is alleged that these acts were done. Mr Sempill had as his helper one Amos Ritchie, a dweller in Woodilee, of whom I had hoped better things, and one Mark Riddel, a new-come tenant of the mailin of Crossbasket. We have had news of this Riddel before. He took a leading part in defending a woman accused of witchcraft in the back-end, and – though it seems that the witch-pricker was a poor creature with some irregularities in his conduct – yet it cannot be denied that the words and doings of the man Mark Riddel on that occasion gave great offence to godly folk in Woodilee and led to the just suspicion that he himself had meddled with unlawful matters. . . . Who think you that this Riddel turns out to be? Who but that Mark Kerr that was a colonel with Montrose and a notorious malignant and has been sought all winter by the arm of the law. Chasehope has riddled out the whole black business, and has those that will swear to the man. Information has been dispatched to the Procurator-Fiscal, and it's like that by this time hands will have been laid on him.'

'I fear that he has gotten clean away,' said Chasehope. 'The word this morn was that there was no reek in the Crossbasket lum.'

'He'll no gang far,' said the Moderator, 'for the countryside will be up against him. Now, Mr Sempill, what say you on this count? Did you ken the true nature of this man Mark Riddell?'

'I knew that he had been a soldier of Montrose. What mattered his past if he were willing to help in a work of Christian duty?'

'Christian duty!' The Moderator's face crimsoned with wrath. 'The words should choke in your throat, sir. You dare to call it

Christian duty to harry the living and perplex the dying for some whim of your own ignorant heart? You found a yoke-fellow worthy of you. It is borne in on me that you and your presumption and your slackness of walk and doctrine have been the cause of this sore dispensation in Woodilee. Upon your head, sir, lie the deaths and sufferings of your afflicted people.'

He checked himself with an effort and proceeded in a calmer tone.

'No evidence need be called on the main counts, for they have been admitted by the panel. By his own confession David Sempill, lately ordained minister of the Gospel in Woodilee, is guilty of the grievous sin of consorting with and abetting the declared enemies of Christ's Kirk in Scotland. Under the specious plea of charity – whilk is a favourite device of the Enemy to delude mankind – he has given shelter to one whose hands were red with the blood of the saints, and has endeavoured to cumber the work of purging the accursed thing from our midst. Moreover, he has lately shown what was in his heart by further and intimate converse with the ungodly. I do not speak of other errors, of harsh and un-Christian conduct towards his congregation, of lack of judgment, and of a weakness in doctrine, whilk, if not actual heresy, is its near neighbour. I deal with the gravamen of the matter, a sin openly committed and indeed acknowledged and gloried in.'

Mr Muirhead pursed his lips, and a sigh of approval rose from his hearers.

'But it is needful at all times,' he went on, 'to temper mercy with justice. Our brother is young and has no doubt been led astray by evil conversation and by over-much carnal learning. There is yet room for repentance, and the Kirk is merciful to the penitent. If he will make full confession of his sins and renounce and abhor them and humbly seek forgiveness from an offended Jehovah, this Court will doubtless be prepared to deal tenderly with him. It would not consist with decency that he continue in the charge of Woodilee, but the matter of excommunication might be dispensed with. For let him understand clearly that if he persists in his contumacy he will be outcast not only from the ministry of Woodilee but from membership of the Kirk of Christ.'

His voice had become sensibly gentler. If his main object was to avoid too great a scandal in the Church, there may have been a spice of pity for the youth and the haggard face of the accused.

'I acknowledge myself most heartily to be the chief of sinners,' said David.

'There must be more than a general confession,' said the Moderator. 'You must condescend upon the transgression. You must in this place confess the heinousness of your guilt on the precise counts I have expounded, admit your grievous errors and your abhorrence of them, and humbly submit yourself to judgment.'

'Nay,' said David. 'I cannot admit that to be sin which I hold to have been my duty.'

Again from the assembly came a sound like sighing, but now it seemed to have a note of wrath in it, as if the breath came through clenched teeth. The Moderator shut his eyes as if to ward off an unbearable spectacle. Then he looked down on David with his brows drawn so that they made a line bisecting his great face.

'Man, man,' he said, 'you are far from Christ. You confess your sin, but you hug to your bosom one darling iniquity which you proclaim a grace. You are blinded and self-deluded, and I see no hope for you in this world or the next. You are an outcast from the commonwealth of Israel.'

He inclined his head to Chasehope, who had plucked at his arm and now said something in his ear.

'I am reminded,' he went on. 'Malignancy is not all the sum of the sins of this unhappy man. There was a charge which I had hoped there would be no need to press, but which in his condition of resolute impenitence I am bound to bring forward. He was seen in the back-end to frequent the Black Wood in the company of a woman, and it is alleged – nay, it can be proved by many witnesses – that in his doubtful work during the time of pestilence a woman was in his company. To public sins he would seem to have added private lusts. Answer me, sir, as you will answer some day to your Maker, who or what was the woman, and where is she to be found?'

The words scarcely penetrated to David's brain, for he had already slipped away from the crowd of moody faces to his secret world. But in the hush that followed the question another voice spoke, a voice high-pitched and tremulous but as startling as a trumpet.

'She is with the angels in Heaven.' Mr Fordyce had dropped his plaid from his shoulders, and stood up with raised arm, his eyes burning in his pale face. His repute as a saint was so well established that at any time he would have comanded silence, but now he spoke in a quiet so deep that his hearcrs seemed to be frozen in their seats. Even the Moderator stopped in the act of settling his bands, and his hand remained at his throat.

'I will speak and not be silent,' said the voice. 'The woman whom you would accuse with your foul tongues is this day with her Lord in Paradise. Well I kenned her – she was Katrine Yester and she abode at Calidon – there was none like her for gentleness and grace. She was the promised wife of David Sempill – and in the time of calamity she left her bien dwelling and her secure life and wrought among the poor folk of Woodilee – ay, as Christ left His Father's house to succour sinful men. . . . She is far ayont us for evermore, and in the New Jerusalem she will be so near the Throne that blessed will I be if I get a glimpse of her.'

The words – which when remembered later were accounted a horrid blasphemy – cast at the moment a strange spell over his hearers. The hush was broken by many turning their heads, as if they could not endure the sight of that prophetic face. Even the Moderator dropped his eyes; Chasehope stared at the speaker with half a smile on his lips.

'Fools, fools!' the voice went on. 'I have been ower long silent because of the infirmities of my flesh. One came among you preaching Christ and you have stoned him, as the Jews stoned

Stephen outside the walls of Jerusalem. I pray that it may be given him, like Stephen, to see the heavens open and their Son of Man standing on the right hand of God. . . . I tell you that there's those among us now that will burn in Hell for this day's work. Blind, blind . . .'

He choked, his face coloured with a rush of blood, he swayed and would have fallen had not David caught him. The cessation of the haunting voice restored the assembly to its senses. Murmurings began, and the Moderator dropped his hand from his throat and found speech.

'This is most unseemly. Our brother is sick and has forgotten himself. Let the work of the Court proceed.'

David lifted the half-fainting Mr Fordyce in his arms. He bowed to the Moderator. 'My presence is no longer needed,' he said. 'I have no more to say and am in the hands of the Court. Meantime I must look to my friend.'

He left the kirk with his burden.

He took him to the little inn in the Nethergate and put him to bed. The landlady was a kindly soul and promised to tend him well; there was no serious illness – excitement and emotion and an unaccustomed effort had drawn heavily upon Mr Fordyce's small reserve of strength – he needed only rest to be himself again. David found a Cauldshaw man just setting off up the water and sent by him a message to ease the mind of Mrs Fordyce, and tell her that her husband would return on the morrow. When he left him he was sleeping.

This business occupied his time till late afternoon, and gloaming had already set in before he rode out of Kirk Aller. The Presbytery business was long since concluded and the kirk on the brae was vacant and locked. The members had departed, for the yard of the Cross Keys, which in the morning had been like a horse-fair, was now empty. The wind, which had been growing in violence all day, had now reached the force of a gale, and as David turned the corner above the gorge where the Aller breaks from the hills into the haugh, it met him full in the face.

He pulled his hat low on his head and looked back. The little town, very bleak and grey in the chill April evening, lay smoking with its hundred chimneys. The sight affected him with a painful regret. It seemed a last look upon the life from which he was now an outcast, a life which eighteen months ago he had so warmly embraced.

He was coming out of his abstraction now and looking at cold realities. Mr Fordyce's outburst in the Presbytery had shattered his secret world. Katrine was in bliss and he was left alone on the bare roads of earth. Very solitary he felt; his father was dead, Mark Riddel was a fugitive, Reiverslaw had failed him, his Church had cast him out; there was no place for him, it seemed, in all the habitable globe, no work to his hand, no friend to lean on. He was looking at life now in a light as bleak as that April day which was now vanishing from the hills. . . . He seemed to have lost the power of feeling. He had no grudge against his enemies, no hatred even for Chasehope; his humility had become so deep that it was almost the abnegation of manhood. He was very tired and had lost the will to contend. 'Katrine, Katrine!' his heart cried. 'I'm not wanted on earth, and there's no comfort here for the comfortless. O my love, that I were with you!'

The night grew colder as it advanced, and the wind, which commonly he welcomed, now cut him to the bone. He drew his cloak round him, and tried to urge his horse to a better pace. But apathy seemed to have fallen on beast as well as master, and it jogged funereally, as if in no hurry to leave the chilly out-of-doors for the manse stable. There was a moon behind the flying rack of the sky, and there was light enough to see the dark huddle of the hills. Only where the track dipped to the trees by the riverside was there any depth of shadow.

It was in one such patch of blackness that David heard the sound of a horse behind him. Presently the rider was abreast of him, and even in the dark it seemed that he recognised him. 'Guid e'en to ye, Mr Sempill,' said a voice, but a gust of wind made it hard to recognise it. The new-comer fell into step beside him, and when in a minute they came out of the trees David saw that it was Chasehope.

'You are late on the road, friend,' he said.

'I had weighty business on hand,' was the answer. The man was in a good humour, for he was humming a tune.

'This has been a waesome day for you, Mr Sempill,' he went on. 'Ye have set yoursel' up against God's law and man's law, and ye have taken a mighty fall. I bear no malice – though weel I might if the Lord hadna gi'en me grace to forgive. What I have done in your case I have done painfully as my solemn duty. But there's pardon even for the chief of sinners, and it's not to be believed that one like yoursel' that had once a title in Christ can be cast away. Seek mercy where it is to be found, Mr Sempill.'

Chasehope spoke fast like one under the influence of drink, but the man was temperate, so it must have been some excitement of the spirit. In the dim light David could not see his face, but he knew the kind of light that was in his eye, for he had witnessed it before.

'I speak in all loving-kindness,' he went on. 'If ye're of the Elect, you and me will meet before the Throne. I would hold out a hand to a stumbling brother.'

David made no answer, but his silence did not check Chasehope's flow, for he seemed to be burdened with that which must have vent.

'What have ye made of it wi' your railing accusations? Bethink ye of that, Mr Sempill. What has become o' your uncovenanted Reiverslaw, and your Glee'd Mark wi' his warlockry, and the bonny may ye trysted wi'? Ane is vanished like a landlouper, and ane will soon ken the wuddy, and ane is under the mools.'

David spoke at last, and had the other had ears to hear he might have detected a strange note in the minister's voice.

'You speak the truth. I am indeed friendless and forlorn.'

'Friendless and forlorn! 'Deed that's the word. And wherefore, Mr Sempill? Because ye have flung yoursel' against the rock o' the Elect who are secure in the Lord's hands. What said the worthy Moderator after ye had gone? He likened the Kirk to

the stone spoken of in Matthew twenty-one and forty-four –
"Whosoever shall fall on this stone shall be broken: but on
whomsoever it shall fall, it will grind him to powder." '

'There was another word spoken – that some for this day's
work would burn in Hell.'

Chasehope laughed his rare and ugly laugh. 'Hoots, man, that
was just puir Mr Fordyce, and a'body kens him. No but what he
has the root o' the matter in him – but he's a dwaibly body wi'
nae mair fushion than a thresh.'

'Nevertheless he spoke truly. Hell is waiting for some, and
maybe this very night.'

Again Chasehope laughed. 'Is Saul also among the prophets?'
he asked. 'Who are you, a minister outed and excommunicat,
that you suld take to the prophesyin'?'

'God makes use of the feeblest pipes to proclaim His will. I
tell you, Ephraim Caird, that this very night judgment may
overtake you.'

This time Chasehope did not laugh, but moved his horse a
little apart.

'Do ye daur to threaten me—?'

'I threaten no man, but God threatens you.'

'Awa wi' you! I have a firm assurance. And if ye daur lift hand
on me—'

'Be comforted. My hand will not be lifted.'

The man seemed to recover his composure, for he edged his
horse nearer and thrust forward his face.

'Ye've aye hated me. I could see it in your een the first day at
the manse.'

'I have never hated you. There is no man living in whose
company I would rather ride this night. I love you so dearly that
I would save your soul.'

'You to speak of savin' souls!' Chasehope began, and then
stopped. For there was something in David which struck a chill
even to his excited mind. The quiet masterful voice cut into his
wild gabble like iron into peat. If there was madness in the man,
there was a fiercer madness in the minister, for in the last

minutes David's weakness had fallen from him like rags and he had quickened to a flaming zeal. It was a flame of such heat that it burned calmly, but the glow of it, radiating from him, made the other's mere wildfire.

David spoke no further word, but a nervous restlessness came upon Chasehope. He blustered and bragged. See to what a pitch of esteem he had come from following the narrow way! And he whined. He had the frailty of all mortals, but it was atoned for by the imputed righteousness of his Redeemer. He seemed to long for a word of confirmation, and he pawed at the minister's sleeve. But no answer came, and the silence of the other began to unnerve him. His voice had a startled note, he quoted texts as if they were supplications to the stony impassiveness of his companion. When his horse stumbled and he almost collided with the minister, he cried out suddenly, as if in fear.

They had crossed Aller half a mile below Roodfoot, and had come to the turning of the ways. The clouds had thinned and the struggling moon showed Melanudrigill before them, rising and falling like an ocean of darkness. David kept his horse's head straight for it, and Chasehope, who had been riding on his left, edged his beast across the path.

'Ye'll be for the short road. I'll gang quicker by the back o' Windyways. . . . Losh, that's an awesome wind.'

'It's the wind of the Lord's anger.'

'Guid e'en to ye, and God send ye a contrite heart!' Chasehope seemed to have recovered courage at the prospect of parting company.

David laid a hand on his bridle.

'Nay, you and I do not twine here. Our road lies yonder.'

'Are ye daft, man?' Chasehope cried, his voice strong again. 'Who are you to order a man like me?' The voice was strong, but in its shrillness was disquiet.

'I do not order you. Look in your heart and you will find the compulsion. It was not for nothing, Ephraim Caird, that we forgathered this night. The Lord ordained it, and in your marrow you know that you cannot leave me. This night we are in a closer bond than man and wife.'

'Havers!' It was the last spasm of bluster, and the voice was weaker than the word. 'I'll do no man's bidding. Tak' your hand from my bridle.'

The hand was raised, and the other cowered to his saddlebow, as if to avert a stroke. But the hand did not fall. Instead it gripped his arm, and the grip seemed to crush his bones.

'You fool,' said the grave voice. 'This night I have the strength of ten men, for the Lord is in me. I could strike you dead if I were minded, but the command is on me that we ride together.'

Chasehope's arrogance had drained out of him, but it had left some dregs of courage. He struggled to compose his voice and recover his every-day demeanour.

'Weel, since ye're so pressin' I'll do your will. There's no half a mile differ in the roads.' But the words did nothing to break the spell which choked him. They were like the wry-mouthed bravado of a criminal at the gallows' foot.

No word was spoken as they crossed the haugh and skirted the Fennan Moss, but had there been anyone to see he would have noted that David rode erect like a trooper, while Chasehope hung like a sack in his saddle, and that David's knee was hard pressed against the other's, as if the two were shackled.

They came to the edge of the Wood, where the road bent to the right among the pine roots towards the glen of Woodilee burn.

'We dismount here,' said David, 'for we cannot ride among the trees. The beasts will find their way home.'

Chasehope cried out, and his voice now was strangled with terror.

'The Wud! No the Wud! Ye daurna gang there . . .' He raised his arm and would have struck, but David caught his wrist. He overbalanced himself and rolled to the ground and in a second David was beside him. The horses, alarmed by the scuffle, dashed up the track.

Fear made the man violent. He flung himself on David, but for all his weight found himself tossed down like a feather. Was this stern figure with the sinews of iron the minister whom he had despised?

The quiet voice spoke.

'You are gross and elderly and I have the exercised strength of youth. At no time could you hope to strive with me. But this night the might of the Lord is in me and I could break you like a straw. . . . You will come with me, though I have to ding you senseless and carry you.'

The man scrambled to his feet and made the place echo with his cries for help. No answer came, except the flap of disturbed night birds.

'Where would ye have me gang?' he whimpered.

'Into the Wood – to the place you know of. Ephraim Caird, this night I give you the chance of salvation. I may have erred – my eyes may have deceived me – it may not have been you that capered and piped in a dog's mask to yon lost crew. If I have been wrong, it will be proven yonder. If I have been right, you will be given a chance of repentance. We go up to the Mount together that you may choose between Abiron and Jehovah.'

Chasehope crouched like a dog. 'I daurna – I daurna,' he wailed. 'I'm a believin' man, but I daurna enter the Wud. . . . It's no the season – there's fearsome things ryngin' in't. Oh, ye dinna ken. . . . Let me gang hame and the morn I'll gang on my hunkers to Kirk Aller and sweir that a' I hae said against ye was a lee. I'll confess . . .'

David's grip was on his arm, but he did not struggle. His legs were loosened, and his whole body dropped like a creature stricken with the palsy.

'I'll make confession – I'll tell ye things that are no to be named – I took the Wud wi' ithers, but I kenned I was a redeemed soul and that the Lord wouldna cast me away. . . . I aye ettled to repent, for I was sure o' the Mercy Seat. . . . It is written that Solomon went after the abominations of Moab, and was yet numbered among the Elect. . . . But I'll hae na mair o't frae this day. . . . I'll tak' my aith on the Word . . . I'll cast my idols ahint my back . . . I'll burn the books . . . I'll forswear the Deil . . .'

'You will do it yonder,' said David.

He had never entered the Wood from this side, and in the darkness the road would have been at all times hard to find, but now he seemed to have a map in his brain and to steer by an instinct. In this backward Spring there was no sprouting undergrowth, but the dead bracken stalks had not yet shrunk to earth, and he waded waist-deep among them. The man beside him had lost the power of resistance. He followed like an obedient hound, without the need of David's grasp on his arm. Often he stumbled, and once he fell into the dell of a burn and had to be lifted out, but he made no attempt at resistance or escape. He walked and sometimes ran, crouching almost double, and as he went he made little moaning noises which might have been prayers.

The wind was wild in the tree-tops, and rushing down the aisles and corries of the hillside made a sound which was now like a great organ and now like muffled drums. Higher they mounted till they reached a broad shelf of more level ground, where the covert was thick and the speed slow. . . . And then, almost before he was aware of it, David found himself looking at an open space with a dark stone in the midst of it.

The moonlight was faint, but the glade was clear in its outlines, a patch of grey turf in a ring of inky shadow. The altar was no longer white as in the summer midnight, but dark with the drenching winter rains. A bleak sodden place, it now appeared to David, a trivial place, no more than a common howe in a wood.

But the other seemed to look on it with different eyes. When he saw the stone he gave one shrill cry of terror and collapsed on the ground, burying his face in the moss as if to shut out the sight. David seized him and dragged him forward till he lay by the altar, and all the while his screams rose piercingly above the wind.

'There is no need for confession,' the minister said. 'You have betrayed yourself. . . . Now I know with the uttermost certainty that it was you I saw here at Beltane and at Lammas.'

The man did not raise his head, but clasped David's legs and nozzled him like a fawning dog, while, like a dog, he gave short, terrified yelps.

'Your sin is proven and acknowledged,' said David. 'Here on the scene of your guilt you will choose your road. I say to you as Elijah said to the people of Israel, "If the Lord be God, follow Him; but if Baal, then follow him." This night you renounce Abiron or renounce Christ.'

The man was silent, as if the extremity of fear had frozen his speech. But as David raised him, a shuddering like an epilepsy shook his body. His legs were limp, and David placed him on his knees so that his brow rested on the stone.

'Renounce your master here in his temple . . . I will give you words if you have none of your own. . . . Say after me, "I abhor and reject the Devil and all his works, and I fling myself upon the mercy of God." Man, man, it is your immortal soul that trembles above the Pit.'

The huddled figure was still silent. Then, after a violent shiver, his voice came back to him. He began to stutter words, words meaningless to David's ear. It may be that it was the renunciation of his gods; but, whatever it was, it was not completed.

For suddenly energy returned to his limbs and he sprang violently to his feet. Madness glowed in his eyes; his head was held for a second in a listening posture.

'They come,' he screamed. 'The dogs! – the red dogs!'

David seized him, but at that moment the maniac's strength far exceeded his own. He tore himself free with a rending of his clothes. His face was a limp vacancy of terror in which the eyes glared unseeingly. He leaped into the air, spun round, fell, laid his ear to the earth, and then with incredible swiftness ran uphill from the glade. Once he halted to listen, and then, so bent that he appeared to run on all-fours, and yelping like a stricken beast, he vanished into the shades. . . . In a pause of the wind David heard his movements grow fainter, and he thought he heard too a murmur of voices as at Beltane and Lammas. It seemed to him that these voices were now like the distant baying of hounds.

Lethargy returned upon David's soul. He had done his duty, and at the last moment, like Samson, had brought down the false temple; but what signified it to one who had no further hope or purpose? He walked out of the Wood as steeled to its awareness as to the other common emotions of man. His heart had dried up within him, and his vitality had run down like an unwound clock. He had but the one thought – to visit Paradise again and Katrine's grave, and this not for comfort but as a step enjoined by duty to complete the heavy weight of his loneliness. After that nothing mattered. His youth was gone and he was become very old.

He crossed the barrier glen, brushed through the catkinladen hazels, and came to his sacred glade. There was the well bubbling darkly, and there beyond it was the fresh-made mound of turf. . . . The sight melted something within him. He flung himself on the grass and his dry heart was loosened in tears. As he wept he prayed, and as he prayed he seemed to live once again the bright days when Katrine had sung to him among the flowers. Fragments of her songs came back to him:

> There's comfort for the comfortless
> And hinny for the bee—

Was there any comfort for a stricken man on this side of eternity? He had a vision of her face with its proud laughing courage, he heard again her voice coming faint and sweet from behind the hills of death. She was smiling, she was saying something too rare for mortal ears to catch, but it seemed to thaw within him the springs of life.

He lay long on the turf, and when at last he raised his head the dawn was breaking. The wind had fallen, and into the air had come the softness of Spring. A thrush sang in the covert – he thought he caught the scent of flowers. . . . Of a sudden the world righted itself and youth came back to him. He saw brightness again on the roads of life and a great brightness at the end of them, where Katrine was his for ever among the eternal fields.

Rab Prentice, limping out in the early morning to see to the lambing ewes in his hirsel, had occasion to take a short cut through the hazel shaws. He was surprised to see a man walking with great strides from the coppice, and more surprised to recognise him as the minister. What did Mr Sempill there at that hour? He watched the figure till it disappeared over the ridge, and then went home much puzzled to his cog of brose.

In after-days Rab Prentice searched his memory for every detail of that sight, and often he recounted it to breathless listeners. For his were the last eyes in Woodilee to see the minister on earth.

TWENTY-ONE

The Going of the Minister

Woodilee was early astir, for it was to be a day of portents in the parish. Word had come the night before of the judgment of the Presbytery – that their minister was deposed and excommunicated and that Mr Muirhead of Kirk Aller and Mr Proudfoot of Bold had been deputed to preach the kirk vacant that very day. There was little work on the farms, for the lambing had scarcely begun, the ploughing was finished, and the ground was not yet dry enough for the seed-bed; so the whole parish waited at the kirkyard gate.

Resentment was still deep against the minister as the cause – under Heaven – of the pestilence, and for his high-handed dealings during that time of trial. There were also the old grievances against him, so that those faithful to him were very few. Isobel was at Calidon, Reiverslaw had gone no man knew where, and only Amos Ritchie and one or two women were left to defend him. Strange news had come about the tenant of Crossbasket. There had been soldiers seeking him with a warrant for his apprehension; it seemed that the decent, quiet-spoken farmer-body was Mark Kerr, a kinsman of the Lord Roxburghe, whose name had appeared in many proclamations of the Kirk and the Estates, and who since Philiphaugh had been zealously sought for through the length of Scotland. Men remembered his masterful ways and declared that they had always known that he was gentrice; they remembered his handling of the pricker and were confident that they had detected his ungodliness. But that he should have lived among them gave them a feeling of distinction and adventure, and the younger people cast curious eyes towards the empty house of Crossbasket.

It was the first day that Spring seemed to have come into the air, and the congregation, waiting in the kirkyard for the arrival of the ministers, were warmed by a mild and pleasant sun. The elders stood by the gate, each in his best attire, wearing – even the miller – an air of ceremonial gravity.

'This is a great day for Woodilee,' said Nether Fennan, 'and a great day for Christ's Kirk in Scotland. We cleanse the tabernacle of an unworthy vessel, and woe is me that some o' the bauldest and stenchest Christians have no lived to see it. Peter Pennecuik – honest Peter had nae broo o' Sempill – clouts o' cauld morality, was his word – Peter has gane ower soon to his reward.'

'What's come o' Chasehope?' Mirehope asked. 'He suld have been here langsyne. He'll surely no be late on this heart-searching day.'

'I heard from the Chasehope herd,' said the miller, 'that Ephraim never cam hame last night. The wife was sair concerned, but she jaloused it would be Presbytery business.'

'But that was a' by and done wi' by three in the afternoon. He would be seein' Edom Trumbull about the new aits. Still and on, it's no like Chasehope to let warldly matters interfere wi' his Christian duty. . . . Eh, sirs, what a testimony Woodilee will bear the day! Mr Mungo is to proclaim the outing, and Mr Ebenezer is to preach the sermon, and on sic an occasion Bold is like a hungry gled and the voice o' him like a Januar' blast.'

Among the women sitting on the flat gravestones there was less talk of the Kirk and more of the minister. Most were bitter against him.

'They may out him and excommunicate him,' cried Jean of the Chasehope-foot, 'but wha will restore me the braw bairn that dee'd in the Pest whilk was sent to punish him? Answer me that, kimmers. I wad be the better pleased if I got my ten fingers at his thrapple.'

'Weel for you, wumman,' said another, 'that Isobel Veitch is no here, or it's your ain thrapple would suffer.'

'There's a queer tale come up the water wi' Johnnie Dow,' said a third. 'There was talk, ye mind, o' a lassie that he met wi' in the Wud, and we a' ken that there was a lassie wi' him in the hinder days o' the Pest – the fairest face, some folk say, that they ever looked on.'

'Tuts, gossip, yon was nae lassie. Yon face was never flesh and bluid. It was a bogle oot o' the Wud, and some says—' The speaker lowered her voice and spoke into her neighbour's ear.

'Bogle or no, Aggie Vicar, it cured my wee Benjie and nae word will be spoke oot o' my mouth against it. The callant is still greeting for anither sight o' the bonny leddy.'

'Haud your tongues and let me speak. Johnnie Dow says the Presbytery had it a' riddled out, and it seems it was nae fairy but a leevin' lassie. And wha think you she was? Nae less than the young mistress o' Calidon.'

The women exclaimed, most of them incredulous.

'But that's no a'. It seems that she and the minister had made it up thegither and she was promised till him. Mr Fordyce o' Cauldshaw telled that to the Presbytery.'

'Heard ye ever the like? Will Sempill be hingin' up his bonnet at Calidon and turnin' frae minister to laird? The lassie will no doubt heir the place, and it's weel kenned that Sempill has walth o' gear o' his ain.'

'He canna weel do that if he's excommunicat. He'll aiblins be for fleein' the country like the auld laird, and takin' the quean wi' him.'

'Ye havena heard the end o' the tale,' said the first speaker. 'Dinna yatter like pyots, or I winna get it telled. . . . The lassie is deid – deid three days syne o' a backcast o' the Pest, and the minister is no to haud nor bind wi' grief. Johnnie said he sat yestreen at Kirk Aller wi' a face like corp and took his paiks as mild as a wean, and him for ordinar' sic an ettercap. Johnnie thriepit that he had maybe lost his reason.'

There was silence among her hearers, and only Jean of Chasehope-foot laughed. 'She's weel oot o' it.' she said, 'and he's weel served.'

'Wheesht, wumman,' said one. 'The lad had sinned, but he's but young, and his punishment is maybe ower sair.'

There was a movement among the crowd, for the ministers were seen approaching. They were received by the elders and conducted to the minute session-house, which was a pendicle on the east wall of the kirk. The congregation, according to custom, now entered the building, whence could presently be heard the sound of slow psalmody. Robb the beadle waited at the single door till the ministers reappeared, Mr Muirhead in Geneva gown and bands, Mr Proudfoot in his country home-spun, for he was a despiser even of sanctioned forms. They too entered, and Robb followed, closing the door behind him, but leaving the great key in the lock.

Amos Ritchie appeared, moodily sauntering through the gate. He had been unable to face the kirkyard crowd, knowing that he would hear words spoken which might crack his brittle temper. He reached the door and was about to enter, when the sound of furious hoofs on the road made him pause. The rider hitched his bridle to the gate-post and strode up the path, and Amos saw that it was Reiverslaw.

'Am I ower late?' the new-comer panted. 'What's asteer in the kirk?'

'Ye're ower late,' said Amos bitterly. 'Yestreen the minister was condemned and excommunicat by the Presbytery at Kirk Aller, and Chasehope was affirmed a saunt for want o' you to testify against him. This day Muirhead and Proudfoot are preachin' the kirk empty.'

'God be merciful to me,' Reiverslaw groaned. 'I only got the word last night, and I've left weary beasts on the road atween here and Langholm. . . . Where is the minister? Where is Mr Sempill?'

'The Lord kens. He's no in the manse, for I was there at skreigh o' day, and he hasna been seen since he left Kirk Aller. . . . What does it matter? The puir lad has his name blastit, and Woodilee loses the best man that ever walked its road. . . . Are ye for in?'

'I'm for in,' said Reiverslaw grimly. 'If I canna help the minister I can mishandle some that hae brocht him doun. I'm thinkin' Chasehope will hae sair bones or nicht.'

The two slipped through the door and stood in the dusk at the extreme back of the crowded kirk. The first exercises having been concluded, Mr Muirhead was reading from the pulpit the finding of the Presbytery. The misdeeds of the minister were set forth *seriatim* with the crooked verbosity of a legal document. Then came the pith:

> Wherefore the Presbytery of Aller, in the name of the Lord Jesus Christ, the sole King and Head of the Church, and by the power committed by Him to them, did and hereby do summarily excommunicate David Sempill, at present residing in the parish of Woodilee, delivering him over to Satan for the destruction of the flesh that the spirit may be saved in the day of the Lord, and the Presbytery did, and hereby do, enjoin all the faithful to shun all dealings with him as they would not be found to harden him in his sins, and so to partake with him in his judgments.

The Moderator read the words with a full voice and with relish. He outlined briefly the civil consequences attaching to excommunication, and dwelt terrifyingly on the religious state of one cut off from communion with Christ and his Kirk. Then he proceeded to depose the minister *in absentia* from the charge and to declare it vacant till such time as a successor was appointed. The appointment would be in the free gift of the people, subject to confirmation by the Presbytery, since Nicholas Hawkshaw, the chief, indeed the sole, heritor, was an outlaw and a fugitive. He concluded with prayer, a copious outpouring in which the godly in Woodilee were lauded for their zeal, condoled with in their sufferings, and recommended for a special mark of the Lord's favour. Then he drew the skirts of his gown delicately around him, and gave place to the minister of Bold.

Mr Proudfoot chose for his text second Kings, the tenth chapter, the twenty-fourth verse, the second clause of the verse:

'If any of the men whom I have brought into your hands escape, he that letteth him go, his life shall be for the life of him.' It was a theme that suited his genius, and never had he spoken with more freedom and power. Scripture was heaped upon Scripture to show the guilt of halfheartedness in God's cause ('Curse ye Meroz, said the angel of the Lord'); the other charges against David he neglected, and concentrated on the awful guilt of unfaithfulness to the Kirk in her hour of trial. The bulk of the world lay prone under the foot of Satan, but in Scotland the Lord had set His poor people erect and committed His cause to their charge, and woe be to them if they faltered in that trust. At this point Mr Proudfoot almost attained sublimity. There was a crusading zeal in his voice; his picture of the stand of the faithful remnant against the world was the vision of a stout heart.

He passed to David and his backslidings. He drew the minister as a weakling, beginning no doubt with an honest purpose, but soon seduced from the narrow path by the lusts of the eye and the pride of life. 'Oh, is it not pitiful,' he cried, 'in this short and perishing world, with the Pit yawning by the roadside and the fires of Hell banked beneath us – is it not pitiful and lamentable that the soul of man should have other thoughts than its hard-won salvation? What signify profane learning and the delights of the eye and the comforts of the body and even good intents toward your fellows, if at the hinder end the Judge of all will ask but the one question – Have you your title in Christ?'

In especial, he dealt scornfully with the plea of charity. There could be no charity towards sin. The accursed thing must be destroyed wherever found, and were it the wife of a man's bosom or the son of the same mother the sinner must be struck down.

The congregation listened as if under a spell. So intent were they that neither the people on their stools nor the Moderator in his chair nor the preacher in the pulpit noticed that in the dim backend of the kirk the door had opened and someone had entered.

But it was in the close of his discourse that the gale came upon Mr Proudfoot's spirit. Now he was at his application. The history of Israel was searched to show how Jehovah the merciful was yet merciless towards error. Agag was hewn in pieces – the priests and worshippers of Baal were slain to a man – the groves were cut down and ploughed up and sown with salt. . . . So rapt were preacher and people that they did not observe that a newcomer was among them moving quietly up the kirk. . . . The minister of Bold concluded in a whirl of eloquence with his favourite instance of Barak the son of Abinoam – how with ten thousand men of Naphtali and Zebulun he went down from the mount Tabor and fell upon Sisera, the captain of the hosts of Canaan, so that not a man was left. He likened himself in all humility to Deborah the prophetess; he called upon the people of the Lord, even as she had called upon Barak, to rise and destroy the Canaanites without questioning and without respite. 'Let us smite the chariots and the host with the edge of the sword, for in this day hath the Lord delivered Sisera into our hand, and let us pursue after the remnant even to Harosheth of the Gentiles!'

'Harosheth of your grannie!'

The minister's voice had stopped, and, in the profound hush that followed, the four words fell with a startling clearness. The blasphemy of them was not decreased by the tone, which was of measureless contempt. The scared eyes of the people saw Mark Riddel, for whom soldiers were now beating the countryside, standing easy and arrogant before the pulpit, and those near him drew away their stools in panic. He had not the look of a hunted man, and though his presence had always won him respect in Woodilee he seemed now to have expanded into someone most formidable and unfamiliar. He wore the same clothes as he had worn in field and market, but he held himself very differently from the friendly crony who had sat in Lucky Weir's. At his side, too, swung a long sword.

Mr Proudfoot looked boldly down on him.

'Who are you that dares to cast scorn upon the Word?' he asked in a firm voice.

'Not on the Word,' was the answer, 'but on the auld wives that pervert it.' He nodded over his shoulder. 'They ken me fine in the parish. I was baptized after the Apostle, and for my surname ye can choose Kerr or Riddel as it pleases you.'

The Moderator sat with a flaming face. 'It is Mark Kerr the malignant. I summon all law-abiding and Christian men to lay hands on him and convey him to a place of bondage.'

But no one stirred. The dark face with the laugh at the lips, the fierce contemptuous eyes, the figure compact and light with a strength which the toil-bent shoulders of Woodilee could never equal, the repute for magical skill – these were things terrible enough without the long sword.

Mr Muirhead rose. 'Then I and my brother will get us forth of this place. Come, Mr Ebenezer,' and he gathered the skirts of his gown.

'Nay, friends,' said Mark, 'ye'll bide where ye are. And the folk will keep their seats, till I give them leave to skail.' He swung the key of the kirk door in his hand as he spoke. 'Sit ye doun, Mr Muirhead. Sit ye doun, worthy Mr Proudfoot. You billies have the chance ilka Sabbath o' sayin' your say and no man can controvert you. This day for a change ye will have to hearken.'

In justice to the two ministers let it be said that it was not the sword that kept them in their places. Neither lacked courage. But this man who stood confronting them, the very sight of whom seemed to paralyse the folk of Woodilee, this shameless malignant had a compelling something in his air. He spoke as one having authority; though he used the broad country speech he had that in his voice which, whether it spring from camp or court or college, means command. Very sensitive to this note in their disciplined Kirk, the two ministers listened.

What fell from Mark's lips was discussed secretly for many a day in the countryside. Publicly it was rarely mentioned, for a more awful blasphemy, it seemed, was never spoken in the house of God. He told two pillars of the Kirk and a congregation of the devout that they had all failed utterly to interpret God's Word; that they were Pharisees faithful to an ill-understood letter and heedless of the spirit; that they were fools bemused with Jewish rites which they did not comprehend and Jewish names which they could not properly pronounce. 'It's nothing but a bairn's ploy,' he cried, 'but it's a cruel ploy, for it has spilt muckle good blood in Scotland. If ye take the bloodthirstiness and the hewing in pieces and the thrawnness of the auld Jews and ettle to shape yourselves on their pattern, what for do ye no gang further? Wherefore d'ye no set up an altar and burn a wedder on't? What kind o' kirk is this, when ye suld have a temple with gopher and shittim wood and shew-bread and an ark o' the covenant and branched candlesticks, and busk your minister in an ephod instead of a black gown? Ye canna pick and choose in the Word. If one thing is to be zealously copied, wherefore not all?. . . . Ye fatted calves!. . . . Ye muckle weans that play at being ancient Israelites!'

This was too much for Mr Proudfoot.

'Silence, blasphemer,' he cried. 'In the name of Him that snappeth the spear asunder I will outface you.' He stumbled down the pulpit stairs, and would no doubt have flung himself on Mark had not old Nance Kello who sat at the foot impeded him and given Mirehope time to catch his coat-skirts. He stopped, breathing heavily, about three yards from Mark, and, as he stood, it was not the sword that a second time deterred him. He felt dimly that this outlaw had come to wear a fearful authority. It was not the tacksman of Crossbasket that spoke but the captain of Mackay's – not the farmer of Jed Water but the kinsman of Roxburghe and the brigadier of Montrose.

Mr Proudfoot turned to his colleague and saw that the Moderator's eye was puzzled and uncertain. He bethought him of his chief ally in the parish. 'Where is Chasehope?' he cried. 'Where is Ephraim Caird?'

The answer came from an unlooked-for quarter. Daft Gibbie sat crouched in a corner of the kirk, and those near him had marked his unwonted silence. He did not gabble as usual, but sat with his great head in his hands, murmuring softly and rolling his wild eyes. But at the mention of Chasehope he suddenly found voice.

'He's up in the hills,' he cried. 'I seen him at skreigh o' day at the buchts o' the Drygrain and he was rivin' a yowe and cryin' that it was a hound o' hell and that it suldna devour him. He was a' lappered wi' bluid, and when he seen me he ran on me, and his een were red and he slavered like a mad tyke and his face was thrawed oot o' the shape o' man. Eh, sirs, puir Gibbie was near his end, for I couldna stir a foot, but afore he wan to me there cam' anither sound, and as sure as death it was like a hound's yawp. At that he gangs off like the wund, and the next I seen o' him he was skelpin' through the flowe moss, cryin' like ane in torment, and I stottered hame to get Amos Ritchie to tak' his flint-lock and stop yon awfu' skellochs. I'll never sleep till I ken that the lost soul o' him is free o' the body.'

'Another has told my tale.' Mark spoke in a voice out of which all scorn had gone, a voice penetratingly quiet and solemn. 'I too have seen him that once was Ephraim Caird and I shudder at the swiftness of the judgment. There is no man or woman in Woodilee that does not ken that he was the leader of the Coven that practised the devil's arts in the Wood, but he had a name for godliness and he had the measure of the blind fools that call themselves ministers of God. – Sit still, sir! I would be loth to draw on an unarmed man, but my sword ere this has punished vermin. . . . He has sworn falsely against the innocent, and yestreen at Kirk Aller he prevailed. But in the night the Lord sent forth His vengeance – ask me not how, for I do not know – and this day he is running demented on the hills, pursued by the dogs of his own terrors. Go and look for him. You will find him in a bog-hole or a pool in the burn. Bury his body decently, but bury it face downward, so that you speed him on his road.'

There was such a silence that the rasp of a stool on the earthen floor struck the hearers like a thunderclap. One voice – it was Amos Ritchie's – came out of the back of the kirk.

'Where is the minister?' it asked.

'He is gone where ye will never see him more,' said Mark. 'A prophet came among you and you knew him not. For the sake of that witless thing that is now going four-foot among the braes you have condemned the innocent blood. He spent his strength for you and you rejected him, he yearned for you and you repelled him, he would have laid down his life for you and you scorned him. He is now beyond the reach of your ingratitude.'

'Unless he be dead,' said Mr Proudfoot, 'he is not beyond the reach of the law, and if he be dead he has fallen into the hands of a living and offended God.'

'Man, man,' said Mark gently, 'you and your like have most lamentably confounded God and Devil.'

'And you yourself,' cried the Moderator, struggling valiantly to assert himself against an atmosphere which he felt inimical, 'are within a span of the gallows.'

'We are all and at all times within a span of death. . . . To you, reverend sirs, I have no more to say. You will gang your own ways, and some day others will play the tyrant over you and give you your ain kail through the reek. In that day of humiliation you will repent of what you did in your pride. . . . To those who have been partakers of the iniquity of the Wood I wish no less than the fate that has overtaken their master. . . . To the poor folk of Woodilee I leave their minister's blessing, and may they have whiles a kindly thought of one that loved them.'

He turned at the door. 'You will bide here till you are released. The ministers can while away the time excommunicatin' me. Guid day to you a'.'

Amos Ritchie and Reiverslaw slipped out after him, and the key was turned in the lock. Amos wept bitterly, and Reiverslaw's dark face was working with suppressed tears.

'You have to live on in this parish,' Mark said. 'I need not involve you in my own peril. Let the bodies out in half an hour. No one saw you enter, so you will get no discredit by this day's work. Say you found the key by the roadside.'

Amos turned on him with a distraught eye.

'Where is Mr David? What have ye done with him?. . . . We ken nocht o' you – ye come and gang like bogfire – there's some says ye're the Deil himsel'. If ye've wiled a saunt doun the road to Hell—'

'Be comforted,' said Mark, laying a hand on Amos's arm. 'I think I have helped to open for him the gates of Paradise.'

Epilogue

The Reverend John Dennistoun in his once-famous work *Satan's Artifices against the Elect* (written in the year 1719 but not published till 1821, when the manuscript came into the hands of Sir Walter Scott) has a chapter on the disturbances in Woodilee. In his pages can be found the tradition which established itself during the next fifty years. He has heard of the doings in Melanudrigill, but he lays no blame for them on the parish. The power of the Kirk has been sufficient to sanctify Chasehope; in Mr Dennistoun's pages he appears as an elder of noted piety, who was the chief mark for the enmity of the Adversary and who was, as that Adversary's last resort, driven crazy by hellish assaults on his person till his life ended in a fall from the rocks in the Garple Linn. There is no mention of Reiverslaw, and Amos Ritchie is treated with respect, for Amos carried his grandfather's matchlock to Ruillion Green, played a notable part in the Killing Time, was an ally of the Black Macmichael, and has a paragraph to himself in *Naphtali*. Mr Dennistoun represents the trouble as a deliberate campaign of the Devil against a parish famed for its godliness, and David as an unwitting instrument. The minister of Woodilee he portrays as a young man of good heart but of small experience, unstable, puffed up in his own conceit. He records that there was faction in the place that took his side, and that his misfortunes, justly deserved as they were, were not unlamented. He mentions as a foolish fable the belief of some that he had been carried off by the Fairies; he notes too, without approval, the counter-legend that he had been removed bodily by the Devil.

On one matter Mr Dennistoun has no doubts. Mark Kerr is
the villain of his pages; the lieutenant of Satan, or, as many
believed, Satan himself; one at any rate who was sold irrevocably
to evil. Of the real Mark Kerr's antecedents he is aware, but he is
inclined to a belief that the figure that appeared in Woodilee was
not Montrose's captain but another in his semblance. He makes
a sinister tale of Mark's doings – his uncanny power over the
minds of the people, his necromancy in the case of the witch-
pricker, his devilries during the Pest (these are explained as
mere purposeless cruelties), his crowning blasphemy in the
kirk, where he outfaced two godly ministers and spoke words of
which the very memory made honest folk tremble. He is
inclined to attribute to him also the warlockries of the Wood.
When he disappeared on that April day he returned to the place
whence he had come.

On this point Mr Dennistoun reflected faithfully the tradition in Woodilee. Old folk for generations, with sighs and a
shaking of the head, would tell of the departure of him who
had so sorely troubled the Elect. The tale no doubt grew in the
telling, and the children would creep close to their mother's
knee, and the goodman would stir the peats into a glow, when
grandfather with awe in his voice recounted the stages in that
journey of the lost. . . . Sandy Nicoll saw him in the gloaming
moving with leaps which were beyond a mortal's power across
Charlie's Moss. Later, at the little lonely alehouse of Kilwauk,
he was observed by a drover to cross the peat-road, and the
drover – his name was Grieve – swore to his dying-day that
beside the traveller moved a coal-black shadow. There was a
moon that night, and Robbie Hogg, herd in Glenwhappen,
saw the fearful twosome – man and shadow, man and devil –
flitting across the braes of Caerdrochit. At one in the morning
a packman, late on the road, saw the figure on the Edinburgh
highway, and, though he had been drinking and was therefore
a doubtful witness, remembered that he could not be clear
whether it was one man or two, and had been sobered by the
portent. . . .

At this point, when all that remained was an awful imagining, it was the custom of a household where the tale was told to sing with dry throats the twenty-third Psalm.

Three hours after the fuddled packman was left rubbing his eyes, two men entered the back room of a little hostelry in Leith within a stone's throw of the harbour. The dust of moorburn and the April roads was on them, and one of the two was limping and very weary.

The only occupant of the room was a man in a great seaman's coat who was eating a hasty meal. He rose to his feet with an exclamation.

'Mark!' he cried. 'In the name of God, man. . . .'

'When does the sloop sail?'

'In the next hour with the tide.'

'The Lord be thanked!. . . . You'll have this gentleman and me as fellow-passengers, Patie. . . .'

'Wheesht, man. They ken me in this place as Jens Gunnersen, a skipper out of Denmark. . . . I'm for Bergen.'

'Bergen be it. All roads are the same for us that lead forth of this waesome land. A bite and sup would be welcome, Patie, and two ship's cloaks to cover our landward clothes. . . . I'm for the wars again, old friend, and I've gotten a braw recruit, but the tale can bide till we're on shipboard.'

But three hours later the telling had not begun. Two men with wistful eyes leaned over the stern bulwarks, and watched the hills of Lothian dwindle in the bleak April dawn.

Glossary

Achan, a man who causes trouble (biblical)
aiblins, perhaps
airt, direction
anent, concerning
ass, ash
assoilzied, absolved
bauchle, shoe
bear, barley
beil, fester
bejaunts, first year student
bielded, protected
bien, pleasant, well stocked
biggit, built
birk, birch
black-avised, dark-faced
blate, shy, diffident
bode, to expect, aim to
bodle, small copper coin
bourtree, elder tree
brandering, grilling
braxy, diseased-sheep salt mutton
brock, badger
broo, opinion
browst, brew, ale
bruit, news
buchts, small sheepfold
buirdly, burly
busses, bushes
byke, wasps'/ant's nest
by-ordinar, unusual
cadger, a hawker
caird, tinker
callant, a youth
caller, fresh
camsteery, unruly
canty, lively, cheerful
cantrip, exploit, jape
carl, bloke
cateran, Highland raider
chief, friendly with
clachan, village

clatter, gossip
clavers, nonsense, idle talk
clypes, tell-tales
cog cogie, wooden bowl
coups the crans, overturns the fishbaskets
craig, neck
crouse, self satisfied
cruisie, an open boat-shaped lamp with a rush wick
cushats, ring-doves
cupples, rafters
cutty stool, stool of repentance in church
daffin, fooling around
deas, seat (stone or turf) outside a cottage
deave, deafen, annoy, bore
depone, testify
dittay, the substance of the charge against a person accused of a crime
doit, worthless coin
dorts, sulks
douce, pleasant, respectable
dowie, sad
dowp, backside
dozened, stupified
dredgy, funeral feast
drugget, coarse wool cloth
drumly, cloudy, muddy
dwam, faint, daydream
dwine, waste away
eident, careful, conscientious
elbuck, elbow
ettercap, spider, poisonous person
ettlin, intending
eldritch, unearthly
fail dyke, turf field wall
feck, the most part
fell, extremely

ferlies, marvels
fernietickles, freckles
fickles, puzzles
fleyed, frightened
floorish, blossom
forenent, opposite
fosy, soft, rotten, stupid
fou, drunk
foumart, polecat
freit, omen
frem'd, unfamiliar
fuff, puff
fugleman, leading soldier
furth, out from
fushion, strength, energy, sap
gait, route, road
gangrel, vagabond
gant, yawn
garr, to cause to do or happen
gash, ghastly
gean, wild cherry
gilpie, lively youth
gimmer, yearling ewe
girnel, meal chest, granary
glebe, minister's plot of land
gled, *kitle*, buzzard
glee'd, squinting
gleg, active, quick
gowk, fool, cuckoo
grieve, farm overseer
grosarts, gooseberries
gude brother/sister, -in-law
guisard, masquerade
grue, shiver, shudder of horror
gyte, mad
hairst, harvest
halflings, green youths
hallin, cottage
hantle, a considerable quantity
haverel, foolish chatterer
heritor, proprietor, parish
  administrator
hind, ploughman; a youth
hinner end, final part
hirplin, limping
hirsel, flock
hoastin, coughing
houghed, hamstrung
howdie, midwife
howms, low-lying land beside a river
howe, hollow
jalouse, guess
jaud, worthless thing, jade
jimp, scarcely

jouk and let the jaw go bye, (duck and
  let the wave go by) to give way to
  superior force
jukes, ducks
kail through the reek, get a scolding,
  come-uppance
kailyard, kitchen garden
kain, produce paid as rent
kebbuck, cheese
kenspeckle, well-known
kerns, Irish footsoldiers
kimmer, old wife
kittle, tricky, touchy
kittled, tickled
kirkton, village with parish church
knock, clock
kye, cow
laigh, low
lameter, crippled person
Lammas, August 1st festival
landlouper, vagabond
lappit, wrapped
lave, the rest
leal, loyal
lear, learning
limmer, rascal
lippen, to trust
loup, leap
lown, mild
lown downsetting, peaceful settlement
mailin, tenant farm
mails, bags
marrow, equal; match; mate
maud, plaid
maukin, hare
maur straik, heavier blow
mell, heavy hammer
mense, courtesy, good sense
messan dog, mongrel
mim, prim
mools, clods of earth
mutch, linen cap
mutchkin, ¼ pint (Scots), ¾
  (Imperial)
nettie wives, women who collect wool
nieve, fist
niffer, bargain, *nowt*, cattle
orra, odd
oy, grandson
paiks, punishment
pat, pot
pease-meal, pease flour
peesweeps, lapwings
plenishin, furnishings

plew stilts, plough handles
preen, a metal pin
press bed, wall recess bed
pretermit, pass over without comment
prie, try, test
pyot, magpie
randan, romp, brawl
randy, beggar-woman, dissolute woman
ratton, rat
rax, stretch
redder's straik, peacemaker's blow
redding, sorting out, clearing up
rede, counsel, advise
reive, raid
rickle, loose pile
rig, furrowed land
riggin, roof ridge
ripit, plundered
rive, tear, split
rouk, fog
roupit, auctioned off
run-rigs, strips of ploughed land
rudas, witch-like
sark, shirt
saugh, willow
scaith, harm
scart, scratch
seilin, filtering
seisin, possession
shieling, shepherd's hut
shilpit, puny
sic, siccan, such
siccar, sure, certain
skail, disperse
skellies, squints
skilly, skilful
skreigh o' day, crack of dawn
smeddum, spirit
smoored, smothered
sned, lop
snowkin, nosing
soorocks, sorrel
sough, sigh, wind, breath
sowens, oat flour porridge
spainins, weanings
speir, ask, enquire
spence, inner room
spleuchan, tobacco pouch
staig, young unbroken horse
steek, bolt, bar
staws, sickens

steer, confusion
stound, pang, throb
stoup, flagon
stour, dust
stramash, commotion
stravaigin, roaming
sweir, stubborn
tack, rent
tak tent, be careful, pay attention
tawpie, scatterbrained girl
teetotum, small toy top
teind, tithe
thack, thatch
thirled, tied
thrang, active, busy
thrapple, windpipe
thrawn, perverse, stubborn
thresh, a rush
thriep, to argue, contend
through-ither, confused
tinkler, gypsy
tint, lost
tod, fox
toom, empty
trams, shafts of cart
trauchled, harassed, burdened
trokins, dealings
tryst, appointment, meeting
tuilzie, struggle
unco, strange, odd
usquebagh, whisky
wabster, weaver
wale, pick
wame, belly
wanchancy, unlucky, ill-omened
wastry, waste
wauf, feeble
waukrife, sleepless
wedder, sheep
wersh, sour
whaup, curlew
wheen, a few, several
widdershins, anticlockwise
wirriecow, hobgoblin, the devil
wud, mad
wuddy, gallows rope
wysed, guided
wyte, blame
yauld, vigorous
yett, gate
yirth, earth

John Buchan Authorised Editions

The John Buchan Story Museum is delighted to be partnered with Polygon Books in the publishing of John Buchan's works in paperback. One of the aims of the John Buchan Story is to introduce John Buchan's works to as wide a readership as possible. The Museum's Trustees are confident that, by collaborating with Polygon Books in producing these authorised editions, the works of John Buchan will indeed reach out to another generation.

Readers are invited to visit the museum, which is housed in the Chambers Institution on the High Street in Peebles. There, through audiovisual presentations and by viewing original artefacts, you can discover more about the life, work and legacy of this remarkable man and his connections with Peebles. For a preview of what's in the museum, visit our website: www.johnbuchanstory.co.uk.

The John Buchan Society, with which the museum collaborates, promotes his life and works. For further information visit their website: www.johnbuchansociety.co.uk.